THE CU

DREA

RE FOR

MING

CAT WINTERS

Amulet Books

NEW YORK

Library of Congress Cataloging-in-Publication Data

Winters, Cat.
The cure for dreaming / by Cat Winters.
pages cm
Summary: In Portland, Oregon, in 1900, seventeen-year-old Olivia Mead, a suffragist, is hypnotized by the intriguing young Henri Reverie, who is paid by her father to make her more docile and womanly but who, instead, gives her the ability to see people's true natures, while she secretly continues fighting for women's rights. Includes timeline and historical photographs.
Includes bibliographical references.
ISBN 978-1-4197-1216-6 (hardback)
[1. Supernatural—Fiction. 2. Suffragists—Fiction. 3. Hypnotism—Fiction. 4. Fathers and daughters—Fiction. 5. Portland (Or.)—History—20th century—Fiction.] I. Title.
PZ7.W76673Cur 2014
[Fic]—dc23
2014012019

Text copyright © 2014 Catherine Karp
Book design by Maria T. Middleton

Image credits: Bettmann/CORBIS: pages vi–vii; Library of Congress, Prints & Photographs Division: pages 40, 78–79, 111, 123, 164, 224, 283, 330, 344–45; Courtesy U.S. National Library of Medicine: pages 55, 90, 204.

The quotation from Mark Twain on page 55 appears by permission of the Mark Twain Foundation.

Printed and bound in U.S.A.
10 9 8 7 6 5 4 3 2 1

Amulet Books are available at special discounts when purchased in quantity for premiums and promotions as well as fundraising or educational use. Special editions can also be created to specification. For details, contact specialsales@abramsbooks.com or the address below.

THE ART OF BOOKS SINCE 1949
115 West 18th Street
New York, NY 10011
www.abramsbooks.com

For Carrie,

MY SISTER AND LIFELONG BEST FRIEND.

KEEP SHINING.

"She was looking thin and pale and weak;
but her eyes were pure."

—BRAM STOKER, *Dracula*, 1897

CHAPTER ONE

A CHARMED INDIVIDUAL

PORTLAND, OREGON OCTOBER 31, 1900

The Metropolitan Theater simmered with the heat of more than a thousand bodies packed together in red velvet chairs. My nose itched from the lingering scent of cigarette smoke wafting off the gentlemen's coats—a burning odor that added to the sensation that we were all seated inside a beautiful oven, waiting to be broiled. Even the cloud of warring perfumes hanging over the audience smelled overcooked, like toast gone crisp and black.

Up in a box seat to my left sat Judge Acklen's son, Percy, in an ebony suit and a three-inch collar that made him look far older than his seventeen years. The electric lamplight shining down on his head coaxed a rich redness to the surface of his auburn hair, which made me think of Father's favorite saying about my mother's strawberry curls: *Red hair is a symptom of dangerous, fiery passions.*

Percy shifted toward the orchestra seats, and I could have sworn, even from that distance high above me, he glanced at me and smiled.

A sharp elbow jabbed me in the arm.

"Stop gawking at him, Livie," said Frannie—my dearest friend, despite the jabbing. "That boy is a vampire."

"A vampire?" I snickered and rubbed my walloped bicep. "Here I thought *I* was the one who'd read *Dracula* too many times."

"Percy Acklen would do nothing but make you feel small and meaningless."

"You never even talk to him."

She patted my hand. "Neither do you, my friend."

I shut my mouth, for she was right. Percy and I had never exchanged as much as a simple *Good morning* or an *Excuse me for stepping on your toe.*

"Forget him," said Frannie, "and enjoy your birthday treat. You're worth a thousand Percys."

Our friend Kate, a dimpled blonde whose married older

sister was supposed to be our chaperone for the evening, plopped down beside Frannie after chatting with other girls at the back of the theater.

"Why is Livie blushing?" she asked, leaning forward.

"I'm not blushing." I fanned myself with my program. "I'm just flushed from the heat."

Frannie frowned up at Percy and twisted the end of her waist-length braid, but she was a good-enough friend not to betray my silly infatuation.

I folded the upper-right corner of the program's front page until the tip of the cream-colored paper met the bold-faced words at the center:

Tonight's Performer
THE MESMERIZING HENRI REVERIE
Young Marvel of the New Century

"Maybe as a birthday present to yourself, Livie," said Kate, flapping open her own program, "you should volunteer to join this Mr. Reverie on the stage. Maybe he'll teach you how to hypnotize your father into being less of a grouch."

"Maybe." I gave a small sniff of a laugh, but I greatly doubted anything could fix Dr. Walter W. Mead.

The lights dimmed, submerging us all in the dark, save for five small candles that flickered inside a row of jack-o'-lanterns in front of the closed red curtain. A hush fell over the audience. Electric footlights rose to life in a fog of white and orange.

A full-whiskered man in a green checkered suit plodded across the apron of the stage, which set off a hearty round of applause from a thousand pairs of gloved hands. The gentleman waved his arms to quiet us down and offered a grin that turned his eyes into tiny crescents.

"Good evening, ladies and gentlemen," he said in a booming voice that rumbled up from the barrel of his round belly. "And a Happy Halloween to all of you. I am William Gillingham, your stage manager, and I'm ecstatic to announce that we have a bewitching show for you tonight. Young Monsieur Henri Reverie, barely eighteen years old, has traveled all the way from Montreal, Canada, to exhibit his enthralling hypnotism skills."

Additional exuberant applause echoed across the theater, and again Mr. Gillingham settled us down with a wave of his hands.

"Thank you, thank you—I'm overjoyed by your enthusiastic response. Some of you sitting out there in the audience will be invited onto the stage to fall under Monsieur Reverie's spell. The rest of you will bear witness to his remarkable powers over the human mind. I assure you, this talented young man will cause your jaws to drop and your eyes to open wide in astonishment. For musical accompaniment, he's brought along his sister, the highly talented Mademoiselle Genevieve. So . . . without further ado, I present to you"—

Mr. Gillingham turned with an upward sweep of his right hand—"the Reveries."

The curtain ascended and revealed two mahogany chairs, facing each other at the center of the stage, and a canvas backdrop painted to look like a star-kissed nighttime sky. On the left, a young woman with long golden ringlets sat in front of a monstrous pipe organ made of dark wood and gleaming copper. The stage lights brightened to their full brilliance, and the girl's peacock-blue evening gown gave off an otherworldly glow that made her appear more spirit than mortal.

She reached toward the instrument's keys and pressed a single D note twelve times in a row—the sound of a church bell chiming midnight. Chills shuddered down my spine. The pumpkins' toothy leers seemed to burn brighter.

Silence swallowed up the theater again, but before we could all lean back into the comfort of the calm, Genevieve Reverie lunged toward the keys and played a series of eerie notes that swelled into a passionate rendition of Camille Saint-Saëns's "Danse Macabre." She hunched her shoulders and plowed her feet into the instrument's pedals, as if she were racing through the streets of the underworld on a tandem bicycle, on which we were all unwitting passengers. I clutched the armrests. My head seemed to spin around and around and around, but I smiled and straightened my posture, for I adored a good Halloween fright.

A cloud of white smoke crept across the floorboards from

both sides of the stage. Genevieve's playing intensified, and the mist grew and billowed into a wall of burning orange that blurred the girl from view. The air tasted like my parlor whenever Father lit the fire in the hearth but forgot to open the flue. Those in the first few rows coughed into their gloves. The rising music warned that something was about to happen—something horrifying. The stage was about to erupt in flames. *We'd all burn up on Halloween night!*

"Are you all right?" whispered Frannie.

"Yes." I nodded with a laugh. "It's just better than I imagined."

The song reached its climax, racing, rising, climbing, higher and higher.

Smoke stung my nose.

I braced myself for fire.

But, no—instead, a young man stepped out of the clouds onto the apron, and the audience drew a collective gasp. A woman in the front row actually screamed. I gripped the armrests with all my might, for the boy looked like the devil—I swear, he resembled Lucifer himself with his black suit and crimson vest and his face shining red in the pumpkins' lights.

"Good evening, *mesdames et messieurs*," said the boy in an accent that sounded French and dangerous and deliciously sophisticated. "I am Monsieur Reverie." He gave a deep bow with his hand pressed flat against his stomach.

Silence greeted him. Our brains took several moments

to absorb the fact that this was our entertainer for the night—Henri Reverie—not the ruler of hell. Weak applause trickled across the theater, but it gained speed and volume as everyone roused from their stupors. Relieved laughter boomed through the crowd. I settled back in my seat, eased my viselike grip upon the armrests, and clapped along with everyone else.

"*Merci.* Thank you." The young man turned toward the reemerging pipe organ and stretched his arm toward the girl at the bench. "Isn't my sister astounding? Please, won't you give a warm round of applause for Mademoiselle Genevieve Reverie."

We all applauded Genevieve's performance, which far surpassed the uninspiring efforts of an amateur organist like myself. Genevieve panted as if she might collapse, and her golden ringlets uncoiled and wilted across her shoulders like limp strands of seaweed. Oh, how I envied her passion.

The applause dissipated, as well as the smoke, and the theater collectively exhaled a calming breath. The stage settled back to normal. Henri Reverie's skin faded to a less-diabolical shade without the orange smoke rising around him, and his short hair, a bit mussed on top and parted on the right, revealed itself as dark blond, a tad lighter than the hue of fresh honey. He was attractive, I suppose, with red lips and a rosy blush of health in his cheeks.

He stepped closer to us and spoke again. "*Merci.* Thank you for coming here today. My name is Henri"—he pronounced his name *On-ree*—"Reverie, and I have been studying the arts of mesmerism and hypnotism with my uncle ever since I was twelve. I use a combination of techniques from the great masters, including animal magnetism, deep relaxation, and the remarkable power of suggestion."

Genevieve played a hushed rendition of "Beautiful Dreamer."

"In a moment"—Henri strolled across the stage, his hard soles clicking against floorboards—"I am going to invite my first volunteer to come onto the stage with me." He placed his hands behind his back, which pulled his coat farther open, allowing the crimson silk of his vest to wink at us in the footlights. "There is no need to be afraid of what you will encounter with me. I am going to temporarily take you away from your worries. You will submerge yourself in a depth of relaxation such as you have never experienced before, and you will awake feeling better than you have felt in your entire life. All your troubles will dissolve into nothingness the moment you let me guide you into the beautiful world of hypnosis."

Despite my previous fear that Henri Reverie was the devil, his words melted in my ears like spun sugar. I needed a temporary escape from life. Yet I wasn't brave enough to say so.

"Is there a young lady in the audience who would like to be my first volunteer?"

A dozen hands flew into the air. And then at least two dozen more. Silhouettes squirmed and arms flailed throughout the darkened audience.

"Let me see—how should I choose?" Henri grinned and scratched his smooth chin. "Tell me, is anyone here tonight for a special occasion? A birthday, perhaps?"

Next to Frannie, Kate shot her hand into the air and shouted, "My good friend over here is celebrating a birthday."

Henri Reverie pivoted our way. Fear stabbed at my heart.

Kate stood and urged me to my feet by tugging on my hand. "She's turning seventeen today."

Murmurs of disappointment over not being chosen rumbled through the crowd. Frannie took my other hand and said, "Do it, Olivia. Don't be afraid. It might be fun."

Henri strutted closer to us. "You have a Halloween birthday, *mademoiselle*?" he called down to me.

I cleared my throat and answered in an ugly, croaking voice, "Yes."

The hypnotist smiled with those red lips of his. "Then legend says you are a charmed individual. You can read dreams and possess lifelong protection against the spirits. Come up here with me, and let us see how you fare with hypnosis."

"Go on, Livie. Don't be shy." Kate steered me toward the aisle as if she were herding a lost sheep into a pen. She then clapped her hands together, which triggered yet another thundering round of applause.

I tripped my way down the center aisle in the dark. Classmates from school called out my name in encouragement, and someone patted my arm as I struggled to figure out how to get onto the stage with the disorienting clapping ringing in my ears.

"Over here, *mademoiselle*." Henri waved me over to the left side, where I found a short flight of wooden steps. He reached out his gloved hand for me to take.

I hesitated a moment, wondering what my father would think of me climbing onto a stage with a young man who had reminded me of the devil only minutes before. Yet I reminded myself of Henri's promise of escape: *You will submerge yourself in a depth of relaxation such as you have never experienced before.*

The hypnotist wrapped his fingers around mine and helped me climb to the floorboards above. Our respective pairs of gloves separated our hands, but I felt the warmth of his skin beneath the smooth fabric. Hot white lights smoked by my feet and glared down at us from the ceiling like an army of small suns. I shielded my eyes while Henri led me to the center of the stage, continuing to hold my hand.

"What is your name?" he asked in a voice for all to hear.

"Olivia Mead," I answered in a decibel only he would be able to detect.

"Do you live here in Portland?"

"Yes. I attend Portland High School."

"Ladies and gentlemen," he said to the audience, "I present to you Mademoiselle Olivia Mead of Portland, Oregon, my first subject of the evening. Do any of you know Miss Mead?"

"Ask her about her father," called a husky male voice from the audience. "Mead the Mad."

I lowered my head and stiffened my shoulders, but Henri gave my hand a squeeze and pretended not to have heard the horrifying remark.

"Is this raven-haired beauty known for her brute strength?" he asked, at which several people laughed, possibly because I was never typically referred to as a beauty. "Would you like to see this delicate young feather of a girl become as strong and rigid as a wooden plank?"

The audience clapped and cheered, and Kate yelled out, "Go on, Livie. Have a bit of fun."

Henri turned to me and said in a quieter tone, "Come with me, Miss Mead. You have nothing to fear."

I drew a shaky breath and allowed him to lead me to the chairs in the middle of the stage. The echo of our footsteps ricocheted across the entire theater and sounded far too loud to my ears. Genevieve transitioned into Brahms's "Lullaby."

"Please, sit down." Henri held the back of the chair on the left.

I seated myself on a springy burgundy cushion, my posture tense and rigid, my back a solid board of oak. I never laced my corset to a point where I couldn't breathe, yet the steel stays dug against my ribs and kept oxygen from settling into my lungs. Every part of me ached and itched.

Henri, still standing behind me, removed his white gloves. "Ladies, Miss Mead will need to remove her gloves and hold my hands directly. I am going to transfer my energy into her, which will enable her to fall into the desired state of relaxation and open her mind to me. I apologize if I offend anyone, but this has been the tradition ever since Franz Anton Mesmer popularized this astounding technique." He stepped around me to the other chair and took a seat. "Miss Mead, please take off your gloves and hold my hands."

I swallowed and hesitated. Prickly beads of sweat bubbled across my forehead. Genevieve's lullaby strengthened in volume, perhaps to assuage my fears.

Don't be rude and delay the show, I scolded myself the way Father would complain whenever I dawdled before leaving the house for an event. *What are you waiting for? Chop-chop!*

I slipped off my gloves with my eyes directed toward my nut-brown skirt. Henri's bare right hand reached my way, and, with trembling fingers, I took it. Our other hands joined as well. His skin, smooth and hot, smoldered against mine.

"Look into my eyes," he told me.

I gave his face a brief glance, noting how blue his irises were, but the idea of staring into the face of a stranger felt unnatural. I tittered and focused instead on the starry backdrop.

"Miss Mead," he said in the gentlest male voice I'd ever heard, "are there any worries you would like to escape?"

My smile faded. My mind skipped back to a scene from earlier that day. I saw a small group of women with yellow ribbons pinned to their left shoulders. They shouted for equality on the steps of the courthouse. My own voice, along with Frannie's and Kate's, rang through the air in support. A barrage of rotten eggs smacked my arms and chest and oozed milky gray yolk down the lace of my blouse with a stink that made me gag. Fierce-eyed men—men who might have known my father—barked at us to go back to our homes where we belonged, and I ran off to scrub away the filth and my guilt until my fingers turned red and raw.

"Miss Mead?" asked Henri Reverie. "Would you like me to take you away from the world for a while?"

I glanced back at him, and his eyes held mine. Such arresting blue eyes—bright river blue, without any flecks of green or gold to distract from the principal color. They pulled me toward them and beckoned me to stay. They wouldn't let me go. Nor did I want to leave them.

"You are going to feel a great deal of warmth pass from my fingers into yours." He squeezed my hands—not enough to hurt, but enough to show me he was there. The balls of his thumbs pressed against mine. "It is going to feel like gentle flames, starting in your palms and fingertips . . ."

Heat tingled down my thumbs and spread across my hands.

"And then it will move into your wrists and slowly, slowly up your arms."

The warmth glided through my blood, past my elbows, and up to my shoulders in a strange, pacifying wave. Henri's blue eyes continued to hold my full attention.

"You may feel your arms grow numb, and that is perfectly

fine," he said, and my arms indeed felt strange and heavy. "The heat and numbness will make you tired. Very tired." He inhaled a deep breath that inspired me to do the same. My lungs expanded with air that soothed me down to my bones.

"As the warmth pours down through your torso like heated milk," he continued, "and travels slowly, gently across your hips and to your legs, you are going to find yourself so relaxed, you cannot keep your eyes open."

My eyelids fluttered.

"Close your eyes."

They fell shut.

"Keep them closed. Fall into a deep, deep sleep."

My hands, weighing several tons, dropped away from his fingers, and my chin slumped to my chest. I sank deep inside the darkness in a languid, dreamlike fall. Nothing hurt or troubled me any longer.

I felt divine.

"As I pass my hands over you," said Henri, "you will travel farther into this wonderful stage of sleep and be unable to open your eyes. Keep going downward, downward, and hear only my voice. Turn off all your other senses. You will only hear, taste, feel, smell, and see if I tell you to do so. For now, just focus on my voice and the magnetic force of my hands passing over your body. Sleep. *Sleep.* Keep going farther into sleep."

Downward I kept sinking. Downward, downward, downward. Gentle nips of heat sizzled across my skin, all the way to my toes, and my body melded into the chair until I became a part of the batting and the nails and the wood.

I continued to hear Henri's voice, directed to the audience. The word *test* came up, and *cymbals*, and *Remarkable, isn't it?* But nothing else mattered until he told me, "Stand up, Miss Mead."

I did as he asked. My eyes remained closed, and my body may as well have been made of stone, but somehow I was able to get to my feet.

"I am going to press my hand against you, and my touch will cause every muscle inside your body to go rigid."

His fingers cupped the back of my head, and a hardening sensation spilled down to my feet, as if he had unscrewed the top of my skull and poured a fast-drying plaster inside me.

"Rigid!" he called near my ear. "You are an iron bar that cannot bend. Every part of you is stiff. Nothing can cause you to falter. You are as solid as a board."

He spoke again to the audience, calling up "strong male volunteers." Firm hands lifted me into the air, beneath my shoulders and legs. I rose up high, my arms glued to my sides, and settled across two bars, one behind my neck and the other below my ankles.

Henri's voice whispered inside my mind. "Lift yourself out of your body, Miss Mead. Float up to the top of the stage, and I will return you safely after you have had some time to enjoy yourself. You can hear Genevieve's organ music again . . ."

The organ filled my ears with a rich and dreamlike melody.

"Open your eyes."

I did.

"See the shine of the lights. Let their radiance beckon you to them. Allow Genevieve's music to carry you away. Do not fight it, lovely girl. Just go."

I rose out of my petrified bones.

"Yes . . . go."

I drifted upward—a weightless feather immune to the burden of gravity, lured by the pull of the vast ceiling above with its rows of metal catwalks and blinding lights that breathed wispy plumes of smoke. Genevieve's music carried me up to the bulbs and allowed me to lie in a foggy bath of golden rays without a worry or a pain. Henri disappeared. Memories of gaseous eggs on my chest disappeared. Fears of what Father would say about the courthouse rally slipped away. I was nothing but a feather.

I floated for hours . . . or so it seemed.

I could have drifted much longer if Henri's voice didn't call up to me. "Miss Mcad," he said. "Are you ready to come back now?"

I tried to hold myself up there in that luxurious land of electricity.

"I need to bring you back so someone else may have a turn. You have done beautifully, but it is time to wake up."

"No," I said, but I felt myself deflating. A withering hot-air balloon with the gas turned low.

"I am going to sweep my hands upward, starting at your feet, and count from one to ten."

"No."

"Yes, Miss Mead . . . and by the time I reach ten, you will feel wide awake and rested." His presence burned at my feet. "One, two—you feel the magnetic force between us fading—"

I sank back to the ground, closer to the stage.

"Do not fight it. Three, four—you are slowly stirring back to life. Five—your senses are returning to your body. You can feel the heat from the stage lights again . . ."

My hair warmed, and my mind was able to recognize the music playing: "Evening Prayer" from the opera *Hansel and Gretel*. The sheet music was part of my collection back home.

"Six, seven—do not fight it, Miss Mead, please do not fight it. Eight—very good, you are almost there—nine . . ." He placed his hot hand against my forehead. "Ten. Awake."

I opened my eyes, and the hum and the glare of the lights made me jump. I found myself standing upright at the center of the stage again.

"Let us give a warm round of applause for the lovely and cooperative Mademoiselle Mead." Henri lifted my hand in the air, and applause assaulted my ears like the blasts of gunshots at a sharpshooter show. My legs wobbled as if made of sand, and I had to grab hold of Henri's coarse sleeve to keep my knees from sinking to the ground.

Henri put his arm around my back and guided me to

the stairs. I resisted the urge to lean against his shoulder to support my drooping head.

The clapping died down.

Genevieve finished her music.

The hypnotist let me go.

He didn't say another word to me as I clutched the handrail and descended from the stage with my gloves somehow back in my hand—not a whisper in my ear or a simple *Thank you for joining me*. At the bottom step, I peeked over my shoulder and caught him watching me, as a doctor would monitor a patient he was releasing from the hospital after a surgery. But then he smiled. A warm smile that heated my blood and made me forget Percy Acklen sitting high in his box seat above the darkened theater.

The hypnotist then turned back to his show.

I returned to my seat.

Our relationship seemed to be over.

CHAPTER TWO

WOMANHOOD PERFECTED

When I sat back down, Kate covered her mouth as if she were stifling a laugh and Frannie whispered, "Oh dear, Livie. That went much differently than expected."

"How do you mean?" I asked, but the woman behind us shushed us, and Frannie murmured that she'd explain later.

The next volunteers ventured onto the stage in a group of ten, and they were a motley collection of males and females of varying sizes, shapes, and ages. Under Henri's spell they waltzed to "The Blue Danube," forgot their names, and performed other embarrassing but relatively harmless feats.

During all the demonstrations, I was nothing more than a heap of melted butter that oozed against my red velvet chair in the audience. I felt as if I had awoken from a hundred-year nap, every part of me rested and content, aside from an odd, smarting sensation in one wrist. I almost possessed the confidence to go home and tell Father I had participated in a women's suffrage rally in the center of the city.

Almost.

"SO, TELL ME, LIVIE," KATE SAID WITH BARELY CONCEALED excitement after the theater lights stirred us back into reality and we rose to our feet, "what did it feel like when lovely Monsieur Reverie was on top of you?"

"I beg your pardon?" I halted in mid-stretch. "What did you just say, Kate?"

"You heard what I said." She smiled with a glint in her hazel eyes. "He instructed you to stiffen, and then he laid you out between those two chairs and stood on your stomach to show how rigid you became."

"What?" I pressed down for signs of bruises below the protective barrier of my corset. "He stood on top of me?"

Frannie nodded and bit her bottom lip. "He did, Livie. That's what I meant by 'Oh dear.'"

"Didn't you feel him?" asked Kate.

"No."

She laughed. "You didn't feel a man at least thirty pounds heavier than you standing on your body?"

"No."

"You were honestly that hypnotized?" Frannie put her hands on her hips. "You didn't hear the cymbals he crashed next to your ears or feel the pins he poked into your wrist to see if you were alert?"

I rubbed my left wrist. "Is that why my skin tingled after I got back to my seat?"

"Oh, Livie." Kate shook her head, her fair curls wobbling across her forehead. "You're always missing the excitement, even when you're smack-dab in the middle of it." She swiveled toward the aisle and held up the hem of her skirt. "Come along, ladies. Let's try to pull Agnes away from her suffragist troops and their election-day plotting and remind her she's our chaperone."

Frannie and I grabbed hands to keep from losing each other in the crowd, and I followed her swaying braid up the aisle, while she followed Kate's bright green-and-black plaid. Strangers stepped on my feet at least three times, and I couldn't help but think everyone was staring at me, the girl who had let a young man balance atop her stomach.

Out in the lobby we had to wait ten minutes to fetch our coats, and then we found ourselves swept along in a warm wave of bodies that pressed toward the theater's exit. On all sides of me people buzzed about Henri Reverie's skills.

"Quite a talented young man."

"Such persuasion. Such power."

"I would have liked to see him try that hogwash on me. My mind is far too sharp and alert for that sort of humbug—I can promise you that."

I glanced over my shoulder, for I thought I heard my name amid the commotion.

"Olivia." An arm waved, flashing a jeweled cuff link. Auburn hair and a handsome face with fine cheekbones came into view ten feet behind me. "Wait," called Percy Acklen.

I squeezed Frannie's hand in the crowd's swift-moving current. "I think Percy is calling to me."

She laughed. "What?"

"Percy Acklen is calling and waving to me."

She turned as well, and although a parade of elbows and shoulders smacked against us, we stood there, frozen.

Percy made his way to where we waited and stopped two feet from me. I could smell his divine, musky cologne.

"May I drive you home, Olivia?" he asked.

"Drive me home?" I looked to Frannie to ensure I'd heard him correctly.

She gaped, her jaw dangling open enough for me to see the little gap between her bottom front teeth.

A rotund gentleman with a heavy black beard fell against Percy, and the force of the blow knocked Percy's chest against mine. He grabbed my arms to steady himself but carried on with his conversation as though we hadn't just crashed together with our cheeks pressed close. "My father bought me my own buggy." He let go of me and stepped back to a more respectable distance. "I'd love to give you a ride."

I cleared my throat to find my voice. "Didn't you come to the theater with your parents?"

"They brought their own carriage. I drove separately."

"Frannie? Livie?" called Kate from the exit, bobbing up and down like a buoy. "Where in heaven's name are you?"

"We're coming, Kate," said Frannie. She glanced my way with concern in her eyes. "You're coming, too, Livie, right?"

My heart pounded. I felt I'd stumbled across a crucial fork in a road after a long journey, and choosing the wrong path might alter my entire life. Going home with my friends as planned would mean safety and comfort and normalcy. Yet driving away with Percy, unchaperoned—Percy who was gazing at me as if I were something rare and enchanting he'd just unearthed—well, that was an entirely new adventure.

I buttoned up my gray wool coat. "I'll go with Percy."

PERCY'S BUGGY WAS AN ELEGANT BLACK CONTRAPTION with fresh paint, a curved roof, and a seat, meant for two, upholstered in padded green leather. He stepped in beside me and rocked the vehicle until he got himself situated.

I tucked my gloved hands inside my coat pockets, for the night air was chilled and damp with the type of mist that stung my cheeks and nose. *Fairy kisses,* my mother had called that type of weather when I was small enough to believe in mystical creatures.

Percy fitted his silk top hat over his head. "Where do you live?"

"Twelfth Street, near Main."

"That shouldn't take long." He gathered up the reins. "Are you ready?"

I nodded. "I am."

"Let's be off, then." He made a clicking sound out of the side of his mouth, and his white ghost of a horse pranced away from the theater with the steady clip-clop of hooves. The carriage bumped and jostled over potholes in the dark, so I grabbed the crisscrossing bars running up to the roof to keep from bouncing out to the muddy street.

"You have a beautiful horse," I said when we were two blocks west of the theater.

"Thank you. His name is Mandolin."

"Oh, that's pretty."

"Thank you."

I leaned back against the seat and wondered what I was doing with exquisite Percy Acklen and his gorgeous black buggy.

Silence ruled our drive across the city, even though I longed to ask him what books he liked to read outside of school and what he thought of hypnotism . . . and Halloween . . . and bicycling . . . and a dozen other subjects. Words failed me, however—as they were apt to do around attractive boys. All my imagined questions struck me as either dull or nosy.

I focused on the glow of the arc lamps dangling from overhead wires and the darkened stores, including my absolute favorite, McCorkan's Bicycle Shop, which featured two pairs of ladies' riding bloomers in the front window. We traveled past rows of houses—oversized gingerbread homes with rounded towers and sprawling porches topped with jack-o'-lanterns that reminded me of Henri Reverie leaping out of smoke. The carriage wheels squelched through soupy puddles and clattered across stony patches of road so poorly paved, the surface might as well have been dirt. The air carried the scent of Halloween bonfires and magic.

We turned left, and Percy urged Mandolin into a fast trot, perhaps to impress me. My backside bounced against the seat hard enough to rattle my teeth.

I clutched the buggy. "Is it safe to go this fast in the dark?"

"Are you scared?"

"A little."

"It's Halloween. You're supposed to be frightened."

"Frightened of the dead arising . . . not of imminent death."

"Ha! I'll slow down, then." He adjusted the reins, and the horse eased back into a walk. The buggy swayed in a gentle rhythm, and I relaxed my stranglehold on the bars. "There, boy," cooed Percy. "There's a good horse."

Our narrow, two-story house came into view to the south, its ugly red clapboards too dim to be seen with the clouds blocking the moon.

"My house is the third one on the right," I said with a nod toward the place. "The skinny one with the big maple in front."

"All right."

We drove close enough for me to see a light flickering behind the lace curtains of one of the side windows in the back. Father's study.

Percy called out another "Whoa," and the buggy rocked to a stop in front of our curb. Mandolin whinnied. Rain pattered against the vehicle's roof, which made me think of poor Frannie and Kate trudging through drizzle and hopping aboard streetcars to get home, and there I was, sitting in the height of luxury on padded green leather.

"Well," I said, "I should probably—"

"You looked beautiful on that stage tonight, Olivia." Percy turned toward me, briefly illuminated by a delicate strand of moonlight that stole through the clouds.

I sat up straighter. "I did?"

"Yes." His eyes—black in the night, a beguiling greenish-brown in the daylight—stayed upon me. "I don't know if you remember it, but that hypnotist laid you out between two chairs. You were as stiff as a board, with only your neck and your ankles supported, and you were as lovely as Sleeping Beauty."

I snickered. "I was?"

He scooted closer to me on the seat with the soft whisper of leather. "My father leaned over to me and said, 'Now, that's womanhood perfected, Percy my boy. That's the type of girl you want. Silent. Alluring. Submissive.'"

My stomach lurched. I tried to appear unfazed by his

father's words, but my mouth twisted into an expression that must have looked as if I were swallowing down those milky gray eggs from the courthouse attack.

Percy laughed. "I said those were my father's words. Not mine."

"Oh." I sighed. "I'm glad. You don't think women ought to be silent and submissive, then?"

"You *are* silent, Olivia. I've never heard you speak one word in any of the classes we've had together."

"That doesn't mean I like to be silent."

Unfortunately, my argument ended there, and I indeed fell silent again. As did Percy.

Down the street, a dog howled. A pitiful wail.

"'Listen to them—the children of the night,'" I said before I could think to regret quoting *Dracula* in the middle of an already awkward moment.

Percy straightened his neck. "What did you just say?"

"I beg your pardon?"

"What about nighttime children?"

"Oh . . ." I wrapped my arms around my middle. "I just . . . I have a strange attraction to horror novels."

"Which ones?"

"I'm reading *Dracula* . . . for the fourth time."

"The fourth time?" He whistled and shifted his knees in my direction. "Doesn't the library mind you checking it out so often? I've heard it's all the rage."

"I saved enough money to buy my own copy as soon as

it showed up in Harrison's Books last year. Have you read it yet?"

"No." He tugged at his stiff collar. "My father only allows classic literature in the Acklen household. Friends have to sneak me copies of anything new and exciting."

"I could lend you my copy if you'd like."

"Really?" He scooted another inch my way. "You'd help corrupt me?"

I sputtered a laugh. "*Dracula* may frighten you, but I doubt it will corrupt you. At least . . . I don't think it will. There are some . . . scenes . . . I suppose some people would find . . ."

"What?" He tilted his head. The right corner of his mouth arched in a wry smile that Frannie would have hated. "What types of scenes are there?"

My face flushed. "I'm not going to say. You'll just have to read them."

"You'll definitely have to lend me your copy, then. Show me what I'm missing." He pressed the side of his arm against mine, clearly meaning for me to feel him.

I froze. My heart rate doubled, and I was certain he could detect my pulse jumping about beneath my sleeve, even with all that fabric separating us.

"Well . . . ," he said.

I lifted my eyes. "Yes?"

"I suppose I should help you down before the vampires

crawl out of their graves and drink your sweet, invigorating blood. What do you think?"

I nodded. "I suppose you should. There aren't any Van Helsings in the neighborhood."

"Who?"

"You'll see."

He shifted his weight and climbed out his side of the buggy, another smile half hidden on his face in the moonlight. His leather soles squished toward me through the shallow mud; then he stopped below me on the damp sidewalk and hooked his fingers around the crisscrossing metal next to my arm. "Thank you for letting me drive you home."

I folded my hands in my lap to keep them from trembling. "May I ask you something about that?"

"Yes."

"Um . . . well . . ." I drew a breath that made my tongue go dry. "You didn't ask to drive me here merely because you liked how I looked when I was in that trance, did you?"

"Well . . ." Percy beamed at me in a way no one ever had before, his head tipped to the left, his dark eyes glassy and wistful. "You really were a beaut up there, Olivia. You should have seen the way the lights shone down on your black hair and your sleeping face."

"But have you ever felt—" My skin warmed over. Words wilted at my lips, but I forced myself to finish my thought. "You've never seemed to notice me before this evening. Am I only attractive to you because I was lying unconscious across two chairs on a stage?"

"No . . . that's not . . . I just . . ." He rubbed the back of his neck. "I'd never thought of you that way before. You've always simply been . . . Dr. Mead's daughter."

"Oh." I nodded. "I see. You're afraid of my father like everyone else."

"No, I'm not afraid. It's just . . . well . . . your father has never worked on my teeth, but he certainly took care of my mother's and father's mouths—I can tell you that much. He fitted them with the finest dentures money can buy."

"And is that so terrible?"

"Your father smiled the entire time he was yanking out my father's molars. As if he enjoyed it."

I swallowed and squirmed. "He's not smiling when he's pulling out teeth. A natural reaction to luring a person into opening his mouth is to make a funny little grimace. I used to play dentistry with my dolls, and my grandmother observed me making the same face."

"I've heard he also enjoys the use of leeches."

"Only to relieve inflamed gums. It's standard dentistry practice. They do the job beautifully."

"They suck blood out of patients' gums beautifully? Is that what you're saying?" His eyes shimmered with amusement. "My goodness, Olivia. You do like horror stories, don't you?"

"You see? This is why I don't talk much in school. You're laughing at me."

"I'm just entertained that sweet little Olivia Mead is defending the use of leeches inside people's mouths." He inched his hand down the metal bar, closer to my skirt. "You have to admit, it is a little shocking."

I picked at my coat's cloth-covered buttons.

"Please, Olivia"—he nudged my leg with the back of his hand—"don't be angry."

"I'm not angry. It's just not easy being the daughter of . . . my father."

"I understand. I've got an infamous father, too. He's been known to make grown men cry in court."

"Oh." I met his eyes again, noting the softening of his expression. "I didn't think of that. I suppose you might truly understand, then."

"I do. I really do." Percy offered me his hand. "It's starting to rain harder out here. We should get you inside before it pours."

"Will you come up to the door with me to meet my father?"

He helped me down from the carriage with a backward glance at the house.

"My father doesn't extract teeth and leech gums just for fun, Percy," I said with a smile. "His home office is solely for emergency treatments, not for torturing his daughter's drivers."

Percy blanched. "He keeps dental tools in the house?"

"I promise, you'll leave here tonight with all the contents of your head intact."

"Oh. Well . . . good." He tucked my hand inside the crook of his elbow. A wind kicked up around us, forcing him to press his top hat against his head with his free hand. "Come on. We're going to get soaked."

We ran up the brick front path just as the rain gained force and pelted the ground with a clatter that sounded like the applause Henri had received when I was standing on the stage with him. Up on the porch, we ducked under the cover of the roof and shook water off our sleeves.

"Come inside for a moment to get dry." I turned the doorknob with an embarrassing squeak and poked my head inside. "Hello? Father?"

Silence met my ears. The only movements within the house were the twitching flames of the entry hall's sconces, which threw shadow and light across the rusty-brown wallpaper. The air smelled of gas from the lamps' hissing jets, and there were lingering whiffs of the pot roast supper Father and I had shared earlier that evening.

"Father?" I called into the silence, stepping inside the entryway with a moan from the unvarnished floorboards. Our home had never seemed so much like the sinister abode of a mad, leech-loving dentist until that moment. "Are you still awake?"

"I need to talk to you, Olivia." Father clomped out from his office at the back of the long hall, dabbing his forehead with his handkerchief the way he usually did when he was anxious. When he saw I wasn't alone, he stopped and blinked, as though trying to clear his head of a brandy-induced hallucination.

"Olivia?" He tucked his handkerchief into his coat pocket and patted down his graying black hair—a longer and scragglier mess than most professional gentlemen's. "You didn't tell me you were bringing a guest home."

"Father, this is, um, P-P-Percy Acklen, Judge Acklen's son. He kindly drove me home from the hypnotism show."

"He did?" Father bounded our way with a jolly smile that rivaled Santa's in my illustrated copy of *A Visit from St. Nicholas*. The leftover stink of one of his cigars muffled Percy's musky cologne. "What a pleasure to meet you, Mr. Acklen." He shook Percy's hand with rapid pumps that jerked the boy's shoulder. "I'm Dr. Mead, a great admirer of your father's newspaper opinion pieces. He's a just and wise man."

"Thank you, sir." Percy slid his hand out of Father's and stretched his fingers with a crack. "He'll have another piece printed soon. A group of women gathered on the courthouse steps this afternoon and protested their lack of a vote in next Tuesday's election."

My heart stopped.

Father's eyes flitted toward me for the briefest of seconds. "Oh?"

"The protest turned somewhat volatile." Percy removed his top hat. "My father yelled out the window for them to all go home before he set the police on them."

"I don't blame him. That must have been appalling."

Father darted another quick glance my way, which turned my stomach into a flip-flopping jumble of nerves.

He knows I was there.

"Well"—Father cleared his throat—"that sort of behavior is inexcusable for a woman. If my own daughter ever dared to throw a tantrum like that on the courthouse steps, I'd pull her out of school and send her straight to a convent." Father snorted. "And I'm not even Catholic."

Percy laughed as if he had just heard the wittiest joke ever uttered, perhaps to humor Father, but he straightened his posture and sobered when he caught my unsmiling reaction. "Oh, I doubt Olivia has ever done anything wrong in her entire life, sir. There's no need to worry about her. In fact, the entire city just witnessed her strict obedience this evening."

Father stiffened. "What do you mean?"

"She was hypnotized. That hypnotist fellow we went to see—Henri Revelry—"

"Reverie," I corrected Percy.

"He called her up to the stage and put her under his spell. She did everything he asked of her."

Father spun toward me. "You were hypnotized tonight, Olivia?"

I nodded. "Yes."

"And you did everything asked of you?"

"Apparently so."

"Well, g-g-good. Good girl." He slipped his handkerchief out of his pocket and dabbed his forehead again. "That's my Olivia. An exemplary model of fine manners and strict obedience."

"And she was positively breathtaking," added Percy. "If I may be so bold, sir, I'd say tonight on that stage your daughter was the loveliest thing I've ever witnessed."

"Really?" Father cocked his head, sounding a little too skeptical that I could have been that lovely.

Percy fussed with the brim of his hat. "May I ask you a question, sir?"

"Of course," said Father.

"I was wondering if I might take Olivia with me to an event Friday night. Sadie Eiderling invited me to her birthday supper."

"Sadie Eiderling?" Father's eyes expanded at the mention of the local beer baron's daughter, and I swear I could see the glow of rich golden ale sloshing about in his dazed irises. "You want to take Olivia to a party at the Eiderling mansion?"

"I realize you don't necessarily know me well enough for me to escort your daughter to such an event, but I'm a respectful young man with a reputation for impeccable behavior."

Father rubbed his lips and seemed to weigh his decision with great care.

"If you need to think about the proposal before answering," said Percy, "I'd understand . . ."

"Yes, let me get back to you before I extend such a privilege to Olivia. I'll send a note over to your house tomorrow evening."

"Thank you, sir. I appreciate your considering the offer." Percy planted his hat back on his head, and I could feel the enchantment of the evening dissolving into the ether. "Well, I hate to scuttle off so quickly, but I need to go home so Mother doesn't worry. Thank you for letting me drive you home, Olivia. Good night, Dr. Mead."

"Good night, Percy," I said.

"Good night, son." Father closed the door and allowed Percy to dart back into the rain and the darkness.

I lunged for the staircase behind me.

"Wait."

I turned and braced myself against the banister. "Yes?"

"After you left for the theater this evening"—Father shoved his handkerchief into his breast pocket—"I received a telephone call from one of my most prestigious patients, Mr. Underhill."

"Mr. Underhill?"

"He owns one of Portland's largest shipping firms."

I shrugged. "I've never heard of him."

"He was at the courthouse this afternoon."

I gulped and turned my attention to the toes of the rain-freckled shoes peeking out from beneath my skirt.

"Olivia," said my father, "look me in the eye."

I did as he asked, raising my chin to bolster my confidence.

He lifted his chin as well. "Why did you humiliate yourself by standing in that crowd of hysterical women? Mr. Underhill said men pelted you with rotten eggs."

"That is correct, sir."

"Why were you there?"

"A friend's sister is a member of the Oregon State Equal Suffrage Association, and I decided to see what all the fuss was about."

"Mr. Underhill said you were chanting *with* the women."

"That is correct."

"Why?"

"Because I would like to vote for president when I'm older."

Father pinched his lips into a scowl that turned his face lobster red, and his entire body quaked, as if blasts of lava were about to spew from the top of his skull. "Olivia Gertrude Mead, my hope for you since the day your mother left was that you would grow up to be a rational, respectable, dignified young woman who understands her place in the world."

"But—"

"You're lucky Percy Acklen's father didn't see you standing out there on his courthouse steps, or that distinguished young man never would have taken an interest in you."

"I—"

"Was he hypnotized into falling in love with you?"

"No!"

"Well, then, if you spoil this unexpected bit of luck you've been handed this evening, I will keep to my word about ending your education and sending you away."

"But—"

"No. You are done talking for the day." He shoved a finger

in my face. "I lost Mr. Underhill as a patient because of you. He was supposed to be leeched tomorrow afternoon, but he demanded to know how he could trust me with his mouth when I can't even control my own daughter. He called me an embarrassment to the men of Portland, and he uninvited me from the election-night ball of the Oregon Association Opposed to the Extension of Suffrage to Women."

"What? That's ridicu—"

"You will go to your room, change into your nightclothes, and turn down your lamps without reading or writing a single word. You will go to sleep while contemplating your poor decision and figure out how you can compensate for your ills tomorrow. You need to prove you won't embarrass me if I let you go to that party with Judge Acklen's son." He lowered his finger and steadied his breath. A bulging blue vein pulsated in his forehead, and for a moment I feared it would burst and kill him right there in front of me.

"Go!" he shouted.

I scrambled up the stairs with thumps and bangs and skids, failing to sound like a "rational, respectable, dignified young woman." I sealed myself inside my bedroom—my cherry-blossom-pink Elysium of lace and literature and freshly dusted china dolls in long satin dresses. Father had already lit my frosted gas lamps, so there was no need for me to fumble in the dark for a match.

I grabbed the little steel hook from the top of my chest of drawers and undid the dozen black buttons running down my ankle boots. "Unfair," I muttered under my breath as I worked to free my cramped feet. "So unfair. I'd like to see *him* silenced for a change and sent off to a monastery. How would he like that?"

My stocking-covered feet broke loose from their leather prisons, and I stretched out my toes across the cold floorboards.

From my bedside table, the Count's dark blue castle on the brown cloth cover of *Dracula* beckoned: *Read me, read me. Only thirty more pages to go before Mina will be saved from Dracula's bloodthirsty curse.*

I slid my arms out of my coat and caught the reflection of my movements in the standing oval mirror by my window. A tired girl with a plain face and a distinct lack of fire in her pale brown eyes peered back at me from the glass. Stray strands of hair the color of wet river sludge had fallen out of my topknot and stuck to my cheeks after my ride through the city and the scramble through the rain with Percy. I brushed the hairs aside with the back of my hand and heaved a sigh that made my shoulders rise and sink.

The only other evidence of mischief on my body, the only sign my seventeenth birthday wasn't quite as proper as it should have been, was a dusty pair of footprints on my dress, right above my stomach and thighs.

"He could see plainly that she was not herself. That is, he could not see that she was becoming herself and daily casting aside that fictitious self which we assume like a garment."

—KATE CHOPIN, *The Awakening*, 1899

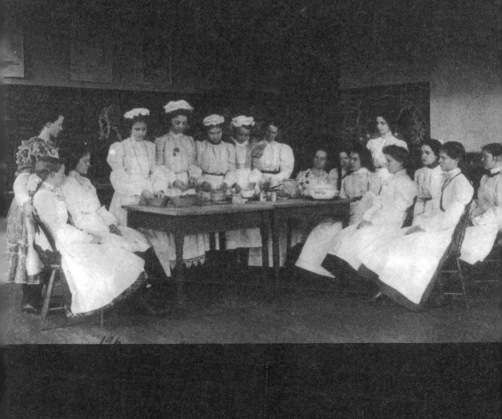

CHAPTER THREE

UNLADYLIKE DREAMS

By the time I had dressed for school and was heading downstairs the next morning, the house smelled like poached eggs, black coffee, and a touch of rosemary from the Macassar oil Father used for slicking down his hair. He was already seated at the breakfast table, below his favorite photograph: an appetite-souring image of a pair of bone dentures, with six of the bottom teeth missing.

"You're in the newspaper, Olivia," he said from behind a sheet of newsprint.

My stomach tightened. "I am? Why?"

Before he could answer, Gerda, the Swedish girl we hired to help with the cooking and cleaning, blew through our swinging kitchen door with the silver coffeepot. She smiled when she saw me, her butter-blond hair and crisp white apron cheery contrasts to our moth-brown walls and dim lighting. "Oh, good morning, Miss Mead," she said in her lovely Swedish lilt.

"Gerda"—Father rustled the newspaper down to the table—"return to the kitchen, please."

Gerda and I exchanged a look.

"Gerda," said Father in a warning tone, "a private family matter needs to be discussed."

"Yes, sir." Gerda nodded and disappeared through the door, which flapped shut behind her as if it were swatting her away on her posterior.

I clenched my fists and prepared for the worst.

Father slid the paper across the table. "*This* is why you're in the newspaper."

My lips parted at the startling image on the front page of the *Oregonian*: an illustrated picture of me, lying supine in my hypnotized state. As Kate, Frannie, and Percy had all told me, I was propped between two chairs, supported beneath my neck and ankles, and my body looked as rigid as the Steel Bridge crossing the Willamette River. A sketched version of Henri Reverie stood on top of me with his arms stretched out to his sides, as if he were balancing on a tightrope instead of a girl.

Below the picture was a caption:

Young hypnotist Henri Reverie stands atop mesmerized
Olivia Mead, daughter of Portland dentist Walter W. Mead.

"I'm so sorry." I scooted the newspaper back across the table and sank into my chair. "Kate volunteered me to go on the stage with that hypnotist, but I didn't even want to do it. I had no idea Mr. Reverie was standing on top of me after he put me in my trance."

Father picked up the paper again, but instead of bristling and grumbling, he sat there with the flames of fascination flaring in his pupils. "Young Mr. Reverie's persuasion over you was clearly quite powerful."

"Yes," I said, a nervous quaver in my voice.

"I'm curious about hypnotherapy myself. I've read several articles about dentists who use trances to subdue their thrashing patients." Father scratched his beard with an audible rustle of hairs. "The article states that between performances, Mr. Reverie is offering his hypnotism skills to help individuals overcome their addictions and fears. He's staying in Portland until next week."

"Oh." I unfolded my napkin. "I'm sure he'll be helpful to men addicted to drink."

"Are you also becoming a temperance crusader, Olivia?"

I looked up, caught off guard by the question as well as the squeak of fear in his voice. "I beg your pardon?"

"I keep reading about that lunatic of a woman, Carrie Nation—the old hag who's smashing up saloons in Kansas with stones and bricks and billiard balls." He stared me down with probing brown eyes that themselves resembled billiard balls. "Do you ever harbor urges to commit violent acts against men?"

"No! Of course not. Just because I want to vote doesn't mean I'm going to turn savage."

"Women who want the vote seem hell-bent on outlawing liquor, too. They're ready to attack."

"Father, I just—"

"I'm considering telephoning this Henri Reverie and hiring him to help you."

I half slipped off my chair. "Help me with what?"

"I want him to put an end to your growing signs of rebelliousness."

"I am not rebellious." I gripped the edge of the table. "I may have gone to a suffragist rally and upset one snobby patient, but no one else has ever complained about my behavior. Not at school—not anywhere. You're just punishing me because of Mother."

"I'm ensuring you won't become like your mother." Father folded the newspaper into two crisp halves. "If Percy Acklen drove you home last night because he has marriage on his mind, what do you think he'll do if he catches word you were at that protest?"

"He probably won't—"

"I'm not done talking, Olivia. If Percy feels he won't be able to command his own domestic ship, if he worries you'll turn wild on him, he'll run as far as he can in the opposite direction. You'll never again have a young man with means and money take an interest in you. You'll have no options for your life."

"I'm only seventeen. I don't care about marriage right now. My schoolwork is good enough that I could go to college and study to be a teacher. Or a writer."

"You are not going to be a teacher or a writer."

"Why not? Plenty of young women are taking jobs these days."

"Only desperate and unfeminine ones. The only reason I even allow you to go to that school is because I hate to think what would happen if you were on your own while I'm at work."

"What?" I gasped. "School is my key to the future, not my nursemaid."

"Your future is to become a respectable housewife and mother. Women belong in the home, and inside some man's home you'll stay."

I squeezed the table's edge until my fingers and my voice both shook. "You're angry because you couldn't keep my mother inside this home—that's what this is all about. But it's not my fault you drove her away."

Father's mouth fell open, and his eyes refused to blink, as if I'd stabbed his heart with the barbed tips of my words.

"I—I—I'm sorry," I said. "Please, Father—please don't hire that hypnotist to remove thoughts from my brain. My mind isn't like a rotten tooth. You can't just take it away."

He stabbed at his egg with his fork, and that angry blue vein from the night before throbbed again in his forehead.

"Father, please—"

"Don't you understand?" He slammed his fist to the table and made the dishes jump. "I'll be making your life easier for you by freeing you of these unladylike dreams. It's for your own good, so don't make me out to be the villain here. The world will seem far less difficult when passions that can never be fulfilled are gone from your stubborn head."

"I don't want them to be gone. I'd rather be able to dream and fail than to never feel the pull of another way of life."

"That's a silly, frustrating way to live."

"But—"

"The subject is closed. If I decide it best to hire the hypnotist, I will."

ON MY WAY TO SCHOOL, I PASSED POSTERS FOR HENRI Reverie's performances, taped to utility posts and shop windows. The corners of the papers curled and fluttered in the cool November breeze, and each notice resembled the other: a black background, tall yellow letters, and a pair of large blue eyes staring out from above the phrase YOUNG MARVEL OF THE NEW CENTURY!

I plodded onward, but every other block, Monsieur Reverie watched me travel through the city.

Up ahead of me, the high school's spire clock tower pierced the gray sky high above the corner of Fourteenth and Morrison, a sight that always reminded me of a postcard my mother sent me from Notre Dame Cathedral on her thirtieth birthday. Our school was actually quite colossal and impressive on the inside, too, with dark wood fixtures, electric lighting, fifteen classrooms, a library, a laboratory, a museum, two recitation rooms, an art room, and an assembly hall. The curriculum was modern. The classrooms were integrated and coeducational.

He sent me to a progressive school. And yet my lunatic father was still considering hiring a stranger to obliterate my thoughts.

Algebra was challenging enough without worrying about a cure for female rebellion, but with that new fear bearing down on me, I failed to complete five equations on the weekly examination. In domestic science I somehow lost my little white baking cap and caused a small grease fire that singed the cuff of my right sleeve. History was a blur of dates and long-dead generals (although, to be fair, that tended to be the case every day in history). And in physical education, down in the musty high school basement, I twisted my ankle when

Mrs. Brueden squawked at us to jog faster in our whooshing black exercise bloomers.

English fared somewhat better.

Percy was in that class with me.

My eyes drifted to the back of his combed auburn hair one row over and three seats up, and with nearly soundless squeaks, I swiveled back and forth in my stiff oak chair, my elbows resting against the steep slope of my desk.

Percy scratched his shoulder with his chin, his eyes turned downward, and I held my breath, wondering if he had caught me staring at him. His eyelashes rose. His gaze met mine. The right side of his mouth curved into one of his sly grins, and I smiled, too, while the back of my neck prickled.

"Mr. Acklen, what do you believe Longfellow meant in this last stanza?" asked Mr. Dircksen, our white-haired teacher with furry sideburns that reminded me of rabbits sticking to his cheeks. His broad shadow loomed across Percy's desk and somehow chilled my own arms with gooseflesh.

Percy returned his attention to his reader and straightened his posture. "Um . . . I think it means, sir, we're all trying to see more in life than what there actually is to see. The moon makes everything look more . . . spiritual. I think."

"Are you positive about that?"

"Yes. That's my interpretation, at least."

"Mr. McAllister, would you care to go one step further?"

Quick-witted Theo McAllister launched into a detailed interpretation of the poem, and Percy's shoulders relaxed.

He peeked backward again to see if my eyes were still upon him—which, of course, they were.

I mouthed three words to him: "I brought *Dracula.*"

"What?" he mouthed in return.

"*Dracula.*" I pointed to my toffee-colored book bag hanging on a hook on the wall next to all the other bags.

"Ah." He nodded, and with an eyebrow cocked, he added, "Corrupt me."

My cheeks burned. Percy snickered.

"Mr. Acklen!" Mr. Dircksen whacked Percy across the head with the palm of his hand, hard enough to knock him out of his chair. "The first rule in this classroom is respect."

Everyone in the room collectively stiffened. My stomach turned with guilt as Percy—red-faced, shoulders hunched—crawled back into his chair and rubbed his ear.

Mr. Dircksen stood up tall above Percy's desk with his hairy neck stretched high. "Turn around in that chair one more time, and you'll be facing the paddle in the principal's office. Do I make myself clear?"

Percy combed his hand through his hair. "Yes, sir."

Mr. Dircksen then pointed a bony finger at me. "You, in the back there. I forgot your name."

I choked on my own saliva.

"What is your name?" he asked in a voice that slapped me on the back and made me cough out the words.

"Olivia Mead."

"Miss Mead"—Mr. Dircksen tapped his reader against his

opened hand—"do *you* require a firm reminder of the first rule of this classroom?"

"N-n-no, sir." I shook my head until the classroom went fuzzy.

"Good. Now, where were we before this interruption?"

I clutched my desk, doubled over, and spent the rest of the class trying to remember how to breathe.

AT PROMPTLY ONE O'CLOCK, MR. DIRCKSEN EXCUSED US. I grabbed my book bag and hustled out to the hallway ahead of my classmates, hoping for a whiff of fresh air, but all I inhaled was the smell of pencil shavings and other students. Even worse, Henri Reverie's eyes haunted me from another black poster that someone had pinned with thumbtacks to the burlap-covered bulletin board across the hall, next to a notice for the school's banjo club. The dramatic yellow letters—all capitals, all screaming to be seen—peeked at me from between the passing hair bows and the male heads with severe parts combed down the middle.

THE MESMERIZING HENRI REVERIE

"I'm glad he didn't wallop your head, too," said Percy from behind me.

I spun around, my book bag sliding to my elbow.

Percy walked toward me, his satchel slung over one shoulder, his hair falling into his eyes. He rubbed his ear again. "I'd use a word to describe teachers like him, but that would guarantee I'd get the paddle."

"I'm so sorry about that. Here"—I dug into my bag and tugged out *Dracula*—"keep it. It's yours now."

"Keep it?" he asked. "But you love it."

"It's the least I can do."

He flipped the novel over and studied the cover illustration of Dracula's angular castle perched atop a lumpy hill. "I like the way the little bats are soaring around the towers. It looks like a corker of a book." His eyes returned to mine. "But I don't know. I think you owe me more than just a ghost story. Don't you?"

I shrank back. "I—I—I don't—"

He cracked a smile and nudged my arm with his elbow. "Don't look so terrified, Olivia. I just meant I think you need to work even harder to persuade your father to let me take you to that party." He reached out and stroked a piece of my hair and, with it, my cheek. "Will you do that for me, Sleeping Beauty?"

"Yes, of course." I peeled my eyes away from his red ear. "I'd be happy to."

"Good." He dropped his hand to his side. "Tell him I won't bite, unlike"—he patted the novel—"your friend Dracula here."

He tucked the book into his satchel and wandered away.

Frannie's face came into view from around the corner to the stairwell, and as she approached she peeked over her shoulder at Percy disappearing down the steps. Without slowing her stride, she grabbed me by the elbow and steered me toward the music room at the opposite end of the second floor.

"So," she said, "was he kind to you when he drove you home last night?"

"Very kind. But something awful happened to him just now."

"What?"

We passed a boy named Stuart from English who was pantomiming Mr. Dircksen's attack on Percy to a group of his friends in front of the library.

I lowered my voice. "Mr. Dircksen smacked Percy in the head in front of the class . . . and he threatened to send him down to the principal for a paddling. Percy and I had just been exchanging whispers about *Dracula*."

"A paddling on the backside?" Frannie lifted her chin, her eyebrows raised. "Well, now. That's highly appropriate."

I stopped and shook her arm off mine. "Why on earth do you hate Percy?"

"It's nothing," she said, but her face went red and splotchy.

I took her by the arm and pulled her aside, one door down from Stuart and his friends.

"It doesn't seem like nothing, Frannie."

"I just . . ." She shifted her weight between her feet. "I just think he's a snob, that's all. And snobs are only fun in Austen novels."

"Are you sure you don't have a particular reason for hating him?"

"Just watch yourself with him—that's all I'm going to say." She hooked her arm again through mine and pulled me toward the opened chorus room doors. "I've heard he flits from girl to girl and doesn't care about their reputations. Watch out for his hands."

"His hands?" I asked.

"On your bottom, you ninny. I've heard he's a grabber."

She tugged me into the music room, and we sealed the subject of Percy closed.

I OPENED MY MOUTH AS FAR AS MY JAW COULD STRETCH and joined my girls' chorus sisters in rehearsing "Silent Night" for the Christmas concert.

In the middle of the second verse, just as my vibrato was gaining strength and feeling good in my chest, my friend Kate entered the room with a folded piece of paper tucked between her fingers. Her new black shoes with buttons on the sides clip-clopped across the floor to the beat of the metronome sitting on Mr. Bennington's piano.

Mr. Bennington stopped conducting and scratched his waxy mustache. "Let us take a short break, ladies."

Kate handed the teacher the note. Mr. Bennington pulled his wire reading glasses out of his striped coat pocket and squinted through the lenses, as if he couldn't quite decipher the words.

"It's for Olivia," said Kate.

My insides liquefied. I wondered why the devil someone was sending *me* a message in the middle of the school day.

"Olivia." Mr. Bennington peeked up at me. "Come read this note and then return to your position."

"Yes, sir." I climbed down from the risers, out of the depths of the deepest altos stuck in the back, and took the piece of paper. Kate patted my back as if I were receiving a summons to the gallows and clip-clopped out of the room.

I unfolded the note.

"Let us take it from the beginning," said Mr. Bennington.

My classmates cleared their throats and stood up tall, while I read two sentences scribbled in Father's squiggly cursive:

> *My daughter, Olivia Mead, must come to my dental office directly after school. She should NOT go home.*
> *Respectfully,*
> *Dr. Walter Mead*

My blood froze. I reread those phrases at least three more times apiece. Our rather somber rendition of "Silent Night" seized the room with a harmony that pricked the little hairs on the back of my neck, and Father's ominous second sentence stared me in the eye.

> *She should NOT go home.*

"He had the calm, possessed, surgical look of a man who could endure pain in another person."

— MARK TWAIN, "Happy Memories of the Dental Chair," 1884

CHAPTER FOUR

THE CURE

I n Father's downtown office, tucked in the heart of Portland's business district, a door with a frosted glass pane separated his mahogany-lined lobby from the windowless operatory in which he tended to his patients' teeth and gums. I could see him moving beyond the glass—a distorted figure in a trim white coat, bending over the silhouette of a man tipped back in the padded dental chair. Laughter erupted from the patient, first in snickers, then in loud brays and hiccups that told me the man had inhaled a bag of nitrous oxide, otherwise known as good old laughing gas.

I seated myself in a rigid chair in the lobby and stared up at Father's four-foot-wide oil painting of a pair of silver dental forceps shining against a green background. I recalled Percy's utter dread of my father's profession (even though Father worried *I* would scare Percy away), and I slunk down a little farther in my spindle-back seat, wishing Father were a bookstore owner like Frannie's pa, or even a chimney sweep or a sailor. Someone who didn't hang pictures of torture devices on his workplace walls or cause men to suffer from fits of laughter while they shouted out, "No! I'm not ready!"—as was happening beyond the frosted glass beside me.

I eyed the main door to the street and debated bolting home. *I can claim I never received the note,* I realized. *I could say that I—*

The front door opened.

Henri Reverie stepped into the lobby.

I drew a sharp breath and averted my eyes. My shoulders inched toward my ears. *He's come to take away my free will. I knew it!*

Henri removed a dark square-crown hat from his head, closed the door, and lowered himself into a chair across from me, below the painting of the forceps. He was dressed in a three-piece suit and tie, all as black as midnight—a shadow with cobalt-blue eyes and blond hair. His complexion was poorer than I remembered, probably due to all the lard-based greasepaint theater people had to wear on their faces, according to my mother. His slumped posture gave him the shifty look of a peddler trying to pass off bottles of booze as magical cure-alls.

"No!" cried the patient in the operatory.

I gave a start—as did Henri.

"Noooo! I'm not ready! Nooooooo!"

Shrieks and loud smacks and another fit of hysterical laughter came from beyond the glass. Henri grabbed hold of his armrests with whitening fingers, and his knees swerved to his right, toward the door, as if he were about to flee.

A smile twitched at the corners of my lips. I relaxed my shoulders and folded my hands in my lap, for I realized something absolutely delightful: Henri Reverie's fear of my father's dental practice gave me the upper hand in our current situation.

Interesting.

"Are you here for an appointment, Mr. Reverie?" I asked.

"Stay still, Mr. Dibbs!" yelled Father from beyond the door. "If you don't stop flailing about, I'll need to clamp your wrists to the chair in addition to your head."

Henri grimaced as if his own head were being clamped to a chair, while Mr. Dibbs cackled and whooped and let loose the screams of a man suffering the tortures of the Spanish Inquisition.

"I said, are you here for an appointment, Mr. Reverie?"

"I—" Henri's blue eyes shifted toward me for a swift moment, but they veered straight back to the bobbing and ducking figures beyond the frosted pane. "Yes, an appointment."

"A bad tooth?" I asked, sitting up straighter, stifling another smile. "Swollen gums? Do you need your tissues leeched of blood?"

A howl of pain echoed through the office walls. "No!" cried Mr. Dibbs in a decibel that made my ears ring. "No! I wasn't ready."

"It's all done," said Father. "The extraction was a success. Hold this ice over the wound and rest a few minutes. You're fine."

The patient sobbed and moaned and then cackled with laughter. "You had a blasted smile on your face, Dr. Mead. You looked like you enjoyed ripping my tooth from its socket."

"Nobody enjoys the sight of a decayed bicuspid rotting away in an inflamed mass of bleeding gums, Mr. Dibbs. Take better care of your oral health, sir."

Father's distorted image came closer to the frosted glass; his beard and white coat grew sharp and clear behind the pane until I could almost see the browns of his eyes. He opened the operatory door and poked out his head. "Ah, good. You're both here. I'll lay Mr. Dibbs on the cot and bring you in."

I jumped to my feet. "I am not going in there like one of your patients."

"Now, don't be difficult, Olivia." Father let go of the doorknob. "Mr. Reverie has kindly agreed to help you accept the world the way it is."

"You actually hired this person"—I pointed toward the still-seated hypnotist—"to extract my thoughts in your operatory, as if my brain were a decayed thing, like Mr. Dibbs's disgusting bicuspid? Do you know how cruel and horrifying this is?"

"Olivia . . ." Father put out a cautious hand and trod toward me as though I were a rabid dog. "I told you, I only want the best for you. Don't have a conniption."

I lunged for the front door, but my father pounced and took hold of both my arms before I could escape.

"Olivia, please." He spun me toward him. "Please behave for me. Your mother—she abandoned the both of us, not just me. She left you behind, too."

"I know that." My eyes smarted with tears, and I saw a blurry version of Henri Reverie turning his face away from us, pretending not to hear, which made me want to cry all the more.

"She said she wanted the vote, too," said Father. "I hear her voice in yours. You can't do that to some poor husband and child one day. I won't let you break people's hearts."

"I'm not going to be like her."

"You've got to change."

"No."

"Think of your future sons and daughters. Think how much better your childhood would have been if your mother had accepted her place in the world and ignored her selfish dreams."

"She did it all wrong." I wriggled my shoulders and struggled to break free of his grip. "I won't be like her, I swear. Please don't pay him to take away my thoughts."

"Please do not be afraid, Miss Mead."

I turned and looked straight into Henri Reverie's eyes—a mistake.

"Do not be afraid," said the hypnotist again in a voice that soothed me as much as when I had succumbed to his anesthetizing words on the stage. Those eyes of his—those potent blue irises that tugged me toward him—swallowed me whole and assured me there was nothing to fear inside that dental office. There was nothing to fear in the entire world. My muscles slackened. My worries evaporated into the sweet nitrous oxide in the air.

Father let go of my arms.

"It is a pleasure to see you again, Mademoiselle Mead," said Henri, rising to his feet. "I can tell you are nervous about my presence here, but I promise, your session in this building will be as relaxing as your trance yesterday. *Ne vous inquiétez pas.* Do not worry."

I exhaled a sound between a laugh and a gasp and tore my eyes from his, an action that hurt as much as pulling a thorn from my finger. "How can I possibly feel relaxed," I said, "when I don't know what's about to happen to me?"

Henri walked toward me with footsteps that scarcely made a sound on the lobby's dusty floorboards. "I swear to you, Miss Mead, you will not be harmed in any way. You will feel the same sense of well-being and euphoria you experienced when you reemerged from my trance on the stage. Do you remember that beautiful sensation?"

He stood in front of me and trapped me again with those unshakable eyes. The flaws in his skin and light stubble on his chin faded to insignificant blurs compared to those two orbs of brilliant blue. My breath grew shallow and fluttery. My veins seemed to flow with hazy waves of Father's laughing gas instead of blood.

Henri took my hand, and a rush of warmth passed between us. I remembered that warmth all too well.

That sensation was my undoing.

He jerked me toward him by my arm and called out, "Sleep!"

My face crashed against the buttons of his coat.

"Melt down, melt down." He cupped his hand over the back of my head, and my body slackened against his chest. "Let yourself go, downward, downward, downward."

He dragged my rag-doll body across the floor and plopped me into one of the lobby chairs, still holding the back of my head. "Keep going down, Miss Mead. Keep easing deeper into sleep. Melt down. Let go, let go."

A lock clicked into place. Curtains clattered closed.

"Teach her to accept the world the way it truly is," begged Father in a voice that trembled and cracked. "Make her clearly understand the roles of men and women."

"I'll try my best, *monsieur*—"

"And tell her to say 'All is well' instead of arguing whenever she's angry. Please. Her rebelliousness has got to be removed if she's going to survive."

I was too submerged in a warm and comfy eiderdown blanket of peace and darkness to care anymore what that silly man was blathering on about. Henri took hold of my left hand, and a numbing shot of heat flowed up my arms and fanned throughout my body to my farthest extremities. I gasped. My chin melted to my chest. The entire world slipped away, except for the soft lull of Henri Reverie's voice.

"You are doing beautifully, Miss Mead. But now I need to take you into an even deeper level of hypnosis. I am going to stand behind you and use my hands to guide your head in a complete circle. Each revolution will send you further and further into the desired state of relaxation."

His warm hands clasped my temples and revolved my head in a gentle, circular motion that slowed my breathing and dropped me down into a tingling world of blackness. My shoulders slumped forward.

"Yes, very good . . . you are melting even deeper now." He rotated my head again, tilting back my chin until my neck was stretched and exposed. "You are doing so well. Keep going . . . all the way down. All the way down . . ."

Two delightful revolutions later, my chest collapsed against my legs.

"Excellent. Wonderful. I am so impressed." He seemed to

shift his position and kneel in front of me. His hand cradled the back of my skull. "You are now submerged in one of the deepest levels of hypnosis. Say *yes* if you understand me."

"Yesss," I mumbled with heavy lips into the wool of my skirt.

"*Magnifique.* Now, Miss Mead, I want you to listen to me, for the next part of my instruction is extremely important." His lips bent close to my ear, and his voice traveled directly inside my head, as if he were taking up residence in the middle of my brain. "When you awaken, you will see the world the way it truly is. The roles of men and women will be clearer than they have ever been before. You will know whom to avoid. Say *yes* if you understand me."

"Yesss."

"Good." He exhaled a feathery sigh against my cheek. "Now, some of the things you see with your new vision might make you angry. However, you will be incapable of uttering angry words. Whenever you are upset, all you will be able to say is 'All is well.' Say it right now."

"All is well."

"Good. All is well. You will see the world the way it truly is. The roles of men and women will be clearer than they have ever been before. Instead of getting angry, you will say 'All is well.' Say it once again."

"All is well."

"Wonderful. I am so glad you understand. I am going to bring you back up again. Let us just take our time and do this slowly. I will count to ten, and you will feel my hands rising up from your feet. One . . . two . . . You feel the force between us cooling, weakening . . ."

The blanket lifted off me, and I rose like a swelling loaf of bread.

"Three . . . four . . . five . . . let it go, you are doing splendidly, Miss Mead . . . let it go . . . six . . . seven . . . eight . . . you are almost back . . . nine . . ." He pressed his hand against my forehead. "Ten. Awake."

I opened my eyes.

"Oh—my Lord!" I sank back against my chair and grabbed the armrests. "Oh, God!"

Henri Reverie kneeled on the floor in front of me, and he had turned into the most delightful creature upon which my eyes had ever feasted. Flawless skin. A perfectly structured nose. Sumptuous red lips that looked ripe and full and ready to be touched. Pure blue eyes with bottomless pools of dark pupils that reflected his sincerity and concern. Concern for me.

"Do you feel all right, Miss Mead?" he asked in a voice like a distant echo, as if spoken from the opposite end of a tunnel. He leaned forward on his knees, and I couldn't help but reach out and sift my hand through his hair, which slid through my fingers like golden threads of sun-bright silk. The rest of the world darkened into shadow around him. All I could do was look at him—really look at him.

"Olivia!" snapped Father, also in a faraway voice. "Why are you touching him?"

I lifted my face toward Father to try to describe Henri's confounding beauty, but my tongue froze when I caught sight of a fiend in a white coat standing in the lobby where my father should have been. The brute's red eyes gleamed bright and dangerous, and his skin went deathly pale and thin enough to reveal the jutting curves of the facial skeleton beneath his flesh. His graying beard resembled the flea-infested fur of a rat.

"What is it?" asked the fiend, his canine teeth as sharp as the fangs of a wolf or the deadly tip of a scythe. "Are you cured or not?"

I clutched the armrests until my fingers ached, and my knees knocked against each other with the thumping of bones and a wild rustle of skirts. I opened my mouth to shout, *You look like a monster! What's wrong with you? Get away from me. I hate you!*

Yet only three limp words emerged from my lips.

"All is well."

CHAPTER FIVE

THE WORLD THE WAY IT TRULY IS

I bolted.

I didn't even wait to see what Mr. Dibbs and his bloody tooth socket looked like back in the recesses of the operatory. The monstrous version of Father shouted something about catching me, but I darted out the front door and down the street before anyone could chase me down.

Outside, the world felt as if it had tipped sideways and knocked everything askew. The air had grown too thin to breathe. Shop windows reflected blinding sunlight that throbbed behind my eyes. The city had turned as bright and vivid as a theater stage at the height of a performance, yet the noises of my surroundings—carriage wheels, trotting hooves, peddlers hawking wares from carts—sounded muffled and tinny. Even my sense of smell dulled as my eyes viewed the world with startling clarity. I saw two women across the street with blood on their necks. A man in a business suit and derby hat came my way, and his face was as gaunt and pale and fanged as Father's.

I panted and slid my hand across the cold sandstone walls for support and somehow managed to run across the street and down the next block—before I stopped in front of an establishment that was caging up women.

Yes, *caging women.*

On a corner lot where a regular storefront should have stood, a giant copper cage held five ladies prisoner. Their shoulders and hats squished together in a crowd of feathers and fine wool dresses, and they buried their noses inside some sort of pamphlet that distracted their attention from the freak-show absurdity of their situation.

Out in front of the entrapment, a female carnival barker—I didn't even know women could be barkers!—in a red-striped jacket and a straw boater hat yelled, "Welcome! Welcome! Come see the only proper place for women and girls."

A young blond woman in a tailored blue suit took a pamphlet from the barker and climbed inside the cage with the other ladies. The barker promptly shut the cage door and locked it tight.

"Miss Mead!"

Footsteps ran toward me, and before I knew what was coming, Henri Reverie grabbed me by my arm. "Are you all right?"

The hypnotist had returned to his shady young showman appearance, and he smelled as dusty and smoky as the letters Mother wrote from backstage dressing rooms. Sounds regained their full volume. Henri's hair lost its brilliance.

"Th-th-they're caging up women," I said. "They're locking them up right here . . ."

I turned and pointed, but instead of the copper cage, I saw a brick building with a wide white banner hanging above the glass door.

HEADQUARTERS
THE OREGON ASSOCIATION OPPOSED TO THE
EXTENSION OF SUFFRAGE TO WOMEN

A slender middle-aged brunette with an entire stuffed quail perched upon her hat—not a strange female carnival barker—stood in front of the opened door, and she caught my eye and said, "Would you like to come inside and see what we're all about, dear?" She held out a pamphlet and smiled with a fine pair of false front teeth, undoubtedly fitted by Father. "Read about the hair-pulling, face-scratching women of Idaho who turned into heathens once their state allowed them to vote. We'll teach you about the proper sphere for ladies."

I yanked myself free of Henri and continued down the block.

Henri followed, and our feet clapped across the sidewalk in near unison. He caught me by my elbow before I could cross another street. "What are you seeing?"

"All is well."

"Tell me." He grabbed both my shoulders and turned me around to face him.

"All is well!"

"I need to know if everything went as planned with our session. Tell me what you see."

"All . . ." A frustrated cry burst from my lips. "All is . . ." Itchy tears filled my eyes, but the more I fought to hold back my emotions, the more a fit of crying longed to break free. A stray tear slipped down my cheek. A sob exploded from my mouth.

"No, do not cry, Miss Mead. Please . . ." He rubbed both my arms with a rapid *swish-swish-swish* against my white blouse sleeves. "Shh. Please do not cry. Try to talk in a calmer voice. Try to relax. Those three words will only come out of you if you're angry. Take a deep breath."

"No, I don't want to do anything you ask of me. You got your money; now leave me alone, you—" A vicious insult burned up my throat, but the words hardened into a lump of simmering coal that lodged in the back of my mouth. I coughed out that stupid phrase again: "All is well." I shook Henri's hands off me. "Never come near me again."

A swift kick in his shin with the pointed toe of my shoe sent him doubling over to clutch his leg. I tore down the street again, away from the anti-suffrage headquarters and Father's cruel teeth and Henri Reverie's disorienting blue eyes.

You will see the world the way it truly is. The roles of men and women will be clearer than they have ever been before. You will know whom to avoid.

HARRISON'S BOOKS SAT THREE BLOCKS NORTH OF THE courthouse, nestled between a dry-goods store and a small hotel, in a row of storefronts Frannie and I affectionately called *Eat, Read, Sleep, and Be Merry*. I panted in front of the bookshop's leftmost display window. When I had caught my breath, I dared a peek inside.

Just beyond the glass the new and successful novels of the season were propped upon low wooden stands—*The Touchstone*, by an author named Edith Wharton. *The Wonderful Wizard of Oz*, the delightful children's book I had read over the summer. *To Have and to Hold. Richard Carvel. A Man's Woman.* And, of course, *Dracula.* My nose bumped against the cool glass, and my shaky breath left a foggy circle on the pane.

A movement beyond the books caught my eye: Frannie's father, with his curly gray hair and little potbelly, passed through the store with a cloth-bound volume in hand. He wore his usual three-piece suit—tan and lined in pale gray stripes—and he fitted his round spectacles over his bulbous nose that was the shape of my rubber bicycle horn.

I dipped down behind the window's display and watched him flip open the book on the front counter, next to the brass cash register. Unlike Father's, his cheeks were pink and healthy. His teeth weren't overly long and barbaric. Everything about him seemed as regular as could be.

I sprang to my feet and pushed my way inside the shop door.

"Oh, thank heavens, Mr. Harrison!" I clasped Frannie's father in a huge hug and buried my face in his itchy striped coat. "You look so normal."

"Hey, hey, hey." Mr. Harrison held me at arm's length and took a long look at my face. "What's all this about, Olivia? Has someone hurt you?"

I nodded but then shook my head in an adamant no. "Is Frannie home?"

"She's doing homework upstairs."

"May I go see her?"

"Of course."

Mr. Harrison dropped his hands from my arms, and I bounded up the staircase that led to the Harrisons' crowded yet homey apartment above the shop.

The front room bustled with the usual whoops and laughter of Frannie's five younger siblings—Martha, Carl, Annie, Willie, and Pearl. They were like a hill of ants, spilling over furniture and books, piling on top of one another, and bumping into the blue-papered walls. Off in the kitchen, around the right bend, someone rapped a spoon against the rim of a pot. I followed a divine scented trail of boiled beef and carrots and found Mrs. Harrison preparing a stew over her big black cookstove, amid a cloud of steam that drifted past her round face. The copper pot spat wet polka dots across the clean white front of her pinafore apron, and she could have used a few more pins to hold down her brown topknot, which was flecked with a scattering of gray hairs. Otherwise, she was perfect.

"Mrs. Harrison!" I threw my arms around her sturdy shoulders. "It's wonderful to see you looking healthy and happy."

"My goodness." Mrs. Harrison patted my elbow with a hand that dampened my blouse. "What's all this about, Livie?"

Frannie peeked up from her McGuffey's Reader at the round kitchen table. "Yes, what is all this about, Livie?"

I let go of Mrs. Harrison, despite her warmth. "I need to talk to you privately, Frannie. As soon as possible."

"All right." Frannie neatened her pile of homework papers and stood. "We'll be up in my bedroom, Mama."

"That's fine, dear." Mrs. Harrison stirred her pot and pressed her lips into a thin smile, but I could tell from her watchful Mama-bird eyes that she sensed something wasn't quite right.

Frannie and I climbed the second flight of stairs, past piles of books perched on the rickety wooden steps—books that always appeared to have wandered in from the shop of their own accord and made themselves at home wherever they found space. The air up there was rich with the perfumes of paper and ink, along with a fine peppering of dust.

Frannie led me into the room she shared with all three of her sisters, a cramped space with two beds, a chest of drawers, and a tall pine wardrobe. She planted herself on the bed that belonged to her and Martha.

"What's wrong?" she asked. "Did your father say something to you?"

"I . . . um . . ." I balled my hands into fists. "I . . . Oh, criminy. When I tell you what just happened, you're going to think I've gone nutty."

"Just tell me. You're clearly not yourself. Wait—" She sat up straight, her brown eyes enormous. "Oh . . . This doesn't have anything to do with Percy, does it?"

"No. It has to do with Monsieur Henri Reverie, *the marvel of the new century* . . . and all that other hogwash."

She knitted her eyebrows. "The hypnotist?"

"Yes. He hypnotized me again, just now, in Father's office."

"What? Why?"

"Father heard . . ." I braced my back against the wardrobe. "He found out I was at the rally yesterday. He thinks I'm turning into my mother. He decided I needed my unfeminine thoughts removed from my brain."

Frannie's mouth fell open. "What? No! Did he really say such a thing?"

"I've heard horror stories of troublesome daughters and

wives getting sent away to asylums. I've read Nellie Bly's *Ten Days in a Mad-House*. What if this is only the first step?"

"What did that hypnotist do to you?"

"Henri told me"—I rubbed my forehead—"I'd see the world the way it truly is, and the roles of men and women would be clearer than they've ever been before. I don't think my father understood what that meant. I'm not sure I do, either . . . Your father looks like someone we can trust. But my father . . ." I tucked my hands behind my back, between the wardrobe and my lower spine, to quiet the tremors shaking through my fingers.

Frannie leaned forward. "Your father what?"

"He looked like a vampire. I swear upon a stack of Bibles, he had fangs and flesh as pale as a corpse's."

Her eyes scanned my face, as if she were waiting for a twitch of my mouth or a flash of laughter in my eyes to reveal I was joking.

I chewed my lip, but I most certainly did not laugh.

"Livie . . ." She let loose a nervous giggle. "You've read *Dracula* at least four times in the past year."

"Yes, I know that."

"And now you're telling me your father looks like a vampire?"

"Yes."

"Don't you think that's a little . . . peculiar?"

"Yes, it is peculiar, but I was hypnotized, Frannie. You saw the power Henri Reverie had over me last night. He's like a sorcerer who changed the world for my eyes alone, and I can't bear the thought of going out there and seeing my father—or any other man—with fangs and bloodless skin and—"

"All right." She sprang off the bed. "I believe you're truly seeing something troubling, but perhaps Mr. Reverie simply stirred up your imagination."

"He's supposed to be *killing off* my imagination. Father hired him to cure me of my dreams."

She winced. "But if these aren't dreams or imaginings . . . what are they?"

"They seem real. They seem true. How can I go home to Father when he looks like that?"

My nose itched as if it required either a cry or a good sneeze. I scratched the tip with the back of one hand.

Frannie walked over to me and coaxed my hand between her palms. "Have supper with us tonight."

I shook my head. "Father will worry when he sees I'm not home."

"We'll ask Carl to run over to his office and tell him we've invited you to stay. And then Carl and I will take you home after supper so I can see for myself if anything looks different about your father. I'll even give you a little sign if he appears to be normal."

"What type of sign?"

"Well . . ." She scraped her teeth over her bottom lip. "I'll say, 'I still can't believe how many times you've read *Dracula*,

Livie. One too many times, that's for sure.' If you hear that, it means what you're seeing is truly just in your mind, and so it must be the work of that malicious, selfish, conniving hypnotist— Oh, wait." She squeezed my hand and looked me straight in the eye. "You didn't tell me how Henri Reverie appeared after the hypnosis."

I groaned and hunched my shoulders.

"What?" She squeezed my hand again. "Was he even worse than your father?"

I shook my head. "That would have made everything far less confusing."

"What did he look like?"

I sighed. "He looked like . . . I can't even bring myself to say it. It almost hurts to admit what he made me feel."

"What?" Her face paled. "What did he make you feel?"

"He looked . . ." I swallowed. "He looked like someone I should trust utterly."

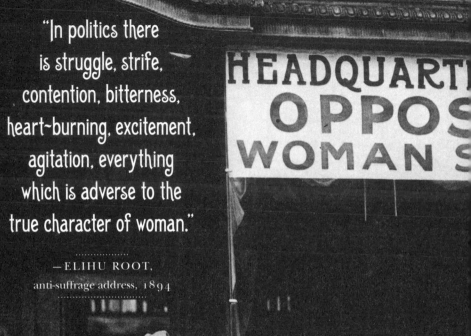

"In politics there is struggle, strife, contention, bitterness, heart~burning, excitement, agitation, everything which is adverse to the true character of woman."

—ELIHU ROOT,
anti-suffrage address, 1894

CHAPTER SIX

THE SILENCER

At supper that evening, the noisy passel of Harrisons chatted and joked about school escapades and camping trips while they stuffed me full of stew and potatoes. Every now and again I caught Mr. and Mrs. Harrison glancing at me with worried expressions, as if they couldn't quite shake the memory of my emotional entrance earlier that afternoon.

After supper, I slid my arms into the thick sleeves of my coat, which, along with my book bag, had been fetched by Frannie's fourteen-year-old brother, Carl, when he went to tell Father I'd be home late. The woolen collar snuggled up to my neck and pervaded my nostrils with the dental office's distinctive odor—a sweet, antiseptic, and metallic potpourri that now flooded me with memories of Henri's hands on my head.

I buttoned up for the outside chill. "How did my father look when you saw him, Carl?"

Carl smiled. "Bloody."

"Bloody?" I asked with a gasp.

"He was leeching some woman, and he had her head locked into a metal contraption to keep her still." Carl tilted his head back to demonstrate, his hands clamped around his temples beneath his curly brown hair. "The leech had wiggled out of the tube wrong and bloodied up the woman's lip, so your father was trying to get the little bugger to travel down to her gums. His hands were smeared in bright red blood."

I lowered my shoulders and steadied my breathing. The fact that the blood was leech related and had nothing to do with fangs and lacerated throats was the best news I'd heard all day.

"I STILL CAN'T BELIEVE HOW MANY TIMES YOU'VE READ *Dracula*," said Frannie from beneath a hissing gas lamp in the dim hallway of my house. "One too many times, that's for sure."

The soles of Father's house slippers whispered their way from his office in the back. I kept my face turned toward the tan rug by the front door as long as I could, but then Frannie gave my back a gentle pat, and I gained the courage to raise my chin.

Father—regular Father, not the cadaverous fiend with the rat-fur beard—frowned at me in the hallway.

"You're not reading that ghastly novel again, are you, Olivia?" he asked. "Haven't you had enough of *Dracula* by now?"

"Yes." I gulped down a nasty taste of bile. "Quite enough."

Carl stuffed his hands into his coat pockets. "You should come to supper again on Sunday, Livie," he said. "Our parents are celebrating—what is it, Frannie?—their hundredth anniversary now?"

"Their twentieth," said Frannie with a roll of her eyes at Carl's exaggeration. "Yes, come. We're planning to sit down at five o'clock. We'd love to have you join us."

"I'd love to be there. Thank you."

Carl opened the door to take his leave, but before following him, Frannie grabbed my hand and leaned in close with a whisper: "Come back to my house if you need anything else. At any time."

I mustered a weak smile. "Thank you."

They closed the door and went on their way.

I stood with my back to Father, facing the exit through which my friends had just vanished while the cool taste of the outside air lingered on my tongue.

"I was so worried about you this afternoon," said Father in a voice cozy and warm with paternal concern.

Despite his tone, I didn't dare turn around.

"Why did you run away like that?" he asked. "You just left me standing there."

"What did you expect me to do? *Thank* you?"

"No—but you made me worry something had gone terribly wrong. Mr. Reverie assured me he found you. He said you had simply been spooked by your new view of the world. But still . . . I was troubled."

I stared at the door.

"Why won't you turn around and look at me, Olivia? Do I look different to you?"

I squeezed my eyes shut and swallowed. "I . . . um . . ."

"What?"

"I . . . I see the world . . . the way it truly is. The roles of men and women are clearer than they have ever been before." I slipped my hands inside my warm coat sleeves and clung to the woolen lining. "I saw a storefront—women, suffrage—a cage."

"What?"

"I saw a cage."

"Suffrage is like a restrictive cage, you mean?"

I pursed my lips. "All is well."

"You understand your place in the world, then?"

I opened my eyes and again peered at the door to the world beyond. "Yes. I understand precisely where I do and don't belong."

Father breathed a sigh. "Thank heavens. It worked."

Another deep sigh, this one accompanied by a small belch. "Well, in light of this new outlook on life, I'll be more than happy to allow you to accompany Percy Acklen to the party tomorrow evening. As long as you promise to be well behaved—and to represent our family with utmost care in front of both Percy and the Eiderlings—I'll have Gerda take a note to the Acklen household tomorrow morning."

"Thank you."

Silence wedged between us again. I assumed he was waiting for me to turn around and face him, perhaps even to fling my arms around his shoulders and tell him, *You were right, Father. My life is so much better now that I hallucinate and can no longer articulate my anger.*

When I showed no signs of moving, he retreated down the hall, his house slippers swishing across the floorboards.

"Time to ready yourself for bed, Olivia," he said as he went. "I'll be finishing my nightcap in my office if you need me."

My stomach clenched into a knot. I steadied myself against the little marble-topped side table we used for collecting mail, and my palm crinkled the copy of the newspaper that featured the illustration of Henri and me. Farther down on the page, a headline I had failed to see that morning jumped out at me in boldfaced letters:

WHY THE WOMEN OF THIS STATE
SHOULD BE SILENCED

The author: Judge Percival R. Acklen.

Percy's father.

I grabbed the paper off the table and tore up the staircase.

Behind my closed door, seated on the edge of my bed, I devoured the entire piece, still buttoned inside my coat and shoes. The letter stated the following:

As nearly everyone knows, in June of this year, the men of Oregon voted down a referendum that would have given the women of this great state of ours the right to vote. As this upcoming Tuesday's presidential election draws nearer, irate females have taken to the steps of the courthouse in downtown Portland to complain about their lack of a voice in American politics—and to bemoan their jealousies over their voting sisters in neighboring Idaho.

What these unbridled women lack is a thorough knowledge of the female brain. Two of my closest friends, Drs. Cornelius Piper and Mortimer Yves, two fine gentlemen educated at East Coast universities, both support the staggering wealth of scientific research that proves women were created for domestic duties alone, not higher thinking. A body built for childbearing and mothering is clearly a body meant to stay in the home. If females muddle their minds with politics and other matters confusing to a woman's head, they will abandon their wifely and motherly duties and inevitably trigger the downfall of American society.

Moreover, we would never allow an unqualified, undereducated, ignorant citizen to run our country as president. Why, therefore, would we allow such a person to vote for president?

Women of Oregon, you preside over our children and our homes. Rejoice in your noble position upon this earth. Return to your children and husbands, and stop concerning yourselves with masculine matters beyond your understanding. Silence in a woman is feminine, honorable, and, above all else, natural. Save your voices for sweet words of support for your hardworking husbands and gentle lullabies for your babes—not for American politics.

I ground my teeth together until my jaw ached. This man—this silencer of women—was raising the first boy who had ever looked at me with longing and affection in his eyes.

Poor Percy.

Poor *Mrs.* Acklen.

Poor Oregon.

We were all being lectured by a buffoon.

I thought of Frannie's mother and everything she did to keep their wild household *and* their bookstore running in tip-top order. A fire kindled in my chest, burning, spreading, crackling loudly enough for me to hear it, until I worried my breathing might singe the bedroom walls. My mouth filled with the taste of thick black smoke.

I pulled a sheet of writing paper out of my rolltop desk, dipped the nib of my pen into a pot of velvety dark ink, and wrote a response to his letter with my neatest display of penmanship.

> *To Judge Acklen:*
>
> *You state that women were made for domestic duties alone. Have you ever stopped to observe the responsibilities involved with domestic duties?*
>
> *What better person to understand the administration of a country than an individual who spends her days mediating quarrels, balancing household budgets, organizing and executing three complex meals, and ensuring all rooms, appliances, deliveries, clothing, guests, family members, and pets are tended to and functioning the way they ought to be? I do not know of any other job in the world that so closely resembles the presidency itself.*
>
> *Moreover, females are raised to become rational, industrious, fair, and compassionate human beings. Males are taught to sow their wild oats and run free while they're able. Which gender is truly the most prepared to make decisions about the management of a country? Do you want a responsible individual or a rambunctious one choosing the fate of our government?*
>
> *You insinuate that women's minds are easily muddled, yet you entrust us with the rearing of your children, America's future. Mothers are our first teachers. Mothers are the voices of reason who instill the nation's values in our youth. Mothers are the ones who raise the politicians for whom they are not allowed to vote. Why would you let an easily muddled creature*

take on such important duties? Why not hire men to bring up your sons and daughters?

I can already hear you arguing that women's bodies were designed for childrearing, but that is not true, sir. Our bodies may have been built for birthing children and nourishing them during their first meals, but it is our minds that are doing the largest share of the work. On a daily basis, we women prove that our brains are sharp and quick, yet you are too blind to see our intelligence.

Furthermore, you have no need to fear that we would forgo our domestic duties if we were to become voting citizens, for we have been trained all our lives to balance a multitude of tasks. We do not let our homes fall into ruin simply because we have been given one more item to accomplish. Worry more about the males who have only one job and no household chores. Their minds are more likely to stray than ours.

Do you call your own mother "undereducated" and "ignorant," Judge Acklen? Was her mind in too much of a muddle to keep your childhood household intact? Was she so easily confused that she was unable to raise a boy who would one day become a judge? I think not. Your mother was undoubtedly a quick-witted, accountable individual who would probably make a far better president than the pampered male you gentlemen vote into office this Tuesday.

I dipped my pen into the inkwell, caught my breath, and read my incendiary words, debating whether the phrasing was too obvious. I tried to imagine what would happen if the writer were identified and made public. Father would likely shove our entire life savings into Henri Reverie's pockets to ensure my mind was altered beyond recognition. There might indeed be a trip to an asylum. I'd even heard rumors of surgeons removing wombs from the bodies of rebellious wives and daughters.

Unthinkable.

But maybe . . . if I was careful . . . just maybe the right anonymous signature would disguise me.

I tested out various examples in my head.

– *An Angry Woman*
– *An Irate Female*
– *Your Long-Suffering Mothers, Wives, and Daughters*
– *A Highly Educated Woman*
– *A Girl Who Refuses to Be Silent*

No. Too emotional for the tastes of stubborn men. I pictured Father shaking his head and calling the letter writer *hysterical.*

I tapped the nib of my pen against the well to dispose of stray drops of ink, sampled ideas for two more minutes, and then wrote the wisest, most reasonable approach.

– *A Responsible Woman*

No. 1.   Upper and Lower Incisors and Canine.

No. 6.   Upper Incisors and Bicuspids.

No. 13.   Right Upper Molars.

No. 14.   Left Upper Molars.

No. 27.   Upper Wisdom.

No. 33.   Lower Incisors, Canines and Bicuspids.

CHAPTER SEVEN

ROTTEN

I dreamt about the hypnosis.

The procedure again occurred in Father's downtown office, this time back in his operatory, at night. The stark wooden room glowed in the light of a bare bulb that reflected off the spittoon and the neat row of dental tools lined on a small oval table. Leather straps clamped my head and wrists to the operatory chair—an uncomfortable piece of furniture padded in worn mauve velvet and braced by four metal feet sculpted like the paws of a beast, as if the chair would one day spring to life and devour some poor, troublesome patient.

Father, his hands still bloody from a leeching, polished the sharp tip of his drill with a white cloth. Behind him in the shadows stood Henri Reverie in his dark suit and a black magician's hat that appeared to be a taller, more ominous version of his real-life hat, but his luminous blue eyes were the only parts of him I could truly see. *Oh, Lord*—those bright and haunting blue eyes.

"Shall we begin?" asked Father, and he leaned over me, reeking of blood and chloroform.

He pulled open my mouth with his thumb, which tasted like everyone else's saliva, and his ears turned as pale and as pointed as the Count's in *Dracula*. Bat ears made of human flesh is what they were—horrifying flaps sticking out from the sides of his pasty-gray head with its fierce and bulging red eyes. He pumped the drill's foot pedal to make the needle spin.

I arched my back and froze against the chair, and that drill buzzed against one of my molars until bitter flecks of tooth sprayed across my tongue. My nerves throbbed with pain. I screamed bloody murder.

"Good heavens, Olivia!" called Father over the grinding and the shrieking. "Your entire head is rotten." He stopped the drill and swiveled around to his little stand of tools. "Let's remove some of those troublesome spots."

"No!" I kicked my feet and tried to wrench my wrists free of the bindings. "Don't take anything away!"

Father picked up a silver instrument, a hybrid of a key and

a corkscrew, with a small metal claw at one end and an ivory handle on the other.

"Let me just get this dental key in there"—both his fanged face and the instrument rushed my way—"so we can break apart that problematic piece."

"No!"

He gripped my tooth with the metal claw and cranked the ivory handle. Pressure mounted on the molar, growing, pushing, squeezing, *CRACK!*—the tooth split in two.

I howled in agony, but Father muffled my cries by digging beneath the crumbling tooth, stirring up blood and more pain, stretching my cheek and lips with cold metal. He then grabbed hold of the shattered molar with a pair of long forceps and yanked each piece straight out of my gum.

"This rotten, broken tooth is your dream of attending a university," he said, and he displayed the decayed rubble on the palm of his hand. "Mr. Reverie, would you please be of assistance?"

"*Oui, monsieur.*" Henri whisked his hat off his head and held it out for Father, who tossed my tooth pieces inside with the sound of rustling gravel.

Father loomed back over me and went in for another molar. Over the high-pitched din of my screams and the thumps of my thrashings he called out, "This is your dream of voting."

Yank, plunk. The second tooth landed in Henri's hat.

He continued onward.

"This is your dream of working for a living."

Yank, plunk.

"This is your dream of becoming 'A Responsible Woman' who publishes letters in newspapers."

Yank, plunk.

"This is your dream of wearing trousers while bicycling."

Yank, plunk.

The list went on and on, and my mouth grew emptier and emptier, until my wails weakened and my heartbeat slackened. My arms flopped over the armrests, my energy spent, and I witnessed Henri waving his gloved hand over the black silk hat with a graceful flick of his fingers.

"You see, Mademoiselle Mead?" He showed me the dark recesses of the hat's interior. At the very bottom lay a mirror that reflected my toothless mouth with blood spilling down to my chin. "If you stay with your father, he'll take it all away."

I awoke with a gasp, my gums sore, but all my teeth, thankfully, intact.

MR. RHODES

ather's fiendish visage did not return during breakfast, thank heavens. I munched my toast without
ever stopping to speak—a good, quiet girl—and
every few minutes Father beamed at me over his
newspaper, quite pleased with my angry silence,
which he clearly mistook for obedience.

He left for work, and I attempted to walk to school—I truly
did. My toffee-brown book bag hung off my shoulder, and
my lunch pail dangled from the crooks of my right fingers. I
made it a full block north before I witnessed a peculiar sight.

Our neighbor Mrs. Stanton exited the front door of her narrow green house on the corner of Main, followed by her three little ducklings: a pair of twin girls in white bonnets and a toddler boy in a navy-blue sailor suit. She sold preserves to grocers in the city, and she and her children often emerged from their house with a wooden pull wagon stocked with jars of brightly colored jams and vegetables swimming in pickling vinegar.

Obviously, all of this wasn't the peculiar part.

No, here was the strange thing that caused me to stop walking and gawk at the woman with my arms hanging by my sides: On this particular morning, Mrs. Stanton was a ghost.

The trees she passed, the white picket fence bordering her house—they were all visible through her skin and clothing and her tea-stain-colored hair, which looked as translucent as the layers of an onion. She was a cobweb woman. Barely there. Almost gone.

A nothing person.

"I FOUND THIS LYING ON THE SIDEWALK OUTSIDE THE building," I said to the statuesque receptionist manning the front desk of the *Oregonian*'s nine-story headquarters on Sixth and Alder.

The female employee, sporting half-lens spectacles and a thick black tie, sat with her posture so impeccably straight, I felt the need to stretch my neck a little higher. Rows of lady workers in tailored dress suits typed behind her in a commotion of clicking keys and high-pitched dings that signified the ends of typewritten lines.

I inhaled a long breath of inky air and handed the woman an unstamped envelope, addressed *Letters to the Editor Department.* "Someone must have dropped it," I said. "I thought I should bring it in." My fingers pulsed with nervous energy.

The woman took my envelope and studied the address through her half-moon lenses. Her hair was puffed so high and her sharp chin held with such confidence that I could have sworn I shrank six inches just from standing in front of her.

She lifted her face and offered a thin smile. "I'll deliver it to the correct department. Thank you for bringing it in."

A gleam in her eye told me she knew the handwriting on the envelope belonged to a seventeen-year-old girl with shaking hands, so I turned and left the building.

NOT ONCE IN MY LIFE HAD I PLAYED HOOKY FROM SCHOOL before that frosty-cold autumn morning. *Not once.* The temptation to be truant had never even occurred to me.

Yet instead of hurrying off to school, I found myself standing in front of the arched brick entrance of the Metropolitan Theater. A haunted sort of feeling squirmed around in my gut, but still I walked inside, my feet motivated by a will of their own.

The empty lobby felt like a hollowed-out husk compared to the hot and buzzing scene from Halloween night. My footsteps clapped across the black-and-white tiles, and the echoing, gilded ceiling above seemed a thousand feet high. I stopped and caught my breath, worried I'd get caught trespassing. I probably shouldn't have even liked theaters so much—not after their allure had spirited my mother away one snowy December night when I was just four years old. When she told us she couldn't breathe in our house anymore.

The pipe organ started up in the auditorium, and my heart leapt into my throat. Beyond the open doorway, someone played "Evening Prayer" from *Hansel and Gretel*, the spellbinding melody Genevieve Reverie had performed when Henri invited me to float up to the theater's catwalks and bask in the warm electric lights. Whoever was attempting to play the song lacked Genevieve's passion and talent, but even the school-recital stiffness of the performance allowed the notes to melt inside my bones and ease my troubled soul.

With silent footfalls, I stole into the auditorium.

The music proved to be the work of a bottom-heavy lady organist with pumpkin-orange hair. She sat in front of the dark wood-and-copper pipe organ, all alone on the stage, her eyes fixed on the sheet music in front of her as if she were just learning the song that very moment. I hunkered down in a red velvet chair in the back row and listened to that mesmerizing melody that reminded me so of Halloween night. My eyelids drooped with each passing refrain. I remembered all the rows of lights hanging above the stage, beckoning me to them, and my cheeks and neck warmed.

Henri Reverie's pacifying voice rose to my ears: "And that's when I leap off the young lady's torso."

I opened my eyes with a start. There he was, on the stage, strolling over to the organist with three pages of notes in his hands, dressed in his midnight-black trousers and vest, without the coat.

Henri Reverie.

He pointed to one of his papers. "If you finish the song early, I recommend transitioning into 'Sleep, Little Rosebud.'"

The pumpkin-haired organist, who for some reason wasn't Henri's sister, withdrew her fingers from the keys and rotated toward the hypnotist. "Do you really stand on top of these ladies, young man?"

"Oui," said Henri, nodding. "But I believe in equality, and I stand on gentlemen, too, depending on what I feel the audience would prefer to see. Haven't you ever heard of the great Herbert L. Flint?"

"No."

Henri stepped back. "You haven't?"

"Do you honestly think I've heard of every two-bit stage performer?" asked the organist.

"But he is not 'a two-bit performer.' He's a well-known and respected mesmerist. We adapted his use of the human plank for our show, and I always open with it. It is my most popular feat."

"And none of these stepped-upon volunteers ever complains?"

Henri shook his head. "None so far."

"Why do you think that is?"

"Well"—he lowered his papers and rubbed his smooth chin—"I never force anyone to come on the stage, *madame.* The volunteers join me up here because they want to, even if they initially demur. I think they want—need—to be seen. To be noticed."

The organist scowled. "And having a hypnotist stand on their torsos, while they're sleeping like pacified infants, is preferable to remaining shrinking violets?"

Henri shrugged. "As I said, they never complain, and the audiences adore viewing them up here. You should hear the applause. Americans gobble up magic and visual oddities, such as viewing a man standing upon a near-floating woman."

"It is scandalous. You may as well be in New York City, debasing yourself in *Sapho,* that *rrr*ibald"—she rolled the *r* in *ribald* with dramatic flair—"theatrical production I keep reading about in the newspaper. The one about the strumpet and her lovers."

"As I was saying . . ." He pointed to his notes again. "This is where you transition into 'Sleep, Little Rosebud.'"

"You ought to be ashamed of yourself."

"Start with an adagio tempo. The notes should be delicate at first."

"Youth these days will be the death of morality." The organist flipped through her sheet music to find the right selection. After a cough and an outward thrust of her chest, she blundered her way through a musical number that would have sounded quite pretty if it were being played by anyone else.

Henri wandered across the stage with his hands in his pockets, wincing and hunching his shoulders as the off-key notes assaulted his ears. His gaze turned to the (almost) empty auditorium, so I ducked my head down farther and inhaled a noseful of dust.

Before I could control myself, a sneeze exploded from my nostrils.

"Who's there?" asked Henri, which made the organist stop playing.

I froze at first, but then I felt like a fool crouching down on the dirty floor that way, my feet stuck in something sticky and my nose itching with the threat of another sneeze. I stood up and let myself be seen.

Henri squinted up at me. "Miss Mead?"

"Yes. It's me—I mean, it is I, to be grammatically—"

"Stay right there. Don't go anywhere." He leapt off the end of the stage and landed on his feet with a thump—a startling maneuver that made me think of illustrations of lions chasing down gazelles.

I turned and lunged for the door.

"No! I need to speak to you." I heard him bounding up the aisle behind me. "Don't go. For your own safety, don't go. I've been worried sick about you."

At those unexpected words, I stopped.

"Please . . ." He skidded to a halt a few feet away from me and held out his arms to catch his balance. "Please tell me—you have *got* to tell me—what terrified you so badly when you saw your father yesterday."

I bit my lip and hesitated.

"Please"—he braced his hands on his hips and regained his breathing—"tell me. I swear to God, you can trust me, Miss Mead."

"My name is Olivia. I have no intention of calling you anything as respectful as Mr. Reverie, so please stop this 'Miss' business."

"What I do on that stage, Olivia"—for some reason his accent suddenly sounded more American, less French—"all that showy stuff, it's just to earn money. I want to help people with hypnosis, not hurt them. I want to cure people of their addictions and fears and—and—"

"And dreams," I finished for him.

"No, not dreams." He swallowed and stepped closer. "Why did you react to your father the way you did? How did he look after the hypnosis?"

"Are you done flirting, young man?" called the pumpkin-haired organist from the stage. "I'm not being paid to watch you fraternize with girls."

"One moment, please, *madame*."

"I have a good mind to tell Mr. Gillingham you're wasting the theater's money—"

"Please—this is important." He turned back to me and

softened his voice to a whisper. "I'm going to tell you something I don't usually share with anyone."

"No! I don't want to become your confidante." I backed away. "I just want you to return my mind to the way it was."

"Listen—"

"No."

"Olivia"—he came to me and took hold of my arm—"my sister has a cancerous tumor the size of a goose egg in her bosom."

My jaw dropped with a gasp of shock.

"It's rare in girls her age," he continued, his eyes moistening, "but it's there. She needs surgery. There's a specialist in San Francisco. His fees . . . they won't be cheap."

"What? No." I wrenched his fingers off my arm. "You're lying. That's a cruel story to tell a person just to get your way."

"You can see the world the way it truly is, so be honest"— he straightened the bottom of his vest with a sharp tug of the black fabric—"do I look like someone who's lying about his sister's health?"

His eyes drew me toward them with a pull that tipped me forward onto my toes. I waved my hands to steady myself, and a second later, like a swift gust of wind, Genevieve Reverie emerged by his side in a white nightgown, her blond head slumped against his arm, her face thin and peaked. The rest of the theater rushed away into a vacuum, and all I saw was the two of them—Genevieve, ill, exhausted, supported by Henri.

I blinked, and she was gone. Her tousled-haired brother stood alone.

"For heaven's sake, Mr. Reverie," called the woman on the stage. "I've had enough of your dillydallying . . ."

"My father looked like the monster in Bram Stoker's novel," I told Henri. "Have you read *Dracula*?"

"Isn't that about a human vampire?"

"Yes, and that's exactly how you made him appear in his office. His skin lacked blood, and his teeth were the fangs of a ferocious animal. I'm witnessing other things as well—disturbing sights—so tell me, please, for the love of God, what in the world did you do to my head?"

"Mr. Reverie," bellowed the organist in a bone-rattling voice that consumed the entire theater, "throw that girl out of here this minute, or I'm asking Mr. Gillingham to cancel your performance. I know of two highly talented juggling brothers who would love nothing more than to take over your booking tonight."

"I'm coming, I'm coming."

He backed away from me, and a topsy-turvy feeling seized me again. My eyes insisted on seeing his hair as more ruffled than before, his dark clothing as frayed and worn. He suffered from fatigue. Distress.

"I'd very much like to discuss this matter with you more, Olivia," he said.

"I don't want to discuss this matter." I rubbed my eyes with the heels of my hands. "I want you to change me back. All is well!"

"I can't."

"You can't? All is well!"

"Not now."

I shoved my hands against my temples and swallowed down my anger so the right words would come. "Do you want to know how *you* truly look, Monsieur Reverie?"

He stopped in his tracks.

"You look like a shifty showman who doesn't really know what he's doing," I said. "And I'm willing to bet the remaining shreds of my sanity that *Reverie* isn't even your real last name."

He frowned and jogged back to the stage—back to his rehearsal with the glowering substitute organist who shook her head as if he were a misbehaving spaniel—and he seemed to ignore my words.

Before he reached the front row, however, he peeked over his shoulder.

He gave me my answer, in an accent that wasn't French in the slightest.

"You're right, Olivia. It's Rhodes. My name is Henry—with a *y*, not an *i*—Rhodes. But as I'm sure you've seen with your own eyes, I am *not* just a shifty showman."

CHAPTER NINE

DEAR, DARLING DAUGHTER

His dual names pulsed in my head all the way home.

Henri Reverie. Henry Rhodes. Henri Reverie. Henry Rhodes.

And then *cancer, cancer, cancer, cancer. Tumor, tumor, tumor, tumor. Genevieve.*

I quickened my pace and managed to find my way back to my house, despite the blurred and rippling sidewalks and the flashes of blue eyes from Henry's theater handbills, watching me from shop windows. Always watching me.

I tripped over the threshold of our front door, and Gerda

raised her head from dusting Father's antique denture collection in the parlor.

"What are you doing home from school, Miss Mead?"

I closed the door and inhaled a deep breath. "I have a headache." I parked my lunch pail on the marble-topped hall table. My book bag slid off my shoulder to the floor.

"*Ja?* A headache?" Gerda lowered the duster. "I left a note with the Acklens. It said that you would go with their boy to the party tonight. Should I not have done that?"

"Oh." I slumped against the wall. "Percy. How the blue blazes did I forget about him?" I massaged the aching bridge of my nose between my thumb and middle finger. "He's going to think I'm an absolute loon."

"Shall I send another note?"

"No. Thank you. I need some sort of reward for surviving this day." I pushed myself off the wall and headed for the staircase.

"Oh, Miss Mead—I almost forgot, your mother's birthday envelope arrived. I put it on your bed."

"Oh? Thank you." My stomach sank. "I suppose I had better go see what extraordinary adventures she's undertaken this year."

I clambered up to my room with the same withered-hot-air-balloon sensation I'd experienced when Henry pulled me down from the theater's ceiling.

Halfway across the bedroom floor, my feet stopped. There wasn't an envelope waiting for me on my pink bedspread.

It was a ticket, a pale brown one with curved edges and the words ONE-WAY PASSAGE TO NEW YORK CITY written across the center in block letters. My skin warmed, and my ears buzzed. I rubbed my eyes and willed away the delusion, for that's what it had to have been.

I lowered my hands. The ticket disappeared, and a plain white envelope came into view, return address New York City. I picked it up and ripped it open.

October 10, 1900

My Dear, Darling Daughter,

Can you really be seventeen years old, my funny little lamb? You're more woman than girl now, which makes your poor mama feel like an ancient crone. My heavens, I was only three months younger than you are now when I became your mother. I hope and pray you don't follow my same path to early mother-hood. Don't rush into relationships with boys, even if they are as handsome as a certain young dental apprentice who wooed me off the stage eighteen years ago. You know as well as I do about the heartbreak that can result when two fools hurry to play grown-up.

On a much happier note, I'm giddy with excitement to announce I'm now established in New York City, playing Tita-nia in a little theater production of A Midsummer Night's Dream. *"Thou art as wise as thou art beautiful." Oh, you should see my costume, my lamb—gold and purple silk, and a heaping crown of flowers upon my red curls.*

I'm settled in an apartment near Barnard College, and I think of you every time I see those smart young women walking around with books tucked under their arms. I remember you trying to read your little collection of fairy tales to me when you were just four years old and how much I marveled at your intelligence. Does your father allow you to be bright? Or does he still insist young ladies ought to be silent idiots?

Oh, my darling, I would love to see what you look like as a grown-up young lady. As usual, I'm slipping a little bit of money into the envelope as a birthday present. If you'd care to come east and visit your wicked old mama, I would open my door to you with outstretched arms and hug away all the hurt I've caused you. I don't believe I did you any good when you were a wee little thing, and I still strongly feel our separation was the best for all of us. However, I certainly know a thing or two about being a young woman, and I could take better care of you now than I did back then. I would even let you take a tour of Barnard, and perhaps I'd allow you to watch that delicious play Sapho, *if the moralists don't shut it down again.*

Happy birthday, my Olivia.

Your Loving Mother

A ten-dollar bill fluttered down to my lap.

A Midsummer Night's Dream must have been paying Mother well—or else she had found herself another wealthy suitor with a fat billfold. I crouched down on the floorboards and slid out one of Father's bright yellow cigar boxes from the dusty depths beneath my bed. Inside I kept my collection of Mother's birthday and Christmas gifts, delivered in little envelopes throughout the years, minus a few missing dollars and coins that had paid for books and hair ribbons.

I counted the cash, including my newest contribution.

"Holy mackerel, Mother," I said, followed by a long sigh.

One hundred twenty-three dollars now waited for me inside that old cigar box.

One hundred twenty three.

I re-counted the stockpile and sat back on my heels, wondering how much tuition would cost at faraway Barnard College, where young women walked around with books tucked under their arms, as if in a marvelous dream.

CHAPTER TEN

"EYES UNCLEAN AND FULL OF HELL~FIRE"

rannie stopped by for a rushed after-school visit.

"Are you unwell?" she asked from our front porch, where long shadows yawned across the scuffed red boards and the scraggly potted plants.

"I had a bad headache."

"I worried the hypnosis made you sick—or that your father sent you away." She hugged me against her chest. "You scared me to death with all that talk about asylums."

"I'm all right." I patted her on the back and let her squeeze me until my collarbones hurt. "In fact, I'm going to go to a party at Sadie Eiderling's house tonight. Can you believe it?"

She stiffened. "I beg your pardon?"

"Percy's taking me."

She dropped her arms and pulled away.

"Don't worry, I'm going to be quite careful of his"—I tipped my face forward and lowered my voice —"grabby hands."

"It's not a joke, Livie."

"He didn't grab you, did he?"

"No!" She blushed so hard, she went practically mauve. "No, I've just heard rumors . . ." She backed away. "I've got to go help Papa at the store. Please be extremely careful with Percy—and your father."

"Frannie?"

"Good-bye, Livie."

She scrambled down the porch steps, and for a moment I thought I glimpsed a white handprint on the back of her blue skirt, below her swinging brown braid.

A shudder and a blink, and the print was gone.

FATHER CAME HOME FROM WORK AROUND FIVE THIRTY that evening. I hid in my bedroom and pinned up my hair for the Eiderlings' party.

"Are you getting ready, Olivia?" he called up to me.

"Yes," I yelled through my closed door. "Gerda is boiling a ham for your dinner, and then she'll help me dress. I can't come down right now."

"Don't take too long. Young men don't like to be kept waiting."

"I won't."

I fussed with my hairpins in front of my mirror, my hands slippery and my mind squalling with fears about the visions. I kept expecting my mirror and my hairbrush to transform into nightmarish abominations—hissing creatures with snouts and needle-sharp teeth that would squeeze around my torso and take a bite.

My hair suffered from all that worrying. Most girls of Sadie Eiderling's caliber were wearing their long locks puffed high on their heads in enormous pompadours, like the fashionable girls in Charles Dana Gibson's drawings. On occasion, Frannie and I would try styling our hair in that manner, but our pompadours always turned out lopsided or collapsed like deflated soufflés—which was precisely the problem at the moment. My pinned-up mess of dark hair sagged as if I had just sprinted through the rain with Percy again. I hated it. Every strand.

"All is well!" I said, and I dropped my hands to my sides and growled.

All is well? Balderdash! Bull dung!

Even worse words entered my head, but they shall not be repeated.

I shoved more hairpins into my topknot, and my eyes drifted to a conjoined pair of silver picture frames that sat on top of my chest of drawers. In the rightmost frame sat a photograph of Mother, just sixteen years old, posed in a brocade Renaissance mourning costume in front of a backdrop of painted vines. A black veil draped over her thick ringlets, which looked brown instead of their natural red in the sepia image. I remembered her explaining to me that she had been playing Olivia, my namesake, in a traveling production of Shakespeare's *Twelfth Night*, and that's how she met Father. Her pretty face—rosebud lips, arched brows, almond-shaped eyes, long lashes—seemed nothing like mine, save for perhaps the round tip of her nose. She looked like the type of person who never lacked confidence about anything.

The accompanying photograph of my eighteen-year-old father, however—*my father*, Mead the Mad—was the spitting image of me, aside from his short hair and mustache, of course.

Good Lord. I was more like him than her.

Good Lord. What if I resembled him in behavior, too?

I snapped the frames closed, pinching a finger in my haste.

A minute later, Gerda joined me and helped button me up in an eggplant-purple gown I'd worn to the wedding of one of Father's cousins down in Salem.

"You look lovely this evening, Miss Mead."

"Thank you, Gerda." I straightened the satin poufs sliding off my shoulders. "I personally think I look like a giant purple bauble someone might hang on a Christmas tree."

She laughed. "No, no, no, you look like an elegant young lady. Your young man—"

"He's not quite my young man."

"*That* young man, then, will fall madly in love with you when he sees you dressed like this."

"Hmm." I chewed my bottom lip. "I'd feel a whole lot better knowing a person was falling in love with me because of me and not because of hypnosis or snug purple gowns."

Gerda tittered again. "You're so funny, Miss Mead. You'll make him laugh, if nothing else. And when men laugh, they feel happy and in love." She hooked the last button. "That's what *Mamma* always says about *Fader.*"

A knock downstairs made my shoulders jerk.

Gerda and I locked eyes.

"He's here," I said in a whisper.

"Put your shoes on." She scurried to my door. "I'll tell them you're almost ready."

Before I could say a word, she was gone, her footsteps padding down the stairs.

Down below the boards of my bedroom, the front door opened with its usual squeak. I heard muffled male voices. My pulse pounded in my ears in the same swift rhythm as the clock on my wall.

"Oh, please look normal," I whispered while facing my closed door. I folded my hands beneath my chin and scrunched my eyes closed. "Please, please, please don't turn out to be a monster."

"Olivia," called Father. "Young Mr. Acklen has arrived."

I opened my eyes, inhaled a deep breath, and dared to leave the safety of my room.

Below me, past the bottom of the staircase, Father and Percy chatted about the upcoming election—the impassioned battle between President McKinley and the Democratic anti-imperialist William Jennings Bryan. I only saw the back of Percy's head, and his auburn hair looked just as handsome and impeccable as usual, with a sheen of pomade glistening in the lamplight. He wore his wool outer coat over a pair of narrow-striped trousers, with a finely knit crimson scarf hanging around his neck. His silk top hat dangled from his right fingers.

Time seemed to freeze for a fraction of a moment. Hope for Percy swelled in my heart. Anything was possible, and if I had my way, we would have remained like that—suspended, innocent, unencumbered by my strange sight—for the rest of the evening.

But then Father's dark gaze—a bit too predatory for my taste—flitted toward me. His voice rumbled through the hall. "Ah, Olivia is here."

Percy turned around.

Normal. He was normal—well shaven and groomed and as beautiful as ever.

My legs gave way in relief, and I had to clutch the banister with both hands.

Percy stepped toward me, the ends of his scarf swaying with the lunge. "Are you all right, Olivia?"

"Yes." I gripped the handrail and proceeded down the steps. "I'm sorry. I got dizzy for a moment."

"Ladies and swooning," said Father with a roll of his eyes. "They can't help themselves, I'm afraid."

"All is well."

"The Eiderlings will have plenty to eat at their party," said Percy, "so you won't feel faint much longer." He fetched my coat from the wall hook and spread it open for me to enter. "Are you well enough to go?"

"Yes, I'm fine." I slid my bare arms inside the heavy sleeves, and a potent whiff of his cologne shot clear up to my sinuses.

Father beamed one of his hearty Santa Claus smiles and opened the door for the two of us. "Take good care of my girl, Mr. Acklen. I'll expect her home by ten." *And don't forget to propose to her,* I thought I heard him add, but he grinned, and Percy grinned, and nobody said a word about marriage.

MANDOLIN'S HOOVES STOMPED ACROSS THE MUD-CAKED street leading north of my neighborhood, and the buggy rocked me in a rhythm that might have made me drowsy if my spine weren't locked upright. Nerves thickened my tongue, and every conversation topic sounded jumbled and stupid in my head.

"How is your ear?" I asked when the silence grew too fierce.

"Better." He glanced my way. "I was only teasing about you owing me more than just a book, you know."

My cheeks warmed. "I know."

"You looked so frightened when I said that to you at school. What did you think I would make you do?"

"I don't know." I fussed with a loose pin in my hair and tried to persuade myself Frannie was mistaken about him. The word *grabber* loitered in my mind like an unwanted guest.

Percy steered Mandolin west, onto Irving. "I read all of it."

"All of what?" I asked.

"*Dracula*, of course."

"Oh." I tightened my coat around my neck. "Did you like it?"

"Yes. But why do *you* like it?"

"What do you mean?"

"Why do you like a horrific story involving so much blood and murder?"

"I don't know. Why does anyone like any literature?" I shrugged as if responding to my own question. "I love that books allow us to experience other lives without us ever having to change where we live or who we are."

He kept his eyes on the lamp-lit road ahead, which was disappearing into a gold-tinged mist that carried the scents of chimney smoke and rain. "You were right about there being certain . . . *scenes*." His mouth turned up in a smile.

My neck sweltered beneath my coat. "Yes, um, well, I warned you."

"And that Lucy character, with 'eyes unclean and full of hell-fire'—holy Moses." He shook his head. "Why would a girl like you want to read about someone like her?"

"The book was about far more than just Lucy."

"Oh, sure, there were also Dracula's lusty wives."

I snorted. "Why are you dwelling on the lewd women in the book? *Dracula* is more Mina's story than anything. Prim and saintly Mina. I'm sure you liked her all right."

"Oh, Mina was just fine. In fact, I think I fell a little in love with her and wanted to save her." He peeked my way. "She reminded me of you."

I met his eyes, which gave off a strange yellow cast in the darkness, the way a prowling cat's eyes appear when it's stalking through my backyard after nightfall. I shuddered and told myself I'd only imagined the phenomenon, even though a sideways sort of feeling washed through me again.

"Mina Harker reminded you of me?" I asked.

He nodded. "She was a lot like you."

"Oh." I took hold of the side of the buggy. "And who are you most like? Jonathan Harker? Dracula?"

"Arthur," he answered without hesitation. "Lucy's fiancé."

My blood chilled. Arthur was the character who had staked wild Lucy. Ferociously.

He looked like a figure of Thor as his untrembling arm rose and fell, driving deeper and deeper the mercy-bearing stake . . .

I wrinkled my brow. "Why would you want to be like *him?*"

"I didn't say I wanted to be like him. But this past summer there was a girl . . ." He straightened his top hat with a clumsy movement of his hand and hardened his jaw. "What am I saying? You don't want to hear about another girl."

"No, tell me. Did someone hurt you?"

"She . . ." He gave a little cough, as though his throat had gone dry. "Her name was Nanette. I met her in Los Angeles when my family was summering down there. She liked to listen to ragtime music and rode around the city on a bicycle. She wore bloomers that made old ladies throw rocks at her in disgust, and she called her parents *Lula and Pete* instead of *Mother and Father*."

"Oh?" My heart drummed with jealousy. Bloomers, no less. Beautiful bicycle bloomers.

Percy huffed a sigh. "I thought I could handle her, but she was a bit much. Her parents believed in free love. Her mother gave birth to her when she was living in some sort of utopian society that shunned marriage. Nanette's father may not even be her father."

He flicked the reins to bring Mandolin to a faster walk. The buggy swayed and bounced and thundered over the uneven road, and wind whistled across my ears.

"It turned out Nanette believed in free love, too," he continued. "I found out she was with two other fellows while I was courting her."

"Oh. I'm sorry." The buggy knocked me to the left, and my hand clutched his arm for support, my nails digging into wool. "And that's why you hate the Lucy Westenra character so much?"

"Olivia . . ." He shook his head. "You're supposed to hate Lucy, too. She drank the blood of children."

"But"—I let go of him and righted myself—"if she didn't have that bloodthirsty side, I'm guessing you still would have hated her. She was hardly a standard young lady with pure thoughts."

"I'm just saying that's why I feel like Arthur. I completely understand the burden of trying to love a devil woman." He eased his grip on the reins. "And that's why I'm more than ready to have an innocent girl in my life. Someone chaste and sweet and docile." He scooted next to me until our arms and hips rocked against each other, while the buggy rolled onward toward the grand mansions of Irving Street that rose up ahead like incandescent palaces. "Olivia . . ."

I waited for him to continue, but when he didn't, I fastened my top coat button and asked, "Yes?"

His foot nestled against mine. "It's my firm belief that you will be the savior of my poor broken heart. You're exactly what I need."

Shadows hid his face too much for me to get a good look at him, but the weight of his expectations—his overconfidence in my sweetness—bore down on my shoulders. I clamped my teeth together.

If he had my vision of the world, if he had seen me the way I truly was, he would have thrown me off the buggy right then and there and kept on driving into the mist.

"Our ways are not your ways,
and there shall be to you many strange things."

—BRAM STOKER, *Dracula*, 1897

CHAPTER ELEVEN

DELICIOUS

Percy slowed the buggy as we approached a sandstone fortress with a terra-cotta roof and a half-dozen turrets. Electric lanterns and chandeliers lit the entire building, and an arched wooden door, wide and thick enough to fend off both hurricane winds and invading armies, guarded the front entrance. Six other buggies stood alongside the curb in front of the castle, and the resting horses exhaled clouds of foggy breath through their wide nostrils.

"Whoooa." Percy tugged on Mandolin's reins and brought

the white horse to a stop behind an enclosed carriage with no driver. He must have been warming up with a mug of coffee in the Eiderlings' kitchen. "There's a good boy," said Percy. "Well done, Mandolin."

The horse nickered, and Percy tossed the reins to the ground and climbed out of the buggy.

I gazed at the mansion beside us, my stomach growling in anticipation of the awaiting feast inside. I remembered the words Kate had shouted up at me when I climbed onto the stage to meet Henry: *Go on, Livie. Don't be shy.* My blood thrummed with expectation.

"Wait until you taste the food here, Olivia." Percy tied Mandolin's reins to a black hitching post shaped like a horse's head. "Mr. Eiderling lets the boys sample his beer, so I always have a crackerjack time at Sadie's parties."

"Oh." I flinched, triggering a small whine from the buggy's springs. "I didn't know you'd be drinking . . ."

"Does that bother you?"

"I don't . . . Maybe."

He peeked over his shoulder with a crooked grin. "What are you, a temperance crusader?"

I threw up my hands. "Why is everyone so concerned about me and the temperance movement? I just don't want to be driven recklessly through the city by someone who's guzzled too much beer."

"Mandolin won't be squiffed, and that's what counts—

unless the butler brings out a bucket of ale for the beasts when we're not looking." He laughed at his own words, his chuckles cracking through the silence of the street.

I fussed with my white kid gloves and noted how every inch of fabric that I wore looked wrinkled and wrong. "Do I look nice enough to be here, Percy?"

"What type of question is that?" Percy strode over to my side of the buggy and offered his hand with a wiggle of gloved fingers. "Come on down, my pet." While supporting my arm and waist, he lowered me off the buggy onto the solid dirt ground and bent his face close to mine. "You have nothing to fear, Olivia. Do you understand?"

"Yes." I nodded, for I didn't see any sights that warned of danger.

Percy planted my hand on his arm and escorted me up the stone pathway to the broad castle door.

In response to Percy's raps with the round iron knocker, the Eiderlings' butler—a portly, gray-haired fellow with the sagging jowls of a bulldog—hoisted open the door.

"Good evening," said the butler, every letter enunciated to perfection.

Percy removed his top hat. "Good evening, Mr. Burber. Mr. Percy Acklen and guest for the supper party, if you please."

"Please step inside, Mr. Acklen. Miss Eiderling has already gathered the guests in the dining room."

"Thank you." Percy handed the butler his hat and scarf and slid his arms out of his overcoat, revealing a gray silk bow tie and a fine black tailcoat that complemented his striped trousers. "I hope we're not too late."

"Miss Eiderling likes to be prompt. I believe she's already asked for the first course to be served."

"Well, she is the birthday girl, after all."

Without responding to Percy, the butler took my coat and hung it on a tall cedar rack that reminded me of a scraggly old tree. An impressive collection of jackets and wraps already dangled from the crooked branches.

Percy offered me his arm again and led me across the grand entrance behind the butler. The soles of our shoes clopped on the polished marble floor that reflected our feet and the swishing hem of my purple skirt. Above us rose lofty, gold-accented walls and a sky-high ceiling that gleamed as white as fresh porcelain dentures.

"I smell oysters and salmon," said Percy, and his stomach rumbled. "And beer. Lovely, lovely beer."

We ventured down a mirrored hall the length of my entire house, toward the sound of laughter and the soft clinks of silverware brushing against dishes. Percy carried himself with grace, his head held high, his shoulders relaxed, his dark evening suit pressed and flawless.

"How do you know Sadie?" I asked before we reached the end of the hall. "Doesn't she go to Saint Mary's Academy?"

"My father helped her father avoid a lawsuit earlier this year. And"—he smiled, and that smile was reflected in the mirror beside us, magnifying his amusement—"I think she's secretly in love with me. That's why she invites me to her parties. I'm a toy she can't have, because her parents consider me beneath her."

I stiffened. "And do you love her?"

"No." He shook his head and lowered his voice to a whisper behind the butler. "She's another wild one. I've heard stories about her that would put both Nanette and Lucy Westenra to shame."

"But—"

"I told you, Olivia"—he pressed his gloved fingers around mine with a squeeze—"I want *you.*"

I bit my lip, unsure how to respond.

We neared the swarming buzz of chattering guests that waited beyond the corner, and the scents of seafood and beer grew potent enough to taste the salt and the bubbles in the air. I gripped Percy's arm.

He patted my hand. "Don't be afraid. No one's going to gobble you up."

We rounded the corner.

My feet halted.

Percy was wrong. So utterly wrong.

Beneath a blinding crystal chandelier, around a lace-draped table, a dozen fanged young guests with ashen skin and lips like blue-black bruises chatted and gorged themselves on appetizers. I heard their voices as muffled nothingness, but I saw them—my word, how I saw them. With sterling silver forks, they scraped oysters from the half shells and devoured the mollusks' slippery gray flesh with slurps and swallows and ripples down their long white throats. Tall, gilded steins sat in front of each boy, but they were filled with blood, not beer. The young men wore black tails and vests the colors of fine jewels; the girls sparkled in dark silk gowns and bright diamond necklaces, but even they were savages.

A bespectacled redheaded creature with long yellow teeth and piercing eyes lifted his head and spotted us standing there. "Percy, you old bore! You're late."

A sea of deathly faces turned our way. All I could hear was the hammering of my heart against my chest.

"Mr. Percy Acklen has arrived, Miss Eiderling," said the butler, sounding bored. And then, as if in afterthought, he added, "And guest." The servant turned on his heel and left the room with footsteps that mimicked the quickening of my breath.

I turned to leave as well.

"Where are you going?" Percy grabbed hold of my wrist.

"I can't do this. They look like they want to murder me." I lunged toward the room's exit.

Percy tugged me back and pressed his mouth close to my ear. "This is embarrassing. Turn around and come back to the table."

"I can't."

"Please. What's wrong with you?" He scowled at me as if *I* were the monster in the room, his teeth so sharp. Fierce. *Oh, God.*

"No!" I gave a small cry and broke free of his grip, but then, with a sudden jolt, the world tipped upright. I leaned forward, regained my balance, and saw the room as a normal room, with more sound, fewer colors.

Fewer teeth.

The throng of faces at the table now belonged to a finely dressed assortment of regular young men and ladies who gaped as though they were encountering an escapee from the Oregon State Insane Asylum.

The girl at the head of the table breathed a curt laugh through her nostrils and scanned me from the top of my drooping hair to the toes of my three-year-old dress shoes. She had reddish-gold locks that rose at least a foot off the top of her head—an impressive soufflé!—and her dress was lined in black and cream stripes, with dizzying swirls on the curves of her bodice.

"Who is this, Percy?" she asked with a wrinkle of her small nose. "And what on earth is wrong with her?"

Percy cleared his throat and guided me toward her. "I'm sorry I was late. This is my guest, Olivia Mead."

Two of the girls snickered. The other guests leaned forward and studied me with watchful eyes.

"Oh! You're that hypnotized girl!" said a sunken-eyed blond fellow, raising his hand as if answering a question in a classroom. "The girl Henri Reverie stood upon at the beginning of the Halloween show. That was the funniest, bawdiest thing I've ever seen."

"*That* was the bawdiest thing you've ever seen, John?" asked the redheaded boy who had first spotted us. "Remind me to show you a certain deck of playing cards, my friend."

"Don't be crass, Teddy," said Sadie. "Even though the presence of certain individuals might suggest otherwise"— she glanced at me again—"this is a lady's supper party, not a North End saloon."

Next to Teddy, a dark-haired girl—a scrawny, bulging-eyed thing—burst into a peal of high-pitched laughter. "You brought the dentist's daughter, Percy? Why?"

"Yesss, why?" Sadie bared her bright white teeth. "Is this a joke, Percy? Did you somehow hear about my surprise guest?"

"What? No." Percy let go of my hand. "What guest?"

Sadie turned her attention toward the opposite end of the table. "Henri Reverie."

My heart dropped to my stomach. I craned my neck forward to better see where she was looking, and there he sat, down at the far end, his face turned toward his plate so I could only see a head of dark blond hair with a few uncombed tufts sticking up on top.

Henri Reverie.

Henry Rhodes.

"Before Monsieur Reverie leaves for his performance tonight"—Sadie shifted her sights back to me—"he agreed to dine with us and then to hypnotize me even more thoroughly than he hypnotized you, Ophelia."

"It's Olivia," I said.

"He's promised to help me sing like an opera ingénue."

"Like Svengali," I muttered without even thinking.

Sadie furrowed her brow. "I beg your pardon?"

"Um . . . I—I—I said"—I cleared my throat to summon my voice, which was retreating down my throat like a frightened rabbit—"he's . . . like the controlling hypnotist in the novel *Trilby*. Svengali hypnotized a girl into singing with the voice of an angel." *Doesn't anyone else my age read popular novels?* I wanted to ask, but I sealed my mouth closed to hide the anxious chattering of my teeth.

"I am not a Svengali, Mademoiselle Mead."

Henry—I could no longer see him as *On-ree*, even though he had slipped back into the counterfeit French accent—lifted his face. "Our hostess hired me of her own free will," he said, "so please do not suggest I am a demon sorcerer."

His eyes held mine, and, despite his defensive words and taut mouth, he brought a sliver of warmth to that cold, hostile room. *I've been worried sick about you*, I remembered him saying at the theater.

"Sit down, Percy," said Sadie with a nod to two empty chairs at the middle of the table, one of them next to Sunken-Eyed John. "There's a seat for your little friend beside you. Speaking of whom"—she took a sip of water from a crystal goblet before continuing, perhaps to create a theatrical pause—"is it true, Mr. Reverie, that dim-witted people are the easiest to hypnotize?"

More snickers erupted down the table, and all heads turned

again to Henry, who lowered his fork to his plate, a small smile on his lips.

"No, that's not true at all," he said. "A clever person, someone skilled at focusing on one subject at a time, is usually the most susceptible to hypnosis."

"A clever person?" asked Sadie with a giggle.

"*Oui*, Mademoiselle Eiderling. The cleverest."

I took the seat between Percy and John and gave silent thanks for Henry's defense of my intelligence, in spite of my Svengali accusation.

"Ah, I see." Sadie squeaked an index finger along the rim of her goblet. "Then I'm sure I'll be as easy to mold as soft putty when I'm in your skilled hands. I'm clever as can be."

"Too clever," said Teddy while chewing on an oyster.

"Thank you, Teddy."

"Tell me, Reverie"—Percy removed his gloves, his eyes locked on Henry—"now that you've hypnotized Olivia once, how quickly could you hypnotize her again?"

"Extraordinarily quickly."

"Really?" Excitement mounted in Percy's voice. "Could you do it in a minute? A half minute?"

"I could put her into a trance in less than one second." Henry dabbed the corner of his mouth with his napkin.

Silence seized the room. I bit my lip and worried he could do exactly what he boasted.

"No, you couldn't," said John beside me. "I think you're full of bunkum, Reverie."

"Am I?" Henry cocked his right eyebrow. "Perhaps I should put you into a trance in the same amount of time, *mon pote*, and set you crowing like a rooster."

The girls all laughed, including Sadie, whose cackles attacked my head like a swarm of screeching insects.

"Prove it by hypnotizing Olivia again, right here," said Percy, resting a wintry palm on the back of my hand.

The laughter quieted. I quaked, for Percy's hand looked as pale as death.

"The way you manipulated her the other night impressed me beyond belief," he continued, his face graying, his voice retreating into the distance. "I would love to witness how you do it—up close."

Anger roiled inside me. I shook Percy's hand off mine and cried out, "All is well!"

Percy wrinkled his forehead, but before that phrase could spew from my mouth again, Sadie clapped her hands and begged in a faraway echo of a voice, "Oh, do it, please, Monsieur Reverie. It'll be fun. We could prop her up next to the buffet table."

"Yes, put her next to the birthday cake, like a delicious tart," said a long-nosed fiend of a boy with a leer that turned my stomach.

"Yes, do it," the bulging-eyed girl chimed in, her canines sweeping over her bluing bottom lip. "How funny that would be."

I glared at Percy, who shrank back and pinked up to his

regular hue, as if he had just then realized he was failing at making me feel comfortable.

"I'll pay you to keep her asleep during the entire meal." Sadie stood to her full height and stared me down with irises that simmered bloody red. Her long black fingernails ripped into the tablecloth. "Name your price, and I'll go fetch my father's wallet right now."

I gasped for air and grabbed the arms of my chair while the room swayed and knocked me about worse than Percy's buggy. *Don't faint, don't faint!* I told myself. *Keep your wits about you. Don't show them you're weak—that's exactly what they're craving.*

"No," I heard someone say, but my tilting brain and failing ears couldn't figure out from where in the room the voice had emanated. I drew long breaths of sour beer fumes and willed the claws and the fangs to disappear, forced the black spots to stop buzzing in front of my eyes, until the room settled back into view. The partygoers ceased being demons once again.

Down the way, Henry peered at Sadie across the fine bone china and gilded steins. "Miss Mead is not an object to be laid out for your entertainment."

Sadie sank back down to her chair. "Prove to us you can put her under in less than one second, or we won't believe you. We'll call you a humbug and send you out the door before you eat another bite." She flapped her napkin across her lap. "You're our entertainer for the evening." She beamed with the smile of a victor. "Entertain us."

Henry backed his chair away from the table with a loud screech, and my heart jumped. He was going to do it. Sadie had harassed him to the point of obedience, and he would drop me into darkness before I could even think of springing out of my seat and fleeing the room.

The hypnotist indeed rose to his feet, seeming to follow her command—but instead of stalking toward me, he tossed his napkin onto his plate. "I will not be bullied into performing hypnosis."

Sadie laughed. "We're not bullying you, you silly, dramatic thing. I just—"

"What do they look like, Miss Mead?" Henry leaned his palms against the table. "What do you see?"

A soundless question—*What?*—formed on my lips.

"They don't look quite right, do they?" he asked.

"What is he talking about, Olivia?" said Percy with a nudge of my arm. "Is he hypnotizing you right now?"

"Is this part of it, Reverie?" asked Teddy. "Can you hypnotize her with just one look?"

A blush seared my cheeks and neck. I directed my eyes toward my empty Wedgwood plate with its swirls of blue flowers—no one had even served me any oysters yet—and squirmed under everyone's scrutiny. If only I could disappear into the wind and blow back through the streets and the darkness toward my own house. If only returning home early to Father wouldn't mean he'd blame me for ruining the evening.

"They look like vampires, don't they?" asked Henry.

I lifted my face, stunned he had asked that question in front of everyone.

"You knew the moment you came into the room that you should avoid them, didn't you?" he added. "I could see it in your eyes. This isn't a curse, Olivia. It's a gift."

I shook my head. "No, this is definitely not a gift. They've got pale flesh and horrifying teeth. I can't stand being around them. All is well!"

Silence befell the room again. I was about to stand and slink out to the hall, mortified, when Teddy slammed his hand on the table and made us all jump.

"Holy Mary," he said. "He did it. He hypnotized her from across the table. She thinks we all look like Count Dracula."

Sadie broke into her awful, screeching laughter again, and the other girls joined her.

"Bravo, Reverie," said Sunken-Eyed John, clapping his hands. "A swell magic trick. How'd you do it?"

"Olivia?" Percy poked my arm. "Wake up. You're babbling nonsense about that novel."

"What about *him*, Miss Mead?" asked Henry, nodding toward Percy. "What does he look like?"

I rubbed the sides of my head, and my whole body went hot and achy with humiliation. "Just hypnotize me, *On-ree*. She'll pay you well, and I won't have to be here anymore. Coming to this house was a mistake."

"Well, that's rude," said Sadie, and then she snapped her fingers and demanded, "Hurry up and make her go rigid as a plank, Monsieur Reverie. I'd like to see if I can stand on top of her myself."

"Oh, yes!" One of the boys applauded with loud smacks of his large hands. "I would pay good money to see *that*."

"Do it, Reverie," said a husky-voiced fellow.

"Yes, do it!" others added.

I shot to my feet, but Sunken-Eyed John grabbed my wrist and pinned it to the table. His fingers squeezed against my bones.

"Let go of me." I struggled to break free, fire smoldering in my chest. "All is well. All is well!"

My ridiculous cries made everyone laugh all the harder, as if my fury were part of the show.

"Let go of her, John," said Percy over the obnoxious guffaws. "She's my girl, you louse."

"All is well!" White steam—the extinguished flames of my actual words—would soon gust from my mouth and nose. I was certain of it. "All is well! All—"

Out of the corner of my eye, I caught Henry approaching, which sent me further into a fit of angry panic. My legs and free arm thrashed about, knocking over my empty chair with a crash. "All is well!"

Henry's footsteps drew closer. The air thinned; my lungs hurt. Percy tugged on my elbow, while John kept my wrist pinned and pinched.

"All is well! All is—"

"It's all right, Olivia." Henry took hold of my flailing arm.

"All—"

"Stop panicking. I'm not going to hypnotize you." Henry yanked John's hand off my wrist, releasing the pain. "Let go of her. You're idiots, all of you. Spoiled brats. Find your own entertainment."

Before anyone could react, he guided me away from the table, toward the breath of freedom waiting beyond the dining room's entrance, and I choked on the fiery pain of embers lodged inside my throat.

"Hey! Reverie!" called Percy behind us. "Where are you taking her?"

We made it halfway down the mirrored hallway before I heard Percy's footsteps jogging after us.

"Where are you going?"

"Away from here." Henry steered me toward the wide front door that would lead to fresh air and escape.

Percy was on our heels. "Come back, Olivia. I didn't even get a chance to drink my beer."

Henry came to a sudden stop and turned on Percy. "Are you Miss Mead's suitor?"

"Yes." Percy pulled at his gray bow tie. "My name is Percy Acklen, and I am courting her."

"Then how the devil can you worry about beer at the moment, *bâtard*? Those people were treating her terribly. One boy called her a tart, and that ugly one next to her was pinning her down and hurting her. You just sat there like an imbecile."

"Now, wait a moment . . ." Percy stepped close. "Don't throw insults at me when you were the one hypnotizing my girl. We all thought you were giving us a show."

"Do you want me to take you home, Olivia?" asked Henry, ignoring Percy, his hand still cradling my arm. "I will explain everything to your father."

"No." I shook my head. "Please, no. My father will be furious if I come home early. He'll make everything so much worse than it already is."

"Oh, to hell with all of this." Percy marched over to our jackets hanging off the scraggly coat rack. "I'm hungry and grumpy and need a good supper. Let's go eat in the city and tell Olivia's father everything went well. Who needs catty birthday girls and overbearing daddies ruining our evening?" He threw his crimson scarf around his neck. "You, too, Reverie. I'm willing to bet you also have a father who's made your life miserable."

Henry lowered his hand from my arm. "No. Just an alcoholic uncle-guardian who got himself killed in July."

"Holy tripe. That's even worse. You're in." Percy clomped back over to us on the loud soles of his oxfords, my coat in hand. "Come join Olivia and me. I'm paying."

"Your buggy only holds two people, Percy," I reminded him.

"True. Well . . ." He helped me into my coat. "Do you have a hired carriage, Reverie?"

"No. Miss Eiderling paid someone to drive me here, but I don't think—"

"Then we'll all squeeze in together. It'll just have to be tight and cozy." Percy offered me his elbow and plunked his top hat on his head. "Come along. Let's get out of here and go toast to youth and vampires and rebellion."

CHAPTER TWELVE

YELLOW~RIBBON GIRLS

Three people did not fit comfortably into a buggy built for two.

Mandolin jostled us through the streets of Portland, and Percy, Henry, and I squeezed together on the padded green seat, my hips too wide to fit between the boys. I had to turn and sit sideways, facing Percy, while half my rump perched on Henry's warm leg behind me.

"Comfy?" asked Percy, shifting his face toward me, his nose an inch from mine.

"Somewhat," I said, and I gritted my teeth against a jolt from a buggy wheel slamming against a pothole.

Cologne and pomade and the scent of wool suits ruled the air around me. *Youth these days will be the death of morality,* I remembered the pumpkin-haired organist complaining earlier that day, and I wondered if she might be right. Wedged between the two young men like that, my chest shoved against Percy's arm and my backside bumping against Henry's femur, I must have resembled the heroine of *Sapho,* the play both the organist and my mother said was causing an uproar in New York City—*the one about the strumpet and her lovers.*

This was not the evening my father was envisioning for his newly tamed daughter.

Percy tipped his face toward mine again. "Is she still hypnotized, Reverie?"

"No," I said before Henry could even think of confessing that my father had paid him to cure my mind. "I'm fine."

Percy turned his sights back to the road ahead. "I'd like to learn a couple of hypnosis tricks."

"They're not tricks, *mon ami*," said Henry with a bite to his voice. "They're skills that require knowledge, compassion, and mastery. My uncle began training me back when I was just twelve years old, and he only did so because he believed I possessed both talent and responsibility."

"Your uncle? The rummy who got himself killed, you mean?"

I nudged Percy in the arm. "That's cruel, Percy."

"Yes. That uncle." Henry shifted the leg that rested below me. "He became the guardian of Genevieve and me after our parents died. And despite his weaknesses of recent years, he was once witty and kind and deeply in love with the arts of hypnotism and mesmerism."

Percy shot him a sideways glance. "You make hypnosis sound like a woman."

"It is like a woman. She's beautiful. She's mysterious." Henry's voice softened to a lush purr that made my stomach flutter. *"Une belle femme."*

"Risqué," said Percy with a chuckle.

"But you have to treat her delicately," continued Henry, ignoring Percy, "and with utmost respect. Or else you'll find yourself waking up in a cold sweat in the middle of the night, realizing"—he paused long enough for me to peek over my shoulder and catch him watching me through the darkness from beneath the curved brim of his hat—"you may have gone too far." He kept his eyes on mine. "You'll be deeply sorry if you've inflicted any harm."

Percy steered Mandolin around the bend to the right, and I forced my eyes away from Henry's.

"Well," said Percy, "despite how sacred you're making stage hypnosis out to be, I would really love to pay you to show me how to perform some of these *skills.*"

"That information isn't for sale," said Henry. "You're just going to have to mesmerize the world based on your own natural charms, Monsieur Acklen."

Percy barked a laugh that seemed to shatter something fragile in the air, and I rocked against them both, wondering if Henry Rhodes would put my mind back the way it was, if he was genuinely sorry for what he had done.

PERCY LED US INSIDE AN ELEGANT TWELFTH STREET establishment with frosted glass light fixtures twinkling over dark wooden booths and tables draped in ivory cloths. Waiters in white coats waltzed about with bottles of wine and steaming plates of fish and beef that made my hungry stomach moan. I'd never stepped inside the place before that moment. Father always preferred eating at home, so we seldom dined in restaurants.

Our host, a tall gentleman with a dusky walrus mustache, took our coats and the boys' hats and led us up two short steps to one of the dining areas. In one of the booths we passed, a woman in a lavender dress picked at a salad with soundless jabs of her fork.

Another vision approached—I could tell, for the air grew hard to breathe, and the colors of the woman's booth bloomed into shades that demanded my full attention. Her supper companion, a bony-faced old coot with a half-dozen gold rings, said something to her that made her blur and fade into fog and shadow.

I stopped in a daze and rapped my knuckles against Henry's arm behind me. "They're disappearing," I said. "Certain women."

"Who's disappearing?" asked Percy. "What's going on with you now?"

I sealed my lips, picked up the hem of my gown, and continued following the walrus-mustached host. The illusion passed. My lungs breathed with ease. Everyone now seemed made of flesh and bone.

The host seated the two young men and me at a round table, toward the back, with the flame of a white candle dancing in a silver holder at the center. We removed our gloves, and the host handed us thick red menus. I heard him describe the evening's specials in a friendly enough voice, but I could no longer pay much attention to the menu or the possibility of food. All I thought about was how I was going to convince Henry to put me back the way I was before I, too, faded like my neighbor Mrs. Stanton and that poor woman poking at her salad.

"Psst—look over there," said Percy in a whisper once the host had left us.

I craned my head toward the booth across the room that had caught Percy's eye. Four young ladies dined there in relative quiet, including redheaded and lovely Agnes Frye, my friend Kate's sister who had lured us high school girls to Wednesday's rally.

My skin prickled, warning of the arrival of yet another hallucination. The ladies' booth seemed to rush toward me for better viewing.

My eyes opened wide.

Lanterns switched on inside all the women's bodies. Their hair glistened with breathtaking luminescence—a light that reflected off the surrounding wood. Their skin flushed with a brilliance that rivaled our candle's flame. I sucked in my breath and watched in awe as they glowed—literally *glowed*—before my eyes.

"See the emblem hanging off their left shoulders?" asked Percy.

Agnes lowered her left arm and revealed a bright yellow ribbon.

My fingers tightened around my menu, and I slouched down in my chair with the hope that she wouldn't see me with the boys and come over. I shook my head to regain control of my brain, as mesmerizing as this particular illusion was. The prickling faded. The ladies' booth dimmed and retreated to its position against the wall. The world tipped back to its normal balance.

"What are the ribbons for?" asked Henry.

"Women's suffrage." Percy frowned. "My sister is like them. She used to wear yellow ribbons, roses, and buttons all the time without any of us knowing what the deuce they meant."

"You have a sister?" I asked.

"Yesss," hissed Percy. "I have two older, married brothers, both respectable lawyers, and a twenty-year-old sister who's no longer a part of our family."

"Because of the—?" I glanced back at Agnes and her friends.

"Yes." He swallowed beneath his stiff collar. "My father learned she helped run a banquet for Susan B. Anthony down in Salem last February, so he forced her to pack up and leave." He closed his menu with a solid *thwack*.

Henry wrinkled his forehead. "You're not allowed to talk to or see your sister anymore . . . just because she wants to vote?"

"That's right." Percy darted another quick peek at the suffragists. "After Father threw her out, she moved to Idaho so she could live the way she wanted and vote as much as she pleased. Mother nearly died from heartbreak and humiliation." He reopened his menu and pressed his lips into a hard line. "My sister is a spinster now, just like every woman in that booth."

"Agnes isn't a spinster," I said.

"Who's Agnes?" asked Percy.

"Shh." I held my menu over my face and slithered down another inch. "The redhead over there is my good friend's sister, and she has a loving husband."

Percy knitted his eyebrows. "How?"

"What do you mean, how? She got married in a church the same way your parents probably did. Her husband is a pro-suffrage man."

Percy snorted. "There's no such thing."

"I'm one," said Henry.

"Pshaw. You're just saying that to charm Olivia. All it does is make you sound like an effeminate French sissy, Reverie."

"Anti-suffrage men are the ones who sound like sissies and cowards," I said under my breath.

"I still want beer." Percy scanned one of the menu pages. "What about you, Mr. Suffrage? Are you drinking tonight?"

"No." Henry shook his head. "I'm performing. No one wants to be hypnotized by a drunk."

"Oh, criminy . . ." Percy laughed. "Can you imagine what that would look like? Oh . . ." He slapped his hand over his mouth. "I suppose you can, what with that sozzled hypnotist uncle of yours."

"I'm sure they serve Eiderling Beer at the bar here." I nudged Percy's arm and wished him away. "Perhaps you should go order yourself one."

Percy laughed again. "I thought you were a temperance crusader."

"You were the one who called me that, not I. If you want a beer"—my desire to catapult him away emboldened my voice—"go get one. You said we're here to toast youth and rebellion, didn't you?"

"Yes . . ."

"Then go." *Shoo*, I wanted to add, but he was already up and out of his seat.

"Don't hypnotize my girl when I'm gone, Reverie," he said with a wink.

"Wouldn't dream of it, *mon ami.*"

Henry and I watched Percy bound down the short flight of steps in his quest for Eiderling booze.

I slammed my menu shut. "Hypnotize me back."

Henry laid down his own menu. "I told you, I can't."

"Why not?"

"Your father only paid me a quarter of his promised fee for your treatment. I can't get the rest of the money until Tuesday evening, before I board a train for San Francisco."

"Why?"

"He wants to make sure the cure takes."

I winced.

Henry reached his hand toward mine on the tablecloth, not quite touching me but near enough to ignite a tingling sensation in my fingertips. "We're so, so close to affording Genevieve's surgery. Your father's payment will get us what we need. It'll give her a chance."

"You don't understand what people look like to me."

"No, I don't, but as I said at Sadie's table, it's not necessarily a curse."

"Of course it's a curse. You try living like this and tell me—" My anger flared; that blasted phrase threatened to shoot from my lips again. I smacked my palm against the table, which prompted two men next to us to turn my way and scowl.

"Hear me out before you get upset with me." Henry's fingers inched nearer. "When your father asked me to hypnotize you, he said he wanted you to *accept* the world the way it is."

"Don't you think I remember what he—?"

"But"—he scooted his chair closer to mine—"I didn't tell you to *accept* the world the way it truly is, Olivia. I told you to *see* it."

"No, you—"

"Think about it. I did."

I sank back in my seat.

"And you *can* see it," he continued, his French accent gone. "Maybe not at every single moment, but when it really matters to you or the person you're viewing, or during moments of intense emotion, you'll clearly see that you shouldn't be with poisonous jackasses like that vampire at the bar."

I sat up straight. "Percy doesn't look like either a jackass or a vampire."

"Yet."

I picked at the spine of my menu. "I want to see and say things normally again, Henry Rhodes. I've never had anyone like Percy show an interest in me before this week, and I don't want to spoil everything by acting like a lunatic."

"What do you mean, 'anyone like Percy'?"

"I know, compared to him, I'm plain and dull and—"

"Plain and dull?" Henry's voice rose to an embarrassing volume. "Is that what your father tells you?"

"Please"—I scooted my chair away from his—"you're talking too loudly."

"It makes me furious when people like that ninnyhammer Acklen make people like you feel inferior to them. Tell me, exactly what type of loving partnership is that supposed to lead to?"

"Please, be quiet. He's coming back."

Henry leaned forward again and grabbed my hand. "He's

not better than you, Olivia, and neither is your father. And you're far from plain and dull."

I pulled my hand away and sat up straight and proper.

"What's going on, Reverie?" Percy swaggered over to us with a mug of beer. "Why are you blushing, Olivia?"

"I should probably go." In his haste, Henry dropped his gloves to the floor. He leaned over to pick them up.

"What happened?" Percy plunked his mug on the table. "Did you say something lewd to her, Reverie? Or"—he bent forward with a grin—"are you attempting to court her by singing suffrage anthems?"

Henry got to his feet. "I can't stay. I'm performing soon and would like to check on my sister beforehand." He slapped his hand on Percy's shoulder and leaned close to his ear. "I said nothing lewd to Olivia, Monsieur Acklen. She's angry because I told her to run away from people who are poisonous to her."

"What?" Percy's brows pinched together. "Who's poisonous to her? What are you talking about?"

Henry fitted his gloves over his hands. "Thank you for the supper offer. *Adieu.* Good night."

And then he was gone, hustling toward the exit as if he couldn't get away from the two of us fast enough.

Percy plopped down in his chair, still wrinkling his brow. "What was all that about? Was he trying to hypnotize you?"

"No . . . he just . . . it's hard to explain. He . . ."

Out of the corner of my eye, I saw Henry returning to us. My neck muscles tensed. "Oh, no, here he comes again."

Henry approached our table and handed me something limp and white that I realized was one of my own evening gloves. "I must have accidentally picked this up when I was fetching my own gloves, *mademoiselle. Je suis désolé.* I am sorry." His eyes lingered on mine and then darted to the glove, as if he were trying to convey some sort of message.

"Thank you," I said, resting the glove in my lap.

"You're welcome." He left us again so swiftly that the air ruffled my hair and made the night feel even more out of whack.

"Criminy . . ." Percy peeked over his shoulder and watched him go. "My father always says theater people are eccentric and ill-mannered . . ."

I sighed. "You keep telling me what your father says and thinks, Percy. Weren't we supposed to be forgetting overbearing daddies right now?"

"I give my own opinions."

"Not really. For instance . . ." I kneaded the fabric of my glove between my fingers and was surprised to hear the rustle of a piece of paper inside the thumb.

"For instance what?"

"For instance"—I set the glove aside on my lap and attempted to ignore that peculiar rustling—"do you truly agree with your father that women shouldn't vote?"

Percy lowered his eyes.

I lifted my chin. "I read his letter in the newspaper yesterday."

He flashed a sheepish grin. "Oh, yes, that letter. Father's public opinion pieces always make me supremely popular with the ladies."

"But what is *your* opinion? Do you think women are inferior creatures to men?"

"I think . . ." He scratched the back of his neck, repositioned himself in his chair, took a swig of beer, and hesitated far too long. "I think volatile subjects are best avoided in fine dining establishments, Olivia. Let me call over a waiter and order you a nice meal, and then we'll talk about a lighter subject more suitable for a sweet little thing like you."

"But—"

"Waiter." He waved over a short server with large ears, who was just darting back to the kitchen. "We're ready to order."

The waiter scuttled over to our sides and asked what we wanted.

Before I could open my mouth, Percy told the fellow, "The young lady and I will have the salmon and a salad and a loaf of fresh bread, and could you cook the fish a little more than you normally would? So that the ends are charred and crunchy."

"Could mine be cooked the regular way?" I asked the waiter.

"Oh, you'll like it my way, Olivia." Percy handed the fellow our menus. "It's the only way to eat it."

"I don't even like salmon all that much . . ."

But the waiter was gone; my opinion hung in the air,

unacknowledged, while Percy dove into a story about his travels.

"Did I tell you we spend our summers down at the beach in California?"

"Yes." I cleared my throat. "You said so when you told me about Nanette."

"I'm a crackerjack swimmer, I've discovered. I've swum nearly a mile off the coast and never once tired from the waves smacking me around."

Percy yammered on, and my heart shriveled into a disappointed little prune. I didn't have to witness his true feelings by seeing any dangerous curved teeth or predatory gleam in his eyes.

I heard it in his voice, clear as church bells—and I'd probably even heard it and ignored it on Halloween night.

Percy thought me inferior.

CHAPTER THIRTEEN

PERCY'S TEETH

B y the light of a streetlamp outside the restaurant, I found two tickets to Henry's Saturday matinee show stuffed inside the thumb of my glove. On the back of one of the tickets was scrawled a smudged note, yet I could still make out the message:

Come to the side door of the theater after the show if you're able. I want you to meet Genevieve.

I heard approaching hooves and looked up to find Percy driving his black buggy around the bend from the side street where he'd parked it. I crammed the tickets into the far reaches of the glove and slid the white leather over my hand, scraping my thumb on a rough edge.

Percy brought the buggy to a stop along the curb next to me and hopped out to the sidewalk. "You're blushing again. It seems you're always blushing."

I shrugged. "I'm just warm."

"It's freezing out here."

"The food warmed me up."

"Or the company, perhaps." He smiled and took my hand to help me into the seat above, but I didn't respond, which I'm sure made me seem like an unfeeling lump of stone.

The ride home started off uneventfully, and the message in my glove kept me from paying attention to our route. In fact, I didn't actually notice our surroundings until Percy directed the horse and buggy down the South Park Blocks, where wide expanses of moonlit grass separated the east and west sides of the street.

Strange, vaporous wisps of air rose off the damp park ground and drifted into the trees like steam rising from a pot—or spirits escaping graves. I'd seen such mist before; the effect wasn't one of my illusions, just a mixture of atmospheric warmth and cold and moisture. The sight unsettled me, though. Between the ghostly fog and Mandolin's footfalls across the soundless neighborhood, I felt like Ichabod Crane venturing through the depths of Sleepy Hollow upon the back of trusty Gunpowder.

"Why are you taking this route?" I asked, staring at the empty path that lay ahead.

"To stretch out the time and make it seem as if we didn't desert Sadie's party." Percy stole a glance at me. "I'm keeping you out of trouble, my pet."

"Oh. Thank you." I toyed with the little pieces of paper wedged beside my thumb. "But I'd prefer not to be called your pet, if you don't mind. It makes me feel like a cocker spaniel."

Percy didn't answer.

We came upon the corner of Park and Main, and he gave Mandolin's reins a firm pull. "Whoa, boy."

I stiffened. "Why are you slowing down?"

"Whoa, Mandolin."

The buggy came to a swaying stop alongside the rising mist. Cold air sliced across my cheeks. My shriveled prune of a heart pounded back to life with throbbing intensity.

"Why did you stop?" I asked. "We're still three blocks away."

Percy shifted his knees toward me, the upper half of his face masked by shadows, his eyes a knife slash of yellow. "Olivia . . ." His arm slid behind me, across the back of the leather seat. "I really want to kiss you." He leaned in close, and his sour Eiderling Beer breath flooded my nose.

"I . . . um"—I inched away—"I don't . . ."

"There's no need to be so nervous." He cupped my cheek with one soft-gloved hand. "I'll be gentle."

"I don't—"

"Do you want to play *Dracula?*" He lifted an eyebrow. "Would that make it more fun?"

My mouth went dry; I shook my head. "No! H-h-how do you mean?"

"I know you're a good little thing, but you have to admit"—his left hand found the crook of my waist, below my coat—"a girl who's read *Dracula* as many times as you have must be aching for the touch of a pair of lips against her neck." With that, he nestled his ice block of a cheek against my face. His breath tickled its way inside my ear. "Do you want to see what it feels like if I place my mouth against your bare skin? Do you want to be my"—he kissed my earlobe—"Mina?"

I closed my eyes and found my thoughts racing back to the Percy Acklen who had waved me down in the theater lobby with the lights glinting off his cuff links. I remembered those green-brown eyes and the mischief on his lips and the way we'd commiserated about our fathers before darting through the rain to my house.

"I d-d-d . . ." My teeth chattered. "I don't want to be with someone who thinks I'm inferior to him."

"I don't think that." His breath cooled the upper regions of my neck, below my ear.

"I don't even like salmon very much, but you never even asked me what I wanted before you ordered for me."

"Olivia . . ." He slid his bottom lip across an inch of my throat—not a kiss, per se, but a tease that gave me unpleasant shivers. "You're making too much of everything. Just have some fun. Play with me. Close your eyes and play."

"I don't—"

"Just play." He licked my neck, which almost made me laugh, if it weren't also kind of awful, but then he cupped his full mouth—wet and soft and warmer than the rest of him—around my neck and sank his teeth against my flesh. Blood rushed through my veins until I seemed to be made of nothing but blood and a pounding pulse—racing, anxious, beating, beating, beating blood he would taste if his teeth bit down any harder. His hand shifted to my posterior and gave a firm squeeze—*his grabby hands! Just as Frannie said!* Every part of him pressed down on me. His mouth, his fingers, his chest. I couldn't breathe.

I pushed him away, and his head smacked the buggy's overhang.

"Ouch!" He rubbed the top of his skull. "What did you do that for?"

"Did you ever grab my friend Frannie's backside?"

"What? Who the hell is Frannie?"

"Frannie Harrison. She goes to our school."

"Jesus, Olivia." He lunged toward me again. "Just close your eyes and let me kiss you. You owe me for what happened in class."

"But . . ." I gasped. "You said . . ."

He grabbed the back of my neck and squished his mouth

against mine. His lips were sloppy and wet, and the beer taste was so obnoxious, I gagged on the fumes.

"All is well!" I pushed him off, and his head clunked the buggy a second time.

His visage changed—oh, God, how it changed. His eyes sank into the blackened recesses of a gaunt and anemic face. His canines lengthened into the grotesque tusks of a wild boar.

"Why do you keep saying that all is well?" he asked, and his mouth seeped my blood.

"Oh, God!" I snatched his scarf from his shoulders and jumped off the buggy.

"Hey! Where are you going? And why'd you take my scarf?"

"I'm saving both our hides, you idiot." I wrapped the yarn around my bare neck and fled down the street. "My father will see your tooth marks if I don't wear your rotten scarf."

I heard the snap of reins behind me and the galloping rhythm of Mandolin taking off after me with the rattling buggy. I cut through side yards, even though the shortcut meant soaking my shoes and skirts with mud. My pulse hammered in my ears. My breathing turned ragged, but I pushed onward across the rain-soaked grass and dirt.

Percy was already parking the buggy by the time I sprinted up my own brick path. Our house's tall front windows stared me down—gawking eyes observing my frenzied arrival in the dark. I turned the doorknob but found it locked.

"No, no, no. You can't be locked. You can't be locked!"

I twisted the knob and banged on the door. My struggle to get inside allowed Percy to hustle up beside me mere seconds before my father swung open the door.

Father widened his eyes at my sweaty hair and muddied shoes. "What happened?"

"She fell out of the buggy," said my escort, who looked like Percy again.

"She fell out?"

I gasped. "All is—"

"She leaned over too far, trying to look at something"— Percy took my arm as if I were an invalid—"and tumbled into the grass. She muddied her dress, but I don't think she's hurt, sir. Naturally, I'll let you, a physician of sorts, make the final diagnosis."

I moved to enter the house, but Father blocked my entrance with his arms.

He nodded toward my neck. "The scarf, Olivia."

A wave of nausea rolled through me. "I—I—I beg your pardon?"

"Isn't that young Mr. Acklen's scarf you're wearing?" he asked.

"Y-y-yes."

"Shouldn't you be returning it to him before he leaves?"

I glanced back at Percy, who had gone pale again, although in a frightened way—an *I'm about to get dissected by dental tools* sort of way—with quivering lips and watery eyes.

"Um . . ." He stammered, "Well . . . th-th-there's no need for her to return it to me right now. She got cold out here and should keep warming up. I don't want her catching her death of pneumonia."

"Oh. Thank you." Father dropped his arms from the doorway. "How very thoughtful."

I leapt inside the house. "Good night."

Father shut the door, but before he could ask details about Sadie's party, I launched myself up the staircase, closed myself in my room, and unwound Percy's scarf until the crimson wool lay in a coiled heap upon the floor. With my head tipped to the right, I approached my oval mirror.

My reflection showed me two sore and bleeding puncture wounds on the left side of my neck—as vicious and angry-red as Lucy's wounds in *Dracula.*

Not real.

Two blinks later, the marks retreated and left a purpling bruise in their stead, which was almost worse.

"But unlike Lucy and Mina," I said to my solid face in the mirror, and I braced my hands around the curved wooden frame, "you will *not* be returning to your vampire for a second bite, Olivia Mead. You will not." I swallowed and nudged Percy's scarf away with my toes.

"[Bicycling] has done more to emancipate woman than any one thing in the world. I rejoice every time I see a woman ride by on a wheel. It gives her a feeling of self-reliance and independence the moment she takes her seat; and away she goes, the picture of untrammeled womanhood."

—SUSAN B. ANTHONY, 1896

CHAPTER FOURTEEN

A RESPONSIBLE WOMAN

The following morning, my plaid wool winter blouse, buttoned clear up to the top of my throat, hid Percy's bite mark from view. On my way downstairs to breakfast, I tested the durability of the top button by twisting it about until I felt confident the little pearl fastening would remain in place. A thin edging of lace tickled like a gnat beneath my chin, but the discomfort was minor—well worth the trouble of avoiding the topic of my virtue with my father.

Father sat at the breakfast table, his face a concealed mystery behind the newspaper, as usual.

"Good morning." I took my seat and unfolded my napkin.

"Good morning, Olivia." The newspaper didn't budge.

"Are you playing billiards today?"

"It's Saturday, isn't it?"

"Yes"—I fluffed the napkin across my lap—"it is."

"Then I'll be playing. What are your plans?"

"I'll probably go to Fran—"

A headline caught my eye and paralyzed my tongue:

OLD MOTHER ACKLEN FOR PRESIDENT?

My heart stopped. Nervous sweat broke out beneath that strangling straitjacket of a collar. I pulled at the lace to breathe.

"What's the matter?" Father lowered the paper. "Why did you stop talking mid-sentence?"

"Is—is . . . ?" My eyes refused to budge from the newsprint. "I think I see a headline about one of the Acklens."

Father closed the paper to get a better view of the front. "Oh, yes. That."

"What does the article say?"

"It's nothing to fret about." He folded the paper in half so I could no longer see the article. "Some silly woman wrote to the editor, suggesting Judge Acklen's mother would make a far better president than either McKinley or Bryan."

I pressed my lips together. "Really? They printed a letter like that?"

"Surprisingly so. They usually keep suffragist drivel out of the *Oregonian*." With a grunt, he unfolded and readjusted the newspaper so that it lay next to his plate with the second page on top. The only items left viewable from my seat were a political cartoon involving President McKinley and an article about the Socialist Eugene V. Debs.

Father raised his steaming mug of coffee to his lips, but before taking a sip, he added, with a quick glance at me, "Please, Olivia, don't even think of reading the letter. It was probably written by a man, anyway."

He sipped his drink.

I raised my eyebrows.

"Why do you think a man wrote it?" I asked.

He lowered the mug to the table with a smack of his lips. "It's too well written for a woman."

Before I could respond, Gerda glided through the swinging kitchen door on a bacon-and-egg-scented breeze.

A smile wiggled across my face. *It's too well written for a woman*, Father had said. *Well written*. He believed my work to be well written.

Gerda set my breakfast plate in front of me. "Good morning, Miss Mead."

"Good morning, Gerda." My smile stretched to an unmanageable width.

She nudged my elbow below the table. "A lovely party last night?"

"Oh. Yes." I lowered my eyes. "Lovely."

"Good. More coffee, Dr. Mead?"

"Not at the moment. Thank you."

"Then I'll let you two eat." She wiped her hands on her apron and made her way back through the door.

I reined in my smile but longed to ask Father more about why he thought the letter was so well written, and if he felt swayed by the argument, and if the writer seemed to live up to her name: *A Responsible Woman.*

Instead, I buttered my toast with a rhythmic *scrape, scrape, scrape, scrape.*

"What did you say you were doing today?" he asked between bites of food.

"I'm bicycling over to Frannie's."

He swallowed the last bite and cleared his throat. "You're getting a little too old to be riding around the city, don't you think? Especially now that a young man is courting you."

"I don't care for Percy as much as I thought. Please don't consider us courting."

"You don't care for him?"

"I learned his reputation isn't as spotless as he made it out to be. I'm a good, chaste girl, so you should be proud of me resisting his charms."

"He tried to"—Father coughed up crumbs—"*charm* you?"

"And what do you mean about me getting too old to bicycle?" I stopped buttering. "I see plenty of women cyclists."

"I don't know why that is, when there are so many households to run."

"Are you saying I can't ride anymore?"

"I'm saying we should perhaps only hire Gerda on the week-days when you're in school. You're more than old enough to be taking care of the cooking and cleaning on Saturdays."

"Gerda is relying on her employment here."

"I'm sure she can find a family who needs a girl to clean only once a week."

"But—"

"It's time you took on more duties, Olivia. You're not a child anymore."

I dropped my knife to my plate with a clank.

"Or are you a child?" he asked. "Am I mistaken?"

I eyed the stack of newspaper pages piled up beside him and thought of my published letter to the editor buried inside. *A Responsible Woman* was what I had claimed to be.

"No, I'm not a child." I dragged my teeth against my bottom lip and tried to still the wanderlust in my legs. "But can the change of her schedule wait until next week? I was planning to offer to help Frannie's mother with preparations for tomorrow's anniversary party."

"Well . . . ," Father grumbled. "I suppose Gerda is already hard at work for the day . . ."

"Thank you."

"But next week, this new schedule must start. And I must say, I'm sorely disappointed by this turn of events with Percy."

"I am, too." I picked at my eggs with my fork.

Father returned to the newspaper and grinned at the political cartoon, his dark eyes sparkling, a chuckle shaking his torso, while I ate my breakfast and rid my head of Percy.

I TIGHTENED THE LONG PINS THAT SECURED MY GRAY felt bicycling hat to my hair, hitched up my black skirt, and mounted the padded seat of my vermilion-red bicycle. Before Father could run outside and change his mind about letting me ride, I took off and pedaled down Main Street, amid horse-drawn wagons delivering fresh Saturday produce to the city's grocers. Nearly a year before, the *Oregonian* reported that the city now boasted one automobile, owned by a German immigrant named Henry Wemme, but I hadn't yet seen the contraption. I'd only heard stories about how it caused horses to rear and bolt when it charged through the city with its motor howling.

Ruts and stones in the uneven road jostled my shoulders, but the ground was dry and firm, aside from the occasional pile of horse dung. Gunmetal-gray clouds loomed over the city, threatening rain, yet they were merciful and withheld their showers.

I turned left on Third Street, before getting anywhere near the sewage stink and unsavory characters of the waterfront district. Feeling the need to go faster, I leaned forward and powered the pedals with all my strength. My calf muscles burned, the bicycle chain whirred below my flapping skirts, and I caught enough speed to lift my feet and cruise past the towering brick buildings and streetcar tracks. Air rushed across my tongue; the wind fought to whip the hat off my head. The company names written on the buildings—INDEPENDENT STEAMSHIP CO., E. HOUSES CAFÉ, EMBERS PHOTO STUDIO, THE J. K. GILL CO., FUNG LAM RESTAURANT, and even METROPOLITAN—streaked into a blur.

To avoid the saloons and gambling dens (and Father) in the North End, I steered left and zoomed up Washington, my heart racing, heat fanning through my face, my arms, my legs. I veered down Sixth and rode three more blocks before turning right onto Yamhill. McCorkan's Bicycle Shop's forest-green awnings came into view, and a Christmas morning sense of elation stirred inside me. My feet slowed on the pedals. The chain *click-click-click*ed to a stop, and I planted my shoes on the road in front of McCorkan's display window.

There they were, prominently displayed on two dress forms.

Bicycle bloomers.

Rational garments.

Turkish trousers.

Whatever one wanted to call them, the garments—so vibrant compared to our black physical-education pants, which were meant for female classmates' eyes alone—resembled beautiful, billowing hot-air balloons that could lift a girl off the ground. One pair matched the blue of the American flag swaying in the wind outside the shop. The other was as shocking red as the bicycle I straddled. The pants swelled wide enough that they would make the future owners appear to be wearing skirts—if the young ladies kept their legs pinned together.

But as everyone knows, bicycling ladies don't keep their legs pinned together.

The shop door opened with the soft tinkle of a bell, and out stepped Kate and her sister Agnes. Both of the Frye ladies had flushed faces and wore the American-flag-blue version of the bloomers. They headed toward two parked bicycles alongside the curb. Kate carried a little satchel tool bag meant for cyclists embarking upon longer rides.

"Oh." Agnes squinted at me through the glare of the sun behind the clouds. "Look, Kate, it's Olivia. Was that you I saw at the restaurant with two boys last night?"

"Um . . . well . . ."

"Are you looking for bloomers?" asked Kate.

"Just admiring them for now."

"You should ask your father to buy you a pair," said Agnes, putting her hands on her bloomers-clad hips. "Turkish trousers don't get caught in bicycle spokes like that dangerous skirt of yours. Besides"—she winked at me—"today's a day to celebrate if you're a Portland woman."

"It is?" I scratched my chin and tried to recall if we celebrated any famous Oregon women's birthdays . . . or if there *were* any famous Oregon women, for that matter. "Why?"

Agnes lifted her chin. "Because that *damned* editor"—she didn't even flinch when she swore like a sailor—"Mr. Harvey

Scott, finally found the courage to print a suffrage letter in the *Oregonian*."

"Language, Agnes," said Kate with a twinkle in her eye.

I gripped my handlebars and tried not to topple over with my bike. "I read that letter, but I—I—I . . . I don't . . ."

"I know, this historic occasion is enough to make a person speechless." Agnes mounted one of the awaiting bicycles—a canary-yellow beaut with a silver horn attached to the handlebars. "I don't know if you realize it, but Mr. Scott's sister is our local suffragist leader, Abigail Scott Duniway. Up until this morning, that stubborn old mule has refused to print anything pro-suffrage in his paper. We blame him for the failure of the referendum."

I shook my head. "But . . . I don't understand. Why do you think he printed this particular letter?"

Agnes shrugged. "Perhaps he thought it was a joke. The headline tried to poke fun at the letter writer, but it failed miserably. Mother, Kate, and I all received telephone calls from friends who read the letter and want to personally toast this mysterious 'Responsible Woman.'"

"Oh." Prickles of both fear and pride crawled across my skin like hundreds of sharp-clawed insects. *What have I done?* I thought. *What the blazes have I done?*

Kate straddled the other bicycle with a swing of her right leg and pumped her pedals into motion. "Well, I'll see you at school, Olivia."

"Ask your father to buy you bloomers," added Agnes,

following her sister into the street. "Tell him you're asking for trouble if you don't adapt to modern safety advances."

The young Frye ladies rode away, their bloomers flapping and billowing in the breeze like the sails of a schooner.

I know it was my eyes deceiving me again—a strange side effect of my awe over my letter's publication, perhaps—but halfway down the next block, the wheels of both the Frye girls' bikes lifted an inch off the ground, and the ladies careered down the street on the wind.

I FOUND FRANNIE PERFORMING HER FAVORITE BOOKSHOP duty: arranging new arrivals in Harrison's display windows. I rapped on the glass, gave her a quick wave, and hurried inside the store. The jangling bell above the shop door announced my entrance.

"Good morning, Livie." Frannie stood up straight with a book in each hand. "Is everything all right?"

I poked my head around shelves to check for eavesdroppers. "Where's the rest of your family?"

"Carl is out delivering a rare book, and the rest of the children are at Grandmother's. My parents took a riverboat ride to celebrate their anniversary."

"I thought they were celebrating with a fancy supper tomorrow."

"They are, but Papa wanted to treat Mother today, since she'll be cooking the meal tomorrow."

I sighed. "Such a good man. Such a beautiful man."

"I beg your pardon?"

I darted my head behind another bookshelf. "There aren't any customers here, either?"

"No, it's just me here at the moment. Why? What's happening? More hallucinations?"

I approached her and lowered my voice, just in case anyone should emerge from out of nowhere. "Frannie . . ."

"Yes?" she whispered back.

I swallowed and summoned a burst of courage. "I'm 'A Responsible Woman.'"

"Yes, of course you are, Livie." Her tone and nod were patronizing. "Except for when it comes to your relationship with Percy Acklen."

"No." I scowled. "I'm talking about the pro-suffrage letter printed in today's newspaper. I'm 'A Responsible Woman.'"

Her brown eyes swelled as round and bulgy as my largest prized marbles. She exhaled with the sound of a deflating bicycle tire. "Egad, Livie. Really and truly?"

"Did you read the letter?"

"Of course I read it. It was the talk of the breakfast table this morning, and every woman who's walked through the shop door has asked for publications by Abigail Scott Duniway or Susan B. Anthony."

"They have?"

She set down the books she was holding and pulled me toward General Literature. "We've sold every single copy of Duniway's women's rights novels in the past two hours. See the gap?" She pointed to an empty space toward the end of the *D* section. "People think she's the one who wrote the letter."

"Holy mackerel." I breathed a sigh that whistled through my teeth. "Maybe this will mean women won't give up the fight. Maybe there'll be another referendum."

"Maybe." She raised her eyebrows. "But does Percy know you're the one publicly making his father sound like a buffoon?"

"Oh. Percy." I growled and held my head between the tips of my fingers.

"The party didn't go well?" she asked.

"Tell me honestly, did he touch you?" I asked in return.

Frannie turned her face away and ran a knuckle across Charles Dickens's spines.

"Frannie?"

"Are you still in love with him?" she asked.

"Not anymore."

"Then, yes." She dropped her hand from the books. "I admit, he grabbed me last year when I was retying the lace of my shoe in the school stairwell. He came up the steps behind me, gave me a spank and a squeeze, and then continued up the stairs without even looking back. I hated myself the whole rest of the day."

"Oh, Frannie. Why didn't you tell me?"

"I was never sure if he simply confused me for someone else, or . . ." She fussed with the end of her braid. "I don't know. It happened a whole year ago. I hoped he might have matured a little."

"No." I folded my arms over my chest. "He's still a grabber . . . and a biter . . . and a terrible kisser."

"You kissed him?"

"He kissed me, and it was awful."

The shop door opened, and a woman and her twin daughters—girls no older than twelve or thirteen—strolled into the store.

"Do you have *The Awakening* by Kate Chopin?" asked the mother.

"I believe so," said Frannie in a professional tone. She reached up and took hold of a tan book with green grapevines laced around the title. "Yes, ma'am. Here it is."

I wandered to one of the front-window displays and thumbed through a Kipling book while Frannie proceeded with business. In addition to Chopin's novel, the woman and her daughters purchased *The Yellow Wallpaper* by Charlotte Perkins Gilman and *A Vindication of the Rights of Woman* by Mary Wollstonecraft. I hadn't read *The Yellow Wallpaper*, but I knew all three of the texts questioned the subordination of women.

After the sale, each of the customers retreated with a book wedged under her left arm, and before they reached the door, a transformation occurred. The little family brightened. Their faces, like those of Agnes and the other suffragists at the restaurant, shone with some sort of internal brilliance, and their hair—fluffed and pinned beneath a small straw hat in the case of the mother, long braids for the daughters— became the bold yellowish orange of firelight.

The door shut behind them, and the little bell punctuated their exit with a jingle. The illusion ended.

"You see what I mean?" asked Frannie, coming toward me. "You stirred up something remarkable with that letter. What does your father think?"

"He doesn't know I wrote it."

"If he finds out . . . do you think . . . what about the hypnosis?"

"I wrote that letter after he mandated that hypnotism cure"—I spat out that last word—"so, clearly, it did nothing but push me into trying things I never would have dared before."

"You're not saying you like being hypnotized, are you?"

"No! It's just . . . Look here . . ." I squatted down and fished around in my right shoe. Henry's theater tickets, along with some quarters I'd brought in case I got hungry, were hidden between the stiff leather and my thick stocking. "I've seen Henry—"

"I thought it was *On-ree.*"

"His real name is Henry Rhodes, and he gave me these tickets so we could stay in contact with each other." I pulled out the tickets and stood upright. "I begged him to end the hypnosis, but he needs my father's money for his sister. She has a tumor that requires surgery. It's cancerous."

Frannie took the tickets from my hand and, with her lips pursed, read them over.

"He can't change me back," I continued, "until my father gives him his full payment on Tuesday. That's when he'll be taking his sister to San Francisco for her surgery."

"He's about to leave town?"

"In three more days."

"Are you still seeing strange sights?"

"Yes." I grabbed for the tickets, but Frannie hid them behind her back. "Frannie?" I tugged on her elbow. "Give those back."

"You're telling me"—she swung her arm away and inched backward—"you're going to keep viewing your father as a vampire, and doing whatever other horrible things that hypnotist is making you do, for three more days?"

"I've got no other choice. That poor girl might die if she doesn't undergo her surgery. The cancer's in her bosom."

"How do you know he's not making up her illness?"

"Don't be mean."

"How do you know, Livie?"

"I trust him."

She stopped and thrust the tickets at me. "Fine. Trust a traveling, mind-altering showman."

"There's no need to get upset." I took the tickets from her.

"I bet he smells terrible, too."

"Frannie!"

"I'm just worried about you. Wait . . ." She squinted at the backside of the tickets and snatched them straight back out of my hand. "What's this?"

"What?"

"This note. 'Come to the side door of the theater after the show—'"

I grabbed the papers so hard, one of them ripped. "Never mind what that says."

"You're going to meet him in private?"

"I don't know." I slunk toward the exit. "I'm not sure what to do about any of this, but I know whom to trust and whom to avoid, so stop frowning at me like I'm an idiot."

"I didn't say you were an idiot, Livie."

"But you're looking at me as if I am one." I turned and pushed open the door.

"Wait! Livie . . ."

The door slammed shut behind me before she could say another word.

I climbed aboard my bicycle and pedaled away, toward the Metropolitan.

CHAPTER FIFTEEN

ALL IS NOT WELL

Henry's matinee performance wasn't scheduled to start until one thirty in the afternoon. To bide the time, I stopped for a ham sandwich across the street in a smoky café with a pressed-tin ceiling and theater posters hanging from knotty-pine walls.

Halfway through my meal, one of the other diners plopped himself across from me in my booth.

"What's a good little girl like you doing all by herself in the city?" he asked, and when I raised my face, I found Sunken-

Eyed John from Sadie's party, grinning at me. "Does Percy know you're not a respectable woman?"

I set the second half of my sandwich aside on the bone-colored plate. "I don't care what Percy does or doesn't think of me."

"Is that so?"

"Yes. I am not his sweetheart."

"Well, that's unfortunate for him." He leaned forward on his elbows, his breath stinking of cheese and ale. "I learned a little secret about you."

I knitted my eyebrows together. "What secret?"

"Well . . ." He ran his tongue along the inside of his cheek. "I told my father about your odd behavior with that hypnotist last night, and he said he knew who you were. Your father used to work on his teeth—before last Wednesday."

My skin went cold. "Who is your father?"

"John Underhill Sr., owner of the city's largest shipping firm. My mother is the president of the Oregon Association Opposed to Women's Suffrage—or whatever the devil that thing's called."

"Oh." My voice cracked with too much of a quaver for the heroine of the morning's newspaper.

A smirk inched up the side of John's face. "Your daddy telephoned my father to brag about a hypnotism cure. It sounds as if Monsieur Reverie has you on the end of a leash, performing tricks like a trained little monkey."

"Why did my father tell him that?"

"I just said, to brag." He leaned back with a broad smile and spread his arms across the upper ridge of his side of the booth. "So, you say you're not Percy's girl anymore?"

"No, I'm not."

"Are you a lesbian?"

"A what?"

"Are you in love with women, not men?"

"No, I—"

"Why don't you come home with me right now"—he slid his shoe across the floorboards and wedged it between my feet—"and I'll thrust the masculinity straight out of you myself. I'll break you like the wild filly you are."

Without even thinking, I raised my right foot and stomped John's toes with my heel.

"Ouch! Christ!"

I tried to stand up with some semblance of dignity, but I banged my knee on the table, which sent my water spilling into the cretin's lap.

He jumped up. "Hey! You little—"

"All is well."

"Oh, God, not that again."

"All is well." I grabbed my hat and pushed my way through a crowd of other young men piling into the restaurant with hunger shining in their eyes and growling in their bellies. Clouds of tobacco smoke and spiced colognes blew in my face, telling me, *You don't belong here . . .*

"Hey, watch where you're going, girlie," cried one of the

men, grabbing my elbow and smiling as if I were part of a bawdy joke.

I shoved his scratchy tweed arm aside and made my way past all the plaid coats and derby hats and waxed mustaches, out into the sweet fresh air.

A MIDDLE-AGED COUPLE WITH ACROBATIC TOY POODLES opened Henry's show, and their yippy little dogs and gaudy sequined costumes sucked every breath of enchantment from the Metropolitan Theater. I could now see that the stage floor was streaked in sawdust and filthy trails of footprints, and the pipe organ appeared shorter and duller than the tower of copper and beauty from Genevieve's ethereal rendition of "Danse Macabre." *Cheap* was the first word that came to mind when I sat in the sparse audience that Saturday afternoon. Cheap. Gaudy. Disappointing. It wasn't even the hypnosis showing me the way the theater truly was. All it took to sour my belief in magic was a lack of Halloween glamour and that disgusting encounter with Sunken-Eyed John.

The poodle couple took their bows to overly generous applause, and after they pranced off to the wings, the organist with the pumpkin-colored hair swaggered across the stage without any special introduction or fanfare. She plunked down on the bench in front of the pipe organ and embarked upon a slow and lumbering rendition of "Sleep, Little Rosebud"—not even "Danse Macabre."

I couldn't stand sitting there, subjected to her ruckus, and

I couldn't bear the thought of Henry's appearance in the show looking fake and lusterless—not when I required him to possess the power to set my world right. I got to my feet and fled to the lobby, where I asked a gray-whiskered gentleman in the box office for a piece of paper and a pen.

At the counter next to the ticket window, while the organ music plodded along in the background, I scribbled down my frustrations on an ivory sheet of theater letterhead.

Dear Henry,

I am writing down my thoughts for you, because yelling at you will only make me say that "All is well," and I am tired of that damnable phrase spouting from my lips. I am not sure if I can last three more days. That meaningless sentence you have forced me to say is turning me weak and putting me in danger.

I just came across that ogre of a boy, John, from Sadie's party, and he got uncomfortably flirtatious with me—but all I could say was "All is well." Someone else left unwanted bite marks on my neck last night (please do not ask why or mention this indiscretion to anyone), and I am sure you can guess which three words shot from my mouth when I tried to shout, "Stop!" I may be able to tolerate my strange visions until Tuesday evening, but I fear I will be allowing myself to become the victim of something even more heinous if my shouts of anger and distress continue to be silenced.

I know you love your sister dearly and fear for her health. I believe your story about her tumor to be true and not a ruse to keep me from complaining about this "cure" of yours. Yet you must imagine what her world would be like if she could never complain about her discomfort or cry out to protect herself. You would never wish such a dangerous fate upon her, would you? If not, then please take pity on me and allow me to stop saying that all is well.

Let me speak my anger again—please! I swear upon my grandparents' graves I will hide from my father my ability to say what I mean. You must change me today. Do not leave me like this.

All is NOT well.

I waited with my letter on the cement steps leading up to the theater's side entrance, ten yards down from the streetcar tracks. The gray clouds continued to do nothing more than hang over the city, teasing of rain but refusing to spit a single drop. I stretched out my legs on the stairs and enjoyed a small sip of sunlight that managed to steal across the sidewalk. My bicycle rested against the rails beside me—my horse awaiting the getaway.

One of the city's electric-powered streetcars whirred to a stop down the way, its brakes squeaking in the damp air, the wheels clenching against the tracks. Only its rounded front end was visible from where I sat, but I assumed departing theatergoers were climbing aboard around the bend.

Behind me, the theater door swung open, and the substitute organist exited. She tramped down the stairs with a gold and green carpetbag hanging over her left arm, and she screwed up her lips when she saw me sitting there, perhaps remembering me from the day before, when I had kept Henry from rehearsing. Her newtlike eyes studied me, as if she were evaluating an apple for bruises and wormholes, finding more bad spots than good.

The wind shifted—or maybe it was just my brain switching directions. In any case, the organist tipped her head a certain way, and her orange hair careened down to her waist in plump curls. Her face slimmed and softened with youth. The carpetbag transformed into a German hurdy-gurdy instrument with strings and a crank, and her frumpy brown dress blossomed into a ruffled blue slip of a gown, like the shocking costumes of lady entertainers in North End saloons.

Without a word, her regular fussy, sharp-eyed looks reappeared, and she wandered around the corner, toward the streetcar. I stared at the place where she had vanished, my mouth hanging open, for I felt I'd just encountered a person much like my mother—a beautiful entertainer trapped in the body of an aging woman. Not an easy place to be, I'm sure. I wondered if my mother also shot bitter glares and unkind words at the young theater people around her.

The door opened again, and I got to my feet when I saw Henry stepping outside in the dark coat from his Halloween performance. He wore his black square-crown hat pulled down over his eyes, as if to conceal his identity, and he chewed on something crunchy that sounded like hard candy.

"Henry?" I asked, and I gripped both the rail and the letter.

He looked up, revealing familiar blue eyes that brightened at the sight of me.

"Olivia, *c'est toi*." He galloped down the stairs until he landed in front of me, smelling of peppermint. "You came."

I slammed my letter against his chest.

He gulped down the last of his candy. "What's this?"

"Just read it. Please."

He unfolded the letter.

I chewed my bottom lip and watched his eyes shift back and forth over my writing. The longer he read, the more his brow puckered in a frown.

He blew out a sigh that rustled his hair and lowered the letter to his side. "Did Percy really bite you?" he asked in the American version of his voice.

"Why do you have two accents?"

"I asked my question first."

Before I could gather enough breath and courage to answer, the pack of squeaky show poodles exited the side door, their exhausted-eyed owners following in a web of leather leashes. Henry and I both stepped away from the theater, and I grabbed my bicycle by the handlebars. Side by side, we headed toward Third Street with the barking ruckus trailing behind us.

"I'd like to see your neck," he said over the commotion of the dogs and the hum of the streetcar breezing off in the opposite direction.

"Are you off your rocker? I'm not going to expose my neck in public." I held fast to my bike, which I walked by my side up Third.

The streetcar's bell clanged at an intersection in the distance, and the poodles yipped to the south while we trekked north. Our section of Third lay empty at the moment, aside from Henry and me.

"Why did he bite you?" he asked. "Was it a romantic bite?"

"No." I blushed with such intensity that my eyes watered. "I'm . . ." I fanned my face with my hand. "I'm trying with all my might not to say that all is well, so please don't ask any more questions about it. The point is, I couldn't tell him no when I was alone with him in the buggy last night."

Henry stopped. "Did he make you do anything else?"

I stopped, too. "As in what?"

"As in . . . um . . ." He nodded as if I should know what he was thinking, his face pinking up. "Hasn't anyone ever told you about . . . ?"

"I don't . . . he didn't . . ." I pulled at my collar and cringed at the memory of one of Mother's detailed letters that instructed how to avoid becoming in the family way. "I'm not sure if you mean . . ."

"Um"—he scratched his cheek—"never mind. Were you able to get away from him after he bit you?"

"Yes. I pushed him off me twice, and both times his head whacked the top of the buggy."

I resumed walking my bicycle.

Henry stayed behind for a moment, but when I glanced over my shoulder, he grinned and caught up.

"*Mon Dieu,* Olivia. You're much stronger than you look. I took you to be a frightened little bird when you came up onstage with me on Halloween."

"Now, there you sound French again. Are you French or American?"

"My mother was born in Paris and grew up in Montreal. My father was from Toronto. My uncle took guardianship over us in Cleveland."

"And French sounds more mysterious and exotic than a Cleveland accent?"

"*Oui.*" He smiled and slipped his hands into his pockets. "Uncle Lewis asked me to sound French whenever I appeared on the stage. I was always good at imitating my mother's accent, and I speak both languages fluently."

"Hmm." I stole a glance at him. My fingers gripped the handlebars.

I summoned a vision of my own accord.

Large rips formed in the underarm seams of his coat and revealed glimpses of a striped shirt underneath. His red vest— the same dazzling garment from Halloween night—drained to the color of underripe cherries, and the black of his suit faded to gray. On his head, his felt hat deflated until it looked battered and squished and as well traveled as an old railroad car. His eyes turned puffy and red.

I shifted my attention to the sidewalk ahead.

"You don't look like the mesmerizing Henri Reverie any-more," I said. "Not when I get a good look at you."

"I don't?" He turned his face toward me. "What do I look like, then?"

"Tired. Desperate. A little like a hobo."

He responded with a weary smile. "That's exactly what I am."

The commotion of the city—the wagons, the workers, the Canada geese honking across the sky toward the Willamette River—filled my ears again. The vision passed.

Henry, back in his regular, intact clothing, hopped into the street at the corner and waved for me to follow. "Come along. Genevieve is in here."

I followed him across the intersection, my bicycle chain spinning as I hustled to avoid a horse-drawn milk cart jangling our way.

On the other side of the street, Henry stopped in front of the four-story Hotel Vernon, which had fuzzy strips of bright green moss growing between the walls' red bricks. I saw two boarded-up windows on the third floor, and a round hole that could have been made by a bullet gaped from a piece of glass on the second story.

I kept hold of my bicycle and craned my neck to look up at the building. "Is this where she is?"

"Yes."

"I can't go into a hotel with you."

"Genevieve isn't feeling well enough to come outside."

"If any of my father's patients see me—"

"Go in ahead of me." He nodded toward the entrance. "We're in room twenty-five on the second floor."

"What about my bicycle? If he passes by, Father might recognize it."

"Here . . ." He took hold of the handlebars and the frame. "I'll take it inside for you and ask if we can park it in the lobby. Go on up and wait by the door to the room. I'll be there soon."

I scanned both sides of the street, and when I didn't see anyone I recognized, I ducked inside the hotel. A sign at the back of the lobby said STAIRWAY, so I made a beeline toward it, passing Grecian pillars, plush armchairs, and emerald-green rugs laid over a diamond-tiled floor. Despite the attempts at finery, a worn and decaying look—and odor—clung to every article in the lobby, including the customers. A woman in a beaver-fur stole sank back in an armchair, and her clothes blended in with the moss-green upholstery, as if she and the chair were becoming one. A hotel clerk with a devilish Vandyke beard was belittling two well-dressed black men who were trying to check in at the front—and I could have sworn I saw the polished counter straight through the guests' striped trousers and coats.

I headed up to the second floor, my heart skipping, and tried to ignore the stink of the place and the nervous twisting of my stomach. Henry's voice echoed down below, asking the clerk if he could park my bicycle in the lobby, his voice smooth and as exquisitely French as fine wine. Less than two minutes later, he was upstairs, coming toward me down the hallway, tugging a gold key out of his coat pocket, while I stood in front of the closed door of room twenty-five.

He moved to insert the key into the lock, but before he could click the metal into place, I blurted out, "Let me see your teeth first."

Henry's hand stopped in midair. "Pardon?"

"Show me your teeth."

"Why? Because you're a dentist's daughter?"

"No, because I want to make sure I can trust you."

I lifted my hand toward his face, but he flinched and shrank back against the gold wallpaper.

"I'm not a vampire, Olivia."

I stepped closer, which made him blink and flinch again.

"Then why are you acting so suspiciously?" I asked.

"Because . . ."

"Because what?"

"I'm worried I'll—" He sidestepped away from me, but I pinned his arm to the wall, lifted his lip past his gums, and wished to see the truth in his teeth.

Normal.

Harmless.

Clean.

His spotless incisors, canines, bicuspids, and molars were actually quite beautiful, perhaps even brushed on a regular basis. His breath still carried the Christmassy scent of his peppermint candy, and his lip felt as soft as a petal against my thumb. Our eyes met, and I dropped my hand from his mouth.

"What were you going to say you were worried about?" I asked in a squeak of a voice while retreating two feet backward.

"I was worried that . . ." He removed his hat and ran his fingers through his hair. "I'm sure there's part of me you still won't be able to trust."

My heart sank. "You're not going to fix me, are you?"

"Come meet Genevieve. We'll discuss what we're going to do after you've spoken to her."

"Of course I'm going to agree to go along with everything when I see your sister."

"Olivia . . ." His voice softened. He took my hand. "Please don't get upset. I'll consider altering the hypnosis if I can figure out a way to keep everyone safe."

"You've got to swear you won't leave me like this." I gripped his fingers. "Swear to me you won't run away to San Francisco without helping me."

"If you help Genevieve, I swear upon my life I'll help you."

A hot tear escaped my left eye before I knew it was even coming.

"I promise, Olivia." He squeezed my hand. "I won't leave you like this. We're partners, not enemies. *Oui*?"

I nodded and wiped my cheek with the back of my hand, tasting salt on my lips. "Yes. *Oui*. Partners."

He turned the key in the lock and led me into a small room

with amber curtains pulled back to expose the dwindling late-afternoon sun. The flowery burgundy paper peeling off the walls soaked up most of the light, but the place wasn't quite the woeful retreat of a dying girl I was expecting. A twin bed, a lime-green sofa made up as a second bed, and an elegant ivory washbasin lent the room a homelike atmosphere. The smell of lilac soap, not fever, sweetened the air.

Something on the far corner of the bed caught my attention: a short blink of candlelight that faded the second after I spotted it, as if someone had snuffed out a flame. I tensed, for I saw a pair of eyes watching from the darkness.

Before I could ask Henry what I'd just seen, the light brightened again, illuminating the face of a girl. A moment later, it flickered away, and the bed lay empty.

"Olivia, this is my sister, Genevieve." Henry came around my side and walked toward the waxing and waning figure on the sheets. "Genevieve, I present to you Olivia Mead."

I couldn't move. One moment, she was clear and vibrant—a golden-haired girl in a white nightgown, crawling toward me across the covers—the next, she was sputtering out, and the bed looked abandoned, save for the indentations of hands and knees on the mattress.

"What's wrong?" asked Henry, his face paling. "What does she look like?"

I gave a shiver. "I see things the way they are, but I can't predict the future."

"What does she look like?" he asked again, his voice taking on a tinny phonograph quality as his sister consumed my attention.

I swallowed. "A candle flame that can't decide if it has the strength to keep burning." I shifted my eyes away from her.

Henry's bottom lip trembled. His arms hung by his sides like two useless extensions of his body. I felt compelled to hug him, but Genevieve spoke before I gathered the courage to do so.

"Henry told me what he was paid to do, Miss Mead," she said. "Please come sit by me so I may talk to you. Don't be afraid to look at me."

I turned and ventured over to the bed while clutching the sides of my skirt. Genevieve continued to flicker and fade, as if she were sitting in a blackened room, illuminated every few seconds by a soundless flash of lightning. My brain went dizzy and fuzzy from watching her come and go like that, and I half expected crashes of thunder to rumble across the walls and make sense of the phenomenon—yet none ever arrived. I sat beside her and steadied my breathing.

"Henry told me you're not allowed to speak your anger anymore," she said during a moment of illumination that revealed the concerned arc of her eyebrows, "and you can see people's true selves, sometimes in frightening forms."

I nodded, still speechless. I discovered that blinking a few times in a row almost made her stay in place. "Are you in pain, Genevieve?" I asked her.

"No." She placed her hand over her upper chest. "The

tumor is simply something I know shouldn't be there, which, I admit, does make me feel a little sick. And tired."

"I'm so sorry."

"And what about you?" she asked, scooting closer with a rustle of sheets. "Are you staying safe?"

"I'm healthy, so I can't complain."

"No, be honest with me. Are you suffering because of Henry's hypnosis?"

"Well . . ." I averted my eyes from hers again, choosing to gaze instead at the wrinkles in my black skirt and the spots of dirt flecked across the hem. "I've just asked him to alter the part about . . ." I shook my head and sighed. "I can wait, Genevieve. It's just three more days. You're a little bit younger than me, aren't you?"

"I'm almost sixteen."

"Sixteen?" I clasped my hand over my eyes. "No, I'll just keep saying that all is well."

"You hinted you weren't safe," she said. "What's happened to you?"

"Someone bit her," said Henry.

Genevieve gasped. "Bit her? Why?"

"It was the boy—the cocky one—who escorted her to that party last night." Henry sank down on the sofa with an uncomfortable sigh. "That type of behavior happens sometimes . . . when, um, *gentlemen* get . . . romantic."

"I assure you, I'm not a loose girl," I said to Genevieve. "I tried to tell Percy to stop, but all I could say was—"

"'All is well,'" Henry finished for me.

Genevieve flickered into view with greater wattage. "Where did he bite you?"

"On my neck."

"Like Dracula?" she asked.

I smiled. "You've read *Dracula*?"

"Of course. It was *magnifique*."

"When did you read it?" asked Henry.

"I borrowed it from the library last year, when you were so busy reading your hypnotism books and fussing over your hair for the girls." She brightened even further, remaining solid and steady for seconds at a time. "How bad of a bite was it, Miss Mead?"

I squirmed and didn't answer.

She shifted her legs over the side of the bed. "Please show me."

I looked to Henry, who pursed his lips as if he didn't know what to say.

"Oh, I don't know about that," I said. "It's an awfully embarrassing thing to share . . ."

"No need to be embarrassed," said Henry. "If I'm an honest hypnotist, which I like to think I am, I should see how much harm I've caused."

I sipped two calming breaths through my lips—*in, out, breathe, deeper*—and lifted my hand to the topmost pearl. Henry stood up from the sofa and trod toward me with hesitant footsteps, making my fingers shake and slide around on the pearl's slick surface before I could twist the clasp loose from the buttonhole. I undid the second button, which allowed the air in the room to cool the skin of my throat, and I exhaled, as if I'd just freed my neck from the embrace of a noose.

The blouse remained taut over the lower half of my neck. I unbuttoned the third clasp and pulled the plaid wool aside to expose my bare skin.

Genevieve whimpered and sputtered out of view. Henry's eyes widened. He came closer and peeled the fabric farther down.

"Is that . . . is it . . ." I attempted to smile away my mortification. "Is that the normal look of a bite from a gentleman who's feeling romantic?"

Henry tucked my blouse back over my skin. "I don't think romance had anything to do with that mark."

"Perhaps . . ." Genevieve surged back into light. "You could maybe consider hypnotizing her father into paying your fee, eh? Then you could immediately end her hypnosis and—"

"What? Genevieve!" Henry froze. "You know full well I can't hypnotize people into giving me money."

"But—"

"Look what happened to Uncle Lewis when he tried that sort of thing. What good would I be to you if I'm lying in some gutter, bleeding to death?"

"But that was all because of a gambling debt," said Genevieve. "This is different."

"Something would go wrong, and I'd end up either in jail or in a coffin." Henry tottered over to the window and scratched his forehead. "I don't know what to do, Olivia. We really can't change any part of the hypnosis before your father sees satisfying results."

"But he's already seen results," I said. "He knows I can't get angry with him. What more proof is he waiting for?"

Henry rubbed his face, but he did not answer.

"What is it?" I rose from the bed. "What do you know, Henry?"

He dropped his hands to his sides and faced me. "I have an appointment to go to your house in an hour. He's asked me to make adjustments to the hypnosis."

"What? More mind control?"

"He wants to show you off to members of some sort of organization—the Association of something or other."

My mouth went dry. "The Oregon Association Opposed to the Extension of Suffrage to Women."

"That's the one." Henry leaned his shoulder blades against the window. "He wants to demonstrate your treatment to some woman who's in charge of the association."

Oh, Lord. Sunken-Eyed John's mother.

"What else did he say?" I asked with my hands balled into fists.

"He mentioned it's the millionaires' wives who are the strongest anti-suffrage voices, and he's terrified of losing his rich customers if these powerful women think you're a suffragist. If he can convince this lady that I've removed your 'unfeminine' beliefs, he'll be invited back to her election-night party, where I'm to demonstrate to an entire crowd that suffragists can be cured."

I stepped back, my breath tight in my lungs. "Am I the suffragist you'll be curing in front of everyone?"

"You'll be there," he said with a grim nod, "but you might not be much of a suffragist by then."

I dropped back down onto the bed with a force that jarred my neck.

Genevieve's hand nestled against mine. "Surely we can get money some other way."

"After both the theater and Dr. Mead pay me Tuesday night," said Henry, "we'll only be two dollars short of the rest of the surgeon's fee. Just two measly dollars! How else am I supposed to legally find that sort of money? Before it's too late for you?"

I sniffed back tears and buttoned up my blouse, nearly forgetting I had left my neck exposed and cold.

"Olivia." Henry stepped toward me on the hard soles of his shoes. He cupped a warm hand over my shoulder. "Please, look up at me."

I did as he asked, my teeth clenched, my every muscle tense and on the defensive.

His eyes locked on to mine. The force of his skills shattered all my barriers. "Close your eyes. Think of nothing but sleep."

I did exactly that, for sleep swept its numbing, dark cloak

over my face and chest and legs—down to the smallest of my toes.

"Relax. Melt down, melt down, until all you hear is the sound of my voice. Calm your breathing."

My lungs relaxed, along with the rest of me.

"Yes . . . that's good. Very good. Let your breathing grow slower. And slower. And slower. Melt all the way down until you feel the utter bliss of deep relaxation."

I collapsed into a heap at the bottom of a cozy black box.

"Now," he said near my ear, "imagine a lamp switching on and finding the two of us seated in the safest room you can imagine."

Gaslight whispered to life, and Henry and I were sitting together at Frannie's kitchen table. A vegetable soup bubbled on the stove, and the Harrisons' bright yellow wallpaper, as well as the children's pinned-up drawings and poetry, surrounded us. Henry reached across Mrs. Harrison's home-embroidered tablecloth and took my hand.

"You no longer need to say that all is well when you are angry." He bent his face toward mine. "You are free to speak your mind, but you will do so with caution around your father. For now, in front of him, you will limit your volatile words only to moments when someone is about to get hurt. Do you understand?"

I nodded.

"Good. You will keep seeing the world the way it truly is so that you may remain alert for danger, but I will give your mind entirely back to you after the election-night show. For it will be just a show, Olivia. This is all merely a temporary spectacle to make your father happy." He squeezed my hand and lifted his head. "Now, I will count to ten, and you will awaken and return to your home, where I will see you in less than an hour—*ma partenaire.*" He squeezed again. "My partner."

"My only doubt was as to whether any dream could be more terrible than the unnatural, horrible net of gloom and mystery which seemed closing around me."

—BRAM STOKER, *Dracula*, 1897

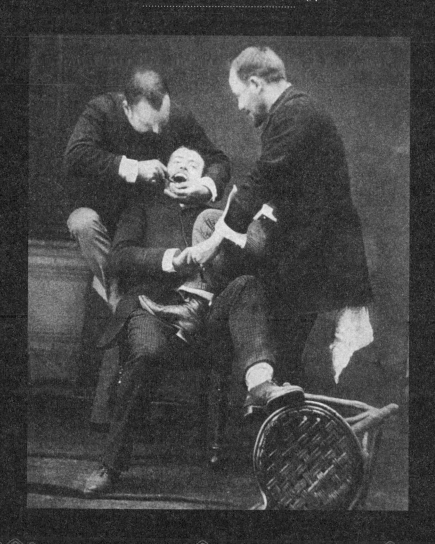

CHAPTER SIXTEEN

THE WHITEHEAD GAG

The hour before Henry's arrival at our house moved with the excruciating slowness of twelve hours. I passed the minutes on the bench in front of my late grandmother's high-backed Beckwith parlor organ. My song of choice: "Evening Prayer" from *Hansel and Gretel.* My fingers lacked Genevieve's skill, but, oh, what a glorious relief when I thrust my troubles into the black and white keys and pumped my anxieties into the foot pedals.

I must have played the song at least five times in a row; I lost track after the second or third round. Halfway through the fifth or sixth go, someone knocked on the front door. My fingers slipped, and the lowest keys belched a deep grumble.

Gerda passed the parlor's entryway on her way to the front door.

"I'll get that, Gerda," said Father from down the hall.

Gerda stopped and tightened her apron strings. "Are you certain, sir?"

"Yes." Father walked into view. "Return to the kitchen. Immediately."

"Yes, sir." Gerda's shoulders slumped, and for a hiccup of a moment, before she bustled back to the kitchen, the poor woman faded before my eyes. Our brown wallpaper behind her bled through her wavering wisp of a body. Her footsteps retreated to the back of the house.

I rose up from the organ bench and approached the hall, my pulse ticking in the side of my neck. Father opened the door, revealing Henry on our front porch, his short black hat in hand.

"Come in, Mr. Reverie." Father pulled the door farther open and clapped the hypnotist on the back as he made his way across the threshold. "Thank you for coming out to my house this afternoon. I know you must be a busy lad."

Henry shrugged. "It is no trouble, Monsieur Mead. I am happy to help if you feel the cure is not to your satisfaction." The French accent was back in place.

Father shut the door and puffed up his chest. "As I said when I telephoned, I require more results." He took Henry's hat from his hand and plunked it on one of our brass wall hooks. "Come to my office for a moment and—"

"Father, I've learned something tragic about Mr. Reverie," I said, and I clasped my hands behind my back to hide the terrible trembling that results when one deviates from the plans of a tyrant.

Father lifted an eyebrow. "'Tragic'? That's an awfully dramatic word, Olivia."

"H-h-his sister . . ." I swallowed and averted my gaze from Henry's startled eyes and gaping mouth. "She requires a surgeon to remove a tumor. It's cancerous. Perhaps you know a local physician who could help her as soon as possible."

Father cocked his head at Henry. "Is this true?"

"I really wish it weren't, sir, but . . . she is sick."

"I'm terribly sorry to hear that." Father tugged at his beard and seemed to search his brain for the name of someone who could help. His eyes softened. The quest for Genevieve's well-being nudged aside his urgency to fix me. I held my breath and prayed this version of Father would remain with us.

"Well," he said, "I don't believe I know any cancer surgeons, unless you're discussing an oral tumor . . ."

"No, it's not that," said Henry. "I appreciate you even considering the matter, but you don't need to—"

"Wait a moment." Father turned abruptly toward me. "How do you know this about his sister?" He placed his hand on Henry's shoulder—not in a firm way, but enough to make my neck sweat beneath my collar.

"I b-b-beg your pardon?" I asked.

"I said, how did you suddenly find out he has a sick sister?" Father squeezed down on Henry, who seemed to shrink an inch. "Mr. Reverie didn't once mention her during your treatment in my office. I doubt he'd announce something so private at his Halloween performance."

"There was a . . ." *Oh, hell.* I hadn't concocted an excuse for that particular detail. *Damn! Damn, damn, damn!*

Father's eyes narrowed. "Have you two spoken with each other since the hypnotism on Thursday?"

"No, sir," said Henry.

"N-n-no, sir," I agreed. "I just—"

"How did you become privy to his family troubles, then, Olivia? Why on earth do you have the intimate details of this stranger's personal life?"

"Father . . . please, don't get upset. The point is, his sister needs help, and I thought—"

Father grabbed Henry's wrist. "Come with me. Do not say a word— No!" He raised a finger with a nail sharp and black. His eyes burned scarlet, and his cheeks sank into the skull of his graying face. "Don't even open your mouth and think of hypnotizing me into giving you extra money."

"I'm not asking for extra money, sir." Henry pulled back and tried to wrench his arm out of Father's grip. "I didn't ask her to say anything about my sister—I swear to God!"

"That's true!" I said. "He didn't ask that at all."

"Quiet! Both of you!"

An awful buzzing rang in my ears. I pushed my hands over them and let out a cry of shock as Father paled even further and sprouted fur on the backs of his hands—part wolf, part corpse, part red-eyed demon.

"If you want me to pay you for your services, boy"—he yanked Henry down the hallway, toward his home office, which he used for drinking and for nighttime emergency treatments—"then shut your damned mouth."

Henry's feet skidded and tripped across the rugs and the floorboards.

"Don't hurt him!" I chased after them. "Please—I didn't mean any harm. I just thought you should know in case you could help . . ." I followed them into the office and braced my hands on the door frame. "His sister isn't even yet sixteen. What would you do if I were the one dying of cancer?"

"You're not dying of cancer, Olivia. Don't be so melodramatic," said Father, but he was no longer anything like my actual father. A clawed devil with spiked teeth and a sharp, hairy chin slapped Henry down into the office's wooden dental chair and buckled his left wrist to an armrest.

"Let me go!" Henry pushed at the creature with his free hand, but Father managed to pin down and shackle his other wrist, too.

"Stop!" I rubbed my eyes, but Father refused to look normal. "Are you really forcing him into that chair? Am I really seeing this?"

"I've offered you a large sum of money, Mr. Reverie." With

one hand planted on Henry's chest, not far from his throat, the horrific version of the man with whom I lived squeaked open a cabinet door. On the shelves gleamed his home collection of dental tools—forceps, clockwork drills, pelicans, chisels, tooth keys. He pulled out a Whitehead gag, a beastly contraption that resembled a bear trap with leather straps. "If you truly do have a sick sister, then I assume more than anything that you'd like me to pay you that money."

"Father! Let him out of that chair!"

"Yes, sir, b-b-but . . ." Henry bent his legs and hovered over the seat, not quite landing his posterior on it. His knees wobbled everywhere, while his wrists stayed strapped to the wood.

"Relax." Father pushed on his knees. "Sit back." He shoved him down by his collarbone, which made Henry's feet pop up on the footrest. "There's no need to panic. I'm just going to fit this gag into your mouth"—he shoved the metal trap between Henry's lips with terrible scraping sounds—"to make sure you aren't verbally manipulating my mind while I give my instructions to you." He yanked the straps around Henry's head, stretching his jaw both vertically and horizontally until Henry groaned in wide-eyed terror.

"Stop it!" I pulled on Father's shoulder and arm. "This is terrible. What type of monster have you become? Just look at yourself."

Father elbowed me away. "Get out of here, Olivia. You're not supposed to be able to argue with me."

"But—"

"Silence!" He pushed me so hard, I banged my lower back against his desk. "Tell me the God's honest truth," he said over Henry, "have you and my daughter spoken since Thursday's hypnosis?"

Henry panted and glanced my way. I nodded, so Henry did the same. He managed a "Yes" that sounded like gargling.

"Is she trying to persuade you to reverse the hypnosis?" asked Father.

Henry nodded again.

Father tipped the dental chair back, raising Henry's feet as high as his hips. "My Olivia isn't the greatest beauty in the world, I admit, but she can break your heart a little, can't she?"

Henry's chest contracted with each shallow breath.

"But, despite feminine wiles," said Father, "we gentlemen must be strong. We must protect the women from their own foolishness. They're fragile and ignorant and need our constant care. I think, if you stuck by my side and ignored my daughter's passionate pleas"—he bent down close to Henry's face with bared yellowed fangs that hung down to his chin— "we could show the world that hypnosis is the key to keeping these modern young women in their proper places. No man will lose a sweet loved one ever again."

"Father"—I held my throbbing head—"you look disgusting."

"Get out of this office, Olivia."

"Take that barbaric thing out of Mr. Reverie's mouth."

"I said, get out!" Father grabbed me by both arms and steered me toward the door.

"No, don't hurt him." I thrust out my foot to try to catch it on the door frame. "Please! Don't hurt either of us."

Father unhooked me from the doorway and pushed me out into the hall. The door slammed shut in my face, and the lock latched.

"Father!" I slammed my fists against the door. "Please, open up!"

"Go wait in the parlor," he called through the wood. "And if you're not sitting there patiently when we both come out, Mr. Reverie will never see a cent of my hard-earned money. You're supposed to be tamed, for God's sake. I was led to believe you were cured. What happened to you saying that all is well?"

I backed away, and the whisper of the gas feeding into the lamps merged with the wheezing of my lungs.

"Is everything all right, Miss Mead?" asked a small voice behind me.

Down the hall, Gerda's blue eyes peeked out from the kitchen doorway.

"If you can find a position with a kinder employer," I told her, "I recommend doing so as quickly as possible."

I turned and staggered into the parlor and clutched my side, which cramped like the dickens from breathing too fast.

. . . . .

THE OFFICE DOOR OPENED WITH A LOW CLICK.

I stood up from my slumped position on our mustard-yellow settee and endured each approaching footstep as if someone were digging his heels into my heart.

Father came into view from around the bend, and as hard as I blinked, I couldn't stop seeing him as a monster—I simply couldn't. Behind him emerged Henry, rubbing his red wrists, his lips bleeding.

"What did you do?" I asked.

"Silence, Olivia." Father held up a hand with the long, rotten nails. "I've said this before," he said through his teeth, "and I'll say it again: This is all for your own good. You do not need to be burdened with impossible dreams."

I wrapped my arms around myself and stared at Henry's bleeding mouth.

Genevieve, I reminded myself. *She's waiting for him in that moldering hotel room.*

"Fine." I swallowed and rocked myself for comfort. "Hypnotize me, Mr. Reverie. Let's get it over with."

Henry stepped forward. "Do not be afraid," he said in a French-tinged voice that possessed a sharp edge.

He held out his hand to mine, and I saw that his nails were as black and hooked as Father's. He heaved a sigh that revealed a pair of canine teeth fierce enough to sever his own tongue.

I pulled my hand away, but his fingers shot out and grabbed

my wrist. He jerked my arm toward him and plunged me into darkness with the firm command, "Sleep!"

"WHEN YOU AWAKEN, YOU WILL HAVE NO MEMORY OF this session."

Henry counted from one to ten in a dreamy rhythm that reminded me of skipping rope with my braids jumping on my shoulders, and then, with his hand on my forehead, he told me, "Awake."

My sandbag eyelids blinked open. I found myself on the settee again, my back slouched against all the scratchy needlepoint pillows my grandmother had sewn decades before.

Henry jumped off the cushion beside me, rustling up a breeze of dusty parlor air, and he exited the room in a streak of black clothing and blond hair. The front door slammed shut, and I wondered if he had even remembered to grab his hat.

Father loitered next to his armchair, his hands stuffed in his pockets, his face turned to the parlor's exit.

"What did you make him do to me?" I asked from the settee.

"Everything was done with your best interest in mind, Olivia." He tugged his handkerchief out of his breast pocket and dabbed his shiny forehead. He looked more man than monster again, but I had seen what he was capable of, and I still believed him to be a fiend. "If all goes well," he continued, "then I'll be satisfied, and young Reverie will get paid. That girl will get her surgery."

A pair of solid footsteps marched toward us from down the hall. Gerda stopped in front of the parlor and untied her white apron. "I'm afraid I must give my notice, Dr. Mead."

"I beg your pardon?" Father straightened his neck. "You're quitting?"

"*Ja.*" She pulled the apron over her head. "I cannot work for a man who pays a stranger to harm his daughter."

"What happened during the hypnosis, Gerda?" I jumped to my feet. "Did you hear them?"

"Were you eavesdropping?" asked Father.

Gerda slung her apron over the parlor rocking chair. "I'd like my final wages, Dr. Mead. I've worked a week and a half since you paid me last."

Father huffed and muttered something under his breath about everyone wanting to take his money. Gerda stepped aside and let him pass. His feet made an awful tromping ruckus all the way back to his office.

"Miss Mead . . ." Gerda grabbed my hands with shaking fingers. "There are certain topics you won't be able to talk about anymore."

"What topics?"

"Please, don't even attempt to say words that feel as if they shouldn't be spoken. And cover your ears if you hear those words uttered."

"What words? What topics?"

"I can't say them out loud to you, either." She glanced over her shoulder. "They'll hurt you."

Father plodded back into view with three floppy dollars in hand. "Here are your wages. Mark my word, as soon as you come to your senses, you'll regret this ridiculous decision."

"Thank you for the wages." Gerda took the money with a polite nod. "There's cold ham and carrots in the icebox. Fresh bread is cooling on the kitchen table. You should be just fine for tonight's supper." She darted a quick glance at me. "I'm sorry, Miss Mead. *Lycka till.* Good luck."

CHAPTER SEVENTEEN

VILE SUFFRAGE

G *o numb,* I told myself from the far corner of my bed, in the crook of my cherry-pink walls. *Don't move. Don't think.*

I pushed the palms of my hands against my temples until my head was as clamped as those of Father's patients in his wicked operatory chair. Moving even the smallest muscle would bring memories and, with them, an anger that burned through the lining of my stomach.

You will submerge yourself in a depth of relaxation such as you have never experienced before . . .

Father knocked on my closed bedroom door. "Olivia? I've prepared supper for us."

I still didn't move, but I asked, "*You* prepared supper?"

"I've lived without a wife for thirteen years now. I have been known to assemble a meal or two." He rapped against the door again. "I know you're angry, but you need to eat."

"What terrible thing am I going to do if I speak the wrong words?"

"I don't want to say."

"Why not? Because you realize how horribly you're behaving?"

"No, because it's for the best if you don't even envision the subjects I've asked you to forget. Now, come down and eat your dinner."

"I'd rather not."

"Olivia . . ."

"No."

"You're not supposed to be arguing with me."

"I'm not supposed to be saying volatile words, which I'm not. I'm speaking quite calmly." I turned on my side, away from the door, and made myself go stiff again.

"Very well. I'll place a plate of food outside your door."

"Like a jailer," I said under my breath as his footsteps creaked down the stairs.

AROUND EIGHT O'CLOCK, WHEN THE GAS LAMPS GLOWED and my stomach growled too much to bear, I brought the plate of food into my room. I sat down on the floor and ate cold ham and carrots. All the while, the yellow cigar box stuffed with money peeked at me from beneath the ruffles of my bed.

I'm settled in an apartment near Barnard College, Mother had said in her letter, *and I think of you every time I see those smart young women walking around with books tucked under their arms.*

And then . . . *I would even let you take a tour of Barnard, and perhaps I'd allow you to watch that delicious play* Sapho, *if the moralists don't shut it down again.*

The box was just sitting there, waiting for me to lift the lid and dip my fingers into the stack of bills both limp and crisp. A train ticket. Rent money to use while finishing my requirements for my high school diploma. A typewriter to help me start a journalism career. College tuition. Textbooks. The possibilities were all there, within my grasp. All I had to do was reach out, grab the thick wad of bills, and escape out the window.

Yet . . .

One hundred twenty-three dollars might also pay for Genevieve's surgery.

It might allow Henry to release me from my treatments that very night.

Before my fingers could stretch forward and touch the smooth lid, Father swung open my door without knocking.

"We have guests arriving."

"What guests?"

"The Underhills." He took hold of me by one elbow and jerked me to my feet. "Do not ruin this for me."

Father steered me out of my bedroom and down the stairs just as someone was clanging our brass knocker. The closer we got to the door, the more the knocking deteriorated into muffled thuds that sounded strange to my ears.

Another vision neared. I sucked in my breath and prepared for the worst.

Father lunged for the door and opened it up to a startling collection of sideshow oddities:

Sunken-Eyed John with his long, crooked teeth.

The bulging-eyed, dark-haired girl with the scrawny neck and blue lips from Sadie's party.

The lady carnival barker in the red-striped coat and straw hat.

A Draculean man with a white mustache, oddly arched nostrils, and teeth that protruded over a ruddy lip.

"Welcome to my house," said Father, and I half expected him to quote the rest of Count Dracula's first spoken lines to the fellow who resembled Stoker's character: *Enter freely and of your own will!* Instead, he uttered a nervous-sounding, "P-p-please, c-c-come inside."

The Underhills passed across our threshold, and my eyes readjusted. The delusion ceased. Our guests became a normal family of four, albeit a garishly wealthy one, with plush silk jackets for the ladies and solid-gold cuff links and pocket-watch chains for the gentlemen. The lady barker again transformed into the brunette woman who was handing out pamphlets in front of the headquarters for the Oregon Association Opposed to the Extension of Suffrage to Women.

The dark-haired daughter snickered. "You were so funny at Sadie's party, Ophelia."

"It's Olivia," I said.

The girl stiffened her arms straight in front of her, and with her eyes wide and dazed, she droned, "'All is well. All is well.'"

"That's enough, Eugenia," said Mrs. Underhill, slapping her daughter's hands. "We're only here for a brief visit. Let Dr. Mcad proceed with business."

"Yes, very good." Father closed the front door and lifted a metal bucket from the little hallway table. "As I already discussed with you, Mr. Underhill, sir, I have found an innovative solution to our state's peskiest problem. Imagine, if you will, your lovely wife no longer needing to manage the Oregon Association—and spending her precious time in more enjoyable pursuits."

Mrs. Underhill arched her slender eyebrows.

"Imagine," continued Father, "never having to worry about your dear daughter choosing the path of social impurity, or your son accidentally getting trapped with a shrew of a wife—a shrew who is only after your money so she can try to buy the vote."

Mr. Underhill's white mustache twitched.

"All of these worries will disappear," said Father, "and

become ancient relics of the past, with Henri Reverie's Cure for Female Rebellion and Unladylike Dreams."

Father pushed the pail into my sweating hands, and I half expected the preposterous name for the treatment to materialize on the side of the container, scrawled in the curved black lettering of traveling hucksters' tonics and cure-alls.

Father lifted a piece of plain white paper from the bottom of the pail. "Mrs. Underhill, will you please do me the honor of slowly reading the words on this page so I may demonstrate the fruits of young Mr. Reverie's work?"

Mrs. Underhill took the paper and again raised her brows. She cleared her throat and looked between me and that bucket, while Sunken-Eyed John and his tall, mustached father blocked my path to the door.

To escape or not to escape . . .

Mrs. Underhill drew in her breath and spoke the first word. "Suffrage."

My stomach moaned loudly enough to make John chuckle. He scratched his nose and muttered, "That's what happens when you dine where you shouldn't."

Mrs. Underhill ignored her son and inhaled another short breath.

"Women's rights."

I gagged and dropped the bucket to the floor with a clank.

Mrs. Underhill's next three phrases pelted my stomach like white-hot bullets.

"Suffragist. Votes for women. Susan B. Anthony."

I covered my mouth and shoved my way to the door.

"College," called Mrs. Underhill after me, and I tore out to the front porch, leaned my chest over the rail, and vomited into the bushes. Sweat dripped off my forehead and nose. Shivers racked my body. I just hung there, my ribs pressed against the rail, and let the fresh night air swim inside my head.

The soles of fine leather shoes pattered out to the porch behind me, but no one spoke a word until I turned around and slid down the splintery rail to the ground with a thump.

"You are most definitely coming to my election-night party, Dr. Mead," said the missus, whose face blurred and wavered before my eyes—veering from slick carnival barker to silken society queen. "It'll be held at the Portland Hotel at seven o'clock. Bring that hypnotist. Bring this girl. And let's end this ridiculous fight for the vote."

"You put me in here a cub, but I will go out a roaring lion and I will make all hell howl."

—SALOON-SMASHING TEMPERANCE FIGHTER
CARRIE NATION, from jail, 1900

CHAPTER EIGHTEEN

TRANSGRESSIONS

I slammed my bedroom door shut behind me. Shelves rattled, wall lamps flickered, and wide-eyed china dolls smacked to the floor. A new sort of growl roared up from the pit of my stomach—not a moan of nausea, but a primal howl.

"I hate this!" I yanked on my hair and pulled out the tight pins. "I hate my life!"

I lunged toward the window and pulled back the curtains, ready to fling up the sash and climb down the trellis, despite my shoeless feet.

Bars blocked my exit. Thick copper bars that shone in the

moonlight, secure as jail cell barriers—or the rungs of an enormous birdcage, as in the popular song.

She's only a bird in a gilded cage . . .

"You're not real." I backed away. "I know you're not real. Stop looking like you're actually there."

I grabbed my shoes and house key, shut my bedroom door, and stole downstairs to our tiny wood-paneled bathroom, a pine-scented closet added behind the kitchen when I was thirteen. Father—probably already sloshing about in a brandy-induced stupor—didn't make a peep from his closed office hideout.

I gave the sink's stiff spigot a twist, and the pipes trumpeted their usual high-pitched racket before water squirted into the cast-iron basin. I washed my face, scrubbed my teeth, and gargled with Holmes's Sure Cure Mouth Wash until my tongue and cheeks burned.

My feet then swished back down the hall, silent as spiderwebs, while I carried my shoes in my left hand. In his office, Father began singing some old ditty from before I was born.

I held my breath and opened the front entrance.

More bars—fat steel ones. I shut the door and bang-bang-banged my forehead against the wood.

You will see *the world the way it truly is—not accept it. You will not accept it.*

I lifted my smarting head with gold specks buzzing before my eyes.

You will not accept it.

I reopened the door. The bars vanished.

Without even grabbing my coat or hat, I closed up the house and leapt into the night.

Out in the side yard, my red bicycle waited for me against the house's chipped planks. After buttoning up my shoes, I hopped onto the saddle like a dime-novel cowboy, wobbled my way across the front yard's sparse and lumpy patches of grass, and pedaled toward the city with legs propelled by wrath.

The streets lay empty and silent, with rows of white arc lamps dangling from wires overhead, guiding the way, whispering, *This way, this way, kill him, kill him.* I pedaled faster, faster, faster, faster, hopping aboard smooth sidewalks to avoid getting slowed by ruts in the streets. A man stumbled out of a tavern and tottered into my path, but I swerved to avoid him and felt the graze of his arm against my elbow. He shouted a curse word, so I shouted it right back at him, even though I'd never cussed aloud in my life.

Outside the great Henri Reverie's hotel, I tossed my bicycle to the ground and threw open the establishment's front door. I marched straight toward the staircase sign at the back of the lobby with my nails sharp and poised to fight.

"Olivia?" asked a voice from one of the lobby's chairs.

I stopped and whipped my head toward the sound.

Henry set aside a newspaper and rose from an armchair with a baffled expression that grew even more perplexed when I walked over and pushed him three feet backward.

"You made me vomit! In public!"

"I told you to trust me."

I pushed him again. "You humiliated me."

"You made your father torture me."

"I threw up in the bushes in front of those people." I kept shoving. "I got sick as a dog."

"Olivia, stop. Be quiet."

"Don't tell me to be quiet. Who do you think you are?"

"Please—"

"You made me vomit, Henry. You're as horrible and controlling a jackass as he is." I raised my arm. "I could kill you!"

My nails sliced down his cheek, and to my horror, blood rose to the surface of four long gashes that stretched from his eye to his mouth.

He cradled his skin and staggered backward, dazed and whey-faced.

"Take your lovers' quarrel outside, you animals!" yelled the hotel clerk with the Vandyke beard, and other voices joined in the commotion—those of concerned guests, a hotel employee in a round cap, and then Henry, who took hold of my arm and tried pulling me away while telling the clerk that everything was fine.

But my feet wouldn't budge.

In a gilded mirror across the lobby, a red-eyed devil stared me down, her dark hair hanging in her face like poisonous black asps, her teeth bared and clenched, the dagger nails of her right hand dripping fresh red blood that stained the green rug below her. Every muscle in my body stiffened at the sight of her—of me—yet I couldn't pull my eyes away.

"Olivia, please! Come outside." Henry gave my arm a good yank and guided me out of the hotel.

The crisp blast of autumn air snuffed out some of the fire blazing inside me. With a whimper of exhaustion, I collapsed against a brick wall beyond the front window and leaned my cheek into a fuzzy blanket of moss. My legs quivered, the muscles and tendons straining to keep me upright.

Out of the corner of my eye, I saw Henry pull a handkerchief out of his breast pocket and cover his bleeding face.

I squeezed my eyes shut and sucked in my breath. "How much blood is there?"

"Hardly any. It mainly stings."

"It looked as if it could turn into gallons."

"You're probably seeing it worse than it is." He stepped closer. "Olivia, I promised you we were partners, not enemies. Why'd you have to bring up Genevieve and let it slip that we've seen each other?"

"I was trying to appeal . . . I just . . . he's still my father. I thought . . ." I rubbed my forehead. "We're not partners. A partner wouldn't allow me to retch in front of strangers."

"Your father gave me those orders when he had that medieval contraption wedged in my mouth."

"But he took out the gag eventually."

"We signed a contract back there in his office. A mutual agreement, saying if I completed the tasks asked of me, he would give me the full remainder of Genevieve's surgeon's fees."

I closed my eyes again. "I'll give you one hundred twenty-three dollars if we end everything tonight and send you on your way right now."

Henry didn't answer, and for a moment I thought he might have run away.

"Are you still here?" I raised my head and found him in the same spot as before, his mouth hanging open, the cloth pressed against his face.

"What are you talking about?" he asked.

"My mother has been sending me birthday and Christmas money ever since she left us when I was four. I've been saving the cash in a box in my room all these years."

"What have you been saving it for?"

I shrugged. "I don't know. I used to imagine heading out on great adventures, circumnavigating the world like Nellie Bly."

"But"—he lowered the handkerchief—"what had you been planning to use it for before Genevieve and I came to town?"

"It doesn't matter."

"Yes, it does."

I hugged my arms around my middle. "I can't tell you what I've imagined doing with the money. You've made sure I'll be sick if I say the word out loud."

"Does it have to do with education?"

"Yes, but I'm not even sure it's enough for one year's tuition. I'd probably have to apply for a scholarship, anyway."

"Olivia . . ." He stepped in front of me. "Look at me."

I peeked up and saw pink fingernail marks on his cheek in the lamplight shining out through the hotel window.

"Listen to me," he said, and his wounds and his lips and his nose blurred away. Only his eyes remained. "Listen carefully, for what I am going to tell you is extremely important. You will no longer feel nauseated and vomit when you hear or say the following words: *Suffrage. Women's rights. Suffragist. Votes for women. Susan B. Anthony. College.* In fact, you feel healthy and fully recovered from what happened to you this evening."

The disgusting tempest in my stomach settled into peaceful seas. The clouds in my head cleared away.

"However," he continued, "you will feel compelled to cover your mouth and make a gagging sound whenever you hear or say those words. *Suffrage. Women's rights. Suffragist. Votes for women. Susan B. Anthony. College.* You will not suffer any pain or nausea. You will simply cover your mouth and make a sound. Do you understand?"

I nodded.

"Good. Now, slowly, gently"—he pressed his hand against my forehead—"awake."

I blinked and wobbled.

Henry lowered his arm and cleared his throat. "I would have liked to do that before, but I couldn't with him watching."

"Thank you."

"I'm not taking your money."

"But . . . election night . . ." I braced my hand against the wall. "Genevieve . . ."

"We have three days left to figure out a way for it to seem that I'm hypnotizing you in front of that election-night crowd—without doing a single thing to you. I want to give a performance that will somehow end up teaching your father and all those antis a lesson."

"How on earth would we do that?"

"I don't know." He leaned his back against the bricks beside me. "But you're obviously smart, and I've had years of experience in putting on a good show. I'm certain we can think of something."

"What about Father?"

"Well . . ." He tucked his hands into his pockets. "Subtlety will have to be the key to this performance. We've got to make him think we're following his directions."

"And then you'll leave and take care of your sister?"

"Yes. I promise. We'll catch the last train south that night." He turned his head my way and pressed his lips together. His forehead puckered, suggesting a flaw in the plan.

"What is it?" I

"You should co

I blinked as if h

your pardon?"

"You could finish

San Francisco. Stanfor

women."

I pushed myself off the

even know you."

I scratched at a small bump

bell and mulled over the id

eyes. An entertaining

A highly entert

snort.

H

"My father's cousin Anne   ve

housing me while Genevieve   surgery. She

doesn't have the money to he   with medical payments,

but she's able to provide a roof over our heads. I'm sure she'd

welcome you, too."

"I cannot run away with you." I walked over to my tossed-
aside bicycle and hoisted it onto its wheels.

"You have money." Henry followed me to the bike. "You

wouldn't have to rely on me or any other man for income.

But I'd be there for you, as a friend, if you needed anything."

"I told you"—I hiked up the bottom of my skirt and swung

my right leg over the bicycle's red bar—"I don't even know

you."

"Think about it, at least. Please, consider joining us."

I tried to roll forward, but he pushed against my handlebars

and blocked my escape with his body.

"I don't want to leave you behind," he said, "when I know

I caused your life in Portland to crumble before your eyes."

on my turtle-shaped bicycle

a of my life crumbling before my

hought struck me during the mulling.

ning thought that led to an embarrassing

ry shifted his weight. "What's so funny?"

Another snort erupted, one that progressed into a full-blown laugh that made my shoulders shake.

"What's so funny, Olivia?"

"I just realized all the things I've done since I've met you and undergone your Cure for Female Rebellion and Unladylike Dreams—in bold, capital letters. Think about it, Henry." I counted off each transgression by lifting my fingers on the handlebars. "I walked out on a formal dinner party. I rode in a two-seater buggy with two young men—and sat on your lap, no less. I accompanied you into your hotel room. I played hooky. I published a suffragist letter in the news-paper—"

"You what?"

"Read the front page of today's *Oregonian.*" I tilted my head at the nail marks on his face. "I scratched you up like a wild woman. I caused a terrible uproar in a hotel lobby. Oh, I even cursed at a drunkard I almost ran over with my bike. And I rode through the city by myself after dark, while my father imagined me sulking in my bedroom. We're not curing *my* dreams."

He arched his eyebrows at the emphasis on *my*. "Are we curing someone else's?"

"My father's. His life is the one that's crumbling, because he's doing exactly what he wanted to avoid—driving me away." I kicked up my foot to find the right pedal and rang my little bell. "Now move, *s'il vous plaît*. I need to ride home before my empty bedroom gets discovered."

I pedaled toward him, but he pushed me backward by the handlebars again and said, "I'm going to escort you home."

"How are you going to keep up with me while I'm riding?"

"You can't ride through the dark streets on your own. If you fall and hit your head, who would know?"

"As I just said"—I steered the handlebars out of his grip—"how are you going to keep up while I'm riding?"

"I'll sit on the handlebars if I have to." He lifted his knee as if he were going to climb aboard.

"No, Henry!" I laughed and managed to back the bike out of his reach. "You'll tip me forward."

"Then let me sit in front of you so I can pedal while you hang on."

"Ha!" I rode the bicycle off the curb with a jolting bump that startled more hair out of pins. "That would be a laugh."

He leapt into the street behind me. "I'll bet *you're* strong enough to pedal us both."

"I don't know . . ." I rode around him in a wide circle. "I'm only a girl."

"I'll just chase after you, then, and try to keep up." He laughed, a throaty chuckle—an enjoyable sound I don't think I'd ever heard from him before. "Stop riding circles around me, Olivia. Let me get on. I'm willing to sit in back."

"You'll probably fall off." I planted my feet on the ground. "I ride fast."

"I bet you do."

I hopped down from the saddle while still holding the handlebars, and—adding yet another transgression to my growing list of sins against my father—allowed Henry to climb onto the seat behind me. He tried putting his hands on the bars, next to mine, but I nudged them away.

"I'll need to steer. You'll make us fall if you're hanging on, too."

He held up his palms. "What should I hang on to, then?"

"I don't . . ." I laughed and blushed and couldn't believe I was letting him sit on my bicycle behind me, pressed up against my back, his mouth so close to my neck. I got chills just from the thought of him breathing against me. "Oh, just put your blasted hands around my waist. Help me push off, and if we somehow stay balanced, put your feet on the mounting pegs on the rear wheel."

I pressed my right foot against the top pedal. "I'll count to three, and then we both need to give a big push. Ready?"

He squeezed his arms around my waist and answered, *"Oui."*

"One, two, three."

He pushed, I pushed, and both of my feet left the ground. We wobbled and tipped, and he had to shove the soles of his shoes against the road more than once to keep us from falling on our sides like a capsizing ship. My legs pumped and strained, and somehow, one block south of the hotel, we managed to gain speed. Balancing became easier; the act of pedaling turned smooth and as simple as riding on my own. Our chances of serious injury increased, but my legs no longer ached from powering us along.

We cruised onward, past the slumbering businesses on Third. My hair streaked behind me and probably smacked Henry in the face, but he never complained—in fact, he chuckled the whole time, and, when I steered us around the corner to Yamhill, he whooped like a French Canadian cowboy.

"You're not going to fall off, are you?" I yelled into the wind.

"Not unless you do."

"In a few more blocks," I called again, "you need to look in the window of McCorkan's Bicycle Shop on our right."

"Why is that?"

"They sell bicycle bloomers. Buying a pair is yet another one of my unladylike dreams."

"I could get you a pair from backstage."

"Really?"

"Really. I've seen them in the costume room."

That grand possibility inspired me to pedal faster, and the

chain buzzed like a mighty industrial machine beneath our legs. Overhead, the moon peeked between the clouds, washing the road before us in swaths of silver. "Beautiful Dreamer" waltzed through my mind, especially the line "Starlight and dewdrops are waiting for thee," which seemed particularly lovely in the lamp-lit splendor of the nighttime streets of Portland.

Henry's arms tightened around my waist.

"I'm not going to stop," I yelled over my shoulder, "because I don't want to fall, but there they are. Turkish trousers."

We sped past the red and blue beauties, which were mere poufs of shadow in the unlit store, and Henry asked, "Is it because you want to dress like a man?"

"Pfft. No. I want to dress like a woman who drives men around on her bicycle."

He snickered near my ear, and we both laughed like grammar school children all the way back to my street, drunk on moonbeams and speed and the incomparable exhilaration of hanging on to another person as if one's life depended on it.

The descent wasn't half as graceful as the flight. Two blocks from my house, we hit a bad bump, and the handlebars jostled in my hands like a thing possessed. Henry dragged his feet across the dirt to skid us to a stop, kicking up dust and tiny pebbles, but the bicycle fought his efforts and dumped us on our sides one block away from home. We landed with a thump in a tangle of arms, legs, fabrics, and metal.

I pushed myself up to my elbows and unwound my feet

from Henry and the bike. A sore spot, bound to become a bruise, formed on my hip.

"Are you all right?" I asked.

My now supine passenger sat up with a dopey grin and wiped dirt off the sides of his coat. "Mademoiselle Mead, I had no idea you were a daredevil."

"My father would call me a scorcher."

"What's that?"

"A reckless bicyclist."

"Olivia 'Scorcher' Mead." He nodded his approval. "I like it." He climbed to his feet and lent me his outstretched hand.

I let him pull me upright, and we faced each other with our hands entwined. A pine tree bobbed a shadow across his scratched-up cheek, and the nail marks faded and glowed with the peekaboo moon.

His smile faded, and his dark-blond eyebrows turned serious. "What will your father do if he catches you sneaking in?"

I shrugged. "What more can possibly happen?"

"That's what has me worried."

"I'll just say I desperately needed fresh air after getting sick." I slid my fingers out of his. "Don't worry about me, Henry. Go home and take care of your sister. How is she tonight?"

"Exhausted. That's why I was reading the newspaper in the hotel lobby. I didn't want to bother her."

I nodded. "Well, you're a good brother. I'm sure she greatly appreciates you."

"I don't . . ." He turned his face downward and grimaced as if his ribs ached.

"What's the matter?" I asked.

"Nothing." He ran his fingers through his hair and tried to smile away whatever was bothering him.

"Tell me, Henry." I inched closer, my soles stirring up bits of gravel in the road. "Are you hurt? Was it the crash?"

"No, it's just . . ." He swallowed with a loud bob of his Adam's apple. "This isn't the life I ever expected to lead, Olivia. I'm beginning to think I'm bad luck."

"Why?"

"I'm certainly not good luck to you. Look what I've done by agreeing to tinker with your mind. And look at my family. Every single person I love dies on me. I feel as if I'm being punished, but I don't know what I could have done that's so indescribably awful."

"I'm sure your parents' deaths had nothing to do with you."

He swallowed again. "My mother died of cancer, the same kind as Genevieve's. My father lost his life to a bad typhoid outbreak when I was twelve. And . . . well, I already told you about Uncle Lewis and his poor choices."

I nodded. "I agree—all of that is bad luck. But it has nothing to do with you."

He released a long wheeze of a breath that had to have hurt his lungs, and he smoothed down the hair he'd just tousled. "Thank you. You're really far too kind to me."

"The scratches on your face don't look kind."

"I know, but . . ." He reached out and wove his fingers through mine. "Thank you."

Another breeze nudged the needles of the rustling pine and toyed with my hair, tickling stringy strands across my cheek. My skirt billowed around my legs and flirted with the knees of Henry's trousers.

"Henry, do I look like a monster to you?" I asked with a squeeze of his hand. "I saw myself in the mirror in the hotel lobby . . ."

He shook his head. "No, you look like someone who's been on a wild ride and could use a rest—that's all. Go get some sleep, and on Tuesday we'll figure out a way to set everything right. And if you let me, I'll take you away from all your troubles."

"I still don't—"

"Olivia," he whispered, bending his face toward mine. "Pieces of me have been dying with each loved one I've lost."

"I'm sorry . . ."

"But that ride through the city"—a grin burgeoned at the corners of his lips—"that daredevil, bicycle scorcher ride, reminded me what it's like to be wide awake and alive. Please, let me do something for you."

I nodded. "All right. I'll think about it."

"Good. I hope you do."

He kept his face close—close enough to kiss—and I wasn't sure if I should give him a peck on the cheek or back away.

"Are you waiting for me to kiss you?" I found myself asking in a voice too high-pitched.

He gave a startled blink and lifted his head. "What? No."

"You were so close . . . I didn't know if . . ." I lowered my eyes.

"No, I couldn't kiss you if I wanted to."

I peeked up at him. "Why not?"

"It's not easy for me."

"What do you mean? Is something wrong with your mouth?"

"No." He gave a strained smile. "Ladies have a habit of saying the only reason they're kissing me is because they're under my spell. They especially say that if they seem to like it but feel guilty about liking it, and if they're a bit older than me."

"Oh." I loosened my hand from his. "Is this a common problem?"

"No, but it's happened twice. A hazard of the profession, I suppose, but it makes me nervous about kissing anybody."

"Oh. Well"—my voice faltered; I tried not to stare at those red lips of his—"I certainly don't want to complicate this odd relationship of ours even further."

"No." He tucked his hands into his coat pockets. "It's for the best if we stick to simpler pleasures, like bicycle rides . . . and buggy outings."

I laughed and brushed my hair out of my face. "Yes, that's much simpler and far less intimate."

"Oh, definitely."

"And we don't need any more transgressions going onto my long list of post-hypnosis sins," I added.

"No, absolutely not. You don't want—"

I placed my hand on his shoulder and kissed him, just to try it with someone who wasn't drunk and Percy—and only because my heart was still thumping so rigorously from the bicycle ride—and because he fascinated me—and because it seemed as if we both desperately needed a kiss. His mouth felt so velvety soft that I let my lips linger. He tilted his head and held on to my waist and returned my kiss in such a way that lovely little prickles tingled across my stomach and down the backs of my legs.

Our lips parted, and I marveled at how hard I had to work to catch my breath. Henry brushed his thumb across the line of my jaw, but I stopped him by taking hold of his hand.

"I need to go home," I said.

He withdrew his fingers from mine, and the absence of their pressure left my hand empty and cold. "All right."

"Henry . . ."

"Yes?"

I smiled. "I had ridiculous amounts of fun on that bicycle ride, too."

His face brightened clear up to the golden tips of his hair. "We'll figure out a way to make Tuesday work," he said. "I promise. Let me know if you concoct any ideas."

I nodded and grabbed hold of the bike.

Without a single other word—or kiss—he slipped his hands back into his pockets and walked away into the shadows, whistling a song that sounded both sad and lovely, like a Pied Piper who pitied the children he was luring out of town.

FATE WAS KIND TO ME THAT NIGHT. DESPITE THE AWFUL creaks that accompanied my footsteps when I snuck up the staircase, Father's bedroom door remained shut, the light within extinguished. I believed I'd made it safely back to my bedroom by the grace of the brandy swimming through his veins.

In the darkness of my room, I hurried to shed my day clothes, climbed into my long nightgown, and threw an extra quilt over the mirror to hide my reflection from myself. My plate of half-eaten supper still waited on my floor, so I hustled it down to the kitchen in fear of mice sneaking into my room to feast.

Back upstairs, I tucked myself beneath my cotton sheets and the piles of autumn blankets that warmed away the chill of the house. My legs still experienced the fluttery sensation of whooshing through the streets of the city, and my just-kissed lips spread into a smile.

On the brink of sleep, when my mind hovered in that strange off-balance twilight between wakefulness and dream, I envisioned a ballroom inhabited by anti-suffrage ladies with Whitehead gags silencing their mouths. Below the peculiar image, like the suffrage caricatures printed in the *Oregonian* most weeks of late, ran a caption:

A TASTE OF THEIR OWN MEDICINE.

My eyes blinked back open.

A grin stretched to my ears.

A taste of their own medicine. The solution to the dilemma of our election-night performance.

CHAPTER NINETEEN

A PLAN

Father distributed Sunday morning's heaping spoonful of bad news, quite appropriately, in the kitchen.

"Now that Gerda is gone," he said from behind me at the sizzling griddle, "you'll need to manage the housework every day of the week."

The flapjack I had been flipping dropped to the floor.

"What about school?" I asked.

"The house needs tending, and we have no one else."

"But you said you worried about leaving me home on my own."

"Your industriousness will keep you active and out of trouble, and the hypnosis will prohibit you from attending any unsavory rallies. But fear not"—he bent over and picked up the crumbling pieces of oatmeal from the floor—"I have a strong inkling you're going to be in high demand Tuesday night. If we find you a young society gentleman, which I'm certain we will when those boys witness your demure personality, you may not ever need worry about cooking and cleaning again. You'll likely acquire a maid and a cook with your future husband. You'll be able to devote your full attention to my grandchildren." He nodded with an optimistic arch of his eyebrows.

An argument rushed up my throat, but the fight wilted at my lips.

You are free to speak your mind, but you will do so with caution around your father, Henry had instructed me in his hotel room. *You will limit your volatile words only to moments when someone is about to get hurt.*

Father moved to leave the room.

"Father," I said before he could go. "Frannie's family invited me over for Mr. and Mrs. Harrison's twentieth anniversary dinner tonight, remember?"

"Yes, I remember."

"Am I allowed to go? I'd prepare your meal before I left."

He picked at the ends of his beard. "I would have to escort you to their front door and pick you up. No bicycling."

"Because it's unladylike?"

"Because I don't want you conspiring with that hypnotist. He's signed a contract with me."

"I—" I bit down on my tongue, for I was about to slip and say, *I know.*

"You what?" asked Father.

"I'm glad you signed a contract. It's a sensible thing to do."

He cleared his throat. "I've forgotten—what time did Frannie say they're serving dinner?"

"Three thirty, I believe." A lie—the dinner was set for five o'clock.

"Then I'll walk you over at three and pick you up at six."

"Thank you, Father. That's very kind of you."

He retreated from the kitchen, and my mouth hissed a gust of white steam—my snuffed-out arguments.

AT THREE O'CLOCK SHARP, FATHER DELIVERED ME TO Harrison's Books, which was closed for Sunday.

"I'll fetch you at six, Olivia," he said with a peek at his pocket watch, as if he were already counting down the minutes.

"Can you make it seven o'clock, Dr. Mead?" asked Frannie from the bookshop's doorway. "Martha and I baked a cake. We'll need time for dessert."

"Well . . . I suppose." Father crinkled his brow. "If you think the festivities will last that long."

"At least that long. Eight might even be better. Papa will likely play his fiddle."

Father frowned. "Eight at the latest."

I patted his arm. "Thank you, Father."

Frannie shut the glass door behind me with a jingle of the bell, and Father retreated down the street with his gray derby bobbing up and down on his thick hair.

I grasped Frannie by the shoulders. "I'm here early because of a plan."

"A plan?"

"I need to go to the theater and speak to Henry."

"But—"

"Wait before you try to talk me out of it. Gerda quit yesterday. Father won't let me go to school anymore."

"What?" She reached up and gripped my elbows.

"Father hired Henry for a second treatment that was even worse than the first, but Henry is helping to alter the effects. Father got himself invited to an election-night party hosted by the Oregon Association Opposed to the Extension of Suffrage—" I involuntarily covered my mouth and belched a horrid, gagging sound.

Frannie grimaced. "Are you all right?"

"Yes." I let my hand flop down to my leg. "Anyway, at this party, in order to receive Father's payment for the hypnosis, Henry is supposed to hypnotize me in front of everyone and prove there's a cure for suffragists." Again, I smacked my hand over my mouth, and I hacked like a cat.

"Why are you gagging?"

I rolled my eyes. "It's all a part of the hypnosis."

"Livie! This is terrible. Are you still seeing terrifying sights, too?"

"Oddly enough, that's the least of my troubles." I clutched her hands. "But never mind that. Here's where I need your help. First, please let me borrow your cloak."

"But—"

"Second, talk to Kate on Monday at school. Let her know that the antis are congregating for some election-night hoopla at the Portland Hotel at seven o'clock. It would be splendid to have a team of suff"—my right hand slapped my mouth again—"ragists, *ack*"—I spat up another foul sound—"standing out front, singing anthems, wearing yellow ribbons. But tell them they must leave the hotel grounds no later than seven fifteen. That part is vital."

She stared at me with unblinking eyes.

"Please, Frannie." I pulled her against me and squeezed my arms around her.

"Livie, what's going to happen to you when the party is over?" she asked into my hair. "How in the world can you keep living with your father?"

I closed my eyes and pulled her so close, her shoulder dug into my throat. "I'll likely leave for New York Tuesday night."

"What?"

"My mother lives there. Near Barnard."

"Your mother has been an absent fool all these years."

"But she doesn't want to transform me into a creature who doesn't even resemble me." I pulled free of our hug. "Please,

Frannie. Help me. I need you. Genevieve needs you, too. I've seen her in her room in the Hotel Vernon. She's fading. The cancer will kill her if it's not removed soon."

Frannie's nose turned red and sniffly, and her chin shook. "I don't want to see you escape clear across the country." She wiped her eyes with the back of her sleeve. "But . . . if you genuinely believe you need to endure all of this rubbish to save this person's life, then, my goodness"—she heaved a heavy sigh—"let's help that girl."

CHAPTER TWENTY

DES PARTENAIRES QUI S'EMBRASSENT

The stage door was locked. At first all I could think to do was grumble and pace about the sidewalk while holding the brown hood of Frannie's cloak over my head. Just as I was about to run to the theater lobby and spin a story about needing to deliver an urgent item to Henry, fate intervened in the form of a few small beasts.

The side door opened. The middle-aged dog trainers and their half-dozen curly-haired poodles burst from the theater in a gust of high-pitched barks.

"Let me hold open the door for you," I said over all the

yipping, and I sprinted up the stairs, nearly tripping over my skirt.

"Thank you, dear," said the man of the group with a tip of his hat.

The flurry of fur and leather leashes and pitter-pattering feet traveled down the stairs, and I slipped inside the theater.

A heart-seizing note from the organ beyond the curtains soldered my feet to the ground. I stood there in the half dark, rooted to the floor, while the force of a loud waltz reverberated up my calves and knees. Laughter boomed from the audience. Lights poured through the black curtains separating the stage from the wings, luring me over . . . *Come see, come see.*

I rounded a small table topped with a pitcher of water and a bowl of peppermint-scented candies and came to a stop in the wings.

My eyes widened.

Three couples were dancing a waltz on the stage, but the women—not the men—were leading, with their hands on the gentlemen's waists. The gentlemen followed, their left fingers lifting invisible skirts off the ground. The peculiar pairs glided around the dusty floorboards with silly smiles on their faces, paying no heed at all to the wild shrieks of laughter from the audience.

"*Mesdames et messieurs*"—Henry strutted into my view, his red vest shimmering in the stage lights—"let us give a warm round of applause for the Reversed Portland Dancers."

The audience clapped and chortled, and I slithered farther into the backstage shadows. The silhouettes of stagehands in caps and suspenders rushed toward the wings.

Henry guided his subjects out of their trances, and an even grander applause swelled for the great Monsieur Reverie. A smoky-smelling fellow showed up a few feet away from me and pulled on a long rope that clattered the main curtain closed.

I held my breath and crept out of my hiding spot.

Henry staggered off the stage, and my eyes beheld him falling apart. Literally. The bottom half of his coat unraveled at astounding speed, and the seams of his pants stretched and ripped from his ankles up to his knees. He grabbed hold of one of the wings' black curtains and rested his forehead against the cloth, inhaling deep breaths that made his shoulders rise and fall.

"Henry?" I unclasped Frannie's cloak from my neck and approached him. By walking and blinking I stopped the illusion of his fraying garments, but he still hunched over as if he might collapse. "Are you all right?"

He lifted his head. "Olivia?"

"I'm sorry I snuck backstage . . ."

"No, it's fine." He let go of the curtain and took my hands. "It's nice to see you back here. Is everything all right?"

"I'm fine, but how are you?"

"I didn't sleep well last night."

A stagehand brushed past us, so Henry led me away from the wings and toward the table with the water and candies.

He poured himself a glass with shaking hands. "Genevieve has a fever."

"Oh, no!"

"The doctor thinks it might just be a regular cold, not her illness, but she's supposed to take a pill and stay in bed."

"Does it seem like a cold?"

"She's sneezing and coughing, but I don't know . . ." He guzzled the water like a man downing whiskey.

I wriggled Frannie's coat off my shoulders. "I'm so sorry, Henry."

He came up for a loud breath. "It reminds me too much of the typhoid—and my mother's illness. I really hate this. Why can't she just be healthy?"

"Is there anything I can do?"

"No." He shook his head and wiped his lips. "Nothing besides what you're already doing."

"If it's of any comfort, I have an idea for Tuesday evening."

"You do?"

"I—" I held my tongue, for the substitute organist lumbered toward us from the wings with stacks of sheet music poking out of her carpetbag.

"Here." Henry gestured with his head toward the back of the theater. "Let's go speak in private. There's something I need to give you, anyway."

He set down the glass, popped a candy into his mouth, and took me by the hand again, while the organist frowned at us and fished her hand into the candy bowl.

Henry and I wound our way through a dark maze of set pieces and sawdust and down an echoing stairwell that smelled of fresh paint and cigarettes. We arrived in a large underground space crammed with props and extra stage pieces packed onto shelves and crowding the passageways. Bare bulbs dangled from the ceiling, casting a yellow light that produced hulking shadows shaped like masks and trombones and Wild West pistols.

Henry led me down a narrow walkway, toward the opposite end of the room, and the feathers of a dangling pink boa tickled across my cheek, making me think for a moment we were walking through a labyrinth of spiderwebs.

"The wardrobe mistress isn't here today," he said. "We all wear our own clothing for this show, but we've been allowed to come back here in case we want to add anything to our outfits." He opened a back door and pushed a switch on the wall that illuminated a room filled with costumes on coat hangers, bolts of fabric, sewing machines, bobbins, and millinery head blocks. He let go of my hand and walked to a rack of clothing both colorful and drab. "I received Mr. Gillingham's approval to give this to you."

My stomach leapt. Henry pulled something off a hanger and returned to me with a pair of garnet-brown trousers.

Bicycle bloomers.

For me.

I dropped Frannie's cloak, covered my mouth, and burst into tears.

"What's wrong?" he asked, but all I could do was hurl my arms around him and tip us both off balance.

He grabbed hold of my back. "Are you all right?"

"They're beautiful. I'm sorry . . ." I wiped my face with the back of my hand. "I don't know why I'm crying. I love the bloomers. But it's so hard. Oh, criminy, I love them so much." I blubbered like a madwoman against the soft lapel of his coat.

"Here, sit down with me," said Henry, and he lowered us both to the floor, which was scattered with threads of blue and white. He fetched a handkerchief from his breast pocket and gave it to me.

I blew my nose and watched tears rain down on the glorious trousers. Henry stroked my arms until my breathing slowed, and his face gradually grew less hazy through my drying eyes. My scratch marks on his cheek were but thin, hidden streaks beneath a covering of greasepaint.

I hiccupped. "I'm so sorry. I don't know why I reacted that way. It's hardly the behavior of a modern woman with bloomers, is it?"

"Don't worry about how you reacted. Who cares? Now"— he bent his head close—"tell me your idea for Tuesday."

I cleared my throat and drew a long breath. "Well, at the election-night party . . ." I coughed into the handkerchief.

"Tell the audience you can cure more than just one rebellious woman. Tell them you can cure a whole crowd of us." I spread the bloomers across my lap and toyed with the buttons on the hems. "When we first arrive, there will likely be women singing and chanting about the vote outside the hotel. Ask the men to go fetch them to prove your abilities."

"All right . . ."

"If all goes well, when the gentlemen come back, they'll say the women are gone. Inform the audience you'll use the ladies at the party as an example instead. Invite them all in front of the crowd, with me included if it helps"—I met his eyes—"and hypnotize them all into silence. Take away their voices."

His face went still. "Permanently?"

"Long enough to scare them. Show them the dangers of living without the ability to have a say in the world. And then, when they panic and beg in writing to speak again, point out the beautiful irony of a group of antis hating the idea of silence."

He cracked a wry smile that gleamed in his eyes. "It's brilliant."

"Do you really think so?"

"It's well worth a try." He laced his fingers through mine in my lap. "We'll definitely need to make sure you're up there with the crowd to make your father happy, but I have a trick to avoid getting hypnotized if you don't want to lose your voice."

"There's a trick?"

"It's easy. Take your tongue"—he showed me the pink tip of his between his teeth—"and wedge it against the roof of your mouth."

I pushed my tongue to my palate. "Is that all?"

"Theoretically, yes. When I'm hypnotizing you, all I'm doing is putting your conscious mind to sleep so I can communicate directly with your subconscious. When you distract yourself with your tongue"—he closed his mouth and seemed to test out the effect in his own mouth—"or when you mentally will yourself against the hypnosis, your conscious mind stays awake. I can't get into the deeper parts of your brain."

"But what if . . ." My face warmed. "What if my subconscious mind . . . enjoys the relaxation part of hypnosis too much?"

"Well . . ." He slipped his hands out of mine. "You've got to ignore that impulse to be relaxed. Be strong. Push me out. Imagine slamming a door in my face."

"You're awfully good at soothing a person, Henry . . ."

"Even if you like it, you've got to block me. Even if your father's standing right there, keep yourself alert. Force me away."

I squirmed. "Now I'm worried."

"Let's practice. Come on." He sat up tall. "We'll try it right here."

"All right." I rolled back my shoulders. "I suppose if you just use your usual techniques, and—"

He retook my hands and looked me in the eye, and I flopped forward and banged my temple against his shoulder.

"Awake! No, Olivia, you weren't even trying."

I shook my head and straightened my posture. "You don't understand. Relaxation is precious to me. And you're talented."

"Be strong—forget the soothing parts. Slam the door in my face." He squeezed my hands. "Look into my eyes."

I did, and my forehead tipped forward as if it were made of a sheet of slate.

"No. Awake."

I righted myself again.

He sighed and furrowed his brow. "My job, Olivia, is to catch you off guard. Your job is to be alert and strong at all times. I don't want him to force me to do anything despicable to you ever again. And I don't want to think that last night . . ."

He stopped and rubbed his hand over his mouth.

I pinched my eyebrows together. "What about last night?"

"The hazard of the profession I was telling you about." He scooted backward on the floor and stared at his folded legs. "Women saying they're under my spell. I don't want to think hypnosis had anything to do with . . . *anything* . . . last night."

"I was in a fully conscious state, Henry. I may be an overly susceptible subject, but I can tell when I'm hypnotized and when I'm not."

"I wasn't sure. I started to worry when I got back to the hotel."

"I kissed you because I thought it would be fun." I pushed my hands against the floor and slid myself toward him. "I thought we could both use a kiss. It had nothing to do with hypnosis or female equality or anything else but the simple fact that we were having a grand time."

"Well . . . good . . . and, well . . ." He scratched his neck. His eyes met mine. "You were right."

"About what?"

"I did need it." He played with the pucker of my skirt above my knee. "I didn't even realize how badly I needed it until it happened."

I gave a soft breath of a laugh. "I understand."

He took my hands again—a tender gesture, not another hypnosis test. A hush came over us. Footsteps moaned against the wood above our heads, but the rest of the world seemed miles and miles away, as if we were holed up in our own private burrow at the center of the earth. Our interlocked fingers nuzzled against one another. Our seated bodies fidgeted until our knees touched and stayed together. The ethereal spell of our moonlit bicycle ride settled over the hats and the costumes and our tipped-together heads, which seemed to be drawing closer on an invisible thread.

This time, Henry kissed me first, his lips soft and warm, even more so than the night before. I set the handkerchief and the bicycle bloomers aside and reached up to his neck, not caring if the gesture seemed bold. The harder we kissed, the faster the demons in the crooks of my mind slipped away. A better escape than hypnosis. Almost better than bicycling. I reached up to his soft hair and pulled his whole body to mine.

He eased me backward to the floor, and my head rested amid remnants of lace and scattered snippets of fabric. I thought I heard the distant music of the pipe organ playing "Beautiful Dreamer," or maybe even "A Hot Time in the Old Town." It didn't really matter. Nothing mattered except for lips and gentle hands and the coarse texture of a black woolen coat beneath my fingertips.

A mirror stood over us—I had seen it when we first entered the room but tried to ignore its intimidating slab of reflective glass. It watched us as we lay there, tasting and feeling each other, like Sapho and her lovers.

I kept my eyes closed. Henry's fingers slid between the buttons of my blouse, and I worried my reflection would show me a ghost of a girl, fading, oppressed, and ruined. My hand strayed to the firm spread of his lower back, below his coat, his vest, and even his shirt, and I feared I'd look like one of the North End prostitutes I'd always heard about, with their rouged cheeks and low-cut gowns. My mouth strayed to the sweet taste of his neck, and I thought of Lucy Westenra and her unclean lips and eyes.

Not knowing how I looked became too much to bear.

I turned my head to the side. My eyes opened. I saw her. Olivia Mead.

Just me—and Henry Rhodes—evading our troubles in the farthest corner of a theater.

Henry lifted his head, his cheeks flushed, his breaths uneven. "What are you looking at?"

"Us."

He peeked at the mirror and met the reflection of my brown eyes. "Why?"

"To see if we look wicked."

He tilted his head against mine. "And?"

"We just look like Olivia and Henry."

He brushed my hair out of my face. "Do you feel wicked?"

"I didn't until I started thinking about it."

He leaned forward for another kiss, but I touched his chin before his lips brushed mine.

"Here's another worry," I said. "I think I may have gotten my start in the world in the back of a theater, just like this."

He snuck in a soft kiss to my cheek. "What do you mean?"

"My mother came to Portland with a traveling theater company when she was barely sixteen. My father was an eighteen-year-old dental apprentice. For all I know their relationship started in this very same theater. Oh . . . good Lord." I cringed and sat up. "I hadn't even thought of that before."

"I'm sorry you did think of it." Henry sat up, too, and removed his coat.

"My mother lives in New York City now." I bit my lip and glanced at him out of the corner of my eye. "I'm thinking of going to live with her after everything's over Tuesday night."

A shadow darkened his face. He dropped his coat to the floor beside him, and the movement reminded me of a rosebush weeping petals.

"I want to be with family," I said. "I know you asked me to go with you and Genevieve, but . . ."

"No." He swallowed and nodded. "I understand."

"Do you?"

"I do." He nodded again, but I could see disappointment dimming the sparks in his eyes.

"Will this change any of our plans we just discussed for Tuesday night?"

"No." His brow creased. "Of course not. No matter what happens, I'm going to help you."

"We're still partners, then? *Partenaires?*"

"*Oui.*" A small smile rose to his lips. "*Des partenaires qui s'embrassent.*"

"What does that mean?"

"It means you should learn more French if you're going to partner with me, *ma chérie.*"

"No, be honest"—I nudged his knee—"what does it mean?"

He smirked and blushed a little. "Partners who kiss."

I snickered. "Partners who kiss?"

"*Oui.*"

"What a marvelous concept."

He smiled, and I smiled, and we both broke into a fit of tipsy-sounding laughter.

Our faces gradually sobered. Silence stole over the room again, aside from those footsteps shuffling above.

I leaned toward Henry and his lovely mussed-up hair and peppermint-scented lips, and for a little while longer, we enjoyed our lives as *des partenaires qui s'embrassent*.

CHAPTER TWENTY-ONE

INNER WORKINGS

I thought I saw Father on my journey northward on Yamhill Street.

I spun around, and with my back to Fourth, I stood with Frannie's hood pulled over my head—a deer freezing to blend in with the trees. None of it seemed right: me hiding from Father, Father fearful for me—or maybe even *of* me. In his view of the world, I likely resembled a fairy-tale witch who baked children in pies. Or, even worse in his eyes, a witch who could destroy both his home and his right to drink.

I strode to Harrison's Books on unsteady legs, looking over my shoulder every few seconds.

Frannie let me inside after I knocked on the glass door. "Is everything all right?" she asked, and she locked the shop back up behind me.

"Well . . ." I sighed and unbuttoned the cloak. "I think we might be ready for Tuesday."

Phonograph music drifted downstairs—a piano song that sounded as old and romantic as the Harrisons' twenty-year marriage.

She took the cloak. "Is this to be a farewell supper, then?"

I couldn't meet her eyes.

"It is, isn't it?" Her voice cracked.

"I'm not sure. I'm worried everything will go terribly wrong."

"Just be careful, no matter what happens. Please promise me that."

I nodded and rubbed my knotted-up stomach. "I promise."

She wiped her eyes with the cloak. "Let me know when I should properly say good-bye, all right? I don't want to suddenly find out you're in New York without me realizing you're gone."

I fussed with the folds of my skirt, which was hiding the bloomers I had slipped over my legs in the theater. "The world is getting smaller, you know. A train ride across the country is so much easier than before."

Frannie sniffed and nodded. "I suppose that's true."

"It is."

Without another word, we linked arms and headed upstairs

to a celebration of two people who had learned to be kissing partners long before Frannie and I were born.

For a short while, all was indeed well.

Bittersweet, but well.

FATHER FETCHED ME AT EIGHT O'CLOCK, AND WE WALKED through the dark streets in silence with the soft swish of the bloomers brushing beneath my petticoat. Near the Park Blocks, I saw our shadows drifting ahead of us in the lamplight and, in them, the silhouette of a little girl with braided hair, sitting on the shoulders of a trim young man in a tall hat. Two steps later, the image shifted, and all that was left were the regular shadows of Father and me, walking three feet apart from each other.

"I miss when you used to carry me on your shoulders," I said, still watching the sidewalk ahead of us.

"Yes, well . . ." Father cleared his throat. "I think you might be getting a little too big for that nowadays."

I couldn't help but laugh, and I could have sworn I heard a low chuckle rumble from above his thick beard.

The wedge soon formed between us again. Our shadows spread farther apart, and they looked hunched and cold and lonely.

OUT IN THE BACKYARD ON MONDAY MORNING, WHILE MY classmates wrote compositions and solved algebraic equations in school, I scrubbed brown soap and Father's undergarments across the zinc grooves of our washboard in the steaming double boiler. Hair fell into my face from the force of all the rubbing, and my hands reddened and absorbed the smell of lye.

After the washing, I pinned the laundry to the clothesline, and little flecks of rain flew at my eyelids and cheeks. "Don't pour, don't pour," I begged of the sky, for I had come too far to lug everything down to our drying racks in the dark basement, where mice skittered about. I rushed to clip every garment to the line, and our backyard became a white wonderland of undershirts, petticoats, and drawers. Ghosts without bodies, just hovering in the mist.

I closed the door on that chore and climbed upstairs to pen a short note at my desk.

November 5, 1900

Dear Madam,

Please accept my deepest thanks for delivering my letter to the editor this past Friday. I was delighted to see the article's publication in Saturday's edition of the newspaper. The reception to the piece far exceeded my expectations, and I am now strongly considering a career in journalism because of the pure joy I experienced in sharing my words with the people of this city. May ALL women one day gain a voice.

Sincerely,

A Responsible Woman

THE TEAM OF FEMALE TYPISTS IN DARK DRESS SUITS AND ties clicked away at their tidy rows of desks in the *Oregonian*'s headquarters, and the same spirit of adventure I had felt on Friday coaxed me farther inside the building.

I noted one striking difference from the week before: a freckled young man with black hair sat at the front desk instead of the statuesque receptionist.

"May I help you?" he asked while unscrewing the cap of a fountain pen.

"I'm looking for the woman who worked at this desk last week."

"She no longer works here." The fellow set to scribbling a note on a sheet of company letterhead.

"She's not here?"

"No, she's been dismissed."

"May I ask why?"

"Yes"—he grinned and peeked up at me—"you may ask, but I will not answer."

"Does it have anything to do with that letter that was printed on Saturday's front page?"

The young man stopped writing. "Oh, Lord. You're not bringing another note of thanks, are you?"

"There are notes of thanks?"

"And violent hate mail threatening to set fire to both that letter writer's house and our building. But mostly ghastly letters of thanks." He reached down beside his desk and hoisted up a canvas sack spilling over with envelopes. "Ladies stuffed them through the mail slot all weekend long. One of our workers slipped on the piles when he first opened the office this morning. Nearly broke his neck. And then an hour ago, another batch"—the young man gestured with his head toward a bag slumped against a wall like a rummy in an alleyway—"arrived from the postman. Our editor, Mr. Scott, is fuming."

My fingers itched to grab all those beautiful stuffed envelopes and rip them open, one by one. "Would you like me to burn the letters for you?" I asked.

The fellow lifted his eyebrows. "Burn them?"

"I'll gladly take them and toss them into an incinerator. I'm opposed to the vote myself."

"You are?" He plopped the rustling sack back on the ground. "I don't come across many middle-class young ladies who oppose the vote."

"Are the bags heavy?" I asked.

"I don't think I entirely believe you're an anti-suffragist."

I covered my mouth and gagged against my palm.

The man gave a start. "What was that?"

"My reaction to that terrible word that starts with an *s*."

He lifted his chin and seemed to squint down his nose at me, even though he was sitting and I was standing. "Who are you?" he asked.

"Who are *you*?" I asked, just to be as impertinent as he was.

He stiffened at my question, and the typists behind him disappeared into ink-colored smudges. The clicks and dings of their typewriters drifted miles away. The man was suddenly dressed in a white lace tea gown, as relaxed and comfortable as can be—as if he thought himself to be more woman than man.

"Oh." I lowered my face, and the typewriters clacked back to life.

"What is it?" he asked, suited again in brown tweed and a necktie.

"I just . . ." I laid my letter for the fired receptionist upon his desk. "Will you please give this note to the woman who used to work here? It's very important."

"Are you a responsible woman?"

I sank back on my heels. "I—I—I like to think of myself that way."

"You know what I mean." He tapped the base of his pen against the desk. "'A Responsible Woman.'"

"Oh . . ." I pushed my envelope his way. "So, you can see straight through me. Well, that . . . that simply makes us equal, Mr. . . . ?"

"Briggs."

"Mr. Briggs. Believe it or not, I can see through you, too."

"I seriously doubt that."

I leaned my palms against the desk and dropped my voice to a whisper. "Deep inside, you're not so different from me. Are you?"

He gazed at me with a face unnaturally rigid—the paranoid

stare of a person whose inner workings were thrust on display against his will. His reaction made me feel cruel, so I stood and turned to leave.

"Here," he said from behind me.

I shifted back around.

He lifted one of the mail bags. "Go burn them, Responsible Woman."

"I will. Thank you." I took the dense bag and dragged it across the smooth tiles, hearing the future jostling about in all those packed-together papers inside.

THE FIRST THING I DID WHEN I GOT HOME WAS TO GO TO my bedroom. I had hardly sat down before I began tearing open the envelopes.

> *Dear Responsible Woman,*
>
> *You put into words exactly what I wanted to say to Judge Percival Acklen . . .*

> *Dear Responsible Woman,*
>
> *I wouldn't be old enough to vote in this year's election, even if women were enfranchised, but I want to thank you for giving hardworking, unsung females like my mother a voice . . .*

> *Dear Responsible Woman,*
>
> *Who are you, and are you already part of the Oregon State*

Equal Suffrage Association? If not, please join us at our next meeting . . .

> *Dear Responsible Woman,*
> *I'm a pro-suffrage man, and although I'm cautious about discussing my sentiments among my colleagues at work, I applaud you for your bravery . . .*

> *Dear Responsible Woman,*
> *As you may already know, in June of this year 3,473 "gentlemen" of Portland contributed to the failure of the state-wide women's suffrage measure. Please write more editorials to awaken the obtuse males of this city.*
> *PLEASE!*

Dozens of people thanked me. Even men praised my eloquence. Other people felt I should be horsewhipped and chained in my kitchen, but for the most part, the handwritten and professionally typed reactions set my hands trembling with gratitude and hope.

I widened my curtains to invite in more light for rereading some of the letters, and even fragile Mrs. Stanton and her wagon filled with pickling jars seemed to shine a little brighter out on the sidewalk.

That afternoon, I fetched my canvas Gladstone bag and packed my clothing—bloomers included—along with the one hundred twenty-three dollars. I then shoved the luggage under the pink ruffles of my bed.

In barely twenty-four hours, I realized, my knees still on the ground, my eyes locked on my hidden belongings, *A Responsible Woman and the Mesmerizing Henri Reverie—Young Marvels of the New Century—will be venturing to the Portland Hotel and putting on one hell of a show.*

CHAPTER TWENTY-TWO

THE LOWEST FLAME

Less than an hour after school would have been dismissed, Frannie showed up at my door with a basket smelling of chicken looped over her arm.

"How are you doing?" she asked.

"Well . . ." I raised the Fannie Farmer cookbook I was carrying. "I'm mastering the fine art of housewifery."

She frowned. "Is that even a word?"

"I looked it up once, after Father used it."

I dropped the book on the hall table and opened the door wider.

Frannie stepped inside. "How are you really doing?"

I shut the door and leaned my back against it. "My bags are packed. I'm ready for tomorrow."

She nodded and bit her lip.

I nudged her basket with my knuckle. "What's this?"

"We had leftover food from the anniversary party, and I thought"—she cleared her throat—"if you wanted to come with me, we could deliver it to Genevieve."

"That's terribly kind of you."

"To be honest"—she closed one eye and cringed—"I want to meet her."

"You mean you want to see if Henry is lying about her."

"That's not what I said."

"But it's what you mean."

"All right"—she lowered her shoulders—"maybe that's a little bit true. But as I said yesterday, if you're concerned enough about her to put up with your father, then I'd like to see what I can do to help. And I asked Mama about that sort of cancer, and she said she'd be surprised a girl could have it that young."

"Henry's not lying."

"No, let me finish. She said if a fifteen-year-old girl did indeed get diagnosed with it, that girl would certainly need extra support and encouragement."

I glanced down the hallway, toward the kitchen. "I'm not sure if I can go. I have to light the stove for supper . . ."

"We'll be quick. I'll even pay for the streetcar so we can get there faster."

"Hmm. I wouldn't mind seeing how she and Henry are doing." I grabbed my coat off the hook. "It has to be extremely quick. Nothing can go wrong."

I KNOCKED ON THE DOOR OF ROOM TWENTY-FIVE AND tried not to breathe too much of the stale cigar smoke filling up the hall.

"I hope I'm not waking her," I whispered to Frannie. "She's had a fever, and Hen—"

The door opened a crack. Henry's blue eyes peeked out. "Olivia. Hello. I thought you might have been the doctor again."

"No, it's just me. I'm sorry if we're disturbing Genevieve's sleep, but this is my good friend Frannie, and she's brought some food."

Henry opened the door a foot wider. "That's awfully nice. Thank you."

"You're welcome." Frannie handed him the basket, which dipped toward the ground during the transfer, for it was heavy—I'd helped her carry it down the street. "There's chicken," she said, "fresh vegetables, bread, and two slices of cake. You can keep the basket until Olivia next sees you."

"That's far too kind."

"Olivia told me what she's doing to help, so I thought . . ." Frannie pulled her coat tighter around herself. "I wanted to do something, too."

"How is Genevieve?" I asked.

"Um . . ." Henry scratched at his ear. "She's, uh . . ." He peeked over his shoulder. "What did you say, Genevieve?"

His sister called something from inside in a voice too soft for me to hear.

"It's Olivia and a friend," said Henry. "They've brought food." He shifted back to us. "A doctor was just here. She's still running a fever. He's still not sure if it's a cold . . . or if . . ." He grimaced. "He's not a cancer expert by any means, but he thinks . . . the tumor . . ."

He rubbed his hand across his forehead, and a vision attacked without warning.

Buckling knees.

Listless arms.

Sickly pallor.

Henry—not Genevieve.

I closed my eyes and kept my voice steady. "Is there anything else we can do?"

I opened them again to see Henry—normal Henry—shaking his head and swallowing.

"I don't think so," he said. And he dropped his voice to a whisper to add, "She's been crying. She always gets upset after doctor visits. I was just about to go down to the lobby so she can sleep and recuperate."

"I should have brought you some books," said Frannie.

"No need for that." He managed a small smile for her. "I'm sure you probably hate me a bit, if we're being honest. But I appreciate your help with my sister."

"I'd like to see Olivia," called Genevieve, loud enough for us to hear.

Henry turned toward her, one hand on the door, the other on the picnic basket. "Are you sure about that?"

"Her friend, too. I want to thank them."

"All right." Henry stepped back and maneuvered the basket out of our way. "Come inside, ladies."

We entered, and I immediately saw her. A weak blue light on the bed. The lowest flame of a gas lamp. Hope seemed to be vacating her body.

Frannie and I walked toward her, and even Frannie, who didn't see what I did, stiffened.

"I'm so sorry you're not feeling well." I cupped my hand around Genevieve's arm, which felt solid, despite its unsubstantial appearance. "This is my friend Frannie."

"It's nice to meet you." Genevieve gave a polite smile, but she remained a low blue glow. "Thank you for the food. I'm sorry I'm such a mess. The doctor was just here . . . and . . ." She turned her face away. Silent tears rushed down her cheeks. "I'm sorry."

"It's all right." I squeezed her arm. "It's all right to cry. Don't be sorry."

"I don't want to worry Henry . . ."

"Neither of you need to worry," I said. "You'll soon be with a physician who knows how to help you. Just get some rest for now. That's all you need to do. Please don't lose hope. Don't be afraid."

I heard sniffling beside me and caught Frannie—who always managed to cry whenever someone else was crying—rubbing the back of her sleeve across her face. She lowered her arm when she noticed me looking at her.

"He's not eating," said Genevieve under her breath.

"What?" I leaned closer to the bed.

Genevieve licked her chapped lips. "Henry's not taking care of himself. I know he's not."

I glanced back at her brother.

"Please tell him to eat and sleep," she said. "I think he'd listen to you."

"Are you not eating, Henry?" I asked.

"I haven't been hungry. But"—he lifted Frannie's basket—"we have good food now."

"Then eat it." I turned back to Genevieve. "And please make sure you try to eat, too. We're almost there."

"I know."

"Get some good sleep." I tucked her blankets over her shoulders. "You'll be on your way to San Francisco soon."

"Thank you. I'm glad you came."

Frannie and I headed back to the door, where Henry still lingered with the basket.

I reached for his hand but remembered we had an audience, so my fingers fumbled and latched on to the cuff of his shirtsleeve instead.

"Please take care of yourself," I said.

"Don't worry." He grinned, but his eyes lacked their persuasiveness. "Everything will be perfect tomorrow night." He tugged on my own sleeve, and his finger brushed across the side of my thumb.

We parted ways. The door closed behind us with a low thud that traveled through my bones.

Frannie and I journeyed down the hotel stairwell, side by side, our feet slow and plodding in the echoing quarters.

By the time we reached the bottom, she was holding tightly to my hand.

"I may not be here to witness the full fruition of this balancing of the sexes, but already we see the promise of its coming, and future generations will reap its blessings."

— SUSAN B. ANTHONY, "The New Century's Manly Woman," 1900.

MODERN.

MRS. NEWORT, *(to Daughter.)* — Goodness me, Kitty! Don't stand there with your hands in your pockets, that way; — you don't know how ungentlemanly it looks!

CHAPTER TWENTY-THREE

ELECTION DAY

NOVEMBER 6, 1900

Tuesday morning, an hour and a half after Father left for work in his operatory, I lugged the canvas Gladstone to its next hiding spot, across the city.

Every neighbor's house I passed filled me with pangs of nostalgia for my life in the city. Each familiar street sign disappearing over my shoulder jabbed at my conscience and chipped away tiny flakes of my heart.

Yet I kept walking.

I passed a brick firehouse with a ballot-box table set up

next to a black and red steam pumper engine in the garage. Out front, a line of men—a hodgepodge of hats and caps, coveralls, dungarees, and smart black suits—waited to exercise their democratic right and paid no attention to me strolling behind them with my overstuffed bag.

Two blocks later, a wagon led by a handsome pair of chestnut horses rolled past me with flags waving and cornets and trombones blaring "Yankee Doodle." Banners hung off the wooden slats in the back, shouting, WILLIAM JENNINGS BRYAN! and ANTI-IMPERIALISM!

"Tell your father to vote for Bryan, little lady," called out a man around Father's age in red-striped suspenders that looked more like Henry's peppermint candies than the American flag.

"I'm not supposed to have any say in politics," I called back, but then I squeezed my lips shut and eyed the nearby pedestrians. My heart jumped around in my chest until I assured myself Father hadn't just witnessed me sassing a political campaigner while wandering the streets with my worldly possessions. I kept my head down and my mouth closed until I reached the front desk at the Hotel Vernon.

"I'd like a room, please," I said to the hotel clerk with the devilish Vandyke beard—the same terrible little man who had belittled the Negro customers and yelled at Henry and me to take our lovers' quarrel outside.

"A room for one?" he asked.

"Yes, a place of my own." Oh, how I loved the sound of

that! "And I'd like to pay in advance to ensure there will be no trouble finding you if I need to check out early."

Even if the clerk did remember me as the screeching lunatic from three days before, he made no complaint about my presence once I plunked a dollar bill onto his desk.

"Room eight," he said with a smile above his pointy umber beard, and he slid a golden key across the polished mahogany.

I left my suitcase in the first-floor room with a quilt-covered bed that appeared to be collapsing on one side. Another whiff of the establishment's mold met my nose, but I had no plans to stay. I shut the door behind me, locked up my possessions, and exited the hotel without checking on Henry and Genevieve upstairs.

The night before, I had awoken in a panicked sweat from a dream in which I smashed a sledgehammer over a gravestone marked RHODES.

Instead of confronting that fear, I preferred to walk back home and cling to the illusion that everything would unfold as planned.

WITHOUT GERDA'S HELP, I SOMEHOW MANAGED TO BUT-ton myself up in the same eggplant-purple dress I'd worn to Sadie's party, the only gown in my wardrobe suitable for an election-night soiree. Gerda must have scrubbed the mud off the hem Saturday morning, for the fabric betrayed no signs of Percy chasing me down in his buggy.

I descended the staircase toward Father, who was reading

the mail in his best wool suit and a crisp black bow tie. The air was rich with the scent of Macassar hair oil.

He peeked up at me. "You're finally ready. Why are you wearing that lace scarf?"

I left the bottom step. "It's the latest fashion."

"Don't be ridiculous."

"How would you know what young ladies are wearing?"

"I know what does and doesn't look garish." He set down the mail on the hall table. "Please take that off."

I pressed the lace against my neck. "I can't."

"You can't?"

"It's covering a blemish."

"There's no such thing as a neck blemish, Olivia. Now, take that thing off"—he reached for the scarf—"before the ladies at the party see you."

He gave a firm tug, and the lace unspooled.

My neck fell bare.

"The marks are from Percy," I said before he could match words to his open-mouthed stare. "He tried forcing himself upon me the night of Sadie Eiderling's party, but all I could say was 'All is well.'" I yanked the scarf free of Father's hands and wound the lace back around my neck. "I worried you'd ask Mr. Reverie to do something more to me if I told you what had happened."

He just stood there, paralyzed and mute.

"Are you ready?" I asked with a glance at the door.

"Um . . . yes." He blinked and fitted his head with a tall silk hat dating back to the Garfield administration. "I've hired a driver and carriage for the night. We're traveling in high style, which ought to tell you how important I consider this event. Behave as if your life depended on it."

"Of course," I said. "My life indeed depends on it."

FIREWORKS LIT UP THE PORTLAND SKYLINE IN BLASTS OF indigo that rattled my seat in the carriage. Along the side of one of downtown's tallest buildings, an enormous projection of President McKinley's clean-shaven face and balding head glowed across a sandstone wall.

"It doesn't actually feel as if my eyes are playing tricks on me right now," I said to Father, whose toes kept bumping into mine, "but I see President McKinley's giant white face watching over the city. Do you see it, too?"

Father craned his neck to get a peek outside the carriage window. "That's a stereopticon slide. The newspaper said that's how the city would announce who's ahead in the election."

"He looks like the Wonderful Wizard of Oz when he was just a huge head sitting in a chair." I gawked at the passing black-and-white image. "How peculiar."

The whimsical rooftop dormers and chimneys of the eight-story Portland Hotel would be coming up next, within a block, across from the courthouse on Sixth Street. I had walked by its opulent grounds hundreds of times.

The carriage eased down the Yamhill Street slope, but to

my consternation, I did not see all those wonderful chimneys. On a tall, lumpy hill, in the erratic shots of light from the streaks of blue fireworks, stood a castle with towers severe and black.

"No, that's absurd." I turned away from the carriage window and covered my eyes with the lace scarf.

"What's absurd?" asked Father.

"It's not a good sign." I squeezed the lace and spoke more to myself than Father. "It shouldn't look like Dracula's castle—and death. I shouldn't be afraid."

"No, you shouldn't." Father shifted his position on his seat with a squeak of leather. "And you should stop reading that damned horror novel. Perhaps that's one more item I should have Mr. Reverie remove from—"

He cut himself off, and at first I wondered if he was about to revise his stance on the hypnosis. A second later, a sound that must have distracted him reached my ears.

Singing.

Women's voices singing.

I lowered the scarf and shifted toward the window again.

Outside our carriage, females of all ages, sizes, and backgrounds lined the lamp-lit sidewalks in front of our beautiful Portland Hotel with its soaring walls of dark stone and terracotta. The women and girls wore yellow ribbons on their coats and their hats, and they belted out a song while raising homemade cloth flags bearing the words VOTES FOR WOMEN!

I slid across the seat and stuck my head into the chimney-scented air to better hear them sing the satirical lyrics of "Oh, Dear, What Can the Matter Be?"

"Put your head back inside the carriage." Father pulled me down to my seat by my shoulder. "If those are the type of women I think they are, you'll get sick to your stomach."

The driver steered the trotting horses into the hotel's circular driveway, a grand roundabout surrounded by shrubberies and ornamental trees, almost as green in the nighttime lighting as during the sunshine splendor of day. The line of singing women and girls stretched clear up to the front doors.

The carriage rocked to a stop, and Father opened the door and clambered out. He turned around to help me down, just as the chorus of females switched to "Keep Woman in Her Sphere," another saucy anthem, sung to the tune of "Auld Lang Syne."

I spotted Frannie and Kate near the hotel's front doors, but I turned my face away and pretended not to notice or hear them, even though my eyes swam with tears of gratitude.

Father offered me his elbow and helped me down to the ground. With my head held high—I swear, I grew four inches—we trod forward to my fate.

A wind snapped at my ears.

The world went black and tipped off balance, and the ladies' voices seemed distorted into muffled wails. The scents of death and decay breathed in my face, and fiery torches guided our way to the hotel's double doors, which stretched open before us like a pair of jaws with jagged teeth.

"I can't do this." I pulled back. "Something's not right. It reminds me too much of death."

"Don't be silly." Father tugged me onward. "Your fears are all in your head."

With a firm pull, he wrenched me inside.

CHAPTER TWENTY-FOUR

A REMEDY FOR REVERIES

A banner for the Oregon Association Opposed to the Extension of Suffrage to Women hung above a white semicircular stage, its letters as bold and red as knife wounds. Below the sign a twelve-piece orchestra strummed their bows at a dizzying pace for the brisk Viennese waltz careering around the waxed parquet floor.

The first dancer I saw was none other than Sadie Eiderling, dressed in a long scarlet gown, whirling about in the arms of bespectacled Teddy from her party. Sunken-Eyed John waltzed with a blond girl in black, while his sister, Eugenia, danced with the leering, long-nosed fellow who had called me a tart. They held their upper bodies as stiff as shop-window mannequins, and their faces appeared handsome and young in the bright wattage of the crystal chandeliers.

Whenever they veered into shadow, however, oh, how they changed. Their teeth, their burning eyes, the black-tinged blood on their lips—all their hidden savagery—triggered an ache in the marks on my neck.

Percy, primped like a peacock in a dark suit and tails, strutted our way with his hands folded behind his back. "Dr. Mead, Olivia, how lovely to see you. Pretty scarf, Olivia."

"Father knows about my neck," I said, and Percy turned and skedaddled to the opposite end of the room.

Father kept me pulled against his side and didn't even mention a word about Percy. "I don't see the hypnotist." He gazed about the throng of Portland's wealthiest, who danced and milled about and drank champagne at round tables draped in red, white, and blue. "Let's go pay our regards to the Underhills."

I scanned the room for Henry as well, but he was nowhere to be found amid all the jewels and stiff collars. Waiters in white coats glided about with trays of savory-smelling appetizers and flutes of bubbling gold liquid, but they and Father were the only non-society men in the entire place.

On our way to the Underhills, we passed Percy's bald father, Judge Acklen, whom I recognized from the newspapers. He sipped a dark drink that resembled a vial of blood and appeared to be alone, until a vaporous haze of a woman, perhaps Mrs. Acklen, slipped into view beside him.

Father pressed onward to Mr. Underhill, who was conversing with another young couple I recognized from Sadie's birthday party. They chatted in front of an eight-foot-tall ice sculpture carved like the Statue of Liberty, propped on a round table with a star-spangled cloth. The air around them chilled me more than our mudroom in January.

"Mr. Underhill." Father thrust out his hand, interrupting their chat. "Thank you again for inviting us."

"Oh. Dr. Mead." Mr. Underhill shook Father's hand, and his white mustache wriggled with a smile. "So you arrived."

"Have you spotted our entertainment for the evening yet?" asked Father.

"I think she's right here." Mr. Underhill gestured toward me with his champagne. "This is the girl I was telling you about, Lizzie. Go ahead, say the word to her—but stand back."

The female half of the young couple, a pretty brunette with glossy ringlets, leaned forward with pouty lips and said with a chirp, "Suffrage."

I slapped my mouth and hacked a deep, retching sound.

The girl squealed and clapped her hands, and her broad-shouldered escort gave one of those firm-lipped sorts of nods that males seem to make when they're feeling especially mannish. I swallowed down my humiliation.

"You haven't seen young Mr. Reverie, then?" asked Father.

"No," said Mr. Underhill. "But all of our guests will be

especially interested in his cure after that disgusting display outside the hotel just now."

"I've always told Mother," said chirpy little Lizzie, "that women like that remind me of freakish men with bosoms."

Her escort laughed. "Lizzie!"

"I'm sorry, James, but it's true. Just look at this one." She nodded toward me.

I picked at the tips of my hot gloves and pretended not to have heard the insult. My blood simmered. My chest felt overly exposed.

Sadie and Teddy strolled our way, arm in arm, and under no circumstances was I about to bear the brunt of *her* wicked barbs, too. I pulled free of Father and veered toward the exit.

Ten feet before I reached the doorway, Henry walked into the ballroom while fussing with his tie.

I released a pent-up breath and stopped in my tracks.

Henry halted, too, and something worse than his usual fatigue weighed down his shoulders. He looked deathly ill—his lips cracked, his face drawn, his eyes devoid of all fire.

Father snatched my elbow and jerked me away before I could ask what was wrong.

"Henry looks sick," I said, twisting my head to see his red vest disappearing behind us.

"You cannot interact with him before the demonstration." Father tripped me over my feet to the farthest corner of the ballroom. "People will think the hypnosis is a fake, and that I'm a fake—or a fool."

"I just want to find out what's wrong with him. I don't think that was an illusion."

"He probably just drank too much last night. Showmen tend to do that."

"Dentists, too, from what I've seen."

Father plunked me down in a cream-colored chair near the stage. "Sit here for now," he said over the frenzy of strings. "Mrs. Underhill will likely let us know when she's ready."

I leaned forward to better see through the throng of dancing bodies and spotted Henry wandering behind them as if he didn't know where to go. The waiters with the trays of food didn't even stop to talk to him. The frantic strumming of the orchestra propelled everyone in the room into a faster-than-average speed; people were flitting and swerving all over the place, rushing, rushing, rushing—except for Henry.

"Go check on him." I tugged on Father's coat. "He doesn't even know where you want him to be. He looks even more out of place than we do."

"We do not look out of place."

"You were the one who wanted him here. Go take care of him."

Father grunted and circled around the dance floor to meet up with Henry on the other side. He then gestured with his arms while speaking to Henry and pointed toward Mrs. Underhill, who had joined her husband by the frozen Statue of Liberty. Henry headed over to the ice sculpture as well, raking a hand through his hair.

Father hurried back to my side. "He hasn't been feeling his best, but he assured me that everything will go as planned. He's going to ask Mrs. Underhill if we should start soon."

"Did he say anything about his sister?"

"No, and please, just sit here and stop fretting about everything. All will be well once we start the demonstration." Father tugged his handkerchief out of his pocket and mopped his forehead.

I rubbed the tops of my legs through the purple sheen of my skirt. "Show me Henry's money."

Father blinked as if he hadn't heard me quite right. "I beg your pardon."

"Prove to me you intend to pay him if I go up there and let him hypnotize me again. I won't play nicely until you do."

His jaw stiffened.

"Please," I said.

He rustled an envelope out of his breast pocket, gave me a quick peek at the cash inside, and then tucked the envelope straight back into the folds of his coat. "He had better remove every last shred of your sass tonight, young lady. I'm getting tired of this."

The orchestra's song dwindled to a much-needed end, and the room slowed its pace and settled to a stop. Mrs. Underhill climbed aboard the stage in a royal-blue gown with a long train that swished behind her like a cat's tail. She waved at the conductor to keep the music at bay and walked to center stage.

"Ladies and gentlemen, welcome to our election-night ball, sponsored by the Oregon Association Opposed to the Extension of Suffrage to Women."

I gagged over the word *suffrage*, while everyone else applauded and cheered.

"To the Republicans in the crowd," continued Mrs. Underhill, "a hearty congratulations. It looks as though President William McKinley and his running mate, Theodore Roosevelt, will be helming the country as we sail into this glorious new century."

Fewer than half of the attendees smiled and slapped their gloved hands together, while the anti-imperialist Democrats folded their arms across their chests and sat there with a wilted air of defeat.

"What we can all celebrate together as a group, however"— Mrs. Underhill lifted her index finger and waited for the applause to fade—"is the continued tradition of men alone voting for president while we women devote our attention to more ladylike pursuits."

An astounding abundance of women and girls clapped at this sentiment, including bold Sadie Eiderling, who seemed far too despotic to be opposed to female empowerment. I ground my molars.

"My sincerest apologies," said Mrs. Underhill, folding her hands together in front of her waist, "for the unpleasant display that greeted your arrival at the hotel this evening. More than ever it seems we need a remedy for the growing army of loud, obnoxious women who insist they are the same as men." She shifted her royal-blue bosom our way. "And I have good news for you on that account. Some wise men in our very own community have used their innovative brains to create such a remedy."

Silence befell the mesmerized crowd.

"My dear friends," continued Mrs. Underhill, "you may have noticed a few extra people at this party whom you may not have expected to see tonight. Dr. Walter Mead, a local dentist." She stretched out her hand in Father's direction. "And Monsieur Henri Reverie, the talented young hypnotist from Montreal, Canada." She extended her right arm to Henry, who stood in front of the opposite side of the stage from us. "Together, they have invented a cure for female rebellion, using the astounding power of hypnotism. Young Monsieur Reverie is going to demonstrate this revolutionary antidote for wayward women right here, right now, in front of all of you. Please welcome to the stage Henri Reverie and his subject, young rabble-rouser Olivia Mead."

The audience's applause walloped me in the face like a sack of rocks, and I couldn't even think to stand on my own. Father had to yank me out of the chair to get me to come to my senses and move.

"Go up, go up," he said, spinning me toward a small staircase at the side of the stage. "He's waiting for you."

I tripped over my skirt and petticoat on my way up the steps, for the whole room spun, and all I could see were crystal chandeliers whisking over my head. A warm hand slipped into mine and helped guide me to my feet.

"It's all right, Olivia," said Henry, putting his other hand around my waist. "I'm here. Just keep breathing."

With his assistance, I regained my balance and found myself wandering with him to the middle of the stage. Unlike the last time I joined him in such a way, it was the audience below us that resembled devils, not he. No matter how hard I blinked, I couldn't shake the sight of sharp teeth, anemic skin, and hungry stares in that sea of sky-high pompadours and slicked male hair that glistened with greasy spiced oils. Sadie Eiderling stood in the front row, peering at me with a viper-toothed grin, her hair a huge and untamed nest on the top of her head.

Henry slid his hand out of mine and turned to face the monsters. After a deep inhale, he rolled back his shoulders, lifted his chin, and with the magic of a metamorphosing butterfly, transformed into the performer version of himself.

"Good evening, *mesdames et messieurs*. My name is Henri Reverie, and I have been studying the arts of mesmerism and hypnotism with my uncle ever since I was twelve. I use a combination of techniques from the great masters, including animal magnetism, deep relaxation, and the remarkable power of suggestion. As you heard from our lovely hostess, Madame Underhill, I recently received the fascinating challenge of curing this young woman"—he half turned toward me—"of her dreams to vote for president. *Un remède pour des rêveries*. A remedy for daydreams." He rubbed his right fingers together in the air and seemed to taste the phrase on his tongue. "The cure for dreaming. A beguiling possibility, no?"

Spellbound, the rapt devil faces in the audience watched him walk toward them across the stage. "Over the past five days," he said, "I have administered two separate treatments to this young woman. When I first came to her, just last Thursday, she was participating in scandalous rallies for the vote and scrambling to finish her high school diploma so she could attend a university."

"You actually met her last Wednesday," called the gaunt and long-toothed version of Percy from the crowd, his hands cupped around his mouth, "when you stood on top of her at your Halloween show."

"Yes, *merci*. Thank you for reminding me, Monsieur Acklen. I first saw Miss Mead the very day she attended the rally, and I subdued her in front of the eyes of Portland that very night. Now she cannot even hear certain words related to the vote and higher education without getting sick to her stomach. Shall I demonstrate?"

The audience, at first, seemed taken aback by his proposal. They darted skeptical glances at one another, chuckled, and shook their heads. My eyes stopped seeing them as monsters. Now they were a crowd in white summer dresses and suits, gathered to witness a miracle maker at a county fair.

Sadie, decked out in a straw hat and red gingham, lifted her hand and asked, "Will this demonstration be disgusting?"

"Only if we badger her with the words too long," said Henry. "Go ahead, Mademoiselle Eiderling. Say something to her yourself. Try the word that starts with an *s*—the one those singing women out there adore."

Sadie shrugged. "Song?"

"No"—Henry helped her along—"s-u-f-f . . ."

"Ohhh." Sadie balled her hands into fists and drew a large intake of air through her nose. "Suffrage," she said with the breath of a birthday-candle wish.

I covered my mouth and made yet another gagging racket, and I glared at Henry out of the tops of my eyes. *Do not prolong this part of the demonstration,* I mentally willed him. *Do not.*

"Susan B. Anthony," called Mrs. Underhill from her new position down below the stage, and I coughed into my hand until my throat hurt. "Votes for women," she also added. "Women's rights."

"Merci." Henry held up his hands. "Thank you, ladies, for helping me with that particular demonstration. I am proud to say that with the subtlest of commands"—he circled around me with solid thumps of his soles—"I have also instilled in Miss Mead a higher moral standard. This virtuous girl before you now possesses a hatred of higher education, bicycle bloomers, and dalliances with the wrong sorts of boys."

I sank my teeth into my bottom lip to keep from grinning at those last parts. My nerves settled a tad, and the audience shifted back to its regular appearance. Rich folk in ball gowns and evening suits.

Henry stopped right beside me and clasped hold of his lapel. "However, as Madame Underhill so eloquently stated, one of the most pressing problems with these suff—" He cut the word short. "The problem with these young ladies is that they are loud. They certainly want to have a voice, don't they?"

"They certainly do," shouted a red-cheeked gentleman in the midst of the nodding male and female heads.

"Wouldn't it be *magnifique* if we could silence these girls?" asked Henry in a tone that worried me a little with its seriousness. "Simply take away their voices and make them as quiet and gentle as women ought to be?"

Another round of applause echoed across the room.

"Would you like me to prove to you that the silencing of wayward young women is a genuine possibility in this modern era of hypnosis?"

The applause strengthened in volume—its vibrations trembled in the soles of my shoes and the surfaces of my teeth.

"Monsieur Conductor . . ." Henry whisked around to face the orchestra. "Would you kindly have your orchestra play a soothing piece of music for me? A lullaby, if you please."

The conductor and the orchestra flipped through their sheet music, and Henry peeked at me for the swiftest of moments. His gallant stage voice and mannerisms failed to conceal the dark circles beneath his eyes or the fact that his bottom lip was so dry and cracked, it now bled almost as much as when Father had gagged him. I wondered when he last took a sip of water, and I sealed my mouth shut so I wouldn't feel compelled to ask.

The conductor must have raised his baton and signaled to his orchestra to commence, for the strings played a lullaby that filled the room with the delicacy of the fog settling over the roofs and the pines and the big-leaf maples of my street.

"Miss Mead." Henry faced me with his side to the audience. He bumped his fingers against my wrist so that I would position myself the same way.

I hesitated. A spark of fear shot through me. Before I could even think to try the tongue trick, he grabbed my wrist and pulled me toward him.

"Sleep!"

My face smashed against his shoulder blade, and I dropped down, down, down, until the orchestra's lullaby folded over me in black sheets of musical ecstasy. Henry turned me toward the audience and tipped me backward, dragging me with my heels skiing across the stage. My arms flopped below me, and my fingertips skated along the wood.

"Olivia," said Henry with his mouth behind my head. The strings of the orchestra nearly swallowed up his voice, but I heard him say, for my ears alone, "You no longer feel compelled to cover your mouth and make a gagging sound when you hear the words *suffrage, women's rights, suffragist, votes for women, Susan B. Anthony,* or *college.* You can argue with your father as much as you'd like and be as angry as you'd like."

He draped my body in a chair in front of the gentle purr of the violins. My utter lack of control over my limbs sent my legs falling open and my head tipping backward, and I could feel him hurrying to close my knees and reposition my torso.

"Stop." He took his hands off me. "Wait, wait, wait. Stop the music. I'm sorry, but this particular feat seems ridiculously easy. Hypnotizing one girl into losing her voice means nothing to the giant world outside those doors. Hundreds to thousands of suffragists are busily working away right now, spinning their webs, making their next plans to slap another referendum onto your ballots. If we want to rid this state and this country of suffragists, I need to prove to you that I can hypnotize an entire stage full of women into silence."

Henry's hand cupped my forehead.

"Awake," he said while sitting me upright. "Please stand, Miss Mead, to allow room for more chairs."

I let him help me to my feet, even though my legs bent and bobbed at all sorts of odd angles.

Henry readdressed the audience. "Would some of you gentlemen kindly fetch at least five of those singing women from outside this hotel? And then I'll need a few more volunteers to help bring some chairs upon this stage."

The young men and their fathers just stood there and stared as if they had never been asked to carry a stick of furniture in their lives. Before long, the poor waiters were setting down their trays, lugging around chairs, and running out to the street to wrangle women.

I pulled at my lace scarf and pleaded to Frannie and the other girls, *Please be gone! Be gone!* My grand scheme for the evening suddenly struck me as ridiculous and selfish, and I hated myself for convincing Henry to conspire with me.

A curly-haired waiter ran back inside from the lobby. "The women left."

I covered a relieved smile with my hand.

"They left?" asked Mrs. Underhill, and other disappointed murmurings and snorts shook loose from the crowd.

Henry held up his hands. "Do not worry, *mesdames et messieurs.* I am still able to show you how to tame a roomful of tigresses into docile, silent kittens. I simply need some of the beautiful ladies in this audience to temporarily stand in as the rebels."

The women froze.

Henry clasped his hands together in the direction of Sadie's bloodstain of a dress. "Mademoiselle Eiderling, would you care to be one of our volunteers?"

Sadie narrowed her eyes. "No."

"I believe I owe you the chance for an operatic solo," said Henry, "which can certainly be arranged while you're up on this stage. I do not think there would be a sound more breathtaking this election night than your sweet voice filling this room with the national anthem."

Sadie folded her arms over her chest and didn't budge.

Teddy slung his hand over her shoulder. "Do it, Sadie."

Sunken-Eyed John raised a champagne flute and said,

"Yes, do it," and his sister Eugenia clapped and added, "Yes, please, go up there, Sadie. What a laugh that would be"—all of them prodding at Sadie just as she had tried to bully Henry at her party.

"All right." Sadie jutted her chin in the air. "But Eugenia and my mother have to come with me, and my voice had better sound like an angel's when I sing the national anthem."

"*Bien sûr*, an angel," said Henry with a wobble in his footing that got me worrying about his health again. "Certainly, *mademoiselle*. Please come up and sit in one of these chairs."

The partygoers cleared a path for Sadie, Eugenia, and an older woman in a gown dripping in ecru lace, her hair a squat version of Sadie's strawberry-gold pompadour. Mrs. Underhill trooped up on stage with them as well, followed by Lizzie—the squeaky girl who had called me a freakish man with bosoms—and her equally sulky-lipped mother.

I perched myself on the leftmost chair and cleared the nervousness from my throat as the six other ladies joined me in sitting up there, all of us facing the audience in front of the orchestra.

"Thank you for helping us, ladies," said Henry, angled toward both us and the crowd below. "Your cooperation will reward you in the future, for when we silence the suffragists—"

I forgot to gag, but Henry's pause pushed me into action. I choked with passion to compensate.

"—you will no longer need to concern yourselves with organizations such as this one. You will be able to devote your time to charities and other, worthier endeavors instead of hushing up women with pluck."

The mothers on the stage nodded their approval, while their daughters fussed with their skirts and slumped as if bored. I folded my hands in my lap and tried to ignore Father's watchful face out of the corner of my eye.

"Ladies and gentlemen"—Henry pivoted toward the audience and raised his hands—"I present to you America's idyllic future."

He swirled around to us ladies and started work on Lizzie at the opposite end of the line from me.

"Close your eyes." He stroked the girl's head of jostling brown ringlets. "You are drowsy. You can think of nothing but sleep. Melt down, melt down into sleep."

He moved on to Lizzie's mother and embarked upon the same routine. "Close your eyes." He kneaded the woman's supple forehead. "Think of nothing but sleep. You feel very sleepy. You are so tired. Melt down."

He continued down the line of women, repeating the same phrases and massaging everyone's skulls and foreheads. This time I had ample warning to keep myself alert. I wedged my tongue against the roof of my mouth. Henry's silky voice alone was already persuading my chin to drop to my chest, but I forced myself to envision slamming a door in his face.

"You feel very sleepy," he said to Mrs. Eiderling next to me. "You are drowsy. Think of nothing but sleep."

Mrs. Eiderling's head and shoulders slumped forward.

Henry moved over to me and put his hands on the sides of my head. "Close your eyes."

I pressed my tongue to my palate with all my might and shut my lids.

"Think of nothing but sleep." He caressed my temples. "Go to sleep."

I held my breath and strained to block out the potency of his words. *Slam the door. Slam it hard!* My thoughts strained toward suffragist anthems, train rides to New York City, moonlit bicycle rides in garnet-brown bloomers . . .

Henry left my side. My mind remained my own.

"You now feel your right arm drifting into the air," he said. "You cannot help it—the arm is simply moving on its own, rising higher and higher."

I played along and raised my arm, my eyes still closed.

"As you can see, ladies and gentlemen," he said, "some subjects are more susceptible to hypnosis than others. Miss . . . what is your name, *mademoiselle?*"

"Lizzie Yves," said the chirpy girl in a wide-awake voice.

"You still seem awake, Lizzie. Stand up, please—and sleep! Go down, go down, you are so tired you can do nothing but sleep. Very good. You are doing beautifully."

I found myself tapping my foot to get him to hurry along with everything, but I stopped myself as soon as I realized the blunder.

"Now, ladies . . ." His footsteps traveled to the center of the stage. "What I am about to tell you is extremely important, so you must listen carefully. When I say the word *awake*, you will open your eyes, and you will not be able to speak. You will have no voice. No matter what anyone says to you, if you try to talk, all that will exit your mouth is soundless air. You will be silent."

I bowed my head and heard the patter of his shoes leaving the stage, as if he were running away from the mess he was about to create.

"Awake!"

We all opened our eyes. Mrs. Eiderling spread her lips apart beside me, but all that came out was an empty gasp. Next to her, Sadie clutched her right hand around her throat and squirmed in her chair until the legs of the furniture tapped against the stage. Mrs. Underhill and Eugenia flapped their lips open and shut like wide-eyed fish.

"This, ladies and gentlemen," said Henry from down in the middle of the crowd, "is the sound of silent women."

The men in the audience let loose applause that threw us back in our chairs.

"Bravo," shouted Judge Acklen. "Well done!"

Mr. Underhill whistled his approval, and his wife sat up with a fierce-eyed glare.

"Go ahead." Henry grabbed Percy by the arm. "Tell those girls what you really think of women. They can't say a word back to you."

"Oh, I don't know about that." Percy lifted his hands and

retreated out of Henry's grasp. "They can still slap, can't they?"

The gentlemen laughed and patted Percy on the back.

Sadie stood and waved her arms.

"Oh, wait." Henry wiggled a piece of paper and a pen out of his breast pocket. "One of them is trying to communicate."

Sadie snatched the writing utensils from his hands and kneeled on the stage to scribble a note. She then shoved the paper down at Henry's nose.

Henry read the note over and shifted back to the crowd. "Well, this is a historic moment indeed. For the first time ever, an anti-suffragist woman has written the words 'Give us our voices!'"

A few gentlemen laughed, but a sobering silence threw a bucket of ice water over the party. Glimmers of suspicion awakened in the eyes of the Oregon Association crowd. The hairs on the back of my neck bristled.

"Ladies." Henry turned toward us, and he swayed for a moment, as if he had moved too fast. "Gentlemen are not kind when it comes to you speaking your minds. You must be cautious about giving us full custody of your voices. I am afraid we will take unfair advantage, *mes chéries*."

Sadie stomped her foot on the stage and made the whole room jump.

"All right, sit down, sit down." Henry waved her back to her chair.

He moved to take a step away from the crowd, but he stopped and tipped as though dizzy, and his eyes rolled toward the back of his head. He fell forward but caught himself by bracing his hands against the front edge of the stage.

I bolted upright in my chair. "Henry?"

He stayed still for a moment, panting as though breathing were a struggle, his head hanging between his arms.

"I'm sorry." He managed to lift his face, now as white as ash. "Oh, God . . . maybe the orchestra . . . I'm really sorry . . ." He staggered backward and collapsed on the waxed ballroom floor.

CHAPTER TWENTY-FIVE

SILENCE

I'm not sure how I got off that stage—I believe I may have taken a running leap and jumped to the hard parquet below. All I remember is Henry's skin growing cold and gray beneath my hands.

"Are you breathing, Henry?" I shook his shoulders. "Oh, God. Please breathe! Please breathe!"

He turned paler by the second. The only thing I could think to do was jostle him.

"Don't die. Don't die. You can't die. Isn't there a doctor in this room? Why isn't someone helping him?"

I peeked up at the crowd and discovered that the floor

around us had cleared. Everyone stood back in their fine tailored clothing, watching me fumble to save his life.

"Why are you just standing there?" I asked. "This isn't part of the show. Someone needs to get him to a hospital. Put him in one of your carriages. Help him!"

Mr. Underhill grimaced at Henry. "He's a theater person. Some of us would rather not have him in our carriages."

"Oh, Christ, you're idiots." I cradled Henry's head against my chest. "If he dies, then your wives and daughters are going to be stuck without voices forever."

Some of the men and boys actually laughed at that statement—*they laughed!*

Claps of thunder erupted from the stage behind me. I gave a start and peered over my shoulder to discover the silenced mothers and daughters hurling themselves down the staircases at the sides of the stage in their long, shimmering gowns. They barreled toward us and shoved me away from Henry. Sadie and her mother lifted him by his shoulders. Mrs. Underhill and Eugenia grabbed his legs. Lizzie and her mother hoisted him up beneath his back. In less than two seconds, those women had his limp body up in the air and were rushing him across the room.

I jumped to my feet and chased after them through the palm-lined lobby and out to the cold night air. With Henry bouncing in their arms, the ladies reached an enclosed black carriage parked near Sixth.

I lunged to help them open the door and told them, "Be

careful," as they maneuvered Henry's head inside and spread him across a padded seat.

Sadie waved her arms at the driver and mouthed the word *hospital.*

The driver shrugged his broad shoulders. "Speak up. I don't know what you're saying."

"You need to drive this carriage to the hospital," I said for her. "Quickly!"

Sadie dove inside the vehicle with her mother and Henry, and the other ladies ran to the carriage behind them. I tried to follow Sadie into her carriage, but the door slammed shut in my face, and the horses trotted away.

"Olivia!" Father stormed toward me with my coat hanging off his arm. "We're going home. That was a shocking thing you two did in there. I'm appalled beyond words."

"What are you talking about?"

He gripped my arm with a squeeze that made me gasp.

"I'm not stupid, Olivia. You're able to speak when the rest of those women were silenced."

"I just—"

"You conspired with that hypnotist behind my back again and put those ladies in peril. What else have you been doing with him in secret, you lying little hussy?"

"I . . . what does any of that matter right now? Something's terribly wrong with Henry. His sister's waiting for him in the hotel. She's supposed to have surgery in San Francisco this Friday."

"That's Reverie's problem, not mine."

"We only conspired against you because he thought what you were doing to me was horrible. Don't punish his sister for our actions."

Father hardened his jaw but eased his grip.

"Please," I said, "she's done nothing wrong, and she's waiting for her brother. Go with me to fetch her so we can tell her about Henry and take her to him."

He puffed a loud sigh.

"Father?"

"All right, I'll give that poor girl a ride, but I'm not paying her brother one cent of my money. Come along." He wrapped my coat around my shoulders. "Let's go find our driver and be quick about this."

GENEVIEVE'S DOOR ALREADY SAT AJAR.

"Oh, no! What's happened here?" I hurried down the hall and pushed my way inside, expecting kidnappers and murderers and chaos.

Instead, I encountered the strange scene of Genevieve, Frannie, Kate, and Agnes sipping mugs of steaming tea on the Rhodeses' hotel sofa. Genevieve—solid and sturdy—wiped away tears with a handkerchief and smiled.

I blinked to ensure they wouldn't all disappear. "What's happening?"

Father strode into view behind me, and all four pairs of eyes seemed to ask the same question of me.

Frannie stood up from the right-hand arm of the sofa. "We raised money for Genevieve, just in case . . ." She looked between Father and me. "In case there was no other money to be had."

Father and I eyed each other.

"Between school, the bookstore, and this evening," said Kate, nestled beside Genevieve on one of the sofa cushions, "Frannie was able to collect close to seventy-five dollars."

"Seventy-five?" I stumbled toward them.

"Isn't it wonderful?" Genevieve rose with her mug. "I don't even know what to say. I never dreamed of such kindness." She stood on tiptoe and peeked over my shoulder. "Where's Henry?"

"He's . . ." I swallowed and clamped my hands into fists.

Genevieve's tea sloshed over the rim. "What's wrong?"

"Your brother," said Father, "collapsed after he and Olivia played a dirty hypnotist trick upon a group of women. He's on his way to the hospital."

Genevieve flickered out.

"I don't know what's wrong with him," I said, rubbing my temples to bring her back into view, "but he's there, and we'll take you to him."

"Is he all right?" she asked, now a weak sputter of light. "Was he able to speak?"

I shook my head. "You had better come."

The mugs were set aside, the door locked, and our six pairs of feet thundered down the hotel staircase.

Out by the carriage, Frannie folded me up in a hug. "You're still leaving after all of this, aren't you?"

"As I told you," I said into her ear, "train rides are faster and easier these days. Thank you for helping Genevieve."

"You're welcome. Please be extremely careful, Responsible Woman." She gave my lips a quick peck and sent me into the hired carriage with Father and Henry's wavering ghost of a sister.

THE LAMP-LIT HOSPITAL ON DARK AND HILLY CORNELL Street appeared to me as a regular brick-and-stone medical building—not a mausoleum or an undertaker's parlor or anything else more funereal than an actual hospital. All the same, a helpless sense of panic gripped my chest when I jumped out of the carriage below the five-story structure. I felt I'd forgotten something, or I'd lost something, and my mind kept racing back to shaking Henry's heavy shoulders as he lay there on the cold parquet floor. If only I'd moved a little faster to reach him, rustled him a little harder. If only I could have kept him from slipping out of reach.

I put my arm around Genevieve, and we climbed the steps to the hospital's tall doorway beneath an archway of bricks, with Father following us.

Inside the lobby—a cold, wood-paneled room I remembered from my grandmother's battle with pneumonia—the Eiderling, Underhill, and Yves ladies paced across a worn beige rug with their hands on their hips. The floral garden of their perfumes melded into the sticky smells of sweet medicine.

A nurse in a small white cap and an apron-covered dress peeked up from the front desk. "May I help you?"

Genevieve and I walked over to her, still attached to each other.

"You just admitted this girl's brother, Henry Rhodes," I said. "Or . . . Henri Reverie, as these ladies might have called him."

"They didn't call him anything." The nurse craned her neck toward the pacing collection of ladies in ball gowns. "What is wrong with their voices?"

"This is all the result of a hypnotism show gone terribly wrong."

"They're hypnotized?"

"How is Henry?" asked Genevieve. "May we see him?"

The nurse shook her head. "Visiting hours already ended, I'm afraid."

"Is he alive?" I asked.

"I'm sorry, but I don't know how he is. I only filled out his paperwork . . . or what I could of it." She glanced at the mute women again. "You'll need to wait here in the lobby, and the doctors will speak to his sister when they have information to give."

I turned and bumped straight into Father's chest.

"Oh, I didn't know you were there . . ."

"I don't want to stay here with these . . . women," he said

under his breath with a sharp eye on Mrs. Underhill. "They're probably plotting a way to murder me right now. We're going home."

"I can't."

"We took care of Miss Reverie. Now it's time for you to leave." He took me by the hand and jerked me away from Genevieve.

"Wait! I need to fix all the messes I've made."

He hauled me toward the door.

"Father, please"—I pushed his fingers off mine—"stop! I need to take responsibility—"

"Do not test me any further tonight," he said through gritted teeth, leaning toward me, "or I swear, I'll—"

"You'll what? What more can you possibly do?"

"Don't you dare complain again about my choice to help you."

"You hired someone to make me sick and helpless."

"I spared the rod and spoiled the child, is what I did."

"I'm 'A Responsible Woman,'" I said, and the words echoed across the hospital's walls and stopped the silenced ladies from pacing. "I'm the person who wrote that letter to Judge Acklen in Saturday's paper, and I'm more of a suffragist now than when you first hired Henry to control me. You struck a match and lit a fire."

Father's chin quivered. "Well . . ." He fumbled for his handkerchief in his coat pocket. "It's a damned good thing Mr. Reverie—or Rhodes, or whatever the hell his name is—

it's a damned good thing he might already be dead, because I would love more than anything to kill him right now."

"No, *you* did this to me. You made me want to fight. And I bet you did this to Mother, too."

"Women belong—"

I covered my ears. "I don't want to hear any more of your theories about women. I want you to go home and live by yourself, because I'm done living with you and cooking for you and worrying about you drinking away your misery. If Henry is gone, then I'm taking Genevieve to San Francisco. If he's able to take her himself, then I'm traveling to New York. My bags are already packed."

"Olivia—"

"All is well." I closed my eyes and kept my hands over my ears.

Father didn't respond. When I raised my lashes, all I saw was an eight-year-old boy in a long evening coat and an oversized silk hat. He backed toward the hospital's front entrance in shoes too big for his feet, his lips sputtering to find something more to say.

A tear slid down my cheek to my mouth.

"You and your mother deserve each other," said the boy, and he slipped out the door—his most painful extraction yet.

CHAPTER TWENTY-SIX

A QUIET VIGIL

A round nine o'clock at night, Mr. Underhill, John, and two waiters from the party lugged in baskets full of leftover food. Mrs. Underhill greeted them with flailing arms and an attack of noiseless mouthed words.

"I don't know what you're saying, Margaret." Mr. Underhill plunked down a bottle of wine on a small lobby table and squinted at his wife's lips. "I know you're upsct we all laughed, but it was funny at the moment, dear."

Mrs. Underhill slugged him in the arm.

"Ouch! Margaret!"

Eugenia shot up and yelled without words as well.

"I don't know what either of you are saying." Mr. Underhill scratched his head. "This is all very frustrating. We'll check back here when you're calmer. Come along, John."

The gentlemen grabbed hold of each other and retreated as quickly as they'd arrived.

Sadie tore open one of the baskets and scooped out wrapped breads, cakes, and crab salad.

My stomach refused to register hunger. Beside me on our shared bench, Genevieve held her arms around herself and shivered.

"Do you know how to undo the hypnosis?" I asked her.

She shook her head. "Uncle Lewis only ever wanted me to provide the accompaniment. At most, he'd make me the human plank and show how he could break boulders with a sledgehammer on top of me."

I winced. "Oh. Well . . . then I suppose I've committed my worst transgression yet."

"What's that?"

I leaned forward and sank my head into my hands. "I made a group of women entirely dependent on a man."

OUR QUIET VIGIL FOR HENRY STRETCHED LATE INTO THE night, with no news of his health from any of the doctors. Mrs. Underhill shared some of the food with Genevieve and me, an act that drove another spike of guilt through my heart. These women were my equals, I realized, as we sat there and dined as a group in the lobby. Despite our differences in wealth and political opinions, they were no better than me.

And . . . I was no better than them.

The nurse at the front desk fetched us glasses of water around eleven thirty, but she left her station at midnight, and the hospital slept. The lobby was transformed into an uncomfortable bedroom for seven females in lace and silk gowns, plus a fifteen-year-old girl in a gray traveling dress who should have been on her way to San Francisco.

I kept my arm around Genevieve on our creaking bench and refused to drift off until I heard her soft snores against my shoulder. Her flushed red cheeks radiated the heat of a fever.

Both Reveries were slipping out of my reach.

AT ONE POINT DURING THE NIGHT, I SLEPT ENOUGH TO dream I was typing up an article for a suffrage newspaper in an apartment overlooking the brick buildings of Barnard College. Below my opened window, young women walked the green grounds with books tucked under their arms.

Mother—her curls still red and soft, her white dress fragrant with the tea-rose perfume I remembered from our rocking-chair days—walked over to me with a smile on her lips.

"This came for you, Livie," she said, and she set a postcard on the desk beside my typewriter.

On the front of the card was an illustration of Market

Street in San Francisco, with cable cars trekking down the center of the road between flag-topped skyscrapers.

I flipped the postcard over to read the note.

All is well, ma chérie.

I awoke with a start and disturbed Genevieve with my elbow.

"What's happening?" she asked—just a shadow of a girl in the hospital's dim, early-morning light.

"Genevieve," I said in a whisper, "do you remember Henry saying, because of my Halloween birthday, I'm a charmed individual who can read dreams?"

"Mmm. I think so."

"Was he making that up?"

"I don't know." She shrugged against my arm. "Sometimes he just seems like a talented boy with a wild imagination. Other times . . . I don't know . . . Sometimes all his magic feels real."

"Well"—I snuggled back down beside her, this time with my head on her shoulder—"if it is true, then we're going to be all right. Soon."

"Hmm. I like your dreams," she said, and we eased back into sleep a while longer.

DAYLIGHT PUSHED THROUGH THE DRAFTY LOBBY WIN-dows sometime after seven in the morning. Across the room from me, the anti-suffragists wilted across the chairs and the benches, their colors as filmy as the delicate wings of moths. Genevieve rested her head against the armrest beside me and wavered between light and shadow.

The echo of approaching footsteps stirred us all out of our melancholy.

A doctor in a white coat similar to Father's dentistry garb approached a new nurse at the front desk—a petite woman with big dark eyes who reminded me of ladies from Coca-Cola advertisements.

"Miss Reverie," called the nurse, and all eight of us lobby dwellers sat up straight.

Genevieve, now a solid streak of a girl, jumped to her feet and walked over to the front desk. The doctor put his arm around her back, rumpling her long golden hair, and whisked her off to the far reaches of the hospital. I imagined her traveling in the central elevator that transported patients up and down floors without them needing to climb out of beds, and I hoped she was soaring upward, not down to the morgue.

Oh, Lord.

The morgue.

I stood up, wrapped my arms around my ribs, and paced the worn rug the way the silent anti-suffragists had done the night before. Sadie and the other girls and their mothers watched me with fear in the blacks of their pupils. When I wiped away tears, their eyes watered, and they sniffed along with me.

"I'm sorry," I said, and I spun in the opposite direction with a swift whoosh of purple satin. "You were all just so cruel. Why'd you have to be so awful to me?"

They didn't answer, of course, so I continued pacing.

"No one should ever be silenced. Not you. Not me. Not any other woman or man. Please, open your eyes and see"—I stopped and swept my gaze across every single one of them—"we're all on the same side. We're all being treated as second-class citizens. Why are you just sitting beside your husbands and fathers and accepting this rubbish?"

Their dead-eyed lack of a response troubled me more than if they had shouted vicious retorts. I left the hospital and walked the length of Irving Street for the better part of an hour, crunching through thick piles of leaves and brushing my hand across brittle overhead branches.

When I returned—no wiser or calmer than when I'd left—I found Genevieve standing on the front steps in Henry's black coat, her hands hidden inside the sleeves. A gentle wind tugged on her skirts and loose hair.

"The fool still wasn't eating or drinking," she called down to me. "The doctor said he had an attack of fatigue and anxiety. They're feeding him his third meal since his arrival right now, and he's dopey with laudanum. His chest hurt him too much to breathe."

A smile stretched across my face. "He's alive, then?"

She nodded.

I ran up the steps. "You saw him?"

"He's eating and restoring those ladies' voices as we speak. The men's ward is a circus, but the staff members were getting tired of seeing millionaires' wives and daughters glaring like vultures in the lobby."

"May I see him?"

She shook her head. "Not until he's discharged. They made an exception for the hypnotized women."

I joined her inside, and another long bout of painful waiting ensued, interrupted early on by the society ladies in their red, white, and blue dresses, parading out to the hospital's exit from somewhere in the back. They spoke again—I heard complaints about sore backs and idiotic husbands mainly—but the return of those voices allowed me to better breathe.

Before she reached the front door with the others, Sadie turned her face my way, and I braced myself for bared teeth or a verbal dart that would make me feel even worse than I already did about the silencing.

She offered neither.

But I saw her—the true Sadie, a newer version. The rest of the hospital dulled around her, and she brightened before my eyes, a girl in plaid trousers and a thick red tie, with a bouquet of yellow ribbons pinned to her left shoulder. I swear she even offered me a smile of camaraderie, but perhaps that was my imagination stretching too far.

In any case, Mademoiselle Sadie Eiderling, the beer baron's daughter, left the hospital that morning a burgeoning suffragist and a modern woman.

Of that, I'm certain.

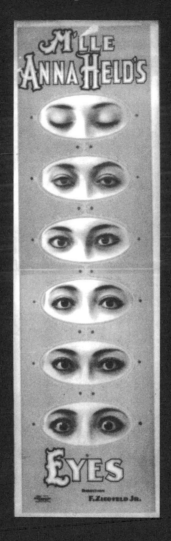

"Perhaps it is better to wake up after all, even to suffer, rather than to remain a dupe to illusions all one's life."

— KATE CHOPIN, *The Awakening*, 1899

CHAPTER TWENTY-SEVEN

AWAKE UNTO ME

Near three o'clock in the afternoon, Henry materialized. Not from a cloud of orange smoke on a stage but from the back hallway of the hospital— a far more impressive feat, considering the state of him the night before. His red vest and black necktie dangled over his arm, and he wore just his striped shirtsleeves and trousers and a pair of brown suspenders.

Genevieve and I sprang up from the bench and hurried toward him. I lagged behind a couple of feet so she could embrace him first.

She clamped his middle like a vise. "Are you all right?"

"I am," he told her. "No need to worry anymore."

She lowered her arms, and Henry moved on to me with an embarrassed-looking smile and a warm hug. His lips nuzzled against my hair near the top of my head.

"That wasn't part of the plan, Monsieur Reverie," I said into the soft sheen of his shirt.

"Those women were in a hell of a panic, weren't they?"

"We all were."

"I know." He rubbed my back. "I'm sorry."

"What about the hospital bill, Henry?" asked Genevieve.

"I told them to send it to Anne's house in San Francisco."

"Did Genevieve tell you about Frannie's collection?" I asked.

"Yes, that was far too kind. I'm deeply grateful." He stepped back and regarded my purple gown, his hand in mine. "You never went home last night?"

"I'm never going back home. Father knows."

"New York City, then?"

"Yes." I gave a small nod and a weak smile.

He swallowed as if tasting a bitter pill.

Genevieve cleared her throat. "Our bags are at the hotel. We still have the rooms if you want to change first. There's a nearby streetcar if you're too tired to walk all that way."

Henry dropped his hand away from mine. "Then let's get going. I don't want to think about this departure much longer."

· · · · ·

BRUSHED AND SCRUBBED AND DRESSED IN MY ORDINARY brown skirt and winter coat, I stood in front of Henry and Genevieve on the vast tile floor of Portland's Union Depot, waiting to purchase a railroad ticket that would take me up through Washington and then east. By the time I reached the ticket counter, my hands were sweating. I dropped my slick coins all over the place.

"I'm sorry," I said to the grandfatherly man working the counter, and I caught a nickel before it clanked to the ground. "I'm a little nervous."

"Going on a grand adventure?" he asked.

"That's my hope."

I sorted out the money, and in a matter of seconds I clutched a ticket between my fingers. The Rhodeses purchased their southbound fares and tucked the papers in their coat pockets.

Henry peeked at my ticket over my shoulder. "Your train leaves soon. We had better walk you out to the platform."

I nodded and ventured outside the depot with the two of them by my side.

A black locomotive breathed white steam on the north-bound tracks, while arriving travelers climbed out of the green passenger cars in their winter hats and traveling coats. Porters in blue jackets and caps lugged large leather bags and pointed the lost in the correct directions.

"Henry." I grabbed his arm before we strayed too far from the bright terra-cotta bricks of the main building. "Don't forget, I'm still under hypnosis."

"Ah." He swung around to face me. "I was wondering if you wanted to let go of that one lingering part."

"Of course I do. I don't want to keep seeing the world the way it truly is."

He cocked his head. "Are you sure about that?"

"Help her, Henry." Genevieve pushed at his shoulder. "Don't you dare leave her stuck like that."

"I want my mind to be entirely my own," I added.

"Olivia 'Scorcher' Mead . . ." Henry cracked a smile, and the corners of his eyes crinkled with amusement. "There's no doubt at all that your mind has remained your own this entire time."

"Do it quickly, eh, before she needs to go." Genevieve backed away with her plump black case—the smallest of their bags. "I'll even leave you two alone for a few minutes if you want to be by yourselves."

"You don't have—"

"Do it." Genevieve turned and wandered off to the opposite side of the platform.

Henry lowered their two larger bags to the ground beside him, which prompted me to set my Gladstone next to my feet alongside my skirt. We stood up straight and faced each other.

"Close your eyes—they're exceptionally heavy." He cupped my cheek, and my eyes fell shut, as if lead lined my lashes. "Keep them closed," he said in a voice soft and lush, and he pulled my body toward him. "Your lids are now stuck together. Try opening them."

I couldn't.

"Good. Very good. I am now going to stroke the back of your neck with my free hand, and each caress will send you deeper and deeper into hypnosis." He rubbed his palm down the base of my neck, over the topmost vertebrae. "Do you feel that wonderful sense of relaxation?"

"Yesss," I whispered from somewhere inside a deep, delicious pocket of darkness.

"Now, listen carefully, because what I am about to say is extremely important." His breath warmed my ear. "You will see the world the way it has always been. You will ensure your mind remains your own and never, ever allow a hypnotist or a domineering suitor or your father—or anyone else—to alter your thoughts beyond your control. Do you understand?"

"Yesss. My mind . . . will remain . . . my own."

"You will not allow people like Percy Acklen to make you feel as though you're lesser than they."

"I . . ." I tried to reach my fingers up to Henry's hand on my cheek, but my arm was built of limp rubber.

"Will you promise, Olivia? Don't let people like him make you feel like dirt."

"I promise."

"Your mind will remain your own."

"Yesss."

I heard him swallow. "I am going to wake you up now. Are you ready?"

I nodded on the wobbly hinge of my neck.

"I'll count forward to ten—we'll take it slowly. One . . . two . . . three . . ."

"I want . . . to make sure . . . you're going to be . . . all right, too."

He lowered his hand from my face. *"Pardonnez-moi?"*

My eyes stayed shut, still too thick and dense to unseal, and my tongue remained heavy and cumbersome. "I feel . . . the urge . . . to tell you . . . things. Waking up . . . might change . . . my boldness."

"It won't."

"You're only . . . eighteen. Hospitalized . . . chest pains. Fatigue. Collapsed. Just eighteen. I can't . . . be with you . . . need to be . . . on my own. But . . . I care . . . about you."

"I'm all right."

"No. Not convinced."

He was silent, and for a moment I just stood there with my arms dangling by my sides, relaxing in the mesmerizing hold of peaceful blackness.

"Are you ready to wake up now?" he asked.

"Swear . . . you'll take care . . . of yourself."

"I—"

"Swear. Let me speak . . . with less heaviness."

His thumb traced my jawline. "All right. You're easing upward to a lesser stage of relaxation. Keep rising up . . . up . . . up. Your tongue is no longer heavy. You can talk with clarity."

My tongue loosened and stretched inside my mouth. I licked my drying lips.

"What did you want to say?" he asked with hesitation.

"There's beauty in this world, Henry, and not everyone dies young. There's so much hope. There's so much work, too—ridiculous amounts of work—but above all, hope. I've seen it out there, alongside the darkness. Look at Frannie and what she did. Look at the times we had together."

He didn't answer. His hand trembled against my face.

"Henry?"

"I'll count forward," he said, a quaver in his voice, "slowly, so you can come up gently. One . . . two . . . three . . ."

"Were you listening to me, Henry?"

"Yes."

"Will you put yourself back together?"

"Yes."

"Promise?"

"*Mon Dieu*, Olivia"—he emitted a weak flutter of a laugh—"are you hypnotizing me while under hypnosis?"

"We're partners, remember?"

"Yes, I definitely remember."

"Then let my words persuade you to become the type of person you're not afraid of looking at in the mirror. If you think your life is a farce, Henry, then change it."

"All right. I'll fix myself up."

"Promise?"

"Yes. If it means that much to you, then . . . yes." A self-relaxing breath loosened his voice. "Um . . . where was I?"

"Four," I said. "And I want you to open up your eyes, too, when we get to ten. Five . . ."

"All right." He took another breath. "Six . . ."

"Seven," I said.

"Eight . . ."

"Nine . . ."

He removed his hand from my face. "Ten."

We awoke, and I took a long look around me. Passengers and porters hurried about, and a train's black smokestack hissed with impatience. In front of me, a boy blinked to keep his eyes dry before letting me go.

"They have to remove her whole breast," he said. "It's a fairly new procedure, but it's the only thing that will save her. She'll have a better chance than our mother did."

I cast my eyes down to Genevieve waiting on a bench with her leather bag. "She looks brave." I peeked back up at him. "And so do you. You'll both be strong for each other."

He nodded without breathing.

I reached up and kissed his lips, which faltered beneath mine. We clasped our arms around each other and hugged instead, and Henry whispered in my ear, *"Un jour, lorsque tu es prête, on se reverra encore."*

"What does that mean?" I asked with the left side of my face pressed against his shoulder.

"One day, when you are ready, we will meet again."

No words found their way to my mouth. My eyes welled with tears and turned Genevieve's brown coat and gray skirt, down the way, into blurs.

A blue-capped conductor checked his pocket watch and called out, "All aboard," and a crowd of people clamored forward to the passenger cars.

Genevieve shot off her bench and jogged past them all to reach me.

"Thank you." She grabbed my face and kissed my wet cheek. "Thank you for your help. Please send me Frannie's address so I may write to her."

"Oh, that reminds me"—I pulled a piece of paper out of my coat pocket—"here's my mother's address." I slipped the paper into Henry's hands. "Please promise to send me a postcard when Genevieve has recovered."

Everyone bustled past us as if they couldn't get on board quickly enough. Time shoved against me.

Henry grabbed hold of my hand, and I kissed him again—a proper good-bye kiss, just in case we were about to turn into mere memories for each other. He pulled me against him by my waist, and we stayed together until the conductor shouted his last boarding call.

I broke loose and climbed aboard the train without looking back at either of them.

A young black Pullman porter in a white coat greeted me at the head of the aisle. "May I help you with your luggage, miss?"

"Yes, thank you." I handed him my bag, and for a moment I saw straight through him to the green floral rug running down the aisle.

No, I told myself, and I rubbed at my eyes. *No—you see the world the way it has always been.*

I followed the porter, and four seats in we passed a man with engorged lips and his dissolving wife, whose neck bled in a bright red bloom.

"No! Oh, no." I turned to leave.

Two young ladies in wide-brimmed hats maneuvered their bags up the aisle and blocked my exit.

"Oh, dear, are you trying to get off?" asked the woman in front, turning sideways.

"I just . . ." I cupped my hand over my forehead and heard the rustle of paper in the left sleeve of my blouse.

"Personally, I think you're traveling in the right direction," said the second woman, who had a distinctive glow in her cheeks. "This train passes through Idaho, where women voted yesterday. That's where we're headed."

"I don't know where I'm going."

I swiveled back around and grabbed hold of the wooden backs of seats to navigate my way down the aisle behind the porter. The floor swayed and bobbed below my feet, as if in a dream. I reached under my left sleeve and drew out a folded piece of paper that had been stuffed up there like the tickets Henry had snuck into my glove while we were in the restaurant with Percy.

Another message, written in the same hand as that previous note, met my eyes.

I believe you have always seen the vampires and the fading souls in the world, Olivia. You just never paid close attention to them before. As I've learned through my own ordeals, once you start viewing the world the way it truly is, it is impossible to ignore both its beauty and its ugliness. Look around you.

You can't stop seeing it, can you?

I glanced up and witnessed a girl near my age with a bruise swelling near her eye. A second later, her body puffed into a thin haze of smoke.

A young bearded man with burning coals for irises glared at the black porter walking by him with my bag, and I swore I saw the man tying a rope into a noose.

My eyes strayed back to the message.

There is some of the unexplainable in me, ma chérie, but there is also a great deal of enchantment in you. Keep telling the world what you see.

Help others to see it, too.

I dropped into an empty seat and slid across the bench to the window. Using my fist, I rubbed a circle against the condensation fogging up the glass.

Down below, Henry and Genevieve roamed the length of

the car with their bags at their sides and craned their necks, as if they were looking for me as well. With a frenzied wave, I caught Henry's eye, and I pressed the letter against the glass. He stopped and gave a small nod.

The train lurched forward, and the Rhodeses stood there on the platform, amid other travelers in black and gray and the faded browns of the autumn leaves. They blended in with the surroundings, and I held my breath in fear of them going one step farther and disappearing.

"Don't fade," I said. "Please don't fade."

Time seemed poised to swallow them up, but before the train chugged past them, a switch flipped. Henry and Genevieve ignited into the blaze of colors from their Halloween performance, Henry in his bold crimson vest and Genevieve in her peacock-blue gown. I pushed my palm harder against the glass to see them more clearly—a beautiful, blinding brilliance.

Another light flared to life in the glass—the reflection of a girl with an ordinary face and unremarkable black hair, but she shone like the brightest stage lights of the Metropolitan.

The train clacked onward, gathering speed. My reflection remained, but the Reveries fell out of my view. I felt them around me, though, in the velvet-padded seats, between the strangers. Henry and Genevieve. Frannie and Kate. Agnes, Gerda, and Mr. and Mrs. Harrison. Even Mother and Father. They were all there, everyone a part of me, by my side, making sure I stayed on that train until I reached my destination.

ACKNOWLEDGMENTS

I'M EXTREMELY GRATEFUL TO THE FOLLOWING INDIVIDU-
als and organizations.

My husband and two kids, my parents, my sister, and the
rest of my close family and friends, for *always* being supportive of my dreams, even when they've seemed impossible.

My agent, Barbara Poelle, for becoming an instant
champion of this book as soon as she read the first chapters.

My editor, Maggie Lehrman, for believing in me a second
time around and for spinning her magic to make my work
shine.

The rest of the team at Abrams: Susan Van Metre, Tamar
Brazis, Laura Mihalick, Jason Wells, Maria T. Middleton
(designer extraordinaire!), Tina Mories in the UK, the
copyeditor, proofreaders, and everyone else who played a
role in making this book as strong as it could possibly be and
putting it into the hands of readers. Such diligent work is
much appreciated.

My early readers, Carrie Raleigh, Kim Murphy, Francesca Miller, Adam Karp, and Meggie, for their enthusiasm and much-needed feedback.

Miriam Forster, Teri Brown, Amber J. Keyser, and Kelly Garrett—my Thursday Morning Coffee and Writing Team—for getting me out of the house!

My fellow members of The Lucky 13s, Corsets, Cutlasses, & Candlesticks, and SCBWI Oregon, whom I can always count on for advice, emotional support, and exuberant cheers of celebration.

The Mark Twain Foundation, for assistance and permission to quote the great Mr. Clemens.

The Oregon Historical Society, the University of Oregon Libraries, the Library of Congress, the National Library of Medicine, and the Women of the West Museum, for their indispensable research archives.

David Burke, Wade Major, Oliver Fabris, and Jamie Lucero for their help with Henri Reverie's French. *Merci!* Any errors in translation are entirely my own.

Last of all, my deepest gratitude extends to every single woman and man who fought to end inequality at the voting polls in the United States and elsewhere. Their sacrifices and struggles to give the silenced a voice should never be forgotten.

May equality spread even farther across the globe in the very near future.

WHEN AND WHERE U.S. WOMEN
GAINED FULL SUFFRAGE

1869 Wyoming territory[1]

1893 Colorado

1896 Utah[2] and Idaho

1910 Washington State[3]

1911 California

1912 Oregon,[4] Kansas, and Arizona

1913 Alaska[5]

1914 Montana and Nevada

1917 New York

1918 Michigan, South Dakota, and Oklahoma

---

[1] Wyoming became a state in 1890, and Wyoming women retained the right to vote.
[2] Women in the territory of Utah were given full suffrage in 1870. In 1887 that right was taken away until Utah became a state in 1896.
[3] The territory of Washington briefly granted women, including African American women, full suffrage in 1883, but in 1887 the Territorial Supreme Court overturned that law.
[4] The men of Oregon voted down suffrage referendums in 1884, 1900, 1906, 1908, and 1910, before approving the sixth measure in 1911.
[5] The territory of Alaska granted women full suffrage forty-six years before it became a state in 1959.

August 26, 1920 The 19th Amendment to the Constitution is signed into law. Female U.S. citizens age twenty-one and older are granted the right to vote in all states.

1924 The Indian Citizenship Act gives Native Americans, both male and female, U.S. citizenship, yet Native Americans will not be granted suffrage in every state until 1962.

1965–2006 The U.S. government passes legislation to protect the voting rights of minorities, Americans with disabilities, and other citizens who had encountered obstacles in exercising their freedom to vote.

1971 The voting age is dropped to eighteen in all fifty states.

RECOMMENDED READING

Bly, Nellie. *Ten Days in a Mad-House.* New York: Ian L. Munro, 1887.

Browning, John Edgar (ed.). *Bram Stoker's Dracula: The Critical Feast.* Berkeley, Calif.: Apocryphile Press, 2011.

Crichton, Judy. *America 1900: The Turning Point.* New York: Henry Holt, Inc., 1998.

Edwards, G. Thomas. *Sowing Good Seeds: The Northwest Suffrage Campaigns of Susan B. Anthony.* Portland: Oregon Historical Society, 1990.

John, Finn J. D. *Wicked Portland: The Wild and Lusty Underworld of a Frontier Seaport Town,* Charleston, S.C.: History Press, 2012.

Lansing, Jewel. *Portland: People, Politics, and Power, 1851–2001.* Corvallis: Oregon State University Press, 2005.

McGill, Ormond. *The New Encyclopedia of Stage Hypnotism.* Bethel, Conn.: Crown House Publishing, 1996.

Nation, Carry Amelia. *The Use and Need of the Life of Carry A. Nation.* Topeka, Kans.: F. M. Steves & Sons, 1908. (*Note:* Newspapers in 1900 spelled Mrs. Nation's name "Carrie," which is believed to be the official spelling. However, she opted to use "Carry" for her temperance campaign and autobiography.)

Ross-Nazzal, Jennifer M. *Winning the West for Women: The Life of Suffragist Emma Smith Devoe.* Seattle: University of Washington Press, 2011.

Sherr, Lynn. *Failure Is Impossible: Susan B. Anthony in Her Own Words.* New York: Times Books, 1995.

Streeter, Michael. *Hypnosis: Secrets of the Mind.* Hauppauge, N.Y.: Barron's, 2004.

Twain, Mark. "Happy Memories of the Dental Chair." In *Who Is Mark Twain?*, 77–86. New York: HarperCollins, 2009.

Ward, Jean M., and Elaine A. Maveety (eds.). *"Yours for Liberty": Selections from Abigail Scott Duniway's Suffrage Newspaper.* Corvallis: Oregon State University Press, 2000.

Winter, Alison. *Mesmerized: Powers of Mind in Victorian Britain.* Chicago: University of Chicago Press, 1998.

Wynbrandt, James. *The Excruciating History of Dentistry: Toothsome Tales & Oral Oddities from Babylon to Braces.* New York: St. Martin's Griffin, 2000.

By the same author

Witold Rybczynski

Waiting for
the Weekend

VIKING

VIKING
Published by the Penguin Group
Viking Penguin, a division of Penguin Books USA Inc.,
375 Hudson Street, New York, New York 10014, U.S.A.
Penguin Books Ltd, 27 Wrights Lane,
London W8 5TZ, England
Penguin Books Australia Ltd, Ringwood,
Victoria, Australia
Penguin Books Canada Ltd, 2801 John Street,
Markham, Ontario, Canada L3R 1B4
Penguin Books (N.Z.) Ltd, 182–190 Wairau Road,
Auckland 10, New Zealand

Penguin Books Ltd, Registered Offices:
Harmondsworth, Middlesex, England

First published in 1991 by Viking Penguin,
a division of Penguin Books USA Inc.

10 9 8 7 6 5 4 3 2 1

Copyright © Witold Rybczynski, 1991
All rights reserved

LIBRARY OF CONGRESS CATALOGING-IN-PUBLICATION DATA
Rybczynski, Witold.
Waiting for the weekend / Witold Rybczynski.
p. cm.
Includes bibliographical references and index.
ISBN 0-670-83001-1
1. Leisure. 2. Recreation. I. Title.
GV174.R94 1991
790.01'35—dc20 90-50760

Printed in the United States of America
Set in Bembo
Designed by Marysarah Quinn

For Shirley Hallam

The days that make us happy make us wise.

—JOHN MASEFIELD

Contents

Waiting for
the Weekend

one

Free Time

Early this morning, before sitting down to write, I listened, once again, to Vivaldi's *The Four Seasons*. I have heard this work so often that the ordered progression of notes holds few surprises, but the melodious singing of the conversing violins still touches me. It is the mystery of music that repeated listenings bring more, not less pleasure.

I am sure I would enjoy the four concertos if they were merely titled Opus 8 (of which they are actually the first part), but like most listeners I am attracted to the images suggested by the lyrical title. My father, who is a musician, disapproves of my admiration for this popular work—I think he considers its conceit maudlin—but I find the descriptive character of the pieces engaging. And, regarding the theme, Vivaldi was explicit, for when the concertos were published, in 1725, he included in the manuscript score the text of four clarifying sonnets—possibly of his own writ-

ing—which he keyed to the music by guide letters. The sonnets depicted the changing climate of the four seasons, and portrayed nature as a backdrop for various rural scenes: a goatherd and his barking dog, peasants celebrating the harvest, a huntsman setting out at first light, the comfort of a winter fireside. The score, in turn, represented these scenes, often imitatively: the solo violin taking the part of the lounging goatherd, and the violas his barking dog; the songs of a goldfinch, a turtledove, and a cuckoo were also musically rendered.

Antonio Vivaldi was a native of Venice, where he was choirmaster at a girls' orphanage. Although he was a priest, he composed secular as well as religious music, and his reputation as a violinist and composer (he wrote more than forty operas) spread throughout northern Italy, where he was known as *il Prete Rosso*— the Red Priest—on account of his red hair. Eventually he was acclaimed in all the musical centers of Europe.*
It is hardly surprising, then, that when *The Four Seasons* appeared, it achieved immediate and widespread popularity. The work was, to some extent, a towns-

---

* Vivaldi's fame was short-lived, and after his death he and his music were forgotten. It was not until the middle of the nineteenth century that his music began to be listened to anew, and more than a hundred years later before it returned to widespread public favor— there is still no separate entry for Vivaldi in my 1949 edition of the *Encyclopaedia Britannica*.

man's celebration of the pastoral—a celebration that is poignant since the composer was sickly and often housebound—and it fashionably reflected the eighteenth century's artistic preoccupation with the idealization of "Nature." But one did not need to be an artist to appreciate the music; its popularity had a lot to do with the familiarity of its subject.

During the eighteenth century, the change of seasons had a considerable influence on everyday life, and for most of Vivaldi's original audience, *The Four Seasons* vividly described a reality that was immediately recognizable. At different times of year one ate different foods, wore different clothes, indulged in different recreations, performed different agricultural tasks, even inhabited different parts of the house—in Italian country villas, for instance, the rooms on the sunny south side were used in the winter, those on the north side during the hot months. The varying length of the summer and winter day in a city such as Venice affected human behavior. Summers were for sitting on the terrace in front of the Caffè Florian; early winter dusk hurried people indoors. Last, and not least, domestic comfort varied according to the season; the cold, damp winters in poorly heated stone apartments made spring all the more welcome.

The comfort of my own home is largely undisturbed by the time of year—electric lighting, efficient heating, and proper insulation have seen to that.

Since, unlike my neighbors, I am not a farmer, the weather doesn't affect my livelihood. Nevertheless, gardening, storing firewood for the winter, raking leaves, walking the dog, and simply eating breakfast on the porch have made me aware of different times of year in a more acute way than when I lived in a city. A patch of gray cloud, glimpsed between tall buildings as one hurried down the street, could be ignored; in the open country, a looming gray sky can affect the course of my entire day. A storm in town always seemed to be taking place somewhere else; here, thunderclaps batter my house unrelentingly, and the lightning is sometimes so close it smells. That is why, although I have listened to this recording of *The Four Seasons* for more than twenty years, the familiar music has recently found a new resonance in my own life.

There are probably several reasons for this delayed appreciation. I was brought up in cities and towns, where seasonal variation was less noticeable—at least to me. With the insouciance of childhood, I was indifferent to the elements: playing in the snow until my fingers started turning numb inside the soggy mittens, or splashing about on a cold Maine beach, happy despite shivering skin and chattering teeth. Of course, I remember the various annual activities— summer swimming, winter skiing, helping my father in the garden in the spring, playing football in the

fall—but these took place in a vague continuum of changing weather to which, like most children, I gave little thought.

The progression itself of the times of year left little imprint on my consciousness. What I remember more vividly is the rhythmic cadence of the week—days at home and days at school. Probably this rotation has stuck in my mind because I disliked school. My earliest recollection (but it may be only a recollection of what was told me later—an oft-repeated family story) is of being taken for the first time to a London convent school and immediately running away, tearfully rejoining my departing father in the street. A companion memory involves Sundays—not accompanying my parents to church, but being sent to a corner pub for my weekly treat: an exotic imported bottle of Coca-Cola. The texture of the heavy, knurled glass bottle and the smell of the oak casks and beer are with me still.

For most of my boyhood, schooldays retained their coercive character. When I was eleven years old, living in Canada, I was sent to a boarding school in Montreal. We lived close to the city, and I was able to return home each Friday evening. I was attached to my parents, and Sunday afternoons unfailingly brought lachrymose departures. What emotion, what unhappiness! I might have been a cabin boy being sent away on a three-year voyage aboard a clipper ship

instead of a grade-schooler going only thirty miles away, and only for five days. But five days was an eternity to someone whose horizon extended only as far as the next Friday evening.

The following year I became a commuter. During the week I rose at six o'clock and bicycled to the train station; in the winter there was a parental carpool. The train journey took about an hour. I liked trains—steam engines still, with real conductors wearing dark-blue uniforms and low-slung leather pouches—and the travel time passed pleasantly enough. There were several of us going to the same school and we sat together, doing homework, reading, and arguing—perfecting our Jesuitical debating skills. I also learned many card games. Still, I looked forward to the end of the week. There was homework to complete, and some household chores (not many, as I recall), but I could sleep late and play with my friends, go on outings in the countryside, or simply stay in my room, reading. For two days, my time was my own.

After my third year of high school I got a summer job on a local weekly newspaper. I worked in the print shop, operating a machine that produced plastic engravings of photographs and illustrations that were then glued to blocks of wood and placed in the form. This did not take all my time, and I also learned to run a terrifying paper-trimming guillotine. Occasionally I was allowed to set the lead slugs that were

spewed out of a rattling Linotype. Once a week, the large flatbed cylinder press that stood at the far end of the shop was started up, and we took turns feeding newsprint into the noisy machine. It was not unpleasant work, since the variety of the tasks assigned mitigated the monotony of what were really dull and repetitive operations. Still, when I pushed my time card into the punch-clock on Friday, I savored the satisfying and conclusive clang that signaled two days of freedom.

When I went to college, the personal liberty that I anticipated I would enjoy as a university student—"The best years of your life," adults assured me—was slow to materialize. I was confronted by a rigorous and crowded classroom schedule that left me little free time during the day. Students of architecture were obliged to take two years of engineering, and I struggled with chemistry, physics, and calculus, subjects for which my classical education had left me unprepared and which consequently engaged me not at all. Nor did it help that the classes were large and anonymous; mine was simply one more unformed face in a crowd of more or less interested freshmen (and in engineering they *were* mostly men), dutifully scribbling notes on their clipboards.

Of course, it wasn't all work. I joined a rifle club, but the initial attraction—I had never owned a gun—wore off quickly, and I soon tired of the noisy and

dark firing range. I became a member of a drama group and happily worked first as a stage manager and later as a set designer. What free time I had was now spent either hanging around the basement office of the Players Club, in rehearsals, or caught up in the excitement of producing plays. The theater not only got me out of the intellectual wasteland of the faculty of engineering and introduced me to Fernando Arrabal and Dylan Thomas, it also brought me into the company of actors, and so allowed me to meet girls.

What with commuting, and attending a boy's school, my experience of the opposite sex was scant, which made my induction into that important university institution—Saturday Night—all the more memorable. I had to learn the unwritten protocols of dating that, during the early 1960s, represented society's vain attempt to control adolescent libidos. There were forms to be observed: the anxious weekday phone call, the formalities of dress, the proprieties of hand-holding, and the delicate progression of necking.

The chief convention of the date was the pretext of going out—usually to a party or to a movie. I developed a taste for jazz, and spent my weekend nights at clubs and bars, listening to visiting American stars: Bill Evans, Charles Mingus, Thelonious Monk, and the great drummer Max Roach. My interest in the last was partly occupational, for I, too, played

drums. Since my two roommates were musicians, we played together on weekends, sometimes at jam sessions, occasionally for pay. Two days a week I was a nocturnal hipster. It was the early sixties, and although we grew beards and wore sunglasses—shades—we did not consider ourselves Beats; like the musicians whom we admired, we dressed in conservative three-piece suits and drank Scotch on the rocks. We took our music more seriously than our studies.

My double life ended when I left the university and got a job—as an architect's assistant, not a drummer, for by then my performing career had faltered. But working in an office, as I already knew from my summer experiences, meant that the familiar five-and-two rhythm persisted, reinforced now by the contractual obligation I had to my employer. I enjoyed my job, and often looked archly down on the crowd of office workers that streamed out of our building punctually at five o'clock at the end of each day. My co-workers and I often kept longer hours, meeting the frequent deadlines that characterize architectural practice; still, were we so different? We would have hated to admit it, but we, too, looked forward to the end of the week.

A historical shift has occurred in timekeeping between Vivaldi's time, and my own—a shift from the pastoral to the industrial, from the natural to the artificial. I could not describe my life in four concertos

but in recurring variations—the Weekend Variations: carefree and playful schoolboy weekends at home; college weekends, livelier now, not just jazz but the sweet fumbling of adolescent infatuation; a young man's nighttime weekends, full of drink, talk, and alternating loneliness and romance.

Because my free time was personally enjoyed, I imagined that it was personally regulated, but this was not quite so. True, I did what I thought I wanted, but certainly not *when* I wanted; I dutifully arranged my recreations to fall in step with the regularly scheduled weekly intermissions that were accorded me. Not that I felt this was an imposition. It was done so automatically, it seemed so normal, that I never gave the presence of the weekend a second thought—it was simply the way life was.

That was twenty years ago. The sovereignty of the weekend has, if anything, grown in the interval, and it now conditions our behavior to an even greater degree. On Monday mornings we recount our weekend adventures and commiserate with one another as we begin a week of labor. By Tuesday, the weekend is slipping into memory. Wednesday is called "Midweek" in German, and it is exactly that—a hiatus. On Thursday we begin to anticipate the weekend. We listen uneasily to the divinations of the weatherman—will there be snow for skiing, or good weather for the beach?—as we anxiously make preparations for

the weekend. "Thank God It's Friday"—a phrase of the sixties—flags the end of the week, or rather the beginning of the weekend. Another signal of the weekend, at least in California, is "Jeans Friday," when many offices suspend their normal dress codes and let their employees dress as they please; in Hawaii, "Aloha Friday" is observed by wearing colorful print shirts.

The word "weekend," which started life as the grammatically correct "week-end," lost its hyphen somewhere along the way, ceasing to be merely the end of the week and acquiring, instead, an autonomous and sovereign existence. "Have a good weekend," we say to each other, never "Have a good week." Where once the week consisted of weekdays and Sunday, it now comprises weekdays and the weekend. Ask most people to name the first day of the week and they will answer "Monday, of course"; fifty years ago the answer would have been Sunday. Wall calendars still show Sunday as the first day of the week, and children are taught the days of the week starting with Sunday, but how long will these conventions last? Sunday, once the day of rest, has become merely one of two days of what is often strenuous activity. Although we continue to celebrate the traditional religious and civic holidays—holy days—these now account for only a small portion of our total nonworking days, and are overshadowed by

the 104 days of secular weekends—more, if you count long weekends.

The long weekend probably began accidentally, when a public holiday occurring on a Friday or a Monday happily added a day to the weekend. One of the first predictable long weekends in Canada and the United States occurred when the first Monday in September—Labor Day—was declared a legal holiday. Columbus Day, and lately Martin Luther King Day, followed suit; so did Thanksgiving in Canada. The American Thanksgiving was set on a Thursday, which for many means a four-day weekend. In the case of traditional national holidays that do not fall on a Monday, such as Independence Day or Canada Day, although official celebrations are held on the appointed date, it is not uncommon for employers to shift the actual day off to make it an appendage to the weekend.

These sanctioned long weekends seem to have whetted our appetite, with the result that additional do-it-yourself long weekends have proliferated. Surprisingly, they have done so at the expense of the traditional vacation. Many families choose to dispense with—or reduce—their two- or three-week holidays, and instead attach a sprinkling of days to weekends throughout the year. The weekend has also expanded in another way, as early-Friday-afternoon office closings have become commonplace, at least during the

summer. The pushy weekend seems destined to nib-
ble away at the week.

This new time structure is important, for it affects
not only *when* we relax but also *how* we relax. For
most of us, life assumes a different rhythm on the
weekend; we sleep in, cut the grass, wash the car. We
also go to the movies, especially during hot weather.
(The sixteen weekends between mid-May and Labor
Day are when Hollywood studios traditionally launch
their summer blockbusters—in 1990 there were fifty
movies jostling each other for box-office primacy.)
But the weekend is not merely an occasion for lazing
about. There are weekend sales to go to, weekend
rates to take advantage of, weekend discount tickets
to buy, weekend clothes to wear. And weekend bags
to pack for weekend invitations, for the weekend
means not only shopping and recreation, it also means
travel. The travel may be distant, but more likely it
takes the city dweller to the countryside on the outskirts of the city, to the cottage and the ski chalet.
There are entire towns and villages whose economic
life is centered on this weekend migration, and many
industries that rely on business generated by the two-
day break, such as do-it-yourself home-repair centers,
boatbuilders, and sports equipment manufacturers.

The weekend is a time for physical exercise and
games. Some of these pastimes, like tennis, have a
long history and a newfound popularity; others,

like whitewater canoeing, windsurfing, or hang glid-
ing, are more recent. Most are distinguished from
nineteenth-century recreations such as croquet and
golf by their relative arduousness and even riskiness.
These periodic bursts of physical activity have their
own consequences, however, and sports-medicine
clinics report a growing number of Monday-morning
injuries as weekend athletes recover from strained tennis elbows, jogging knees, and twisted skiing ankles.
Scraped elbows and peeling, sunburned noses are as
much a weekend institution as the lakeside cottage,
the yard sale, and the Sunday brunch.

And, of course, the Sunday paper. The first Sunday paper was the London *Observer,* which started in
1791, and soon had many competitors. The first
American Sunday paper was published in Baltimore,
in 1796, but it folded after one issue—the religious
tradition against selling papers on Sunday proved too
strong. In the post–Civil War era, attitudes changed
and Sunday editions of dailies appeared; by 1900 there
were 639 of them. The Sunday paper owes its present
form to Joseph Pulitzer, whose gaudy *Sunday World*
pioneered colored comics and the color supplement,
and included book reviews, exotic travel articles,
dime novels, women's pages, a youth department,
and a science column—something for everyone in the
family. The *Sunday World* was a great success (de-
partment-store advertising made it a money-maker)
and circulation was huge, more than five times that

of the daily edition, for Pulitzer realized that on Sunday readers wanted something different. The weekdays were for news; Sunday was for leisure.

The chief Oxford English Dictionary definition of leisure is "Time which one can spend as one pleases." That is, "free" time. But in one of his popular columns in the *Illustrated London News*—a Saturday paper—G. K. Chesterton pointed out that leisure should not be confused with liberty. Contrary to most people's expectations, the presence of the first by no means assured the availability of the second. This confusion arose, according to Chesterton, because the term "leisure" was used to describe three different things: "The first is being allowed to do something. The second is being allowed to do anything. And the third (and perhaps most rare and precious) is being allowed to do nothing." The first, he acknowledged, was the most common form of leisure, and the one which of late—he was writing in the early 1900s—had shown the greatest quantitative increase. The second—the liberty to fashion what one willed out of one's leisure time—was more restricted, and tended to be confined to artists and other creative individuals. It was the third, however, that was obviously his favorite since it allowed idleness—which was, in Chesterton's view, the truest form of leisure.

Perhaps only someone as portly as Chesterton—Maisie Ward, his biographer, estimated he weighed almost three hundred pounds—could rhapsodize over

idleness. More likely, inactivity attracted him because he was the least lazy of men; his bibliography lists more than one hundred published books—essays, poetry, biographies, novels, and short stories. He was also a magazine editor, and a popular lecturer and broadcaster. Although he managed to cram this all into a relatively short life—he died at sixty-two—as his physique would suggest, it was a life replete with material enjoyments, and surprisingly unhurried. Not a life of leisure, perhaps, but carried out at a leisurely pace.

Chesterton's observation—that modern society provided many opportunities for leisure but made it "more and more easy to get some things and impossible to get others"—continues to be true. Should you want to play tennis or golf, for example, courts and courses abound. Fancy a video? There are plenty of specialty stores, lending libraries, and mail-order clubs. Lepidopterists, on the other hand, have a difficult time finding unfenced countryside in which to practice their avocation. If your pastime is laying bricks, and you do not have a rural estate—as Winston Churchill had—you will not find a bricklaying franchise at your neighborhood mall.* Better take up golf instead.

---

* Churchill was a skillful and prolific bricklayer. At Chartwell, he built two cottages, a play house, and several walls. In one letter he wrote: "I have had a delightful month building a cottage and dictating a book: 200 bricks and 2,000 words a day."

16

Chesterton argued that a man compelled by lack of choice—or by social pressure—to play golf in the afternoon, when he would rather be attending to some solitary hobby, was not so different from the slave who might have several hours of leisure while his overseer slept but who had to be ready to work at a moment's notice. Neither could be said to be the master of his leisure. They had free time, but not freedom. To press this parallel further, have we become enslaved by the weekend?

At first glance, it is an odd question, for surely it is our work that enslaves us, not our recreations. We call people who become obsessed by their jobs workaholics, but we don't have a word for someone who is possessed by play. Maybe we should. I have many acquaintances for whom weekend activities seem more important than workaday existence, and who behave as if the week were merely an irritating interference in their real, extracurricular lives. I sometimes have the impression that to really know these weekend sailors, mountain climbers, or horsewomen, I would have to accompany them on their outings and excursions—see them in their natural habitat, so to speak. But would I see a different person, or merely the same one governed by different conventions of comportment, behavior, accoutrement, and dress?

I'm always charmed by old photographs of skiers that show groups of people in what appear to be street clothes, with uncomplicated pieces of bent wood

strapped to sturdy walking boots. These men and women have a playful and unaffected air. Today every novice is caparisoned in skintight spandex like an Olympic racer, and even cross-country skiing, a simple enough pastime, has been infected by a preoccupation with correct dress, authentic terminology, and up-to-date equipment. This reflects a concern for status and consumption, but it also suggests an attitude to play that is different from what it was in the past. Most outdoor sports, once simply muddled through, are now undertaken with a high degree of seriousness. "Professional" used to be a word that distinguished someone who was paid for performing an activity from the sportsman; today the word has increasingly come to denote anyone with a high degree of proficiency; "professional-quality" equipment is available to—and desired by—all. Conversely, "amateur," a wonderful word literally meaning "lover," has been degraded to mean a rank beginner, or anyone without a certain level of skill. "Just an amateur," we say; it is not, as it once was, a compliment.

The lack of carelessness in our recreation, the sense of obligation to get things right, and the emphasis on protocol and decorum do represent an enslavement of a kind. People used to "play" tennis; now they "work" on their backhand. It is not hard to imagine what Chesterton would have thought of such dedication; this was just the sort of laborious pursuit of

play that he so often derided. "If a thing is worth doing at all," he once wrote, "it is worth doing badly."

Chesterton held the traditional view that leisure was different from the type of recreation typically afforded by the modern weekend. His own leisure pastimes included an eclectic mix of the unfashionable and the bohemian—sketching, collecting weapons, and playing with the cardboard cutouts of his toy theater. Leisure was the opportunity for personal, even idiosyncratic pursuits, not for ordered recreation, for private reverie rather than for public spectacles. If a sport was undertaken, it was for the love of playing, not of winning, not even of playing well. Above all, free time was to remain that: free of the encumbrance of convention, free of the need for busyness, free for the "noble habit of doing nothing." That hardly describes the modern weekend.

What is the meaning of the weekday-weekend cycle? Is it yet another symptom of the standardization and bureaucratization of everyday life that social critics such as Lewis Mumford or Jacques Ellul have warned about? Is the weekend merely the cunning marketing ploy of a materialist culture, a device to increase consumption? Is it a deceptive placebo to counteract the boredom and meaninglessness of the workplace?

Or is this the heralded Leisure Society? If so, it is hardly what was anticipated. The decades leading up to the 1930s saw a continuing reduction in the number of hours in the workweek—from sixty to fifty to thirty-five. There was every reason to think that this trend would continue and workdays would grow shorter and shorter. This, and massive automation, would lead to what was then starting to be referred to as "universal leisure." Not everyone agreed that this would be a good thing; there was much speculation about what people would do with their newfound freedom, and some psychologists worried that universal leisure would really mean universal boredom. Hardly, argued the optimists; it would provide opportunities for self-improvement, adult education, and a blossoming of the creative arts. Others were less sanguine about the prospects for creative ease in a society that had effectively glorified labor, and argued that Americans lacked the sophistication and inner resources to deal with a life without work.

Universal leisure did not come to pass, or at least it did not arrive in the expected form. For one thing, the workday appears to have stabilized at about eight hours. Automation has reduced jobs in certain industries, as was predicted, but overall employment has increased, not decreased, although not necessarily in high-paying jobs. Women have entered the workforce, with the result that more, not less, people are

working; since housework still needs to be done, it could be argued that, in many families, there is really less leisure than before.

There may not be more leisure, but there is no doubt that the development of the weekend has caused a redistribution of leisure time, which for many people has effectively shortened the length of the workweek. This redistribution—coupled with more disposable income—has made it possible to undertake recreation in a variety of unexpected ways—some creative, some not—and not only at annual intervals, on vacations, but throughout the year, every weekend.

All this has called into question the traditional relationship between leisure and work, a relationship about which our culture has always been ambivalent. Generally speaking, there are two opposing schools of thought. On the one hand there is the ideal, held by thinkers as disparate as Karl Marx and the Catholic philosopher Josef Pieper, of a society increasingly emancipated from labor. This notion echoes the Aristotelian view that the goal of life is happiness, and that leisure, as distinguished from amusement and recreation, is the state necessary for its achievement. "It is commonly believed that happiness depends on leisure," Aristotle wrote in his *Ethics,* "because we occupy ourselves so that we may have leisure, just as we make war in order that we may live at peace." Or, to put it more succinctly, as did the title of

Lover Boy's 1982 hit song, we are "Working for the Weekend."

Opposed to this is the more modern (so-called Protestant) work ethic that values labor for its own sake, and sees its reduction—or, worse, its elimination—as an unthinkable degradation of human life. "There is no substitute for work except other serious work," wrote Lewis Mumford, who considered that meaningful work was the highest form of human activity and who once went so far as to liken the abolition of work to a malignant Final Solution. According to this view, work should be its own reward, whether it is factory work, housework, or a workout. Leisure, equated with idleness, is suspect; leisure without toil, or disconnected from it, is altogether sinister. The weekend is not free time but break time—an intermission.

But I am getting ahead of myself. I want first to examine something that will shed light on the relation between work and leisure: how we came to adopt a rigorous division of our everyday lives into five days of work and two of play, and how the weekend became the chief temporal institution of the modern age. And how, in turn, this universally accepted structure has affected the course and nature of our leisure—whether it involves playing golf, laying bricks, or just daydreaming.

two

Week After Week

Listening to music, lying on the beach, being caught up in some pleasurable activity, we sometimes feel that we have lost track of time. "Time flies when you're having fun," we say, underlining the carefree and spontaneous character of play. It is ironic, then, that our chief occasion for leisure—the weekend—is the direct product of the mechanical practice of measuring time.

Counting days in chunks of seven now comes so naturally that it's easy to forget this is an unusual way to mark the passage of time. Day spans the interval between the rising and setting of the sun; the twenty-four-hour day is the duration between one dawn and the next. The month measures—or once did—the time required for the moon to wax, become full, and wane; and the year counts one full cycle of the seasons. What does the week measure? Nothing. At least, nothing visible. No natural phenomenon occurs every seven days—nothing happens to the sun, the moon,

or the stars. The week is an artificial, man-made interval.

Generally speaking, our calendar is a flexible affair, full of inconsistencies. The length of the day varies with the season; the duration of the month is likewise irregular. Adjustments need to be made: every four years we add a day to February; every four hundred years we add a day to the centurial year. The week, on the other hand, is exactly seven days long, now and forever. We say that there are fifty-two weeks in a year, but that is an approximation, since the week is not a subdivision of either the month or the year. The week mocks the calendar and marches relentlessly and unbroken across time, paying no attention to the seasons. The British scholar F. H. Colson—who in 1926 wrote a fascinating monograph on the subject— described the week as an "intruder." It was an intruder who arrived relatively late. The week was made the final feature of what became the definitive Western calendar sometime in the second or third century A.D., in ancient Rome. But it can be glimpsed in different guises—not always seven days long, and not always continuous—in many earlier civilizations.

The oldest calendar is that of the Egyptians; if one includes the Copts, Parsis, and Iranians, who all adopted variations of the Egyptian calendar, it has been in use for five thousand years. The Egyptians divided the year into three seasons—inundation, seed-

time, and harvest—which reflected the annual progress of their Nilotic, agricultural society. They also divided the year into months, first ten and later twelve. Day and night had twelve hours each. Daytime hours were counted by means of shadowclocks; at night the hours were reckoned according to the movement of thirty-six different stars. The particular stars used for timekeeping changed every ten days, and as a result the thirty-day Egyptian civil month was sectioned into three ten-day periods called decades, which roughly corresponded to the waxing, middle, and waning of the moon. It is tempting to describe these ten-day intervals as "weeks"; unfortunately there is little evidence about their civic or religious functions, and they may have been only an astronomical convenience.

The Mesopotamian calendars of Sumer, Babylon, and Assyria likewise divided the year into twelve months. Each month of twenty-nine days was further divided in two by a special day—*shabattu*—which commemorated the full moon. This produced a time-interval of fourteen days. By the seventh century B.C., the seventh, twenty-first, and twenty-eighth days of the month were also assigned special importance, and on these days many common work activities were proscribed.

This septenary scheme has led some scholars to refer to the interim periods as "lunar weeks." In fact,

the Mesopotamian month varied from twenty-nine to thirty days, and each of the four seven-day periods was followed by a one- or two-day break, which made the seven-day periods, unlike the true week, discontinuous. Nevertheless, the idea of a relatively short period of time followed regularly by a day or two devoted to leisure, is strikingly similar.

Like the Egyptians, the Athenians divided the month into three periods of about ten days each. The first was called "the waxing moon," the last "the waning moon," and the middle period was unnamed. The days within each decade were numbered, as in "the second day of the waxing moon" or, "the fourth day of the middle period." The days of the third decade were counted backward, however, which indicated how many were left until the end of the month, customarily the time for settling debts and paying bills. Unlike the week, however, the decade did not measure the interval between civic holidays, which were set according to a different calendar.

The republican Roman calendar designated three special dividing days in each thirty- or thirty-one-day month. The first of the month was called the Calends, the fifth (or seventh in one of the four long months) the Nones, and the thirteenth (or fifteenth) the Ides. The three "marker days" were special days for important public events, when religious ceremonies were carried out and certain activities pro-

scribed. Although the intervals were of markedly differing duration—three days, seven days, sixteen days (in a short month)—they performed a function similar to that of the week.

Two other well-known ancient calendars are those of the Chinese and Mayan civilizations. The Chinese calendar included a cycle of individually named days, which resembled the week in its recurring progression throughout the year but which was much longer—sixty days instead of seven. The Mayan civil calendar included a succession of thirteen-day periods, numbered to indicate the thirteen gods of the Mayan upper world. These periods were repeated twenty times—the Mayas were obsessed by the number twenty and used a vigesimal mathematical system—to complete a full cycle. This thirteen-day period—a kind of week—seems to have had no civil function, and was used primarily for religious and ceremonial purposes.

The common feature of ancient calendar-making was a recognition of the waxing and waning of the moon. It took no sophisticated instruments to observe the moon; nor was a knowledge of mathematics or astronomy required to note that the phases of the moon, from the arrival of the new moon to the disappearance of the old, were regular. The origin of the Roman marker days, for example, is considered to have been lunar, for they would have fallen on the first sighting of the new moon, the first quarter, and

the full moon. The twenty-nine- and thirty-day lunar months—"mooneths"—became the basis for the so-called lunar year used by the Babylonians. The lunar month continues to control both the Jewish and the Islamic calendars, as well as the allocation of Hindu festivals.

The lunar cycle was memorable because it was relatively short—it takes about twenty-nine and a half days for the moon to make its circuit—and so it was more practical as a timekeeper than the annual movement of the sun or the change of seasons. There was a problem with the 354-day lunar year, however. It takes the earth about 365 days to perform one revolution in its orbit around the sun, or, to put it another way, it takes about 365 days (a solar year) to complete a cycle of the four seasons. This means that there is roughly an eleven-day discrepancy between the lunar and the solar years. Hence a calendar based on the phases of the moon slowly retrogressed through the year, relative to the seasons, repeating only every thirty-two and a half years. The practical implication of this fluidity was a lack of concordance between the month and the time of year—sometimes December occurred in the winter, sometimes in the summer. To keep the lunar months in step with the seasons, it was necessary to add several days at the end of each year, which is what the Egyptians, Greeks, and Romans all did.

Week After Week

It was Julius Caesar who, with the aid of the Greek astronomer, Sosigenes, totally reformed the Roman calendar, in 46 B.C. The Julian calendar was based on the solar year, and although it kept the traditional names of the twelve months, which we still use, these were no longer lunar months, but varied in length so that they added up to 365 days. Since the solar year is really six hours longer than 365 days, an extra day was added every fourth year, the leap year. A slight imprecision was rectified by Pope Gregory in the sixteenth century, otherwise the Julian calendar has proved remarkably durable.*

Strikingly absent in the Julian calendar was anything resembling the week. Since the Julian months varied—twenty-eight, thirty, and thirty-one days— they could not be neatly subdivided into decades (as could the thirty-day Egyptian civic month). And yet, within two hundred years or so, almost all Roman citizens were familiar with the seven-day week. How did this happen?

To begin with, there were many "sevens" in the ancient world: the Seven Names of God, the Seven Pillars of Wisdom, the Seven Labors of Hercules, the Seven Sleepers of Ephesus, the Seven Against Thebes,

---

* The Gregorian calendar was adopted first by Roman Catholic countries in 1582, and eventually spread to Protestant northern Europe; Britain, insular as ever, held out until 1752. It was adopted in Japan in 1873, in China in 1912, and in Russia as late as 1918.

the Seven Sages of Greece, and the Seven Wonders of the World. There was a cycle of Roman stories called the Seven Wise Masters that also occurred in Greek, Arabic, and Sanskrit. And, of course, the imperial city was built on seven hills.

Seven appeared as a magical number first among the Babylonians, as early as the third millennium B.C., and played an important role in their calendar.* One of the roots of this septenary fascination was mathematical; seven is a prime number. Another was astronomical. There were seven heavenly bodies with apparent motion in the night sky—the "erring seven," the "seven wanderers," that is, the planets. These were Saturn, Jupiter, Mars, the Sun, Mercury, Venus, and the Moon (which the ancients considered a planet), to give them in the usual order of their decreasing distance from the earth. Whether the seven planets of antiquity suggested the belief in the magic number or merely reinforced it is not clear. In any case, as astronomy—and astrology—spread from Babylon to Greece, Egypt, and Rome, the seven heavenly bodies became identified with the great gods of the pantheon.

---

* The cult of the magical number seven has been found in virtually every part of the world, including India and China. In some places, such as Africa and the Pacific, it has been attributed to Islamic or European influences; its presence among many American Indian tribes is more difficult to explain.

Astrology maintained that the movements of the planets represented the activities of the gods themselves, and that every earthly occurrence was influenced by the position of the stars and other heavenly bodies. Individual planets were identified with metals, colors, and animals. The sun, for example, was associated with gold, the color yellow, the cock (which crowed at dawn), the lion (which was tawny), and with certain spices such as cloves and cinnamon. Each of the seven ages of man (infancy, childhood, adolescence, youth, manhood, early old age, old age) was governed by one of the planets. Not surprisingly, each day was likewise under the influence of a different planetary god, and since there were seven planets, this produced a cycle of seven days. Or so we assume, for there is no surviving information regarding the earliest manifestation of what became known as the planetary week.

The actual order of the days in the planetary week did not follow the usual order of the planets, however. The first hour of the first day was assigned to Saturn, who thus ruled that day; the second hour to Jupiter, the third to Mars, and so on. The eighth hour started the series all over again. Following this progression, the twenty-fifth hour, that is, the first hour of the second day, turned out to belong to the Sun, which thus ruled that day. This produced a planetary week as follows:

Dies Saturni (Saturn)
Dies Solis (Sun)
Dies Lunae (Moon)
Dies Martis (Mars)
Dies Mercurii (Mercury)
Dies Iovis (Jupiter)
Dies Veneris (Venus)

Of course, the Jews already kept a seven-day week, organized around the observance of the Sabbath. It is possible—although disputed by many scholars—that the Jews adapted this method of time-keeping from the Babylonians during their exile in that country in the sixth century B.C., and converted the Babylonian *shabattu* into their Sabbath, a day of religious observance when all work was proscribed. Or they may simply have been influenced by the Babylonian belief in the magical number seven. Either way, the correspondence between the Babylonian practice of dividing the lunar month every seven days and the Jewish observance of the Sabbath on every seventh day is surely not coincidental.

There is evidence that by the time of the restoration of Judah, in 140 B.C., the celebration of the Sabbath was a well-established institution. The adoption of a successive seven-day cycle was unusual, and exactly why the Jews evolved this mechanism is unclear. According to the Old Testament, the Sabbath

was "their" day, given to them—and them alone—by Jehovah. Unquestionably, its very singularity appealed to the exiled Jews as a way of differentiating themselves from the alien Babylonian Gentiles who surrounded them. The fact that the Sabbath occurred on every seventh day, irrespective of the seasons, was a powerful idea, for it overrode all other existing calendars.

Religious sects often adopt a temporal distinction to solidify their fragile identities and to detach themselves from other faiths. The early Christians, for example, deliberately chose a day other than the Sabbath as the holy day of their week. So did Muhammad, who designated Friday as the Islamic holy day; indeed, Saturday and Sunday are regarded as unfortunate days by Muslims. So did the Adventists who, after the second coming of Christ failed to occur on October 22, 1844, as they had foretold, decided to observe Saturday instead of Sunday as the holy day of the week. The Quakers emphasized their distinctiveness by replacing the planetary names of the days with numbers: First Day, Second Day, and so on.

The exclusiveness of the Jewish faith precluded the widespread adoption of the Sabbath by others, and for centuries the seven-day week remained a uniquely Jewish institution. Or almost so. The Jews were a small but influential minority in the Roman Empire, and their observance of the Sabbath did not go un-

noticed by the superstitious Romans. There is some evidence that both Greeks and Romans came to associate the Jewish holiday with Saturn, the unlucky planet, which confirmed it (in their eyes) as a day on which it was prudent to do as little as possible. In any case, in towns where there were large numbers of Jewish traders and shopkeepers, it was convenient for everyone to observe the same holiday.

Historians have been unable to fully unravel the relationship between the planetary week and the Jewish week. The Jewish week is obviously connected to the planetary week, but how? In the planetary week each day is devoted to a different deity and is considered important; for the Jews, the week in itself was merely the interval between the Sabbaths. They called Sunday, Monday, and Tuesday the days "after the Sabbath," and Wednesday, Thursday, and Friday the days "before"; in the modern Jewish calendar the weekdays are assigned numbers (first, second, third, and so on), not names. If the Sabbath did not inspire the planetary week, perhaps it was the other way around? There is a theory that the Jews rearranged the planetary week to start on the Sun's Day—instead of Saturn's—after the Exodus, as an expression of their hatred for their Egyptian oppressors, and when they adopted the Sabbath (the seventh day) it fell on Saturn's Day.

The origin of the planetary week is likewise ob-

scure, as regards both place and time. Dio Cassius, a Roman historian who lived in the third century A.D., thought that the planetary week was conceived in Egypt, but modern scholars dispute this claim; more likely it was a Hellenistic practice that migrated to Rome. Dio Cassius maintained that the planetary week had been a relatively recent invention. There is some evidence, however, of a planetary week during the Augustan period—two hundred years before—and it may have originated even earlier, although probably not much earlier. What is certain is that not long before the time of Dio Cassius, the habit of measuring time in cycles of seven days was already commonplace in private life throughout the Roman Empire.

More curious than the origin of the seven-day week is the question of how it spread. In a relatively short period of time, the "intruder" insinuated itself into the Julian calendar and became common in most of Europe. One would imagine an imperial edict as the starting point. Or, as had been the case with astronomical time-reckoning, one might expect the week to have been the subject of scholarly study and debate. But there is no evidence pointing to either of these. As F. H. Colson pointed out, "There is a complete silence as to any official endorsement or even recog-

nition of the planetary week, and this is a matter in which silence does imply non-existence.''

The planetary week did not coincide with any formal rite or celebration, at least not for most Roman citizens. There were some exceptions, but they were not numerous. The early Christians, who adopted the Jewish custom of gathering once every seven days, chose the day after the Sabbath, probably to commemorate the Resurrection of Christ, which was supposed to have occurred on that day. This corresponded to the Sun's Day of the planetary week. That day was also celebrated by another religion—Mithraism. This Persian creed had been brought to Rome in the first century A.D.; it grew in popularity, especially among common people, and eventually received imperial endorsement from Constantine. The magical number seven was important to the Mithraists, so it was not surprising that they, too, celebrated every seventh day; since Mithras, like the sun, was the god of light, they naturally identified with his day of the planetary week.

One should not make too much of the presence of these religious groups in the Roman Empire while the planetary week was spreading. The Jews, for example, were not objects of universal admiration. Nor were the Christians. The Christian church did play a role in the spread of the seven-day week and the observance of Sunday, but that happened much later; in

the second century A.D.—when the planetary week was adopted, the Christians were a tiny, persecuted minority. A slightly stronger case can be made for Mithraism. It was particularly popular among soldiers, and this may have assisted the spread of the planetary week in the Empire. It is equally possible, however, that Mithraists simply adapted themselves to an already popular custom. It is unlikely that the influence of *any* of these minority religions would have been powerful enough to explain the widespread adoption of the week.

Judging from the absence of any written record, the week appears to have been spread by word of mouth and adopted by common people. They left no written account, and we can only guess about their motivations. Ordinary people had no exact knowledge of astrology; nevertheless, as Colson suggests, their belief in the influence of the planets must have been profound. The planetary week, in which days were under the sway of compassionate and malevolent deities, may have developed as a kind of superstition, like the belief in the misfortune that is attached to black cats or to the number thirteen. That the week has superstitious overtones is evident in the old nursery rhyme:

Monday's child is fair of face,
Tuesday's child is full of grace,

Wednesday's child is full of woe,
Thursday's child has far to go,
Friday's child is loving and giving,
Saturday's child has to work for a living,
But a child that's born on the Sabbath day
Is fair and wise and good and gay.

Monday's child reflects the beauty of the moon; Friday's loving child is under the influence of Venus, the goddess of love; and Saturday's unlucky child falls under the influence of Saturn, the dimmest and slowest of the planets.

Typically, superstitions exhibit an appealing logic—or, more often, an equally appealing lack of it. It makes sense to avoid walking under ladders, but why avoid cracks in the sidewalk? Black cats do look ominous; on the other hand, so do crows. A horseshoe on the wall should be U-shaped to catch luck—if it is mounted upside down, the luck pours out. That *sounds* reasonable, but why a horseshoe, rather than some other found object? Thirteen is ill-starred, eleven is not; salt, not sugar, is thrown over the shoulder, and the left shoulder, not the right. It is possible to discover the original sources of some such practices, but such knowledge is extraneous to the belief itself—the core of superstition is acceptance, not understanding.

I would speculate that the planetary week met with

the same sort of easy acceptance. The people who embraced the week did not ponder why it was seven and not eight days, or why it should be named after the planets rather than some other group of deities, or a different set of astrological star signs. Superstitions emerge out of daily practice, not scholarly inquiry. They are learned at a grandfather's knee, or with one's playmates, not in school. And the fact that they evolve out of a general consensus, rather than being imposed, makes them all the more enduring.

Unlike most superstitions, though, the planetary week was not something that grew out of a local tradition—it was a novelty to the people who so quickly adopted it. But as we have seen, the idea of clustering days into bunches, which generally varied from five to ten—what Daniel Boorstin so charmingly calls bouquets of days—was not unprecedented. The decade attests to the need for a shorter time interval than the lunar month. The observance of regular non-working days was also common in many societies. This coincided, in most cases, with a practical desire for a shorter regular intermission, whether for religious or social reasons.

There is no historical evidence that the planetary week first used in Greece and Rome began or ended with a holiday. But such a pattern is visible in another part of the world where the planetary week became a popular institution. The planetary week arrived on

the Indian subcontinent early in the fourth century
A.D.; it appears to have been borrowed from Hellenistic sources. The week did not arrive as an integral
part of an imported time-reckoning system. The
Hindu calendars (like the Greeks, they had several)
were—and are—a complicated mixture of Hellenistic,
Babylonian, and Chinese influences, as well as indigenous practices. At some point, Hindus began to observe the first day of the week, *Adivara,* as a day on
which it was considered unlucky to start new endeavors. It was therefore a holiday and a market day.
The Sanskrit *Adivara,* like the names of the other days,
corresponded to one of the planetary gods, in this case
the god whom Hindus worshiped every morning—
the god of the sun. It is a curious coincidence that
Hindus should have chosen Sunday as a day of rest,
long before contact with Christian missionaries or
British colonizers.

At about the same time as the week arrived in
India, the Emperor Constantine officially proclaimed
the planetary week and designated the Sun's Day as
a special holiday and as the first day of the week,
altering the earlier tradition that began the planetary
week with Saturn's Day. There were later attempts
to divest the week of its pagan planetary origins by
substituting numbers for planetary day names, and
numbered days still survive in the Portuguese, Greek,
and Slavic languages. On the other hand, the Italians,

French, and Spanish stubbornly maintained the original Roman names for the days of the week—except for Saturday, which was called the Sabbath. The English, German, and Dutch kept the planetary names, but they substituted some of their own analogous deities for the Roman gods. For Mars, Mercury, Jupiter, and Venus they used the Teutonic gods Tiw (or Din), Woden, Thor, and Fria. These differences between the Romance languages and those of northern Europe are illustrated below:

Latin	Italian	French	English	Dutch
Dies Solis	domenica	dimanche	Sunday	Zondag
Dies Lunae	lunedì	lundi	Monday	Maandag
Dies Martis	martedì	mardi	Tuesday	Dinsdag
Dies Mercurii	mercoledì	mercredi	Wednesday	Woensdag
Dies Iovis	giovedì	jeudi	Thursday	Dondersdag
Dies Veneris	venerdì	vendredi	Friday	Vrejdag
Dies Saturni	sabato	samedi	Saturday	Zaterdag

There are different names even for the Christian Sabbath. In English, Dutch, German, and the Scandinavian languages, it has remained the planetary Sunday. Italian, French, Spanish, Portuguese, and Gaelic all use variations of the Latin *dominica* (the Lord's Day); so does modern Greek, although the term is translated. In Russian, Czech, and Polish, on the other hand, Sunday follows neither convention, and is called "not-working day."

There is only one European language that exhibits

41

a complete and consistent set of Roman planetary names—Welsh. All the rest have incorporated mixtures of planetary names (sometimes derived directly from the Latin root, and sometimes not), religious references, numbers, and a few secular descriptions. Germans, for example, used the Teutonic deities for the names of the week, except for Wednesday, which is "midweek" instead of Wodin's Day, and Saturday, which is the "eve of Sunday." In the Scandinavian languages, which otherwise resemble English, Saturday is not Saturn's Day but "washing day." In Gaelic some days are planetary, but Friday is called "the great fast." Even when days are numbered, there are inconsistencies. In Polish and Russian, since Monday is the "first day," Sunday comes at the end of the week, as in the Judaic calendar. In Portuguese, which also uses numbers instead of names, Monday is called the "second day," as it is in modern Greek. This variety demonstrates that while the adoption of the planetary seven-day week may have been universal, the *meanings* attached to the days of the week were not consistently planetary. In fact, the root of the English word "week" (wicu, wike, wyke, wek, wok) is ancient and predates the planetary week.

This multiplicity of meanings is another explanation for the week's popularity: it was many things to many people, sometimes many things to the same people. It was magical and practical both. A superstition at first, it survived as a social convention, the

same way that shaking hands with the right (that is, the lucky) hand has endured because there was a need for a gesture to represent friendly feelings to a stranger. The week was a short unit of time around which common people could organize their lives, their work, and their leisure. At the same time, the week provided a simple and memorable device for relating everyday activities to supernatural concerns, whether these involved observing a direct commandment from Jehovah, or commemorating Christ's resurrection, or recognizing the influence of a planetary deity, or, just to be safe, all three.

The fact that the week was so adaptable undoubtedly facilitated its worldwide spread. For Constantine, who decreed its use throughout the Roman Empire, the week was a Christian (and some say a Mithraist) institution; for the Hindus, it was a planetary concept that they grafted onto their accommodating, heterogeneous calendar. Early in the seventh century, the week received another religious endorsement, from the prophet Muhammad, who established a lunar calendar that was very different from both the Christian and the traditional Arab calendars. Nevertheless, he kept the seven-day week, although he shifted the holy day from Sunday to Friday.

The last major civilization to jump on the bandwagon was China, where the week arrived as a result of the 1911 Revolution. To the Chinese, the Western calendar was one of many "modernizing" reforms,

and the week was adopted pragmatically, and in a curious fashion. Weekdays were numbered, not named; the seventh day was a civic holiday, and was called, in Cantonese, Sun Day. This was probably a matter of convention, not religious conviction, although some political leaders had been educated in mission schools and were, like Sun Yat-sen, the first (provisional) president of the new republic, baptized Christians.

Things went less smoothly for the week during an earlier revolution. The French Revolution produced an entirely revised calendar, whose object was to divorce the months, days, and weeks from their traditional Christian associations and, at the same time, to rationalize (that is, decimalize) timekeeping. To begin with, the republican calendar did away with Anno Domini; henceforth dates were to be reckoned from the proclamation of the republic—1792, or Year I. The solar year was maintained, and the extra day of the leap year was consecrated to a festival of the Revolution, the four-year period being called a *Franciade*. The months, too, were renamed. This task was entrusted to Philippe-François-Nazaire Fabre d'Églantine, a poet, who concocted a sort of twelve seasons—the winter months, for example, were called *nivôse* (snowy), *pluviôse* (rainy), and *ventôse* (windy).*

* Typically, for France, this represented Parisian weather.

44

There were still twelve months, but, as in the civil Egyptian calendar, they were all of equal thirty-day length. The five days left over were devoted to an end-of-the-year public festival.

Under this system the week fared badly—it was done away with altogether. Instead, each month was now divided into three ten-day periods. The days of the revolutionary week, or *décade,* were given numerical designations: *primidi, duodi, tridi,* and so on. The tenth day—*décadi*—was a holiday.

Voltaire wrote that "if you wish to destroy the Christian religion you must first destroy the Christian Sunday," and that was precisely what the secular week set out to do. Since the vast majority of peasants remained believers, one must imagine that celebrations of the Lord's Day, and hence the seven-day count, continued, albeit in secret. The same must have been true for the Jewish Sabbath, especially since the "universal" rights of the revolution did not extend to Jews. But even among confirmed *sans-culottes,* the new week cannot have been popular; it deprived them of sixteen public holidays for which the five festival days did not make adequate recompense. In any event, the ten-day week lasted only until Year XIV, when Bonaparte restored the traditional Gregorian calendar in France.

The French revolutionaries underestimated the potency of the week. This was largely because they

45

misjudged the extent of the religious sentiments of most of the population, for whom the seven-day week and Christianity were inseparable. But they also failed to understand that the week was a deeply held social convention. Ordinary people were prepared to put up with ten-hour days, and hundred-minute hours—in any case, few owned timepieces. The ten-day count, however, was lackluster and mechanical, and had none of the mystery and individual richness of the planetary week. Grounded in an intellectual idea, the new week had no cultural roots, and even had the Jacobins survived, it is unlikely that the *décade* would have persisted.

The most recent attempt to undo the seven-day week occurred in the Soviet Union. In the autumn of 1929, the regime of Joseph Stalin completely restructured the Soviet calendar. The new scheme resembled the French republican calendar in many respects; it, too, had twelve months of thirty days each, the extra days being public holidays. Unlike the French, the Bolsheviks retained the traditional names of the months, for the main target of the reform was the week itself. Henceforth, factories would operate continuously, without a break. There would be no more universal rest day—in fact, no more week at all; workers labored four days, on staggered shifts, and had every fifth day off. This increased the annual number of nonworking days from fifty-two to seventy-two.

The four-day shift may have been less onerous than its six-day Tsarist predecessor but it was unpopular. Since everyone worked on a different schedule, families and friends could seldom enjoy the same day off. Supervisors and managers were obliged to work on many of their free days, so that committee and board meetings could take place. Schools, banks, and administrative offices became disorganized—staff members were never present at the same time. Machinery and equipment were neglected, since no one was personally responsible for their operation. Of course, the abolition of the traditional week was also unpopular with the deeply religious peasants, as well as with the large urban Jewish minority.

The stated purpose of the new calendar was to increase industrial and agricultural production. After less than three years, it became clear that the four-day shift was having the opposite effect, and the five-day week was canceled. Now each month was divided into five weeks of six days each, with every sixth day a common holiday. This arrangement lasted for nine years, when it, too, was abandoned. In June 1940, the Soviet Union returned to the Gregorian calendar and the seven-day week. The official reason given was that a longer week would permit an improvement in factory production, and a reduction of staff. Unofficially, the Bolsheviks would have had to admit their defeat; their campaign to undo the traditional week, the

mainstay of the Russian Orthodox Church, had failed.

The week has proved remarkably resilient to such official challenges—as well it might, if one believes that it was ordained by God. Or are we still attracted by the magical properties of the number seven, which continues to find resonances in our collective subconscious? There were seven deadly sins, and seven seas; today we have Snow White and the Seven Dwarfs, the Seven Sisters (elite American women's colleges), and the Group of Seven (Canadian painters). We buy 7-Up at the 7-Eleven. There are also an unusual number of movie titles that include the number seven: *Seven Brides for Seven Brothers*, *The Seven Year Itch*, *Seven Beauties*, and *The Seven Samurai* along with its American counterpart, *The Magnificent Seven*. The persistence of the number seven in popular culture attests to the durability of the belief in its magical power.*

There may be another explanation. One of the rhythms that modern biology has identified follows a period of about seven days. These so-called circaseptan rhythms have been detected in several functions of the human body: heartbeat, blood pressure, oral temperature, the acid content of blood, the amount of calcium in the urine, and the quantity of

---

* Nowhere has this belief been carried as far as in Isma'ilianism, a breakaway Islamic sect whose members became known as "Seveners." They believe in seven cycles of history, seven major prophets, and in the coming of the unknown seventh Imam.

cortisol in the adrenal glands. The evidence is incomplete, but it is certainly within the realm of possibility that the seven-day week is an instinctive attempt to establish a social calendar that more or less corresponds to an internal biological fluctuation.

The roots of the week lie deep, too deep to fully understand. An air of mystery surrounds the week; perhaps that, too, is part of its appeal. It is an observance that has been distilled over centuries of use, molded and fashioned through common belief and ordinary usage. Above all, it is a *popular* belief that took hold without magisterial sanction. This, more than anything, explains its durability. Less an intruder than an unofficial guest, the week was invited in through the kitchen door, and has become a friend of the family. A useful friend, for whatever else it did, the seven-day cycle provided a convenient structure for the repetitive rhythm of daily activities; not only a day for worship but also a day for baking bread, for washing, for cleaning house, for going to market—and for resting. Surely this over-and-over quality has always been one of the attractions of the week—and of the weekend? "Once a week" is one of the commonest measures of time. The planetary week is not a grand chronometer of celestial movements or a gauge of seasonal changes; it is something both simpler and more profound: a measure of ordinary, everyday life.

three

A Meaningful Day

The roots of the Sabbath go back at least to the time of Moses. According to the Book of Exodus, the Fourth Commandment enjoined the Jews: "Six days you shall labor, and do all your work; but the seventh day is a Sabbath to the Lord your God, in it you shall not do any manner of work." For the last sixteen hundred years, Christians, too, have set aside one day out of seven as a day free from labor. A similar day is present in Muslim societies. Although the origins of the day of rest are clearly religious, the fact that Hindus, Buddhists, Taoists, and Marxists alike have adopted such a schedule suggests that the weekly break has other resonances in the human condition.

The ancient Greeks did not celebrate Sundays, but they did have many regular festivals, which Plato called breathing spells; he suggested that the gods themselves had appointed festival days, out of pity for toiling humans. The Romans had a similar atti-

50

tude. "Let contentions of every kind cease on the sacred festivals," wrote Cicero, "and let servants enjoy them with a remission of labor; for this purpose they were appointed at certain seasons." Whether they believe that Sundays (or Saturdays, or Fridays) were ordained by divine intervention or not, most people would agree that the distinguishing characteristic of the weekly day off is that, like any holiday, it is a time without work.

This sounds obvious. Work, after all, dominates the world. "Work and its product, the human artifact," wrote Hannah Arendt, "bestow a measure of permanence and durability upon the futility of mortal life and the fleeting character of human time." Work represents the everyday routine; rest is a temporary interruption. Moreover, the workday appears paramount not only because it dominates the calendar numerically but because it is work that makes rest possible—not the other way around. The weekly day of rest is, in a material sense, a kind of surplus, paid for by labor already completed. Its status is underlined by the way in which we consider the weekend a reward for having worked. "I deserve a holiday," we say after a hard week.

There has never been a human society that did not recognize the need for regular days off, although some have tried to reduce them to a minimum. These spoilsports have usually been regimes that glorified

labor and begrudged their citizens the "unproductive" time away from work. During the sixteenth century English Protestant society frowned on the excessive number of traditional nonworking days (Sundays and holy days), of which there were more than two hundred; the second Book of Common Prayer, approved by the English Parliament in 1552, reduced them to seventy-nine. The *décade* of the French revolutionary calendar cut the fifty-two weekly Sunday holidays to thirty-six; the ninety annual days off, as well as the thirty-eight saints' days, were also drastically reduced. The Bolsheviks made a dramatic abbreviation in the number of public holidays, and by instituting the staggered holiday effectively relegated the weekly day of rest to a distinctly inferior status. Probably the most extreme example of a leisureless society was Cambodia in the late 1970s, when the Khmer Rouge turned the entire country into a work camp, and reportedly allowed only every tenth day to be a nonworking day—for the long-suffering citizens of Kampuchea, a breathing spell indeed.

Ancient societies were more generous. The Egyptians proscribed work on a total of about seventy days a year, once every six days on the average. The Athenians celebrated fifty or sixty annual festivals, but in some wealthy Greek city-states this figure was more than three times higher. The Romans in the time of Augustus (27 B.C.–A.D. 14) had sixty-six days off each

year, but by the fourth century the number of holidays had been expanded to 175. In Tsarist Russia, there were well over a hundred religious holidays every year, and in some parts of Galicia, where religious festivals followed both the Greek and Roman calendars, the number of nonworking days was reported (in 1909) as exceeding two hundred. In so-called primitive societies, the number of rest days varied. In Hawaii, before American colonization, work was forbidden on more than seventy days. The Hopi Indians of the Southwest reserved more than half the year for leisure. A similar statistic was noted in Ethiopia by a visitor in the early nineteenth century. In Ashanti, now Ghana, the number of holidays reached almost two hundred.

Most North Americans enjoy about 130 days off each year—fifty-two weekends, eleven or twelve public holidays, and about two weeks of personal vacation—which happens to be the historic mean. By contrast, in the People's Republic of China, where Saturday is still a workday and there are only seven public holidays, the number of annual days off is much lower—fewer than seventy.

Anyone who believes that the holiday is a reward for successful work might point out that China is much poorer than the United States, and hence can "afford" fewer days off. The gradual increases in the number of annual holidays in ancient Greece and

Rome suggest that increased wealth allows for more free time. But if days off were a result of prosperity, why did the workingman in industrialized Victorian England have many fewer holidays than did his counterpart in the less affluent Middle Ages? And why, at the turn of the century, when the United States was a much richer country than its neighbor Mexico, did Americans enjoy less than half as many days off as Mexicans, who celebrated 131 public holidays each year? If leisure were tied to prosperity, one would expect that Japan, which has achieved global economic preeminence, would have the largest number of holidays. Not so. A recent study found that the average summer vacation taken by Tokyo residents is 5.2 days, compared with twelve days for New Yorkers.

Of course, the reverse could also be argued, that societies that prosper do so precisely because their citizens work longer. This certainly is at the root of the popular belief that the economic success of the Japanese is linked to a propensity for hard work, or that the poverty of most South American societies is largely the result of long siestas, frequent festivals, and a general preference for merrymaking over work. But while it's true that Brazil and Colombia do have many annual public holidays (twenty-one and sev-

enteen days, respectively), so do Japan (nineteen days) and Israel (fifteen days). No one would seriously suggest that the French standard of living is lower than that of the United States because French family vacations are two and three times longer than those of Americans. Long summer vacations—a tradition in France and West Germany since the 1950s—do not seem to have had any ill effect on the economic growth and prosperity of these two countries. The relationship between the duration of time off and the wealth of a society is not straightforward. The quantity of days off work is neither a simple product of affluence nor a mark of cultural indolence. Its significance lies elsewhere.

In 1914, as part of the war effort, British industry introduced Sunday work, as well as longer hours and overtime. The result was not, as had been hoped, greater production but the opposite: reduced efficiency on the part of the workers, disciplinary difficulties, labor disturbances, and, most surprisingly, an actual drop in overall output. A short time later, when the Sunday holiday was reluctantly reinstated and the twelve-hour day was reduced to ten hours, not only did hourly output increase, to everyone's surprise, but so did gross weekly production.

The implication was obvious—the amount of pro-

duction was not only a function of how long people worked but also of how long they did not work. Greater attention began to be paid to the effects of the duration of work on productivity, and on the importance of external factors such as fatigue. The chief result of this research was a call for short, intermittent, daily rest periods—which produced, among other things, the coffee break, a sort of Protestant siesta. Since the Sunday holiday was an established tradition that, under normal circumstances, was unlikely to change, little research was done to shed light on the weekly break itself.

The fact that periodic days of rest have existed throughout history suggests that they might be the result of a physiological imperative—that intermittent days off represent a weekly maintenance break, analogous to the body's requirement for a certain number of regenerative hours of sleep or for a given amount of food and water. Such, at least, was the assumption in the nineteenth century, when scientists began to study human fatigue.

Angelo Mosso, an Italian physiologist, published a popular book on fatigue that appeared in English in 1903, in which he described various kinds of fatigue brought on by both physical exertion and by intellectual work, including stressful activities such as writing examinations and lecturing. Mosso drew his evidence from both anecdotal material and his own

experiments. He constructed an apparatus that measured the effect of fatigue on muscle strength, which showed that intellectual work also produced a consistent corresponding reduction in physical strength. In the case of one Dr. Maggiora, a professor of medicine who had to administer an arduous series of oral examinations, muscle strength flagged after an afternoon of examining but revived partially after dinner. A night's sleep restored the professor, but another afternoon of examining students brought the same results. After several days, however, the night's rest was no longer enough to return his strength to normal. Following the fifth and final day his forces were, in Mosso's word, "exhausted." As part of the experiment, Dr. Maggiora was then asked to spend two days in the country in "complete idleness." On his return, he demonstrated, as one might expect, a full revival of muscular force. The case of the tired professor showed the recuperative powers of the five-and-two schedule, although two-day weekends were unusual at this time.

We now know that Mosso's thesis—that physical and cerebral fatigue produces a chemical imbalance in the brain—was mistaken, but no simple alternative explanation has presented itself. Medical researchers agree that fatigue has to do with a person's physical and mental state; where the difficulty lies is that the latter "is little reflective and very elemental, almost

subconscious by definition, and largely inaccessible to rational analysis," according to one textbook on the subject. Moreover, fatigue at work appears to be the function of a great many associated factors such as working conditions (lighting, ventilation, noise), the degree of worker involvement, and the nature of the work, particularly if it is monotonous. Fatigue remains, in the words of one researcher, "a most mysterious phenomenon." We have not advanced far beyond Mosso's observation that after three or four uninterrupted days at his writing desk, he often had headaches, slept badly, and generally felt tired. At that point, he said, "I shut my books, set aside my papers, and after twenty-four hours' rest I find that I am cured."

Common sense suggests that a periodic day off from our regular occupations is required to combat mental and physical fatigue, stress, and boredom. Although there is no scientific evidence regarding the exact frequency necessary, on the strength of the historical record it would appear that such a break is needed roughly every five to ten days. But we should be careful of jumping to conclusions. A British author, Donald Scott, points out that studies of different industries have shown that output drops to its lowest level at the end of the week, just before the holiday. On the other hand, output is also low at the beginning of the week, when everyone is supposedly rested. He

speculates that factors other than fatigue—for example, an improvement in the worker's skill as the week progresses—are at play. But this period of adjustment, for that is what it is, also underlines the essential discontinuity that exists between work and leisure. Jeremy Campbell suggests that the "Monday-morning blahs" are the result of sleeping in on the weekend, which is a way of readjusting the body's twenty-five-hour circadian rhythm to the twenty-four-hour cosmic schedule. On Monday the inner biological clock, which has been allowed to run free, is abruptly brought back into line.

We may require a day off from work to alleviate our fatigue, but to describe holidays only as the antithesis—or consequence—of workdays misses the mark. To call the holiday either an interruption or a reward ignores the wealth of words that have traditionally described the period devoted to leisure—holy day, festival, feast, carnival, celebration—and reduces them to merely two: work stoppage. This is like defining comfort as merely the absence of discomfort; it fails to convey the essential positive quality of the elusive experience. In his book on festivity, Josef Pieper pointed out that the key to grasping the nature of the holiday lay precisely in divorcing it from work and other external influences and goals, and understanding that the holiday is meaningful in itself.

Over time, the meaning of the weekly break has

varied. The carefree modern weekender takes the days of rest as a pleasurable interlude from a hectic work schedule, and also as an opportunity to engage in personal hobbies. He considers the day off as a day when he is not *required* to work (at least, not for others, for the weekend is also a time for household chores); this is different from describing the day off as a day on which one is required *not* to work.

It was the prohibition of work that characterized the earliest regular holidays. An Egyptian calendar that has survived from about 1200 B.C.—the Papyrus Sallier IV—lists a series of forbidden activities for each day or part of a day for the entire year. These include injunctions against travel, sexual intercourse, washing, and eating certain kinds of food. Among the most frequent injunctions is "do no work." A Babylonian calendar, possibly belonging to the age of Hammurabi, describes the seventh, fourteenth, nineteenth, twenty-first, and twenty-eighth days as "evil days," on which various activities were proscribed, including, according to some scholars, business transactions. Unlucky days, on which all important work stopped, were also identified in the Greek and Roman calendars. "Egyptian days," which were considered ill-favored for various activities, were observed in Europe throughout the Middle Ages and until the Ref-

ormation. The current prejudice against Friday the thirteenth is a survivor of such superstitions.*

It is often hard to decipher the exact meaning of these ancient customs, but it helps to look at analogous beliefs in "primitive" societies. During the nineteenth century, European travelers made contact with many indigenous cultures in Asia and Africa, where the observance of lucky and unlucky days was actively practiced. The most extreme example was in Polynesia, where everyday life was governed by a vast and complex system of prohibitions, known as *tapus* or *tabus*. These taboos governed people, places, objects, activities, dress, and food, and were supported by supernatural authority. Their violation supposedly resulted in supernatural punishment.

Propitiatory tabooed days could arise as the result of particular events—the outbreak of an epidemic, a natural calamity, or any unusual occurrence. A taboo could occur automatically as the result of a birth, a death, the construction of a house, or before an important hunt. It could also be invoked (by the priest)

---

* Friday has been considered an unlucky day since the Middle Ages, and it remains so in many cultures. Macedonian folk lore proscribes cutting hair and nails on Fridays; Slavic peasants believe that any work begun on the day of "Mother Friday" is bound to finish badly; Indian Brahmins and Parsis consider Friday to be inauspicious, as do the Burmans. Some Islamic societies, which celebrate the Sabbath on Friday, also consider it an unlucky day for certain activities.

as a punishment for a religious or civil transgression, and it could affect an individual, a household, or the entire community. Taboos could last a few days, a few months, or, rarely, several years.

They were also part of everyday life. Traditional Hawaiian religion observed four regular tabooed periods a month: the third through sixth nights, the time of the full moon, the twenty-fourth and twenty-fifth nights, and the twenty-seventh and twenty-eighth nights. During these periods, sexual intercourse was prohibited and various activities—cooking, rowing a canoe, going outside the house—were proscribed.

There were also regularly scheduled seasonal taboos against fishing and hunting, for example, which had a beneficial effect on maintaining food stocks, and on nonagricultural work during the planting and harvesting periods, which ensured that the entire community pitched in for these crucial times. This has led some observers to wonder if taboos had a utilitarian origin, but since identical taboos were imposed on many different occasions, with no apparent practical end in mind, this explanation is unconvincing. If the taboo did serve a practical purpose, it was of a more general kind. Like any belief system, it provided the satisfaction of knowing that one had observed the correct forms. Communal taboos also contributed to a sense of social cohesion and self-discipline, which bound the members of the community together.

A Meaningful Day

The core of the tabooed day was that everyday activities stopped, especially those that involved labor.* Because of this, tabooed days are sometimes called holidays or festivals; as contemporary descriptions make clear, there was nothing festive about them. Work, like certain prized foods, singing, dancing, or sexual intercourse, was forbidden because it could not be safely or beneficially undertaken on these unlucky days. The regularly scheduled tabooed days, which occurred four times a month, resembled the weekend, but the atmosphere of these work breaks was not one of rest and recreation. Fear, not celebration, was their hallmark. These were gloomy days, during which all activities stopped and people stayed at home in an anxious mood of apprehension.

Once the taboo tradition was identified in the South Seas, anthropologists and sociologists found examples of it among indigenous peoples throughout Asia and Africa, and historians identified taboo traditions in the ancient world.† Their recurring features, especially

---

* The Polynesian word *tapu* signifies "specially marked," but *tapua'i* is more explicit and means "to abstain from all work, games, and so on."

† For example, the Romans had special holidays following earthquake tremors, when propitiatory rites were carried out and all public business ceased.

the ban on work, prompted some to point to evidence of taboos in contemporary industrialized societies such as our own. "In economic theory," wrote Thorstein Veblen in his famous book on the leisure class, "sacred holidays are obviously to be construed as a season of vicarious leisure performed for the divinity or saint in whose name the tabu is imposed and to whose good repute the abstention from useful effort on these days is conceived to inure. The characteristic feature of all such seasons of devout vicarious leisure is a more or less rigid tabu on all activity that is of human use."

Discounting Veblen's sly use of "obviously" and "vicarious," his characterization of the prohibition of work on religious holidays as a taboo, and hence as something fundamentally archaic (although probably intended mockingly), was not inaccurate. The Pentateuchal code of the Jews contained many Sabbatarian provisions—not lighting fires or cooking—which most historians agree derived from the taboo beliefs of the Babylonians and Egyptians. The link between the sacred day and the tabooed day was also evident in Polynesia, where New England missionaries tried to introduce a strict observance of Sunday. They were surprised at how easily the natives accepted this foreign practice, not realizing that among their new converts, Sunday was popularly known as *la tabu*.

Veblen's characterization of religious holidays as

tabooed days is misleading, however, for although the holy day undoubtedly borrowed from the earlier taboo tradition, the two were not identical. The holy day emerged as part of the evolution from animism to polytheism, and involved, as the anthropologist Hutton Webster pointed out, a distinction between two contradictory beliefs, that of the "unclean thing" and that of the "holy thing." The former held that work and other secular activities could contaminate the sanctity of the holy day and should be avoided. But at the same time, the day that was consecrated to a divinity was not unlucky—on the contrary, it was considered holy. The observance of its sanctity took the form of various religious rites and rituals, including an abstention from work—not in a spirit of apprehension or atonement but as a form of worship.

Among the Romans, there were two types of holidays, or *feriae:* private family celebrations following a birth, marriage, or death, on which work was proscribed for all (including servants, as Cicero observed); and annual, public *feriae* (of which there were sixty-one in republican times), which were chiefly religious, although some, which fell on *dies religiosi,* were considered merely unlucky (in both cases, work was prohibited). The *feriae* combined elements of both the tabooed and the holy day. With time, the former gave way to the latter. This blending of traditions was not unusual; as Webster observed, it is "a universal

tendency of the human mind to dwell with special emphasis on the festive aspects of a holy season, and by some subtle alchemy of the spirit to convert what was once a day of gloom and anxiety into a day of gladness and good cheer."

This conversion of a tabooed day into a holy day is evident in the evolution of the Jewish Sabbath, in which the early, taboo-like proscriptions were replaced (in post-exile times) by a more tolerant attitude that forbade fasting and promoted a more joyous festivity. It became a moral obligation to enjoy oneself on the Sabbath, and the Sabbath meals were occasions for delicacies and special treats. Hymns acclaimed the Sabbath as "a day of rest and joy, of pleasure and delight." This interpretation was in turn replaced by Pharisaic legalism, which tried to reinstate a complex of Sabbatical regulations. It was in opposition to this view that Jesus Christ taught that "the Sabbath was made for man, and not man for the Sabbath." In other words, that it was a rest day for the benefit of mankind, not a tabooed day to be feared.

The early Christians, especially those who were Jews, observed both the Sabbath and the succeeding Lord's Day, when they assembled to break bread. By the time of St. Paul, Sabbath observance was greatly diminished. This did not mean that one replaced the other, though; initially the Lord's Day had few Sabbatarian characteristics. The faithful gathered for the

Eucharist, in commemoration of the Resurrection, but otherwise it was an ordinary working day.

There was another weekly holiday that was different from either the tabooed day, or the holy day—the market day. There was an old tradition among the Romans, perhaps dating back to the Etruscans, that every eighth day was set aside for holding town meetings, conducting public business, and bringing goods to market. The legal character of this day—the nundine (that is, the "ninth day," counting inclusively as the Romans did)—was eventually lost, but the market and leisure function survived. The nundine was a useful device, since ordinary farmers and townspeople, who did not have access to astronomical time-reckoning devices, needed a simple way to schedule public markets. Any interval would have done, as long as it was reasonably short, since food without refrigeration spoiled rapidly in hot climates.

There are two differences between the Roman nundine and our seven-day week. For one thing, the Romans didn't give names to individual days. For another, there was a casualness about the exact length of the period between markets; the nundine was held in different parts of the empire at different intervals, although eight days was the most common.

The eight-day Roman nundine is the oldest known

example of a market week, but it was not unique; analogous periods have been observed in agricultural societies around the world. In West Africa, for example, four-day market weeks were common, and, unlike the nundine, the individual days were usually named; the fifth day was market day, and one more day was set aside as a day of rest. The Akikuyu of East Africa held a market every four days, and in a predetermined rotation in different locations. There were five-day market weeks in Java, Bali, and Sumatra, as well as in ancient Mexico and parts of Central America. In Assam, the market week was eight days long. In pre-Hispanic Colombia, the market week lasted only three days; in Peru, it lasted ten. In old Mexico, markets were held in different villages every four days; sometimes a greater fair was held on every fifth interval, that is, every twenty days, which produced a year of eighteen "market months."

The lengths of the intervals between markets were remarkably consistent—usually between four and eight days, never less than three or more than ten. The main purpose of the market week was to provide a timekeeping device for a regular succession of market days when farmers could gather to exchange goods. But it was more than that. Lacking regular holidays, farmers needed a day of rest. The lives of fishermen and hunters were—and still are—alternations of intensive labor and enforced idleness. The

responsibilities of the shepherd or cowherd precluded a day off, but his toil was slight when compared with the exertions of the farmer. Heavy and continuous physical labor—plowing, digging, cultivating, and harvesting—required a regular intermission, and market day provided precisely such a break.

There is explicit evidence for this theory. In Dahomey, in the mid-nineteenth century, every fourth day was a market day and a holiday, "not kept holy, but devoted to the will of the working class; in short, a sort of remuneration to the slave for the three days' labor," observed one British visitor. The tenth day of the Incan week was also a holiday and a market day, which was said (by an old chronicler, himself of Incan descent) to have been conceived "in order that labor might not be so continuous as to become oppressive." Peruvian peasants were required to come to the market to "hear anything that the Inca or his council might have ordained." As in ancient Rome, market day was not only an opportunity for trading and a break from work, it was also a public, social occasion. Goods were exchanged, but so was news, information, and knowledge, for the market gave farmers a chance to break their rural isolation and come into contact with itinerant merchants, tinkers, and entertainers.

The seven-day week has replaced the market week in most of these societies, but the market day persists.

I have attended markets in the town of Benue, in central Nigeria, where despite the presence of video-cassettes and plastic buckets, the atmosphere was much as it must have been in the past: a holiday, characterized by loud trading, gossip, music, and playfulness. The open-air bazaar had not the least re-semblance to the scrubbed solemnity of the modern supermarket but reminded me instead of a garage sale or a church rummage sale—or, for that matter, of a seasonal country fair of the type that is still held in American and Canadian rural towns and villages.

The first Sunday law can be dated with certainty. In A.D. 321, the Emperor Constantine decreed that, throughout the Roman Empire, magistrates, city peo-ple, and artisans were to abstain from work "on the venerable day of the Sun." He pointedly exempted farmers from this obligation, since there was a Roman tradition that even on *feriae* necessary agricultural work was permitted. Historians disagree on whether this legislation was the result of Constantine's Chris-tianity, his acknowledgment of the growing accep-tance of the planetary week, or his recognition of the popularity of Mithraism. In any case, there was no mention of the Lord's Day, neither then nor four months later, when the strict law was amended to permit various public acts, since "it seemed unworthy of the day of the sun, honored for its own sacredness, to be used in litigations and baneful disputes."

The first imperial edict to specifically mention the

A Meaningful Day

Lord's Day was issued sixty years after Constantine's decree. As Christianity spread, the Christian Sunday assimilated the day of the sun and became a civic holiday, free from work. At the same time, the ecclesiastical authorities began to proscribe various Sunday activities. In 436, the Fourth Council of Carthage, for instance, discouraged Sunday attendance at games and circuses, although it did not ban them outright; the Third Council of Orléans judged it "better to abstain" from all rural work, "so that people may the more readily come to the churches and have leisure for prayers."

The term "Christian Sabbath" was first used in the twelfth century, and it marks the beginning of the church's grafting of the Sabbatarian tradition onto the Lord's Day. It became a mortal sin to do any unnecessary work on Sunday, as the clergy, with the help of civil laws, attempted to drape a pall of Pharisaic gloom over the day. In practice, though, Sunday was still a festive day. Part of Constantine's edict had involved shifting the nundine from the eighth day to the day of the sun, and this tradition continued strongly in many parts of medieval Europe, in spite of clerical attempts to forbid it.* The reemergence of Sunday shopping (mainly in the United States, and more gradually in Canada) is a return to this market tradition.

---

* This tradition is recalled by the Hungarian word for Sunday, which means "market day."

Medieval Sundays were both holy days and civic holidays; work was generally forbidden, but other activities took place, including sporting events, tourneys, plays, pageants, festivals, feasts, parish ales (where much of the substance was consumed), and various other public amusements. The day happily combined the social recreations of the market day and the celebratory, religious festivity of the Sabbath—as so often happened in the Middle Ages, the secular and the profane merged one into the other. In any event, Sunday was only one holy day among a multitude of festivals and saints' days, and did not carry the full weight of religious observance.

The character of Sunday was greatly altered by the Reformation. Some, like Calvin, considered that religious services could be held on any day of the week; although he did preserve holy Sunday as a practical measure, Calvin himself bowled after services. Others placed the Sunday service—and so the entire day—at the center of religious life. "Everything is governed and ordained by the Gospel, baptism, and Sunday prayer," preached Martin Luther. Sunday was the occasion not only for devotions but for instruction; most Lutheran adults attended catechism classes after church.* The day acquired a wholly religious

---

* The Counter-Reformation, too, stressed attendance at Sunday Mass and, by the eighteenth century, Sunday vespers as well.

character, and, given the inclination of the Protestant faiths for seriousness and simplicity, it also lost its medieval gaiety. This character found its ultimate expression not on the Continent but in England, where Puritans (and, to a lesser extent, the Church of England) eventually made Sunday into a gloomy festival, a veritable tabooed day.

Before the Reformation, Sunday churchgoing had been a religious, not a civic obligation. In 1551, the British Act of Uniformity made absence from Sunday services punishable by a fine. The Sunday Observance Act of 1677 went further and forbade "tradesmen, artificers, and laborers" from carrying out any business. This law was applied in the widest possible way and prohibited even boatmen from plying their trade. In 1781, a law was passed that made it a serious offense to hold any form of public entertainments on Sundays for which people were charged an entrance fee. This ban stayed in force for 150 years. As late as 1856, when free Sunday band concerts began to take place in London parks, the Archbishop of Canterbury objected, and they were stopped. That same year, the House of Commons refused to consider a suggestion that the National Gallery and the British Museum stay open on Sunday afternoons.

It was not surprising that English settlers, many of whom were Puritans, brought their strict Sunday customs to the colonies. The first Sunday law enacted

by the Colony of Virginia, in 1610, enjoined all
men and women to attend divine services in the morning and catechism in the afternoon. The penalty for
a first offense was losing a week's provisions; for the
second offense, whipping; and, for the third, death.
The latter punishment was unusual, but laws requir-
ing attendance at Sunday services and prohibiting
work, travel, sports, and other frivolous pastimes also
existed in Maryland, Massachusetts, and Connecticut.
They became a distinguishing feature of all the new
American colonies—the Carolinas as well as New
York, Pennsylvania, New Hampshire, Maine, and
New Jersey.

"Blue laws"—named after the blue paper on
which a Sunday edict had been written in New Haven
in 1781—were widespread. Although a strict Puritan
interpretation of blue laws lapsed after the War of
Independence, the Sabbatarian tradition has continued
to the present day. It remains strongest in states such
as Massachusetts and Maryland, but, as late as 1985,
thirty-nine states continued to restrict Sunday activities, either by a general ban on all commerce and
labor (twenty-two states) or by restrictions on specific
activities. The latter make a curious list. Every Sunday, somewhere in the United States, it is illegal to
barber; bowl; play billiards, bingo, polo, or cards;
gamble; race horses; hunt; go to the movies; sell cars,
fresh meat or alcohol; organize boxing or wrestling

matches; hold public dances or sporting events; or dig oysters.

"The festive quality of a holiday depends on its being exceptional," wrote Josef Pieper. I can recall my own childhood Sundays as days apart from the rest of the week. To begin with, we slept in, and breakfast was later than usual. Like my parents, my brother and I put on special clothes—our Sunday best. We went to church, which took most of the morning and established the mood for the rest of the day—not necessarily one of sanctity but of singularity. What I remember more clearly than Sunday Mass is the ride home after church, the pleasurable feelings of satisfaction that a serious obligation had been fulfilled (and sin averted) and the relief that this serious part of the day was over.

Sunday lunch was also special; at least, it was an occasion for special food. Not roast beef and Yorkshire pudding—my parents' Anglophilia did not extend that far—but more elaborate dishes than on a weekday. Sunday lunches were also the occasion for guests, when my father, with some ceremony, placed wine on the table. I realize now that this "Sabbath meal" was really a celebration, and hence an implicit part of the holiness of the day.

Sunday the family stayed at home. I don't recall

Sunday afternoon drives, although there must have
been some, at least when I was a youngster and automobile ownership was still a novelty. Sometimes
we children bicycled to the Yacht Club (despite the
grand name, there were no boats—the river pier was
used only for swimming), where there were tennis
courts.

There was a final punctuation before Sunday was
over—*The Ed Sullivan Show*. We watched it religiously. The word is not altogether inappropriate, for
in addition to acrobats, jugglers, and comics, there
was usually a "serious" act, a choir or a dramatic
reading, which tempered the burlesque atmosphere
and was, I think, an implicit recognition of the special
day. This was family entertainment, but it was also
Sunday entertainment, and the host's notoriously delicate sense of decorum was influenced by the latter as
much as it was by the former.

Ed Sullivan—like most of what we saw on television—had the added exoticism of being foreign, for
we lived in Canada. Or more precisely, in Quebec,
French Canada, which was predominantly Roman
Catholic. Catholicism traditionally imposed few of
the Sunday inhibitions of Protestantism—most European Catholic countries, for example, never instituted Sunday laws.* This was not the case in Quebec,

---

* In Spain, for instance, bullfights are traditionally held on Sunday
afternoons.

however, which came under English Sunday legislation in 1774 during the reign of George III, but since the ordinances were never strictly enforced, Sunday traditions were more relaxed there than in the rest of Canada.

The difference in Sunday observance between French and English Canada went unnoticed until it was dramatically underlined during the vociferous 1906 countrywide debate on national Sunday legislation. The conflict between Catholic Quebec and Protestant Ontario—the chief protagonists—recalled the arguments that had divided papists and Puritans in seventeenth-century England. The Protestant Lord's Day Alliance wanted to put an end not only to all Sunday commerce but to Sunday streetcars, rail travel, and "public spectacles." But the prime minister, Sir Wilfred Laurier, the first French Canadian to hold that office, told a Protestant Member of Parliament, "In the province of Quebec we have a different way of observing the Sabbath, and I am not pretending that we observe it in a better fashion than other people. Everybody in our province goes to church in the morning, and in the afternoon he is at liberty to engage in those contests. The young people play baseball, which I know is objectionable to some Christian communities. For instance, in the constituency of my honorable friend it would be a high moral offense for a young man to play ball on a Sunday."

As has happened so often in Canadian history, the resolution of this cultural conflict was a compromise. The Dominion Lord's Day Act was passed in full, but an amendment was added that left enforcement to the discretion of the provincial attorneys general and that furthermore allowed the provinces to pass modifying legislation. In Quebec, this made the federal Sunday law a dead letter.

As in the past, neither sports nor public entertainments were banned in Quebec, and although large businesses like offices and factories were closed, small shops could stay open. The day had some of the features of the festive medieval Sunday, and, as in the Middle Ages, the church frowned on this levity. In 1922, inspired by a pastoral letter decrying the lax observance of Sunday as a day of rest, the Ligue du Dimanche (Sunday League) was formed. For fourteen years the League agitated for Sabbatarian legislation, particularly against cinemas, but politicians, sensing the public mood, resisted efforts to impose stricter rules, and the province remained the only place in Canada where movie theaters stayed open on Sunday.*

---

* The Sunday League's chief success—and it was a shameful one—was to force the abrogation of that part of the law that had permitted Jews to carry on their business on Sunday. This was the result of a general anti-Semitic climate that existed in Quebec during the 1920s and 1930s.

A Meaningful Day

The contradictions between Sunday legislation, the lenient application of laws, and the strict teaching of the clergy continued in Quebec for several decades. When I was a boy growing up there in the 1950s, I could go to movies and sporting events on Sunday; had I been older, I could have bought a drink in a restaurant, or (illegally) a bottle of beer at the accommodating corner store. At the same time, the atmosphere was not one of unbridled gaiety—the parish priest saw to that. Except for morning churchgoers, the streets were empty, as empty as the clotheslines awaiting the Monday wash. People avoided being seen doing yardwork or household chores; there were no Sunday papers.

I remember Sunday as an idle day—no housework was done, no vacuuming or clothes washing, no digging in the garden. This custom was not followed strictly, for I was asked, one Sunday, to mow the front lawn. An earnest catechism student, I knew this sort of work was forbidden, and as a prim adolescent I was scandalized by what the neighbors would think of this flagrant, public flaunting of the day of rest. As I pushed the mower over the small patch of grass I imagined secret eyes behind drawn curtains—I might as well have been made to wear a scarlet letter.

My childhood Sunday was not the festive celebration of the Middle Ages, the somber holiday of the Puritans, or the unlucky day of the Polynesians.

Or, rather, it was all three: a curious combination of day of rest, holy day, and tabooed day. This amalgam of traditions suggests that in one form or another, Sunday—or whatever name we choose to give this meaningful day—will continue to punctuate the course of time. It may evolve into more of a rest day, an introspective retreat from the busy workweek, not because of physical exhaustion but out of mental fatigue or boredom. If material pleasures wane, it could reaffirm its religious, celebratory function. Or it could become more secular—Sunday at the mall, not Sunday with the catechism, a market day instead of a tabooed day.

four

Sunday in the Park

There have been scores of Sunday painters, but there is one great Sunday painting: Georges Seurat's *A Sunday on the Grande Jatte*. For six months, beginning in the late spring of 1884, the young artist went daily to the Île de la Grande Jatte to work on studies and sketches for the final painting. During the week he concentrated on the landscape elements that formed the background to his subject. One can imagine him shifting his attention on Sunday, when the previously empty park filled up with crowds of holidaying Parisians.

The island of Grande Jatte lies in the middle of the Seine, upstream from Asnières and Clichy, where the river loops around to encircle the northwest edge of Paris. Today this area is completely citified, the skyline dominated by the futuristic architecture of the nearby La Défense, but in the nineteenth century it was the site of a different type of modern novelty— the suburb. The Parisian suburbs, or *banlieues*, were

a result of the rebuilding of the city that had been undertaken in the 1850s, during the Second Empire. The boulevards and avenues that were cut through working-class neighborhoods in the center of Paris displaced many people. When the new railways made it possible to live outside the encircling fortifications that had traditionally defined the city, many—including the working poor—moved there. At the same time, industrialization was attracting people to the city from the countryside; by 1900 Paris would have 2.5 million inhabitants. The physical expansion occurred in concentric rings: first, closest to the city, were the industrial slums of the workers; next, slightly farther out, the tidy houses of the middle class; lastly, at the perimeter, beyond the reach of the railway (and hence of the masses), one found the fashionable homes of the *haute bourgeoisie*.

The better residential suburbs of Paris were in the south; to the north of the city, the suburbs were mainly industrial. Such was Clichy, on the main railway line to the Channel ports and served by the barges that plied the Seine. The town contained workshops and factories, a smoke-belching gasworks, as well as rows of squalid tenements. Asnières, across the river, was a *petit-bourgeois* residential area, half-country, half-town. The narrow island of Grande Jatte lay between the two. Too small to be of practical use, it had been left in its natural wooded state, and had

become, as Richard Thomson described it, a "no-man's land, between bourgeois propriety and proletarian dereliction."

Throughout the second half of the nineteenth century, Grande Jatte was a favorite destination for Parisians who wanted to spend a day in the country, or at least in a countrylike setting. It had been first a boating center, later a place for strolling and picnics. The location was convenient for short excursions, only two and a half miles by train from the Gare Saint-Lazare; those who lived near the Place de l'Étoile could take a horse-drawn omnibus straight down the Avenue de Neuilly. For the adventurous, the velocipede was an alternative, and if they could afford a new bicycle, with the pneumatic tires made by the Michelin brothers, it was a comfortable ride.

Like many Parisian painters, Georges Seurat was attracted to the outer suburbs and their peculiarly odd mixture of images—pastoral and industrial, field and factory. This interest started early; his father owned property in the northeast suburbs, and some of Seurat's earlier drawings were made there. In 1881, when he was twenty-two, suburban subjects began to appear in his work, and two years later he started to make regular painting excursions to Asnières. Seurat probably took the train, since he lived in Montmartre, not far from the Gare Saint-Lazare.

Seurat's first major painting was the masterful

Bathing, Asnières, which shows a group of young men swimming in the Seine. Some are in the water; others sit or recline on the grassy bank. The mood is summery. The island of Grande Jatte can be seen in the background, its verdure contrasting with the bridge and the smoking factory chimneys of Clichy on the far shore. Despite the clash of images, however, there is no social comment. Without irony, Seurat, a bourgeois, represented a *petit-bourgeois* scene. The swimmers in the scene, judging from their clothes—bowler hats, a straw boater, white shirts, elastic-sided boots— and their decorous postures, are not factory hands. They are store clerks or office workers, inhabitants of Asnières who have come to the grassy riverbank after work for the fresh air and relaxation, for a swim, to enjoy the view of the pleasure boats on the water. This is a portrayal of the suburb as a setting for leisure.

Seurat began work on his next painting immediately. This time he chose a location directly across the river, on the island itself. *Sunday on the Grande Jatte,* completed in 1886, was more ambitious both in the choice of theme and in its composition. On the riverbank, among young trees, whose long afternoon shadows dapple the ground, Seurat disposed many human figures—men, women, and children. Some were walking, some standing, some sitting on the grass. Most were facing the water, gazing across at Asnières on the far shore. The small stretch of river

glimpsed through the trees was no less crowded and included several sailboats, a rowboat, a four-man scull, a steam launch, a tug, and the Asnières ferry, with a tricolor at its stern.

Seurat crammed his large (six and a half by ten feet) canvas with more than forty figures. One woman stands beside the water, hand on hip, holding a fishing pole; nearby, a girl and a man are posed motionless, like statues, at the water's edge. A couple holds an infant in swaddling clothes. Two soldiers stroll side by side; a little girl in a white dress primly accompanies her nanny; a dumpy figure in a wet nurse's bonnet sits mutely with a companion, paying no notice to the nearby solitary man playing a trumpet. The atmosphere is sunny but lethargic—a dog-day afternoon. The sense of movement is arrested, and yet so strongly implied that for the modern viewer it is like watching a movie in which the film speed has been turned down almost to zero and the action unfolds imperceptibly, frame by frame.

Seurat's methodical technique and careful composition—he made three preparatory canvases, thirty painted studies, and about twenty-six drawings— went well with his choice of subject: a Sunday scene of bourgeois decorum and propriety. Or is that too simple a reading? "The *Grande Jatte* is one of those great pictures in which every generation finds the meaning best suited to it," wrote John Russell. For

many, the painting's significance lies in its delicate rendering of light, its masterful composition of simplified forms, and, of course, its pointillist technique. When the painting was first shown, many critics considered Seurat's style too primitive, verging on caricature. Others felt this was intentional; the painter was satirizing his subject. "The painting has tried to show the toing and froing of the banal promenade that people in their Sunday best take, without any pleasure, in the places where it is accepted that one should stroll on a Sunday," wrote Alfred Paulet in his review of the Eighth Impressionist Exhibition, where *Grande Jatte* was first shown. "The artist has given his figures the automatic gestures of lead soldiers moving about on regimented squares." Since there is no record of any explanation of the painting by its maker, the viewer must decide for himself whether Seurat is mocking these Sunday promenaders or merely observing them. It is revealing that the title he himself gave to his painting was so specific, not only as to the location (which was not unusual) but also as to the day of the week. In *A Sunday on the Grande Jatte,* Seurat dealt deliberately, and in great detail, with a subject that fascinated him, as it did many of his contemporaries: the nature of popular urban leisure in an industrial age.

Seurat portrayed a scene whose ingredients are recognizably modern: escaping the city for an after-

noon, walking in the park, sitting on the grass, sailing on the river, fishing by the shore, taking pets for a stroll. The languid Sunday atmosphere, too, is unmistakable. Update the costumes, take away the parasols, add some boys playing with a Frisbee and a teenager lugging a boombox, and this could be Central Park, or Mount Royal in Montreal, on a summer Sunday afternoon.

More than a hundred years have passed since *Grande Jatte* was painted, and, in some ways, not much has changed. This would not be true if we traveled a further hundred years back. Hugh Cunningham, a British historian, wrote, "In 1780 no one could have predicted the shape of leisure a century ahead. In 1880, by contrast, the lines of development are clear . . . There is nothing in the leisure of today which was not visible in 1880."

What happened, according to Cunningham, was the so-called Industrial Revolution. It is common to consider this a cataclysmic occurrence, a watershed, with the modern world on one side and preindustrial society on the other. Such a view can be misleading, however. The term "Industrial Revolution" itself, popularized by Arnold Toynbee, implies sudden and dramatic change, whereas industrialization was a process, one that lasted a hundred years or so. The changes that took place in the period between 1780 and 1880 were the result not only of industrial inven-

tions but also of social and commercial innovations, many of which had occurred earlier.

But Cunningham is right about one thing: by the 1880s, when Seurat was painting his suburban scenes, leisure had assumed a character that could be called modern. A hundred years earlier, it had had a different form. How did this evolution occur? Let's go back to the period immediately before industrialization began, the first half of the eighteenth century, to England, where industrialization first appeared, and take a look at the nature of popular leisure.

This period, roughly 1700 to 1750, was a time of great prosperity for England, which had replaced Spain and Portugal as the world's dominant sea power, hence commercial power. The economy boomed; goods flowed to Britain from India, Asia, the West Indies, and North America, as well as from the Continent, which still accounted for the biggest share of England's trade. Since affluence is a prerequisite for leisure, we would expect this to be a time when the pursuit of pleasure was given importance. Expenditures on the home increased dramatically and produced an extraordinarily refined domestic architecture, pottery and porcelain of unparalleled elegance, a generation of furniture makers whose work continues to be prized, and the eighteenth-century garden.

What was novel about the early eighteenth cen-

tury was that this prosperity was widespread—or at least more widespread than before. The "leisured classes" included not only the aristocracy and the landed gentry but also the middle class. It was the latter who inhabited the Georgian terrace houses and who were the patrons of Chippendale, Hepplewhite, and Wedgwood.

Nothing characterized this new age better than the growth in popularity of three luxury goods: coffee, tea, and tobacco. Coffee had been introduced to England in the 1650s and had quickly become fashionable—by 1700 there were two thousand coffeehouses in London alone. Tea, which arrived at about the same time, took longer to catch on, as it was expensive; but when trade from the Far East increased, and prices fell, tea consumption increased enormously. Eventually tea became cheaper than coffee, and much cheaper than chocolate, another fashionable drink. Twenty thousand pounds of tea were imported in 1700; sixty years later it was 5 *million* pounds (that was the official figure—probably an equal amount arrived illegally from France). The third popular "poison" of the time—for so it was that many contemporary critics considered these products—was tobacco, which was smoked, chewed, and taken as snuff.

Coffee, tea, and tobacco had all been known before, but during the early eighteenth century, con-

sumption surged on the Continent as in England. Why these three substances should have been received with such enthusiasm at this particular time is hard to explain. The French historian Fernand Braudel has suggested that coffee, tea, and tobacco, which are all stimulants, were meant to compensate for dietary deficiencies. This may have been the case in France and Germany but was hardly true in England, where caloric intake was generally high, and even less so in prosperous Holland, the country that had introduced tea to the English, and a nation then famous for overeating. Another, more likely explanation is that the new popularity of coffee, tea, and tobacco reflected the growing availability of leisure time. They were not, after all, dietary staples: all three were—and are—associated with relaxation and "taking a break" from work.

The increase in consumption of such luxuries was the result of the prosperity of many individuals, encouraged by the increased marketing skills of entrepreneurs. Napoléon later dismissed the British as a nation of shopkeepers; they would have been better described as a nation of customers. That is the most striking thing about early-eighteenth-century leisure, not merely that it was enjoyed by many but that it gave many the opportunity to consume a wide variety of both material goods and culture. "The cultural poverty of late-seventeenth-century England was

vast," writes the eminent historian J. H. Plumb. "No newspapers, no public libraries, no theaters outside London, no concerts anywhere, no picture galleries of any kind, no museums, almost no botanical gardens, and no organized sports." During the next hundred years, all this changed.

The number of people who read for pleasure is a good indicator of leisure, since reading requires the availability of not only money but, more important, time. What people read, in addition to newspapers (the first English daily was founded in 1702), were magazines. The magazine was a Georgian invention, and there were dozens of them. Most were of general interest, such as *The Gentleman's Magazine, The Lady's Magazine, The Tatler, The Rambler, The Idler,* and the famous *Spectator* (a daily); in addition, there were magazines that dealt with such specialized subjects as fashion, music, and gardening. The most successful monthlies did not have large circulation by modern standards—only about ten thousand copies—but their readership far exceeded this number, since bound copies were available in coffeehouses and taverns, or for a small fee from so-called newsrooms, as well as from the circulating libraries that were becoming common in the provinces.

The magazine was a product specifically designed for leisure. Like the newspaper, it informed: but it also entertained. It was more opinionated than its

modern descendants, and was often written entirely by one person: in the case of *The Rambler* and later *The Idler,* Samuel Johnson; Daniel Defoe produced three issues of *The Review* each week. Magazines contained essays, political views, advice on self-improvement, fashion plates, social satire, gossip, and serialized fiction. It was this last, as published in *The Spectator,* that is generally considered to be the precursor of the eighteenth century's greatest literary innovation—the novel.

The novel derived its form—and its name—from northern Italy, but first achieved prominence in the English language in the 1740s. Samuel Richardson's *Pamela* and *Clarissa,* Tobias Smollett's *Roderick Random,* and Henry Fielding's *Joseph Andrews* and *Tom Jones* all appeared in that decade, and introduced the genre to an immediately enthusiastic reading public. The novel was, from the first, a commercial venture. *Pamela,* arguably the first modern English novel, and its author's first literary effort, was commissioned by two London printers. It was a great success and went through four editions in six months; in true entrepreneurial spirit, Richardson produced a sequel. With an eye to the market, eighteenth-century printers devised the "part-book," which reduced the price of each book for the poorer reader—of whom there were many—and also increased profits, always assuming the public was hooked. This was how the immensely

popular *Clarissa* appeared—two volumes the first year, two the next, and the last three just in time for the following Christmas. Another example of part-book publishing was Laurence Sterne's *Tristram Shandy,* which appeared in nine volumes over a period of eight years.

There is no more leisurely occupation than reading a novel. It requires calm surroundings, a comfortable chair, and long periods of uninterrupted time. Magazines and newspapers could be read in noisy coffee-houses, but the novel was a different creature. It signaled the arrival of a new type of leisure activity—introverted, intimate, personal, and private—and undoubtedly accounted for the growth of domesticity during this period.

Widespread private leisure was a thing of the future, however, and most entertainments were still public. The eighteenth century saw an explosive growth in the number of playhouses, both in the large cities and in smaller provincial towns. Between 1700 and 1750 more than a thousand new plays were produced; nor was attendance limited to the rich, as the popularity of cheaper "after-hours" performances shows. The general public was also provided with comic opera, pantomime, and puppet theater. In the second half of the century, the number of theaters continued to increase dramatically, and the quantity of new plays doubled.

New popular entertainments were devised, the most striking of which was the circus. The word circus comes from Charles Hughes's "Royal Circus," an enclosed amphitheater which was built in 1782, but the real inventor of the circus was Philip Astley, who presented the first circus performance in 1768. Astley was an equestrian, but he soon expanded his show to include pantomime, tumbling, acrobats, and clowns. His circus was based in London; the winter was spent performing in Paris, under the patronage of the queen, Marie Antoinette. Soon there were permanent circus buildings in all the large cities and, by 1800, there were dozens of smaller, traveling troupes—usually run by people trained by Astley—that took the spectacle to the provinces.

A parallel popularization occurred in music, with the introduction of musical societies and subscription concerts. The first regular public concerts in London had begun in 1672, organized by John Bannister, a violinist. A few years later, Thomas Britton, a coal merchant, converted a loft in his warehouse into a "concert room" and presented weekly recitals that attracted notable performers (among them Handel) and introduced the London public to the music of such Continental favorites as Vivaldi. Taverns and inns often had small music rooms, and by the middle of the eighteenth century there were many famous locales such as the York Buildings and Hickford's,

where the young Mozart played. Eventually larger halls were built that were no longer improvised spaces but designed especially for musical performances.

Concerts and plays were operated as a business, and, like all commercial entertainments, they needed publicity. This the newspapers and the magazines provided, not only in the form of reviews but also through advertising, another Georgian innovation. "Puffery," as it was derisively called by its critics, played a key role in the popularization of public leisure by attracting the public to theater and music—and new books—and by promoting sporting events.

The popularity of horse racing, for example, grew, thanks largely to newspapers, which not only advertised races but carried news of the results. The early 1700s saw a local recreation turn into a national industry: the Jockey Club, established in 1725, enforced standard rules; the Racing Calendar regulated meetings nationwide; the General Stud Book documented pedigrees. Another sport that became popular during this period was cricket. Although a version of the game had been played two hundred years earlier, the first definite match of which there is a record was in 1700. This record, aptly enough, is to be found in *The Post Boy,* the first nonofficial commercial London newspaper. Newspaper advertising played an important role in publicizing cricket matches, which eventually attracted large crowds—not because the game

95

was a rousing spectacle but because it was particularly suited to gambling, both for stake money and for continuous side bets. The game itself was also highly commercialized—many of the players were professionals, paid from subscriptions raised from cricket club members, from prize money, and from gate receipts (unlike horse-racing courses, which had unrestricted access, cricket grounds were usually fenced). The promoters of the sport were entrepreneurs such as Thomas Lord, who established the famous cricket ground that still bears his name, and innkeepers like George Smith, who ran the Artillery Ground where crowds of up to twenty thousand paid tuppence a head to eat, drink, wager, and noisily amuse themselves.

If one had to choose a characteristic Georgian recreation, though, it wouldn't be cricket or novel reading but animal baiting. Blood sports were hardly invented in the eighteenth century; cockfighting had arrived in England a hundred years earlier, and bearbaiting was older than that. But the same commercial forces that impelled the growth of theater, reading, and horse racing also advanced the popularity of the cockpit and the bear garden. Just as innkeepers provided premises for social clubs, musical and theatrical evenings, political societies, even libraries, they also were pleased to maintain locales for prizefights and for a variety of blood sports.

Here was an opportunity for a crowd of men—

public leisure was still mainly a male preserve—to drink, shout, wager, and revel in the sight and smell of blood. Even more than wrestling and prizefighting, which were also popular, contests between animals (cocks and dogs) and between dogs and an unfortunate bear, badger, or bull fascinated the public, rich and poor.

Undoubtedly the chance to wager had a lot to do with it, for, like all prosperous societies, this was a betting society. The excitement of the spectacle was also an attraction; the Georgian public was by all accounts an impassioned one, whether it was rallying behind Richard Nyren, Hambledon's leading cricketer, or cheering a bird in one of the cockpits on London's Birdcage Walk.

What contributed mightily to the excitement was the consumption of alcohol, mainly cheap gin. It has been estimated that between 1700 and 1735 the annual amount of gin legally produced in England grew from four hundred thousand gallons to more than 4 million; to this must be added the considerable output of illicit gin shops, and homemade stills.

The popularization of gin, brandy, rum, and a host of other grain alcohols throughout Europe was the result of eighteenth-century technological developments in distillation, which reduced the cost of production and allowed alcohol to be distilled from a variety of local, inexpensive, fermentable materials:

rye, wheat, corn, barley, sugarcane, potatoes, apples, and many other common fruits. In England, the rapid rise in the consumption of gin—and later rum—was aided by the business acumen of tavernkeepers, who discovered the profitable symbiosis between drinking, betting, and public sports.

The first half of the eighteenth century saw the beginning of what J. H. Plumb has called the "commercialization of leisure," a trend that would continue throughout the Georgian and Victorian epochs. What's striking about this commercialization is it didn't mean, as one might expect, the commercialization of traditional or amateur recreations. It was businessmen who promoted the growth of cricket, music, circuses, theater, magazines, novels, and horse racing. This is worth pointing out, since our conventional view holds that commercial leisure activities— and today almost all leisure has a commercial component—are somehow a crass distortion of "pure" leisure.

Public houses and taverns were important centers of public leisure, whether they were promoting prizefights, cricket matches, or musical concerts. There was one inevitable problem, however, with the otherwise happy combination of commerce and play: excessive drinking. As Fernand Braudel put it, "By the

early eighteenth century, the whole of London society, from top to bottom, was determinedly getting
drunk on gin." Drunkenness reached unprecedented
heights in the eighteenth century and had many adverse effects—not only public disorder and rowdiness,
and familial misery, but also a generally poor state of
health. The high mortality rates that characterized this
period were due in no small part to the immoderate
consumption of spirits, especially homemade spirits,
which were often poisonous.*

The reason for the popularity of spirits was their
extremely low price—unlike beer, they were taxed
only lightly. Desultory efforts were made in the 1730s
to tax alcohol—desultory because the outcome was
widespread rioting. In 1751, the Gin Act raised the
tax and imposed controls on retail sales by distillers.
This did have a dampening effect on consumption,
but it wasn't until a hundred years later, when Gladstone imposed extremely heavy taxes on spirits, that
popular consumption of alcohol diminished and beer
drinking regained its traditional primacy.

Since drinking was intimately linked to so many
recreational activities, the condemnation by social reformers and church groups of the former led to dis-

---

* Drinking on the job was customary, and remained so until the
middle of the nineteenth century. Nor was it done secretly—a bottle
was generally purchased communally, and different trades had different drinking traditions: printers preferred rum; tailors favored gin.

approval of the latter; before the mid-nineteenth century, sporting events and athletics in general were not considered respectable by the middle class. Blood sports, in particular, became a target of religious and social reformers, although it took many years before laws were passed prohibiting bearbaiting (1835) and cockfighting (1849). Prizefighting, too, was under attack, though it persisted even longer; the Queensberry Rules, forbidding bare-knuckle pugilism, were adopted only in 1866. Of course, this did not mean these activities died out immediately—in fact they continued illicitly—but they did diminish.

Horse racing, which provided many chances for wagers, was appropriated by the upper classes for their own amusement rather than being banned. The improvised country races often staged by tavern-keepers were replaced by large organized events on permanent tracks. A 1740 Act of Parliament restrained the number of small local races and promoted the sport among the aristocrats. They became its chief patrons, breeding the horses, hiring the professional jockeys, and making races such as the St. Léger, the Derby, and the Oaks—which were all founded in the 1770s and would become part of the five "classics"— into important social occasions. At the same time, formal public betting came into existence at several tracks, which further encouraged the involvement of the lower classes, who, if they did not have access to

the boxes of the rich, could at least mingle with the toffs and nobs at trackside.

The appropriation of popular sports by the wealthy continued in the nineteenth century. Professional touring cricket teams were replaced by an organization of county teams, which consisted of upper- and middle-class players, all amateurs. The dominance of county cricket, which occurred in the period 1860–80, was literal—the amateurs simply outplayed the professionals. This was a result of the introduction of cricket to the exclusive Victorian public (i.e., private) schools. Amateur cricket turned a raucous and noisy sport into a polite pastime for gentlemen. Beginning in the 1840s, football, previously a workingman's pastime, started to become an upper-class sport. The rules were altered and formally codified and eventually the game (now called rugby) came to be adopted in this form by many of the public schools. The traditional version of the game, in which the ball cannot be picked up, became known as association football, or soccer, and remained the proletarian favorite.

The nineteenth century saw the increasing privatization of leisure by the middle classes, who elevated the status of the home to a previously unimagined level, spent large amounts of money on architecture and decoration, and spent much of their free time in

a domestic atmosphere. Around the same time, another leisure institution made its appearance. Belonging to a private club, for men, was also a way of keeping the crowd at bay. The changes in such sports as horse racing, cricket, and football all reflected a general desire on the part of the better-off to distance themselves from the general population.

But leisure was also a way of asserting status in a public way—hence the popularity of such pastimes as fox hunting and shooting, which by law and custom were unavailable to ordinary people. The pastime of yachting, which grew in popularity during the first half of the nineteenth century, was ideally suited to conspicuous consumption. It was expensive, hence exclusive. The yachtsman could distance himself from the crowd simply by sailing out into the middle of a lake—there was no need for fences or enclosures. At the same time, it was—and remains—a gratifying opportunity to be seen, admired, and envied by the plebeians on the shore.

The segregation of leisure according to social class was not wholesale, however, and during the mid-Victorian period there were several opposing influences. One was the rational recreation movement. Initially a middle-class phenomenon that promoted circulating libraries, literary societies, and public lectures, it eventually turned its attention to the public at large. The general idea was to offer the workingman

an ordered, educational, self-improving alternative to the attractions of the tavern and the gaming house. This was, of course, an uphill battle, but it did produce some tangible results such as free museum admissions on holidays, and the passing of statutes that made it possible for municipalities to create a variety of public leisure institutions: libraries, museums, and parks. Although the physical realization of the ideal—public places of recreation accessible to all—took many years to achieve, the shift in perception was an important one. Leisure, previously a commercial affair, was becoming a public concern.

Another democratizing influence on nineteenth-century leisure, especially Sunday leisure, was train travel. Trains transported entertainers—whether circus performers or theater troupes—more quickly and conveniently than before, and provincial audiences could now enjoy almost the same quality of entertainment as metropolitan ones. More important, as the cost of travel came down, more people could afford to go farther for a spectacle. This ensured the growth of large recreational enterprises such as fairs and pleasure gardens, and of the major racecourses, which could now draw spectators of all classes from a considerable distance. It's important to note that, as Cunningham points out, during the nineteenth century "working people used the trains not to get to work, but to travel for pleasure." When the Crystal

Palace was reerected at Sydenham, in 1854, it was reached from London by rail, and the idea of taking the train for "a day in the country" caught on. Railway companies made concerted efforts to attract the public by reducing fares on holidays and by organizing Sunday excursions not only to fairs and racecourses but also to the seaside. Previously exclusive resorts such as Brighton and Blackpool began to fill with crowds of day-trippers.

Georgian leisure had always been an antidote to work—it removed the participant from the humdrum, everyday world of the workshop and placed him in the exciting atmosphere of sport and public spectacle. Thanks to the railways, this dislocation became literal, taking the Victorian factory worker out of the confines of the industrial city and into more congenial surroundings.

The immense changes that Sunday—and leisure—had undergone by the last quarter of the nineteenth century were admirably depicted by Seurat in *Grande Jatte*. The wooded island, a short train ride from the Gare Saint-Lazare, offered precisely the amenities that attracted the Sunday crowd: fresh air and verdure, opportunities for boating, fishing, and picnicking— an escape from the center of Paris, which, like London, was increasingly congested and crowded. Most

homes were cramped, dreary, poorly lit and ill-ventilated. The city was an unhealthy place; until the turn of the century, outbreaks of typhoid, cholera, and smallpox were common in Paris. Little wonder that most people looked forward to getting away, even if only for a day.

What did they do on their outings? At first glance, most of the figures in *Grande Jatte* do not appear to be doing anything except strolling. The nineteenth century took the idea of "a walk in the park" seriously. Walking was physically healthful, and walking surrounded by nature was held to be spiritually uplifting—thus the growing popularity of mountain climbing and hiking. The first public parks were intended only for walking and contained no other facilities; they were deliberately introduced as a "civilizing" alternative to other recreations. One Manchester writer approvingly observed that "on Sunday, instead of loitering in the fields, dog-fighting, playing at pitch-and-toss, or being in the beerhouse, they [the public] go to some of those parks." He added, "They are also induced to dress better."

The island of Grande Jatte was not a formally planned park, but it had much in common with such places. Certainly the promenading figures that Seurat observed were well dressed: gentlemen in frock coats and top hats, ladies with fancy bonnets and parasols, exhibiting the curious silhouette that came from wear-

105

ing a bustle, which was then the height of chic. But among these fashion plates in their Sunday best are other figures, whose costumes suggest a lesser social pedigree: the two hatless young women sitting on the grass, for example, or the nanny with the child. On closer inspection this "bourgeois scene" is not that at all, for it also includes working-class participants such as the wet nurse and the conscript soldiers. Or the reclining man in the foreground, whose billed cap, sleeveless singlet, and clay pipe mark him as a factory hand. At the other end of the social spectrum are the yachtsmen and the team of rowers, indulging in gentlemanly pastimes that were restricted to the prosperous bourgeois.

The mixture of social classes demonstrated the extent to which the middle-class ideals of the rational recreation movement had come to dominate French Sunday leisure. This domination was not total, however, for Grande Jatte was not only a place for boaters and picnickers, it also offered commercial entertainments. The island was the site of several cafés and skittle alleys, and of a dance hall that had a slightly risqué reputation. These entertainments are not visible in the picture, but Seurat has alluded to them, in typically circumspect fashion.* The busty woman in the

---

* Seurat's origins were bourgeois, and he exhibited many of that class's characteristics: perseverance, sobriety, and reserve. Degas's nickname for him was "the notary."

foreground, accompanying the elegant boulevardier, has a monkey on a leash. Art historian Richard Thomson has suggested that Seurat was making a cunning visual pun, for in contemporary Parisian slang *singesse,* or female monkey, meant a prostitute. He also points out that the well-dressed female figure at the water's edge, anomalously holding a fishing pole, may be an allusion to a common French metaphor that referred to prostitutes as "fishing" for clients (the French words for "fishing" and for "sin" sound the same).

The presence of strumpets in the park is a reminder of an earlier time, when the only women who frequented dance halls, as well as other places of public leisure such as taverns, pleasure gardens, casinos, and even music halls, were assumed to be—and generally were—prostitutes. The proper place for proper women was the home—public leisure was exclusively a male domain. This began to change when sports and recreations became upper-class leisure activities. Then, too, the popular Sunday outing was a family affair. After the middle of the nineteenth century, the respectable recreations of the seaside—and of the park—could safely be indulged in by women of all classes, as Seurat's painting demonstrates.

It is a mixture of sexes and classes that has come to enjoy a Sunday afternoon in the park. Nevertheless—or maybe because of this democratic rubbing of shoulders—the individuals in this calm setting choose to ignore one another, and appear engrossed in private

reverie. They are all together, yet apart. This was yet another nineteenth-century change. Public leisure ceased to be local, class-bound, and familiar, and became instead increasingly communal. In the process, it also became more impersonal, almost anonymous. Now one went *away* to rest, and on the beach, or in the park, one took one's leisure in the company of strangers.

five

Keeping Saint Monday

The Oxford English Dictionary finds the earliest recorded use of the word "weekend" in an 1879 issue of *Notes and queries,* an English magazine. "In Staffordshire, if a person leaves home at the end of his week's work on the Saturday afternoon to spend the evening of Saturday and the following Sunday with friends at a distance," the entry goes, "he is said to be spending his week-end at So-and-so." The quotation is obviously a definition, which suggests that the word had only recently come into use. It is also important to note that the "week's work" is described as ending on Saturday afternoon. It was precisely this early ending to the week that produced a holiday period of a day and a half—the first weekend. This innovation—and it was a uniquely British one—occurred in roughly the third quarter of the nineteenth century. To understand how and why the weekend appeared when

it did, let's examine how the nature of free time changed during the previous hundred years.

Throughout the eighteenth century, the workweek ended on Saturday evening; Sunday was the weekly day off. The Reformation and, later, Puritanism had made Sunday the weekly holy day in an attempt to displace the saints' days and religious festivals of Catholicism. Although the taboo on work was more or less respected, the strictures of Sabbatarianism that prohibited merriment and levity on the Lord's Day were rejected by most Englishmen, who saw the holiday as a chance to drink, gamble, and generally have a good time.

Only one official weekly holiday did not necessarily mean that the life of the average British worker was one of unremitting toil. Far from it. Work was always interrupted to commemorate the annual feasts of Christmas, New Year, and Whitsuntide (the days following the seventh Sunday after Easter). These traditional holidays were universally observed, but the length of the breaks varied. Depending on local convention, work stopped for anywhere from a few days to two weeks. In addition to the religious holidays, villages and rural parishes observed their own annual festivals or "wakes." These celebratory rituals, which dated from medieval times, were mainly secular and involved sports, dancing, and other public amusements.

Towns had their own festivals, less bucolic than those of the countryside. Stamford, in Lincolnshire, celebrated a special holiday; each November 13th, thousands of men and boys gathered in the streets for bull running, an event reminiscent of the famous festival that still takes place in Pamplona. The British today deride the Spanish passion for bullfighting, but their sensibility in this regard is, at least culturally speaking, recent—the Stamford run ended with the bull's being pushed off a bridge into the river, and then fished out and killed. The Stamford run is famous because it lasted the longest (well into the nineteenth century), but similar runs took place in many English towns. In London, bull running involved workers and apprentices in the Spitalfields weaving trades, who merrily chased and goaded the animal, provided by a local butcher; the popular event persisted until 1826 and it took several violent police actions to stop it.

Annual festivals like the bull run were not the only days off. There were also communal holidays associated with special, occasional events such as prizefights, horse races, and other sporting competitions, as well as fairs, circuses, and traveling menageries. When one of these attractions arrived in a village or town, regular work more or less stopped while people flocked to gape and marvel at the exotic animals, equestrian acrobats, and assorted human freaks and oddities.

The idea of spontaneously closing up shop or leaving the workbench for the pursuit of pleasure strikes the modern reader as irresponsible, but for the eighteenth-century worker the line between work and play was blurred; work was engaged in with a certain amount of playfulness, and play was always given serious attention. Moreover, many recreational activities were directly linked to the workplace, since trade guilds often organized their own outings, had their own singing and drinking clubs and their own preferred taverns.

Eighteenth-century workers had, as Hugh Cunningham puts it, "a high preference for leisure, and for long periods of it." This preference was hardly something new; what *was* new was the ability, in prosperous Georgian England, of so many people to indulge it. For the first time in their lives, many workers earned more than survival wages. Now they had choices: they could buy goods or leisure. They could work more and earn more, or they could forgo the extra wages and enjoy more free time instead. Most chose the latter course. This was especially true for the highly paid skilled workers, who had the most economic freedom; but even general laborers, who were employed at day rates, had a choice in the matter. Many of these worked intensively, often for much more than the customary ten hours a day, and then quit to enjoy themselves until their money ran out.

Of course, the amount of regular free time varied according to local custom and the strength of each trade union. But many—too many—were left out. The poorest people, especially women and children, who were paid the lowest wages, did not share in the prosperity and were obliged to work continuous and unremitting days, often twelve to fourteen hours long. Sunday was their only opportunity for rest, and for some, who were obliged to work seven days a week, not even that break was available. But the occupation that offered the least chance for leisure had nothing to do with factory work—it was domestic service. Servants were at their masters' beck and call and had little time of their own. One afternoon a week was the typical maid's day off.

Whenever people had a choice in the matter, however, work was characterized by an irregular mixture of days on and days off, a pattern that the historian E. P. Thompson described as "alternate bouts of intense labor and of idleness." This irregularity was exacerbated by the way holidays were prolonged. The London bull run, for example, which traditionally took place on Easter Monday, was almost always extended to the following day; other runs began on Sunday and continued for one or two days thereafter. Village wakes followed a similar pattern. It was not unusual for sporting events, fairs, and other celebrations to last several days. Since Sunday was always

the official holiday, it was usually the days following that were added on. This produced a regular custom of staying away from work on Monday, frequently also on Tuesday, and then working long hours at the end of the week to catch up. Among some trades, the Monday holiday achieved what amounted to an official status. Weavers and miners, for example, regularly took a holiday on the Monday after payday—which occurred weekly, or biweekly. This practice became so common that it was called "keeping Saint Monday."

The origin of the Saint Monday tradition is obscure. Like the seven-day week, it was a custom that spread rapidly, despite the fact that it lacked any official sanction, because it appealed to people. Like the week, it was an institution whose genesis was explained by legends and folktales. According to some, keeping Saint Monday originated among tailors, whose shops were generally closed on Mondays. According to another story, the custom began with cobblers, tradesmen who were not held in high esteem since they, unlike real shoemakers, had only enough skill to mend shoes.* These slow-witted fellows were supposed to have forgotten the exact date of the feast day of their patron, Saint Crispin; remembering only

---

* Hence something "cobbled together" is considered to be clumsily or poorly made.

that it occurred on a Monday, they celebrated each "Saint" Monday instead. It is a charming tale, though unlikely to be true, for the Monday tradition also existed in France, Belgium, Prussia, and Sweden. Its widespread observance suggests that it may have been a popular reaction against the loss of the cherished medieval saints' days, which had been eliminated by Reformation clerics in Protestant countries and by demanding employers in Catholic Europe.

Cobblers had a reputation as great tipplers—"cobbler's punch" was a cure for a hangover—and in some versions of the story they were said to have needed the Monday holiday to recover from their Sunday excesses. That part of the legend rings true, for the custom of keeping Saint Monday was undoubtedly linked to heavy drinking. The eighteenth century's propensity for heavy drinking has already been mentioned; if anything, the consumption of alcohol increased during the first half of the nineteenth century, and did not begin to decline until the early 1900s. Since binges rarely lasted only one day, those workers who chose to "do a lushington" found themselves unable to get to work on the Monday morning. Here is Benjamin Disraeli writing about the fictitious industrial town of Wodgate, in his novel *Sybil, or the Two Nations*: "The men seldom exceed four days of labour in the week. On Sunday the master workmen begin to drink; for the apprentices there is

115

dog-fighting without stint. On the Monday and Tuesday the whole population is drunk."

The habit of keeping Saint Monday was not ancient—it probably started at the end of the eighteenth century. It was directly linked to industrialization, since it was a way for workers to redress the balance between their free time and the longer and longer workdays being demanded by factory owners. This improvised temporal device also allowed the worker to thumb his nose at authority and assert his traditional freedom to come and go from the workplace as he willed. Once the practice of keeping Saint Monday took hold, it was hard to dislodge. It was still common when Disraeli published his novel, in 1845, and it lasted for decades more. Thomas Wright's well-known book on the habits and customs of the working classes, which appeared in 1867, describes Saint Monday as "the most noticeable holiday, the most thoroughly self-made and characteristic of them all . . . that greatest of small holidays." Wright described himself as a journeyman engineer, that is, a mechanic, and his views are therefore those of someone who was not unsympathetic to his subject. On Monday, he wrote, "[the workers] are refreshed by the rest of the previous day; the money received on the Saturday is not all spent; and those among them who consign their best suits to the custody of the pawnbroker during the greatest part of each week are

still in the possession of the suits which they have redeemed from limbo on Saturday night." Dressed in his Sunday clothes, with a few shillings in his pocket, the idle worker could go out on the town and enjoy himself. Not a small part of this enjoyment was meeting friends and fellow tradesmen who were engaged in the same recreation.

According to E. P. Thompson, Saint Monday was observed "almost universally wherever small-scale, domestic and outwork industries existed"; it was also common among factory workers. Saint Monday may have started as an individual preference for staying away from work—whether for relaxation, for recovering from drunkenness, or both—but its popularity during the 1850s and '60s was ensured by the enterprise of the leisure industry. During that period, most sporting events such as horse races and cricket matches took place on Mondays, since their organizers knew that many of their working-class customers would be prepared to take the day off. Saint Monday was not only a day for animal baiting and prizefighting, however. Since many public events were prohibited on the Sabbath, Monday became the chief occasion for secular recreations. Attendance at botanical gardens and museums soared on Monday, which was also the day that ordinary people went to the theater and the dance hall and when workingmen's social clubs held their weekly meetings.

Michael R. Marrus, a British historian, defines leisure as "a free activity which an individual engages in for his own purposes, whatever these may be." The implication is that not all free time should be considered as leisure time, and that what distinguishes leisure from other recreations is the element of *personal choice*. This exercise of individual choice became a reality for a significant number of people for the first time during the late eighteenth and early nineteenth centuries, partly as the result of prosperity, partly as work habits changed, and partly as leisure activities passed from the world of custom and tradition (which offered little real choice) to the commercial world of the marketplace.

Chesterton maintained that the truest form of leisure was the freedom to do nothing. This was precisely the choice that the worker who kept Saint Monday made. This involved not only taking a particular day off but also the idea that it was the individual who was the master of his—and, more rarely, her—leisure. Because of its association with personal liberty, Saint Monday is sometimes described as if it were a preindustrial custom, like Maypole dancing or the village wake. Although this description is chronologically inaccurate, it is true that the ability to exercise the personal freedom to do nothing reflected preindustrial mores and stood in sharp contrast to the late-Victorian attitude to work, which stressed discipline and reg-

ularity, promoted creative recreation, and was critical of inactivity and idleness.

Saint Monday was a reflection of old habits, but it was also a premonition of what was to come. The "small holiday" prepared the way for the weekend. First, because it accustomed people to the advantages of a regular weekly break that consisted of more than one day. Second, because it served to popularize a new type of recreational activity—travel for pleasure.

Until the coming of the railway in the 1830s, modes of travel had been basically unchanged since ancient times. Short distances were covered on foot; longer trips were undertaken on horseback (although only by young and fit males) or in a horse-drawn carriage. Both involved bad roads, mishaps, and, for a long time, the perils of highwaymen. By the early 1800s, the last was no longer a problem, but travel continued to be something undertaken out of necessity, rarely for amusement. In Jane Austen's *Emma*, Mr. Knightley frets about the "evils of the journey" that he and his family are about to undertake from London to Highbury, and about the "fatigues of his own horses and coachmen." The modern reader is surprised to discover that the journey is a distance of only sixteen miles. But sixteen miles, by coach, took almost four hours, and it would have been an exceedingly unpleasant and uncomfortable four hours, swaying and bumping over rutted, muddy country

roads.* In the same novel Emma's father, Mr. Wood-
house, has a horror of carriages and hardly ever travels—except on foot; Emma's sister visits Highbury
from London, but she does so infrequently. Most
houseguests in *Emma* stay at Highbury for at least a
week or two, since the slowness and discomfort of
coach travel makes shorter visits impractical.

The time involved, as well as the expense, ensured
that travel was a luxury, if not exactly enjoyed by,
then at least restricted to, the moneyed and leisured
classes. But the railway and Saint Monday changed
all that. According to Douglas A. Reid, a historian at
the University of Birmingham in England, cheap railway excursions in that city began in the summer of
1841. The custom established itself quickly, and in
1846, twenty-two excursions (many organized by
workers' clubs) took place; more than three quarters
of them occurred on a Monday. The train furnished
the workingman and his family with a rapid and cheap
means of travel, and the weekday holiday provided
an entire free day to indulge it. "Eight hours at the
seaside for three-and-sixpence," announced a contemporary advertisement. The Sunday-to-Monday holi-

---

* *Emma* was written in 1816. It wasn't until the 1830s that metaled
roads became common, at least between major cities, and coach
travel, in turn, became somewhat more comfortable and more rapid.
On a good road, with frequent change of horses, a coach could attain
the unprecedented speed of ten miles per hour.

day also meant that people could leave on a trip one day and return the next. This was not called "spending a weekend," but it differed little from the later practice. It only remained to transpose the holiday from Monday to Saturday.

The energy of entrepreneurs, assisted by advertising, was an important influence not only on the diffusion and persistence of Saint Monday but on leisure in general. Hence a curious and apparently contradictory situation: not so much the commercialization of leisure as the discovery of leisure, thanks to commerce. Beginning in the eighteenth century with magazines, coffeehouses, and music rooms, and continuing throughout the nineteenth century, with professional sports and holiday travel, the modern idea of personal leisure emerged at the same time as the business of leisure. The first could not have happened without the second.

Saint Monday had many critics. Religious groups actively campaigned against the tradition which they saw as linked to the drinking and dissipation that, in their eyes, dishonored the Sabbath. They were joined by middle-class social reformers and by proponents of rational recreation, who also had an interest in altering Sunday behavior. They wanted their countrymen to adopt the so-called Continental Sunday, a day on which French and Germans of all classes mingled together in easy and decorous intimacy in promenades

and pleasure gardens—the kind of civilized Sunday in the park that was depicted a little later by Seurat in *Grande Jatte*. These were the sorts of Sunday activities that were promoted by such improving societies as the newly founded Young Men's Christian Association, the Sons of Temperance, and especially by the P.S.A., or Pleasant Sunday Afternoon. For all these groups, Saint Monday, and the popular working-class entertainments of which it was an integral part, was an enemy.*

One of the organizations that played a role in the debate was the Metropolitan Early Closing Association, established in London in 1842. Its members, who were drawn almost exclusively from the middle class, were concerned with the labor conditions of shop assistants, whose workday lasted up to eighteen hours. At that time, shops generally stayed open until ten or eleven o'clock in the evening, and even later during the summer months; the Association lobbied for a six o'clock closing time. It organized meetings and public appeals, and in a short time, chapters sprang up in Manchester, Birmingham, Liverpool, and all the other major English cities. Eventually its demands were made on behalf not only of shop assistants but

---

* The religious reformers and the proponents of rational recreation were not always on the same side, however, for the latter called for Sunday museum openings and band concerts, which were anathema to the Sabbatarians.

also of clerical workers in offices and warehouses.

The aims of the Early Closing Association, as it came to be called, were humanitarian but also religious. Since Sunday was the only holiday for the hardworking clerks, they used it partly for sleeping in and partly for recreation—understandably, church attendance was not a high priority. The hope of the Association was that a less arduous week would encourage more participation in Sunday worship. In 1855, this led to the suggestion of a one o'clock closing time on Saturday, which left a half-holiday for household chores and social activities—an evening at the dance hall or the pub—and permitted Sunday to be used exclusively for prayer and sober recreations. Since shop assistants had no union, this change required the voluntary acquiescence of individual shop owners, whose reactions varied considerably from city to city. Some types of shops—booksellers, druggists, and clothiers—adopted the shorter hours more readily than others.

The Early Closing Association must be credited with introducing the idea of the half-Saturday to the general public, but it achieved few other victories during its more-than-fifty-year life. There were some inherent contradictions in its aims. The more other off-duty clerks used Saturday afternoon for shopping, the more the remaining shops were encouraged to stay open. There was also the drawback that the As-

sociation was a top-down movement—the organization was initiated by the wealthy, and actually involved few clerks or shopkeepers. It relied on moral suasion rather than industrial action, and never managed to develop a strong political base.

It's unlikely that the Saturday half-holiday would have spread so rapidly if it hadn't been for support of the factory owners. It was becoming apparent to them that it was expensive and inefficient to operate machinery, especially steam engines, on a stop-and-go schedule, and it was impossible to plan production properly—and profitably—when a good part of the workforce might at any time disappear, without notice, to participate in some local celebration. Absenteeism was endemic, but efforts to impose disciplinary measures—locking out employees who did not appear, substituting women workers—had been ineffective, so ineffective that many owners just gave up and used Monday to effect repairs and maintenance on their idle machinery.

Employers had little to gain in insisting on a six-day week of twelve-hour workdays if, on some days, so few workers showed up that the factory had to be shut down anyway. The proposal of the Early Closing Association for a Saturday half-holiday offered a way out, and it came to be supported by factory owners, who were prepared to trade a half-day holiday on Saturday for a commitment to regular attendance on the part of their employees. Half-Saturdays and

shorter workdays became the pattern followed by all later labor negotiations, and by legislation governing the length of the workday.

There were historical precedents for the Saturday half-holiday, which had existed for some time among certain trades in Scotland and the north of England. For weavers who worked at home, for example, Saturday afternoon was "reckoning time"; their weekly production was brought in to be counted, which naturally resulted in a shorter workday. Early Saturday closings are reported among cotton workers as far back as 1816, and also among paper workers in Lancashire and in the west of Scotland. Textile workers traditionally stopped work early on Saturday—payday—although this practice had died out by the nineteenth century. It was revived by the Ten Hours Bill (1847), a law that regulated the length of the workday in the northern textile industry, legislating a return to the customary ten hours—from six in the morning until six at night, with two hours off for meals. At the same time, the Bill mandated a "short Saturday" of eight hours. Several years later, the Factory Act required that Saturday work cease even earlier, at two o'clock in the afternoon. Over the next twenty years this practice spread across England, and came to include builders, lace workers, and many other trades. In 1874 a law was passed that reduced the length of Saturday work for all large industries throughout the nation to six and a half hours.

In his essay on the decline of the Saint Monday tradition, Douglas A. Reid suggested that the achievement of the Saturday half-holiday also depended on the acquiescence of the workers themselves, for "men had to wish to be converted and unless they did evangelism was not bound to succeed." But why did they agree to the new schedule? Giving up a full Monday holiday in exchange for a half-Saturday was not exactly a bargain; one might also expect that there would have been opposition to the loss of personal freedom—no longer being able to choose when to work and when not to. Opposition there was, but it was not universal. Only the elite trades, skilled and better paid, earned enough to absent themselves from work at will, and many of these did resist the loss of Saint Monday, continuing to work irregular days. But many workers couldn't afford to take Monday or any other day off. For the poorly paid laborers who worked six long days a week, an additional half-day holiday was a welcome break—they had nothing to lose. For others, keeping Saint Monday became impractical as a result of child-labor laws, which limited the number of daily hours children could be made to work, and deprived the individual artisans, who relied on young assistants, of the option of working extra-long hours at the end of the week to make up for the lost production of Saint Monday.

But often, the choice of the better-paid trades to exchange their freedom for more regular employment

was voluntary. Spending habits were changing, and the growth in consumer demand and acquisitiveness, and hence in the importance of saving money, resulted in a higher value's being placed on regular wages. The attraction of money was displacing the attraction of free time. Then, too, the gradual spread of middle-class values meant that there were many workers who were critical of the profligate Saint Monday tradi-tion—the excessive drinking and gambling—and whose clubs and societies supported the idea of a more disciplined and progressive work schedule.

For the social reformers, the difference between a Saturday and a Monday holiday was crucial. In crit-icizing Saint Monday they were not just suggesting that leisure activities be shifted from one day to an-other—they were trying to alter the nature of those activities.

Attacked on all sides, the Saint Monday tradition suffered a decline—though not all at once and not everywhere at the same rate. The idea of a Monday holiday did persist in the Bank Holidays Act of 1871, which required that three of the four new official na-tional holidays fall on a Monday.* A few trades, such as cutlers, printers, and potters, held fast to Saint Monday until the turn of the century; E. P. Thomp-

---

* This raised the total number of bank holidays to eight. Lest this appear magnanimous, it is worth noting that before the first Bank Holidays Act of 1834, banks were closed on certain saints' days and anniversaries—thirty-three days every year.

son tells of British coal miners' keeping Saint Monday as late as the 1960s, but that was unusual. Sometimes the old custom managed to coexist with the new. As late as 1874, the American consul in Sheffield wrote that "every Monday is so generally a holiday, that it has come to be called Saint Monday . . . And this holiday is, in thousands of instances, protracted through the next day, so that large numbers of the workmen, stopping work on Saturday noon, do not commence again until the following Wednesday." But on the whole such behavior, once so common, was becoming the exception. For more and more workers, the week was assuming its modern shape: regular workdays followed by a regular period of leisure.

It was in the 1870s that people began to speak of "week-ending" or "spending the week-end." The country houses of the wealthy were generally located in the Home Counties, in the vicinity of London, and were now easily reached by train. It became fashionable to go there on Friday afternoon and return to the city on Monday, and these house parties became an important feature of upper-class social life.* Weekend

---

* According to Ralph Dutton, the Victorian weekend was a backward step; whereas eighteenth-century country-house life had provided a leisurely setting for visiting poets, painters, and writers, who would stay one or two weeks, the emphasis of the abbreviated house party was on entertainment, not culture.

outings, often to the seashore, were also available to the lower classes, although their weekend was shorter, extending from Saturday afternoon until Sunday evening.

According to one contemporary observer, Thomas Wright, "that the Saturday half-holiday movement is one of the most practically beneficial that has ever been inaugurated with a view to the social improvement of 'the masses,' no one who is acquainted with its workings will for a moment doubt." He approvingly described a variety of activities that working people indulged in on the Saturday half-holiday. The afternoon began with a leisurely midday meal at home, and was often followed by a weekly bath in the neighborhood bathhouse, an important institution at a time when few homes had running water, and one that was common in British and North American cities until well into the twentieth century. The rest of the daytime hours might be spent reading the paper, working around the house, attending a club, or strolling around town window-shopping. Saturday afternoon became a customary time for park concerts, soccer games, rowing, and bicycling. And, of course, drinking in the local pub, for despite the hopes of the reformers and Evangelicals, drinking was still the main leisure pastime of the working classes, whether the holiday occurred on Saturday or on Monday.

Wright emphasized that the afternoon was usually brought to a close in time for five o'clock tea, to leave plenty of time for the chief entertainment of the week—Saturday night. This was the time for an outing to the theater; most people brought their own food and drink into the cheap seats in the gallery. The music hall, an important influence on the spread of Saturday night, began as an adjunct to taverns but emerged as an independent entity in the 1840s, and proceeded to dominate British entertainment for the next eighty years. Like American vaudeville, the music hall presented its working-class audience with variety entertainment, chiefly songs. One of these catches the spirit of the new holiday, and of a new ritual:

> *Sweet Saturday night,*
> *When your week's work is over,*
> *That's the evening you make a throng,*
> *Take your dear little girls along.*
> *Sweet Saturday night:*
> *But this hour is Monday morning—*
> *To work you must go*
> *Though longing, I know*
> *For next Saturday night.*

Michael R. Marrus provocatively suggested that "for the broad masses of Europeans, leisure became

a reality only in the nineteenth century." This is a slight exaggeration, since many recreational habits were established a hundred years earlier, and the Saint Monday tradition was already a kind of improvised leisure. But it is true that the nineteenth century saw, for the first time, a conception of leisure that was markedly different from what had come before. This was not the elite leisure of the aristocracy and landed gentry, for whom recreations such as shooting and fox hunting had become an all-consuming way of life. Nor was it like the traditional mix of leisure and work of ordinary people. No longer were work and play interchanged at will, no longer did they occur in the same milieu; there was now a special time for leisure, as well as a special place. Neither play as work nor work as play, middle-class leisure, which eventually infiltrated and influenced all of society, involved something new: a strict demarcation of a temporal and a physical boundary between leisure and work. This boundary—exemplified by the weekend—more than anything else characterizes modern leisure.

six

A World of Weekends

In the United States, unlike in Britain, there was no formal Saint Monday custom to uphold or to oppose; still, the American workplace before the nineteenth century was marked by casual attendance. Monday absenteeism was not uncommon, and, as in England, "blue Mondays" were the result of heavy Sunday drinking. Gradually employers imposed discipline in the workplace, and their employees retaliated by demanding shorter hours in exchange for regular attendance. On the whole, they were successful. In 1830 the workday was more than twelve hours long; over the next fifty years the workday grew shorter, and by the turn of the century some people worked as little as nine hours a day. The Sunday holiday was far from universally observed, however, certainly less than in Europe. Many industries—steel, for instance—operated on a seven-day schedule.

It wasn't until after World War I that the early Saturday closing began to be common in America, although by 1900 there were Saturday half-holidays during the summer months. Their exact origin is unclear, though the connection between a shorter Saturday and outdoor recreations such as swimming, boating, and baseball is obvious. Then, too, most North Americans had much warmer summers to contend with than Europeans; in the absence of air-conditioning, the summer heat in factories crowded with workers and machinery was close to unbearable.

There's no way of knowing whether Americans were aware of the British custom of stopping work at one o'clock on Saturday. In any case, different forces were at work on this side of the Atlantic. There were church groups and middle-class reformist organizations similar to the Early Closing Association, but the Saturday half-holiday came about largely as a result of the demands of working people themselves.

The shorter workweek was an integral part of the general trade-union agitation for shorter hours—specifically an eight-hour workday—a movement that started in the 1860s, after the Civil War. Its slogan was "Eight Hours for Work, Eight Hours for Rest, and Eight Hours for What We Will"; it was a goal that would take a long time to achieve. The average length of the workday in 1850 was about eleven hours; by 1900, thanks to the efforts of the labor movement, it was down to about nine hours, and continued to decline for the next three decades.

So-called short Saturdays began with the Typographical Union, which represented workers in job printing and in the newspaper and book trades. The nature of the newspaper business—at least that end of it—did not necessitate long hours. Print compositors had to finish their work in the late afternoon so the newspaper could appear the following morning, and so these workers led the fight for shorter work hours. By 1907, following several major strikes, the eight-hour day was a reality. Or almost. Many workers chose to follow a long-standing custom in the book and job trade and work an extra three quarters of an hour each weekday so that they could stop at noon on Saturday. Later this practice was officially recognized in the union's insistence on a forty-four-hour week: eight hours a day, and only four on Saturday. Other trades made similar demands. As early as 1912, a thirteen-week strike by New York City furriers forced employers to accede to a Saturday half-holiday.

Many union members wondered whether a six-day week of shorter days wasn't preferable to longer days and half-Saturdays off. Nevertheless, as in England, the appeal of a full afternoon holiday that was linked to Sunday was strong, and the custom spread. And spread rapidly. According to Roy Rosenzweig's study of workers and leisure in Worcester, Massachusetts, by the early 1920s a "growing number of firms . . . required only a half day's work on Saturday." It was not only blue-collar workers who wanted

early closing. By 1929, the American Federation of Labor, in its call for a reduction of hours for federal government employees, made the shorter week a primary demand, "inasmuch as private business has now generally adopted the Saturday half-holiday practice throughout the year." A famous 1934 social study of suburban leisure patterns in Westchester County, New York, describes the Saturday half-holiday as a "standard" feature of the workweek for the "gainfully employed."

The largest adult occupational group in Westchester was classified as "white-collar," which underlines the widespread observance of the half-holiday not only among the trades but among clerical workers. By the 1930s, most offices in New York City closed their doors at noon on Saturday. The popularity of the custom must be attributed to a general demand for more time off by all classes of workers. This extra leisure was given over to a variety of pastimes. In the Westchester study, more than ninety percent of the leisure time of the admittedly middle-class occupational groups was taken up by seven types of activities: eating, visiting friends, reading, listening to the radio, sports, motoring for pleasure, and various types of public entertainment—a mixture of old and new. The first four activities could be enjoyed after work, during the week, but Saturday afternoons were for outdoor sports such as tennis and golf, and

for pastimes like motoring. The half-day holiday was also convenient for shopping, especially at a time when many states still had restrictions on Sunday store openings. There were many things to do on a Saturday afternoon, but one big advantage of the half-holiday was that it coincided with the emergence of an important leisure institution: Saturday night.

In Britain, the popularity of Saturday night was helped along by the music hall; in the United States and Canada, this role was taken by a different urban entertainment—the movie theater. Movies had arrived on the urban scene just after the turn of the century as full-fledged mass entertainment in the form of the nickelodeon—a half-hour film for a five-cent admission. The low price (a ticket to a Broadway play cost more than a dollar) and the short duration gave it the appeal of fast-food restaurants today. People could drop in to see a one-reel melodrama or a slapstick comedy during their lunch break, after work, or, despite the protestation of religious groups, on Sunday, when many nickelodeons stayed open illegally. Although the public entertainments of choice for working people were still the saloon and the dance hall, the number of nickelodeons grew quickly, and by 1908 daily movie attendance in New York City was estimated at two hundred thousand people.

What happened next was common in the history of leisure: when too many people had too much fun,

someone eventually objected. Play is rarely "harm-less," at least from society's point of view. The "let-ting go" that is a fundamental attribute of play is a letting go of everyday behavior, but also, sometimes, of everyday morality and social conventions. In his classic study of play, *Homo Ludens,* Johan Huizinga observed that since play is older and more original than civilization, it is fundamentally antithetical to it. This opposition becomes more evident the more evolved, and the more serious, civilization becomes, and periodically leads to conflict. Play is often the loser. This is what happened in the Middle Ages to the popular anticlerical festivals, many of which came to be banned by the church, and later to the bull runs. The nickelodeons met with the same fate.

In 1908 the mayor of New York closed all 550 movie houses and nickelodeons in the city. His action reflected the outrage that many felt toward the new form of public entertainment. Respectable people considered movies an affront and a challenge to es-tablishment sensibilities, not only because of their lowbrow and sometimes racy subject matter, which flew in the face of middle-class values and morality, but also because they did not accord with middle-class conceptions of leisure. The American equivalent of the British rational recreation movement did not find anything edifying in the distinctly proletarian en-tertainments of the nickelodeon, which often ridiculed

authority figures such as policemen and politicians. That movie houses were often linked to saloons did not endear them to social reformers, nor did their attractiveness to children—and single women—and their flaunting of Sunday-closing laws. There was also an undercurrent of racial prejudice in the crusade against movies, for the inexpensive nickelodeons were particularly popular with European immigrants—you didn't need to understand English to enjoy a silent movie (in any case, more than half the films were foreign: French, German, and Italian)—and many of the theater owners were Jewish.

The aim of what became a great reforming campaign was not to prohibit movies but to "clean them up." As a result of expensive licensing fees (which went from $25 to $500), stricter building requirements and regulations, and review boards that scrutinized—and censored—movies, the nickelodeon was transformed. Movies became respectable family entertainment, and in the process turned into a major industry. Not only did the audience grow to include the middle class, but the films themselves expanded into full-length dramas such as D. W. Griffith's celebrated *The Birth of a Nation,* released in 1915 and a huge box-office success.

Griffith's aspirations were artistic and polemical—his films have been described as both messages or warnings—but it was his economic achievements

that impressed entrepreneurs, for *The Birth of a Nation* grossed over $13 million. With the establishment of a West Coast filmmaking industry, mainly by Jewish-European immigrants—Adolph Zukor, Louis B. Mayer, Carl Laemmle, William Fox, the Warner brothers—movies abandoned Griffith's reformist Protestant course and returned to their original roots: entertaining the public. "The public pays the money," said Samuel Goldwyn. "It wants to be entertained. That's all I know."

By the 1920s, going to the movies was the chief public amusement of Americans. More money was spent on movies than on any other recreation. In only a decade, New York City alone acquired eight hundred movie theaters; there were more movie houses in the United States than in all Europe. The "Big Eight" producers, who owned most of these theaters, turned out more than seven hundred movies a year, large extravagant creations featuring "stars" whose offscreen lives in the adroitly mythologized world of "Hollywood" were as important to their fans as their film performances.

The movie had evolved from fast food to a three-course meal, and it was a fancy spread. Nickelodeons were small, sleazy storefront operations, seating no more than three hundred; movie theaters, which were located along prominent streets rather than in lower-class neighborhoods, were usually more than three

times larger. At first the buildings were designed in the classical style—like libraries, museums, and other civic buildings—which accurately reflected the cultural aspirations of the reformed cinema. Eventually this decor proved too sedate, and the movie theater was transformed into the movie palace. Luxury replaced propriety. Flashy lobbies and uniformed ushers greeted the moviegoer, and a full orchestra accompanied the film. Baroque, rococo, Moorish, and Chinese interiors provided a glittering and sumptuous setting for what had become a glamorous event.

The movie palace provided an experience of luxury and wealth. People dressed up to go to the movies, just as they did to go to a restaurant or club, for, as Lary May astutely observes in his history of the early period of the motion picture industry, theater owners had consciously begun to associate moviegoing with nightlife. The brightly lit marquee, the chandeliers, the increasingly opulent interiors, and the spectacle of "opening night" all contributed to this effect.

More elaborate movies cost more to make, and admission prices rose accordingly. Higher ticket prices didn't discourage the public—quite the opposite, they raised the status of movies as entertainment. And since films were much longer, one no longer dropped in on a whim. Going to the movies now involved a "night out," for both women and men of all classes and ages. Frequently women and men to-

gether; movies were explicitly romantic, and so was going to the movies. Especially on Saturday night, since, for many people, Sunday was still a taboo day for courting. As for weekday evenings, not everyone felt like playing after a full day's work. The Saturday half-holiday, which left an early evening available for leisure activities, neatly coincided with the phenomenal popularity of moviegoing. Although movies and weekends developed independently, they reinforced each other. Movies were the main form of urban recreation, and Saturday night became the chief occasion for this celluloid excursion.

In Britain, the half-Saturday holiday emerged in the 1870s, and took sixty years to expand to a full day off. The American half-holiday appeared in the 1920s, and its expansion was, if anything, more rapid. Often, the weekend arrived in its full, two-day configuration. The first factory to adopt a five-day week was a New England spinning mill, in 1908, specifically to accommodate its Jewish workers. The six-day week had always made it hard for Orthodox Jews to observe the Sabbath, for if they took Saturday off and worked on Sunday, they risked offending the Christian majority. Moreover, as work patterns became increasingly standardized through union agreements, many Jews did not even have a choice, which threatened the

Sabbath tradition. The five-day week—in which both Saturday and Sunday were holidays—offered a convenient way out, and it came to be supported by Jewish workers, rabbis, community leaders, and some Jewish employers. In 1929, the Amalgamated Clothing Workers of America, composed largely of Jewish workers, became the first union to propose a five-day week.

At first the five-day week was common in only three industries: the (predominantly Jewish) needle trade, building construction (where well-organized unions had been aggressive in seeking shorter hours), and, to a lesser degree, printing and publishing, where the change from the half-Saturday to a full holiday was slower in coming. There were a few isolated cases of employers who voluntarily adopted the five-day week. The earliest and most notable of these was, curiously enough, Henry Ford, a staunch anti-unionist. In 1914, Ford reduced the daily hours in his plant from nine to eight; in 1926 he announced that henceforth his factories would also be closed all day Saturday. His rationale was that an increase in leisure time would support an increase in consumer spending, not the least on automobile travel and automobiles. This was a prescient view, for the weekend did eventually become associated with outings and pleasure trips. But in 1926, that was still in the future, and Ford was alone among businessmen in espousing

the weekend. He was roundly criticized by both the National Industry Council and the National Association of Manufacturers.

The idea of a five-day week was denounced as not only uneconomic but irreligious. A 1926 newspaper cartoon by "Ding" Darling, who drew for the *New York Herald Tribune* and the *Des Moines Register,* captured the mood of the time. He depicted an overalled worker, representing the American Federation of Labor, sitting next to a pile of stone tablets—the Ten Commandments. One tablet, the Fourth Commandment, was cracked in two, and, as a horrified Moses looked on, the worker was enthusiastically carving a new one. The new inscription read: "5 days shalt thou labor and do all thy work, but the sixth & seventh days are your own to do anything you darn please." Darling pointedly included the hood of a Model T in one corner of the drawing.

In the end, what finally consolidated the two-day weekend was not altruism or activism or, paradoxically, prosperity; it was the Great Depression of 1929. Shorter hours came to be widely regarded as a remedy for unemployment—people would work less, but more people would have jobs. In 1932, the Goodyear Tire & Rubber Company of Akron, Ohio, instituted a thirty-six-hour week—six-hour shifts, six days a week. This arrangement, which became standard for many rubber workers, remained in force for several

decades. Six-day weeks were unusual, however; most industries adopted a combination of shorter days and a five-day work schedule. Eventually New Deal legislation embodied in the Fair Labor Standards Act of 1938 mandated a maximum forty-hour week, although it was mute about the length of the workday. By 1940 the eight-hour day was customary and the five-day week had arrived. Wartime production caused the workday to be lengthened to ten hours during the 1940s. This was temporary, however, and during the postwar period, as the economy returned to normal, the workday shortened again and finally stabilized at about eight hours.

Benjamin Hunnicutt, a sociologist at the University of Iowa, characterizes the period between 1920 and 1940 as one during which the movement for shorter hours faltered, and ended. That is true, but although the length of the workweek in 1949 was not much different than it had been in 1929, the shape of the week had been altered dramatically. After World War II, people weren't willing to return to a six- or even five-and-half-day week—they had become used to the five-and-two rhythm. The five-day week, and the two-day weekend, were now a fixture of American life.

Like the planetary week, the idea of the weekend emigrated from place to place and adapted to different

circumstances. And like the planetary week, the weekend spread quickly. The Early Closing Association put forward the idea of a short Saturday in 1855; a hundred years later, the two-day weekend was routine in Britain and America, and short Saturdays were common in most European countries, which adopted the full weekend ten or twenty years later. A 1979 study of leisure in the European Community found a remarkable consistency in the length of the workweek. According to a survey of collective agreements, no country exceeded a forty-hour week (in West Germany and Belgium the workweek was even shorter), and all countries observed the weekend.* But this consistency is deceiving, for the weekend arrived in each country in a different way.

In most places it's impossible to date the arrival of the weekend with any accuracy. This is not the case in Italy, where the weekend arrived precisely on June 20, 1935. Twelve years earlier, less than six months after the coup d'état that brought Mussolini to power, the Fascist government passed a bill that for the first time limited the length of the workday, to eight hours; the workweek continued at six days, its mandatory maximum length since 1907. In 1935, taking its cue from the Early Closing Association, the

---

* This despite a great variety in the length of annual paid holidays in different countries: in 1979 they ranged from a low of three weeks (Ireland) to as long as six weeks (West Germany); in Denmark, the *minimum* legal holiday was five weeks.

regime passed a nationwide law that established the *sabato fascista* and declared that henceforth the work-week would end at one o'clock on Saturday.

The Fascist weekend was a state institution. The government promoted a host of *dopolavoro* ("after-work") organizations to see to it that the new leisure was not squandered in the "banal imitation of bourgeois vices." There were special Saturday matinee performances of the opera (*sabato teatrale*) at greatly reduced prices, limited, by government directive, to low-income workers and pensioners. Saturday afternoon and Sunday were also occasions for special trains that took the masses on excursions to the countryside and the beach. Sports and outdoor activities were emphasized; when it came to leisure, the Fascists, like the Early Closers, were social reformers whose goal was to provide not merely free time but the right kind of free time.

Despite these attempts, the weekend asserted its individual character. Traditional pastimes—card playing, dominoes, American movies—remained popular. The languid game of *bocce,* denounced at first as lacking in manly vigor, proved resistant to reform, and was finally declared a national sport. Attempts to invent a new sport, called *volata,* which was to be an indigenous version of English soccer, failed. The *dopolavoro* proved more successful at appropriating traditional forms of play than at creating new ones. In

her fascinating study of leisure in Fascist Italy, Victoria de Grazia concludes that "there does indeed appear to be much that was not specifically 'fascist' about the regime's organization of leisure-time activities."

During the 1930s, state organizations similar to the *dopolavoro* were instituted in other European right-wing dictatorships: Salazar's Portugal, Franco's Spain, and Metaxas's Greece. The model for all these efforts was Nazi Germany. Immediately after coming to power in 1933, the German National Socialist government took several measures to combat unemployment: expanding the military, instituting a compulsory six-month labor service for young men, and encouraging women to leave the workforce. As in America, the length of the workweek was reduced drastically; anyone working twenty-four hours a week or more was ineligible for social benefits. Unions were abolished and replaced by the Labor Front under the direction of Dr. Robert Ley, who was also given the responsibility for the *Gleichschaltung* ("bringing into line") of free time.

Ley founded the *Kraft durch Freude* ("Strength through Joy"), a state organization that co-opted existing sports and hobby clubs, provided cheap tickets to the theater, opera, and concerts (there was a traveling KdF symphony orchestra), and instituted cheap, collective holiday travel for workers. Ley established special seaside and ski resorts, yachting and riding

schools, and even operated a fleet of ten cruise ships that sailed the Baltic and the Mediterranean. Thanks to such initiatives, one German worker in three was able to take part in some sort of vacation travel. Between 1932 and 1938, tourism doubled.

Unlike in Italy, there was no official sanction of the weekend; the emphasis of KdF was on holidays of one to two weeks. This is not surprising, since the Nazi conception of leisure, although it has been described as bourgeois, was really collective and not individual—hence the promotion of tourism rather than domestic relaxation. Even so, the weekend might have infiltrated the Third Reich had a famous project reached fruition. In 1938, the Labor Front was put in charge of building the Volkswagen—Hitler's brainchild, lifted from Henry Ford—also known as the KdF car. This inexpensive automobile would take workers and their families on short jaunts over the newly constructed autobahns. But preparations for war brought an end both to the Nazi car and to the nascent Nazi weekend. By 1936 there were labor shortages, and official reductions to the workweek had ceased; by 1938 factories were working overtime producing war matériel, the workweek was up to more than forty-seven hours, and the KdF car was transformed into a military vehicle.

The weekend finally arrived to Germany after the war; in France developments were equally slow.

During the 1880s, when more and more British workers had Saturday afternoon off, the French working
people depicted in Seurat's painting still had only Sunday as a weekly holiday—on Saturday the island of
Grande Jatte would have been empty, except for some
middle-class boaters. Even Sunday was not a compulsory holiday; not until the early 1900s was legislation passed limiting the length of the workweek to
six days. As for the workday, it was set at a long
twelve hours. It was only after World War I that the
eight-hour workday was introduced, and it was
longer still before the Saturday half-holiday arrived.
When it did, in recognition of its origin, the new five-
and-a-half-day work schedule became known as *la
semaine anglaise*—"the English week."

There were attempts to introduce a universal five-
day week by the Popular Front government in 1936,
but these were curtailed by the demands of defense
production. Most French workers worked six days a
week; some, if they were lucky, had Saturday morning off. The English week lasted fifty years; as late as
1965, the French workweek was still five and a half
days, and averaged forty-six hours. In 1968, however,
it was reduced, and, over the next decade, the workweek fell to forty-one hours, chiefly as a result of the
arrival of the two-day weekend.

The two-day weekend was taken up belatedly but
with enthusiasm. Not that leisure time was lacking

in France. Unlike in England, where the weekend preceded the vacation, in France the middle class had been taking long summer holidays at seaside resorts, health spas, and Alpine hostelries, which were easily accessible by railway, since the turn of the century. The summer vacation traditionally lasted the entire month of August and had an importance unknown in English-speaking countries. Nevertheless, the appeal of a regular weekly break was strong. In France, as in America, the shorter workweek resulted from a combination of labor union demands, economic prosperity, and individual car ownership. The influence of the latter should not be underestimated. Automobile touring had long been popular in France—Michelin began publishing its guides in 1900—but had been restricted to the wealthy. Between 1950 and 1965, car ownership jumped from ten percent of all French households to fifty, vastly increasing the popularity of short weekend excursions.*

One society that showed reluctance to adopt the weekend was Israel, despite the fact that the Jews could claim to have invented the seventh-day leisure

---

* By 1967 weekend automobile traffic—and the accompanying carnage on the highway—was enough of a French fact of life to be savagely parodied by Jean-Luc Godard in a film titled *Weekend*.

break, and despite the fact that Israel was a country
that adopted many Western institutions. In the new
state of Israel, in 1948, the Sabbath was the only
weekly holiday, prescribed by both religion and cultural tradition. For a long time there was little interest
from either legislators or labor unions in shortening
the workweek. This probably resulted from the economic pressures of building a country from scratch
and the prevailing and necessary pioneer work ethic.
Israelis also feared that increasing consumption on
recreation might fuel inflation, and that an extra day
of leisure might in some way devalue the Sabbath.
Interestingly, Orthodox Jews, who were a significant
minority, supported the establishment of the weekend; like the British Early Closers, they hoped that a
second day of rest might provide an outlet for the
sort of profane activities that, they felt, dishonored
the Sabbath.

A 1970 survey found that fully two thirds of the
Israeli population were in favor of a five-day week,
and its authors took this as firm evidence that "sooner
or later the five-day week will come." It's been a slow
process. Today, the weekend is still far from universally observed in Israel, although it is making head-
way. The army still operates on a six-day schedule,
and so do schools; only in the last five years have
major enterprises begun to give their employees the
weekend (Friday and Saturday) off. But the weekend

is already having a major impact on Israeli life: weekend driving has increased, as have recreations such as camping and skiing.

Many of Israel's first immigrants came from Russia and Poland, where most people worked six days a week. In prewar Poland the half-day Saturday holiday did exist—it was known as "English Saturday"—but it was generally restricted to management. The Communist regime continued the custom, fixing the official workweek at six days of eight hours each. During the 1970s, one and then two free Saturdays a month were gradually introduced by certain industries, although these were not really holidays, since the extra time off had to be made up during the week.

This situation changed radically after the Solidarity strikes that began in the Lenin Shipyard in August 1980. A key demand of the strikers was for "free Saturdays without the need to work them off later," which became a clause of the famous Gdansk Agreement between Solidarity and the government. A few months later, in January 1981, the government announced it would be impossible to implement free Saturdays, owing to the worsening state of the national economy. This statement enraged the workers, and wildcat strikes broke out in many towns. Feelings were so strong on the issue that even Solidarity's charismatic leader, Lech Walesa, was unable to convince his membership to return to work. A last-minute

compromise (three free Saturdays a month) averted a general strike that probably would have resulted in the declaration of a state of emergency and possibly even Soviet military intervention.

The turmoil over free Saturdays did have one less happy consequence—as a result of the civil disturbances and the evident weakness of the regime, an army man, General Jaruzelski, was appointed prime minister. By the end of the year the general had launched a military coup, instituted martial law, and brought Solidarity to a (temporary) end. The reforms to the workweek remained, however, and the weekend became a part of everyday Polish life.

A survey of Polish leisure habits in the years 1976 to 1984 shows that this extra free time was not used exclusively for leisure, since many people worked overtime or took second jobs. Saturdays were also an opportunity for shopping, a time-consuming activity involving long shop lines and hours spent seeking out black-market opportunities. If they were not working or shopping, most Poles spent the weekend at home. A lack of money meant that they could afford only those leisure activities that could be done cheaply, such as chatting with friends, reading, inexpensive hobbies, listening to the radio, and watching television. Only two types of free-time activities seem to have been widely practiced outside the house: going for walks and going to church.

The types of entertainments (movies, theater, restaurants, sporting events) that served to promote the weekend in prosperous societies were unavailable to most Poles, and actually declined in importance during the 1980s. So did participation in leisure activities that required expensive equipment (tennis, boating) or travel (skiing, hiking). Although car ownership started to rise in the early 1970s, gas rationing discouraged holiday travel, and for most people, even public transportation was too expensive. The result was that the weekend excursions so closely associated with the two-day holiday in Britain, America, and France played only a minor role in the development of the Polish weekend.

In 1980, when Solidarity members demanded more free time on weekends, there were no entrepreneurs serving up a smorgasbord of leisure activities for the two-day break, no railway companies promoting weekend destinations, no saloons or dance halls. What there was—what is always a component of the weekend, even if it's sometimes hidden under layers of glossy diversions—was the promise of personal freedom. The limited number of leisure activities available, or affordable, was undoubtedly a frustration for some—"doing nothing" quickly loses its appeal when it is imposed and not freely chosen—but the lure of time for oneself was as strong in Poland as anywhere else. If Polish workers couldn't do "any-

154

thing they darn pleased" on the sixth and seventh days, they could at least do some things, which was attraction enough.

The absence of commercial blandishments in the chaste Polish weekend is unusual. It contradicts the general tendency of the weekend to arrive in societies at moments of prosperity, when a wide range of entertainments and recreations is becoming available to people who, in turn, want a regular weekly break to pursue them. But even more unusual is the relationship between the weekend and the people with the highest per capita income in the world—the Japanese.

Industrialization came late to Japan, and the country lagged behind others in its work legislation. It wasn't until 1926, for example, that a law was passed limiting the length of the workday for women and young children, and even so, it was set at eleven hours and allowed fifteen-hour days under certain circumstances. In 1939, when the eight-hour day and the five-day week were already common in the United States, the average Japanese worked more than ten hours a day, six days a week. The traditional values of Japanese society stressed conformity and discipline—no absenteeism or Saint Mondays here, and no confrontational unions to demand more free time.

The six-day week persisted throughout the diffi-

cult postwar reconstruction period, which was to be expected. But even during the 1960s and 1970s, when an increasingly wealthy society might have relaxed, there was no easing of this hardworking schedule. In 1978, the average Japanese outworked the average American by more than 200 hours a year. That same year, Herman Kahn published *The Japanese Challenge*, in which he observed that although Japan lagged behind other industrial countries in reducing the length of the workweek, he expected the current prosperity to soon produce a great increase in the availability of leisure time. "As Japan gets richer," he wrote, "like other affluent countries, it will almost inevitably pay more attention to welfare, consumption, and leisure."

Kahn was right about the first priority, partly right about the second, but wrong about the third. A decade later, most Japanese still work eight- and nine-hour days, Monday to Saturday. A few Japanese companies—about six percent, or about twenty-eight percent of employees nationwide—have instituted a five-day workweek, but this figure is deceptive since many people work on Saturdays for the overtime.

And the lack of weekends is not compensated by long vacations. Although Japanese law requires annual paid holidays of between six and twenty days, these are irregularly observed. According to sociologist Ezra F. Vogel, the typical salaried worker is hesitant to take all the free time to which he is entitled:

"If he were to request his full vacation time, he would be regarded as selfish and disloyal by his co-workers and by his superiors." Others have suggested that the Japanese are simply too absorbed in their work to take vacations. Whether it is caused by social pressure or personal choice, the result is the same—except for the so-called Golden Week, a period in early May when several national holidays in a row give everyone a four- or five-day break, many Japanese never have a vacation.

The most common explanation for this national reluctance to relax is that the Japanese are drones who prefer work to play. Certainly they seem to have an impressive capacity for hard work, which is generally felt to be the chief ingredient in the country's economic success. This attitude to work begins early. Children attend school on Saturday morning, and most take extra night classes. Summer school vacations are short, a month shorter than in America. Opinion polls regularly show that "being a hard worker" rates high among people's aspirations. Some sociologists have made a case for the existence of a "Protestant ethic" in Japan, although most of the population is not religious. There are, indeed, many parallels between modern Japan and the nineteenth-century industrial revolution, but one obvious difference: it was Protestant Britain and America that pioneered the weekend.

It's true that the Japanese language has no word for "leisure" and uses the English equivalent (just as it has adopted the French *vacances* for "holidays"), but the suggestion that the Japanese are not interested in play is contradicted by the extremely wide variety of commercial recreational activities available to them. Most popular sports, like baseball and golf, are recent imports from abroad, but adult comic books (*manga*), which go back to the beginning of the eighteenth century and are now a huge industry, are uniquely Japanese. So is *pachinko,* a sort of vertical pinball that is played for money and is as ubiquitous in Japan as lottery tickets are in France. It's also worth recalling that Japan is the home of the Walkman, the home video camera, Nintendo, and a host of electronic gadgets intended specifically for leisure.

The average Japanese family has increased its spending on leisure activities eightfold since 1965. But unlike Poles, who had free time, but empty shelves, the Japanese have to work long and hard to take advantage of the array of consumer goods—much longer and harder than Americans. According to James Fallows, a journalist who has written extensively on the Far East, restrictive trade tariffs and cartel-based prices mean that Japanese consumers pay almost twice as much as Americans for the same products. Put another way, high prices at home support low prices abroad. When the high cost of consumer goods is coupled with the cost of food and housing,

A World of Weekends

abnormally high (by European and American standards), the Japanese propensity for putting in overtime at the office and factory makes more sense.

While the Japanese enjoy much less free time than European and American workers, there is also a difference in the role of leisure in their lives. In contemporary Western societies leisure has become an antidote to work; there are physical and temporal distinctions between the two. In Japan the line between work and leisure is often blurred, especially for salarymen—white-collar workers in large corporations. Eating and drinking after work are often done at company expense, and much free time in the evening is spent in the company of one's workmates. In some ways this situation is like the one in eighteenth-century Britain, when workers engaged in drinking, sports, and games not with families or friends but with fellow tradesmen and guild members.

Observers of Japanese daily life suggest another reason for long hours at the office: the Japanese workplace is invariably larger and more comfortable than the home. Japanese housing is cramped and notoriously lacking in amenities, despite its high cost. According to a recent survey, the top five leisure activities in 1984, 1985, and 1986 were dining out, driving, domestic travel, drinking (out), and going to the zoo, botanical garden, aquarium, or museum—all pastimes that take place outside the home.

In Poland the weekend was almost completely a

domestic institution. Even in Europe and America, where there were plenty of public entertainments, and possibilities for weekend travel, the evolution of the weekend was linked to the growing importance of home-life. Saturday night out was an important tradition, and so was going for a Sunday outing or drive, but people spent most of their free time at home. Maybe the weekend's lack of popularity in Japan can be explained in part by the inadequacies of the Japanese home. After all, most of us spend at least a good part of our weekends relaxing at home— still the best place to "do nothing"—and if one's home is poorly heated, noisy, uncomfortable, and crowded, the pleasures of the weekend are considerably diminished.

Old habits die hard, but the Japanese may still get the weekend whether they like it or not. In April 1990, the Japanese government signed a trade agreement with the United States that included, among other things, a promise to shorten the workweek for its employees to five days and to encourage private companies to do the same. This "vow of future sloth," as one sarcastic American editorialist called it, reflects an attempt by American trade negotiators to narrow the trade gap between the two nations by demanding that the Japanese work less hard—or at least less long. It's unlikely that a shorter workweek will restrain the productive Japanese economy, but it will be interest-

ing to see what effect it will have on Japanese everyday life. It will likely be different than elsewhere. After all, the weekend has traditionally been considered a reward; this is the first time it will be imposed as a punishment.

seven

Retreats

Several miles from my house, beside the road I take to drive to the village, I pass what is locally known as a *terrain de camping;* one of several such installations in the vicinity. The other campgrounds are identified by colorful roadside billboards with evocative names like Coolbreeze and Acapulco, but this one, inexplicably, is named Canne de Bois, or "the wooden walking stick." This makes it sound like a refuge for the elderly, but its occupants are mainly families with children. It's also inaccurate to describe it as a campground, for there are no tents here. When it opened, forty-five years ago, Canne de Bois did provide space for campers. Today, instead of temporary canvas shelters, there are dozens of small cabins and permanently parked house trailers, not shiny Airstreams but small, weathered caravans that haven't seen the open road for decades. Mixed among them are newer recreational vehicles, a few mobile homes, and even two or three small houses, perched

precariously on piers of cement blocks. This motley architectural collection is located partly in open ground and partly among trees, around the edges of a man-made pond.

Despite its attractive natural setting, the general appearance of Canne de Bois is not exactly pretty. The house trailers are shrouded in a carapace of verandas, screened porches, lean-tos, and other homemade additions that attest to years of gradual and fragmentary accretion. It doesn't help that the building materials are flimsy and inexpensive—metal sheeting and painted plywood—or that the workmanship is slapdash. There's an atmosphere of impermanence—everything appears to be awaiting completion or to have been left unfinished. What little space there is on the tiny plots, which are surrounded by low fences and hedges, is crowded with an assortment of garden furniture, picnic tables, swings, concrete patios, decks, prefabricated garden sheds, barbecues, and lawn ornaments. The narrow, unpaved roads that snake around the settlement have streetlights and even street names, but this attempt at urbanity only accentuates the makeshift character of the whole.

Although Canne de Bois consists of individual homes on individual plots of land, its heterogeneity makes it unlike any suburban development I have ever seen. Nor does it exhibit the contrived picturesqueness of a Club Med. Instead, it reminds me of the

shantytowns that I've visited on the fringes of cities in the Third World. This comparison is not intended critically. What these gritty, do-it-yourself neighborhoods lack in urbanity and visual coherence they make up in a liveliness that mirrors the resourcefulness of the occupant-builders, who are struggling to make a place for themselves with extremely modest means. The same spirit of individual enterprise and ambition is evident in the improvised homes of the Quebec campground.

The similarity between shantytowns and campgrounds was noticed first by the Dutch architect John Habraken, who observed that in both types of settlements the emphasis was on the unfettered creation of private and family spaces, while the public and communal domain was secondary and consisted of whatever was left over. This, Habraken pointed out, was almost exactly the reverse of what happens in most planned housing developments, where opportunities for personal choice are severely limited and the individual householder is required by zoning ordinances, building regulations, and other rules to adjust himself—and his dwelling—to the needs of the community.

Canne de Bois differs in another important respect from most conventional communities. Throughout the long Canadian winter the house trailers and cabins are empty and blanketed in snow, the pond is frozen over, and the bare trees reveal the surprising spread

of the settlement, which extends more than half a mile from the highway. After the spring, which comes suddenly and offers a brief transition to full-blown summer weather, the "campers" appear. They remove the plywood sheets that cover the windows, fill up their propane tanks, and take the lawn furniture out of storage. The spaces in front of the homes sprout awnings and colorful umbrellas; the access road fills up with cars, and the pond fills up with swimmers and pedal boats. At night, street lamps and porch lights illuminate the previously dark space. Some people have attached strings of Christmas-tree lights to their homes, and the settlement takes on the festive air of an amusement park or pleasure garden.

From May until September, Canne de Bois accommodates 320 families, but these temporary residents make surprisingly little impression on the life of the village. Most arrive late on Friday night and leave on Sunday evening; in the interval, they generally stay in the campground. I sometimes see them in the supermarket on Saturday morning, buying cases of beer for the weekend, or in the convenience store picking up a newspaper. They are identifiable by their colorful attire and their Bermuda shorts and sandals—the local farmers favor green work clothes and baseball caps—and by their noisy behavior and lighthearted demeanor. One can hardly begrudge them their jollity—they are, after all, on holiday.

Just as altered dress and behavior distinguish the

weekenders from the permanent residents, the little cabins and caravans also have a distinctive character. Some plots are entered through a romantic trellised gateway, and the gardens contain many conventional symbols of rusticity—decorative fences, improvised gazebos, imitation wells. Lest there be any confusion about the meaning of these architectural elements, one camper has put up a hand-carved sign outside his modified caravan. *Royaume des biches,* it reads— "Kingdom of the Hinds."

The naming of country retreats has a long tradition. Almost two millennia ago, Pliny the Younger named his famous villa "Laurentum." Villa was a Latin word that the ancient Romans used to describe the country estates they maintained on the outskirts of their cities. There they would go in the summer to enjoy the cooler weather, and at other times of the year to savor the tranquil, pastoral atmosphere. Pliny, who lived in the first century A.D., devoted one of his many letters to a description of his own villa, in Latium, on the shore of the Tyrrhenian Sea not far from Ostia Antica, the port of Rome.

With becoming modesty Pliny described Laurentum as "large enough for my needs but not expensive to keep up." By modern standards, however, it was a large complex of buildings. Pliny was a successful lawyer and public administrator who at a young age was appointed consul, or chief magistrate, the highest

bureaucratic post in the republic, and his villa reflected his status and wealth. The spread-out country house contained a gymnasium, a warmed swimming bath (with a view of the sea), a ball court, several public rooms, a banqueting hall as well as a dining room, apartments for himself and his guests, and slave quarters.

On one side of the compound was a terrace, "scented with violets," that overlooked the sea and was flanked by a covered arcade leading to a small building that contained Pliny's private suite. He was particularly fond of these rooms, since he had them built himself (one has the impression that the rest of the house was built by an earlier owner). "*Amores mei, revera amores,*" he wrote of them—"really and truly my favorites." This self-contained pavilion was divided into three rooms: a bedchamber, a *heliocaminus,* or sun-room (usually a roofless space, protected from the wind), and a sitting room, or, rather, reclining room, for the Romans used couches. From his couch Pliny could enjoy views on three sides: adjacent woods, neighboring villas, and the sea itself. Here, undisturbed by the bustle of his household, he could retire to read and write, or indulge, as he once wrote, in "that indolent but agreeable condition of doing nothing."

Of Pliny's villa there is no trace save the written record, but the environs of Rome are dotted with the

ruins of such villas—that of Hadrian, at Tivoli, is the most famous. The practical Romans did not build their estates for pleasure alone; villas were usually the seats of large farms worked by tenant farmers whose rents were an important source of income for the wealthy landlords. Pliny himself, who would be reckoned a millionaire today, owned a large estate at Tifernum, in the present-day region of Umbria, about 150 miles north of Rome. But he described Laurentum, which had no farm, as his favorite country house. "For there," he wrote in another letter, "I do most of my writing, and, instead of the land I lack, I work to cultivate myself; so that I have a harvest in my desk to show you in place of full granaries elsewhere."

Laurentum was not surrounded, as most villas were, by fields and vineyards. Sitting on his terrace, Pliny gazed out not at his possessions but at the sea—ever the pragmatic Roman, he noted that it provided few fish of any value. When he went for a walk, it was not among his crops but on the beach. This made Laurentum an unusual villa, a thoroughly modern idea of a city dweller's refuge: unencumbered by practical function, quiet, relaxed, and natural.

By the time of the Renaissance, the distinction between farms and country retreats was explicit. The fifteenth-century architect Leon Battista Alberti de-

voted two chapters of his ten books on architecture to the subject of country houses. He differentiated between rural houses that were intended for farmers and villas for gentlemen; farmers, he suggested, required homes designed for utility, gentlemen for pleasure. Pleasure here included the rustic diversions of fishing and hunting, horseback riding, swimming, walking, reading, and "the delights of gardens"; in other words, exactly the pastimes that are still associated with a weekend in the country.

Neither the Florentine patrician that Alberti had in mind nor a Roman gentleman such as Pliny observed weekends, of course, but both would have used their villas more like weekend cottages than like vacation houses. Villas were generally built close to the city; in fact, the villa districts around Rome, such as Praeneste or Tusculum—where Cicero had a summer house—constituted the first suburbs. Laurentum was not one of these fashionable spots. It was slightly farther away from Rome—seventeen miles—but good roads made this a shorter and easier journey than that undertaken by Mr. Knightley in *Emma*. Pliny, who spent a good part of each summer at his Umbrian estate, traveled frequently to Laurentum during the winter. He described the trip as "rather heavy and slow-going if you drive [by carriage], but soft and easily covered on horseback," short enough that "it is possible to spend the night there after necessary

business is done, without having cut short or hurried the day's work." In a similar vein, Alberti pointed out that "if the villa is not distant, but close by a gate of the city, it will make it easier and more convenient to flit, with wife and children, between town and villa, whenever desirable." Commuting to the cottage clearly has a long history.

The weekenders at Canne de Bois also visit their homemade villas regularly. They come from the city—that is, from Montreal, less than an hour away by car, a shorter trip than Pliny made to reach his villa. The pond replaces the emerald Tyrrhenian Sea, a horseshoe pitch the marble ball court, and an outdoor picnic table the banqueting hall. The gardens are decorated with cement birdbaths and fiberglass urns instead of with Hellenic statues. The environment is different, but the sentiment is similar. Indeed, the little cabins, although undoubtedly less elegant, are like Pliny's private pavilion—intimate, self-made, cozy little sanctuaries.

The chief difference is one of wealth. Like most working-class Montrealers, the inhabitants of Canne de Bois inhabit walk-up flats in the tall, narrow row houses that make up most of the city's housing and which give older Montreal neighborhoods the appearance of a nineteenth-century European town. Since most of these people are tenants, the caravans and cabins of Canne de Bois are not "second homes"

but—in terms of ownership—first homes.* This is not unusual. The weekend cottage is frequently the only way people of modest means can own a home. Indeed, as urban housing prices soar to new, unapproachable levels, the weekend house may become, for many, the only real estate they will ever own. Rural land is inexpensive, and rudimentary rural building regulations—or their lack—allow the individual to build slowly, inexpertly, and hence cheaply. In that sense, a summer colony like Canne de Bois acquires greater significance than first meets the eye. What appear to be improvised "play" houses carry a sense of real seriousness, for although they are not inhabited continuously, for their owners, at least, they embody a sense of permanence and attachment.

The idea of having a "place in the country" probably entered human consciousness at the same time as people began living in cities. It was a reaction to the constraints of the rules and regulations that governed behavior in urban society, and was also a way to temporarily escape the curbs that city living inevitably put on the individual. In Italy villas continued to be built by patrician families throughout the Renaissance, often in the same places as their Roman

---

* The plots at Canne de Bois are rented, but the structures are privately owned. If a homeowner moves, the building is sold to another "tenant"; if the home has been enlarged or improved, the builder recoups his investment with a profit.

predecessors. Nor was the country house restricted to the upper classes. In 1598, when John Stow published *The Survey of London,* he remarked that people were erecting "summer-houses" surrounded by gardens just outside the city walls. These buildings probably belonged to merchants and wealthy shopkeepers.

Stow was critical of these summer houses, which were festooned with quaint turrets and fanciful chimneys, and he deplored their lack of any function save "show and pleasure." He had missed the point. These early versions of weekend cottages were not intended to be serious, and their freedom from architectural convention was not a sign of "the vanity of men's minds," as Stow maintained, but a reflection of their owners' temporary liberation. In these playful houses they had the freedom to behave as they liked, to do what they wanted and when they wanted. They could discard the uniformity of the city in architecture as they did in dress.*

The expressiveness and fantasy of the villa, or the summer cottage, are qualities not usually found in urban domestic buildings. Whether it's the gaily painted caravans of Canne de Bois or the extravagant log concoctions—euphemistically called "camps"—that William West Durant built for upper-class New

---

* Both Pliny and Alberti singled out informal dress as an advantage of villa life.

Yorkers in the Adirondacks, country retreats have always been an opportunity to break loose from the architectural constraints of the city.

Pliny loved the rustic surroundings of his villa and the simple life he led at Laurentum. The building itself, however, was as elegant as his city house, and contained all the comforts a sophisticated Roman could want. The idea of making the country retreat itself rustic grew out of the European Romantic movement, at the end of the eighteenth century. In architecture, as in painting and literature, Romanticism encouraged an awareness of the countryside and of traditional rural building styles. One consequence was the so-called *cottage orné* (ornamented cottage) that became fashionable in England during the Regency, and was the model for the holiday retreats of the middle class. Rambling, picturesque, and above all, rustic, the *cottage orné* provided an appropriate architectural image for anyone seeking an antidote to city living.

The search for the picturesque often led to a bizarre exoticism, and the villas of the wealthy took on more and more eccentric forms, forms that would have appalled Pliny: Swiss chalets, Norman keeps, medieval castles, Chinese pagodas, Gothic ruins, Moorish mosques, even Hindu palaces such as the Royal Pavilion at Brighton. The frankly fake rusticity of the *cottage orné* did not please Coleridge, for example, who

ridiculed the "cottage of gentility" as a sign of "pride that apes humility." That sounds like Stow's complaint about the "vanity of men's minds." It is true that many of these cottages overdid it, with rough tree trunks supporting porch roofs and elaborate decors hidden under thatched roofs and behind cob walls.

Probably the first *cottage orné,* or rather *village orné,* was the famous hamlet built for Marie Antoinette at Versailles, in about 1781. A few years earlier, Louis XVI had given the queen the summer house of Petit Trianon, built by his father a decade before. Marie Antoinette surrounded the exquisite house with gardens in the fashionable "English" style, planted to resemble the natural landscape. She made twice-yearly "trips" to her retreat, in the spring and summer, to get away from the public life of the palace.

Petit Trianon was used like a summer cottage, but it was really a miniature château. Seeking something more natural—or, as Jean-Jacques Rousseau taught, seeking "to return to nature"—the queen had built nearby a mock-Norman village of romantic thatched cottages. Set in an lovely, naturalistic landscape, the charming structures, designed by the architect Richard Mique, included a mill, a dairy, and a dovecote. Despite their names, these buildings had purely recreational functions—they were for informal dining, billiards, backgammon, and dancing.

It's easy to make fun of a queen who pretends to be a country lass, eating ice cream off marble tables in the "dairy," picking flowers in the garden, or standing with a fishing pole at the edge of an artificial pond. But were her affectations really so different from what many modern city dwellers do on weekends: stockbrokers wearing old clothes and driving tractors, office workers in checked shirts chopping wood at the cottage, bus drivers putting on camouflage gear and going hunting, or pharmacists in sou'westers messing about in boats? Marie Antoinette's hamlet was a make-believe world, but so are all country retreats.

If I were to ask the inhabitants of Canne de Bois why they come here each weekend, they would answer, "To get out of the city, of course." Pliny would probably have given the same response, and for the same reasons that he once confided to a friend, in a letter written from Laurentum: "You should take the first opportunity yourself to leave the din, the futile bustle and useless occupations of the city." The attractions of a country retreat have changed little: peace and quiet, privacy and relaxation.

At no time was the din and bustle of the city greater than during the nineteenth century. Industrialization meant, above all, urbanization, and the growth rate for cities in Europe and America was

explosive—analogous to that of Third World cities today. As national populations grew—Britain's doubled between 1800 and 1850—large numbers of rural people were obliged to move to cities and towns where expanding factories provided their only chance for gainful employment. In the early 1800s, London, with a population of about a million, was several times larger than either Vienna or Paris, and was already the largest city in the world; by the end of the century it was approaching five million. Because they were newer, American cities were smaller, but their growth was equally dramatic—the result of both a depletion of the countryside and the arrival of large numbers of European immigrants. Between 1835 and 1870, New York grew from less than two hundred thousand inhabitants to a million; Chicago's population tripled.

The rapid expansion of the nineteenth-century industrial city was bought at a great cost. Lewis Mumford likened the urban destruction and disorder of the period between 1820 and 1900 to a battlefield. Railroads cut indiscriminately through the older urban fabric, smoky factories surrounded residential areas, and inhuman slums surrounded the factories. As buildings grew higher and denser, streets became more congested. The traditional water and waste systems proved inadequate; aqueducts and underground sewers, as well as organized garbage collection, would eventually resolve these problems, but that took time.

(The first underground sewer was constructed in the 1850s, in Brooklyn; most cities did not have proper sanitation until the end of the century.) In the meantime the city became a dirty, noisy, crowded, unsafe, and unhealthy place.

Montreal was no exception. Beginning in the middle of the nineteenth century, the city underwent the first of a series of periods of spectacular growth. The change was more dramatic there than elsewhere, for when the British conquered the French colony, a hundred years earlier, Montreal had been little more than a fur-trading town with fewer than nine thousand inhabitants. With British immigration, and the influx of loyalists after the American War of Independence, the town grew to a city of twenty-two thousand by 1825. The introduction of steamships turned Montreal into the main seaport of Canada—it was soon the largest port in North America—and the Lachine Canal, built in 1825, linked ocean shipping with inland navigation from the Great Lakes. Railways joined the port to the major cities of the Eastern Seaboard, first to New York, later to Portland and Boston. Thanks to these advantages, which provided jobs for large numbers of immigrants, over the next two decades Montreal's population doubled, then doubled again. By 1910 the city contained half a million people. Twenty years later it would reach a million.

It was during this period that the newly prosper-

ous merchant families of Montreal, like their coun-
terparts elsewhere, began to treat themselves to
second homes to escape the increasingly crowded metropolis. Some built large log houses in the Laurentian
Mountains, north of the city, but these were really
elaborate fishing and hunting lodges, not weekend
homes. Grand family summer mansions sprang up in
the suburbs, on the west end of the island of Montreal,
a carriage ride of one or two hours from the city.

For some, this was not far enough. Each decade
of urban growth redefined the boundaries of the city
and relentlessly pushed its perimeter farther and farther into the surrounding countryside. This was typical of nineteenth-century cities, whose sheer physical
extent had a major impact on urban life. It's easy to
forget the small scale of the preindustrial city. Eliz-
abethan London, for example, stretched along the
Thames for little more than a mile. Going to the country was a matter of a short walk. Two hundred years
later, Mozart's Vienna, with a population of roughly
two hundred thousand, was still a walled city, also
about a mile square; that meant that it was only a ten-
minute walk to the line of fortifications, beyond
which lay the country. The city of London and Vienna's Innere Stadt were densely built-up warrens of
narrow streets and twisting lanes lined with tall houses
built tightly one against the next. But for the inhabitants of these small, compact homes, the respite of

the open countryside was never more than a short stroll away. This ceased to be true in the nineteenth century, or, rather, it ceased to be universally true; access to the now distant countryside had become a luxury.

There were practical reasons to want to escape the congested Victorian city. Those who had the means had another motivation: the wish to experience the beauties of nature, preferably in their pristine unadulterated state. This appreciation for the wilderness was also something new. John Ruskin first saw the Alps in 1833, when he was fourteen years old—and he was overwhelmed. Describing the experience in later life, he wrote that his emotion "belonged to the age: a very few years—within the hundred—before that, no child could have been born to care for mountains." Ruskin's insight is important. The Romantic movement altered not only artistic principles but also people's sensibilities. Mountain vistas and seashore views, which had previously been ignored, were now sought out as rewarding aesthetic experiences.

Montreal was an inland city, but it did have a great river. Near Montreal, the Saint Lawrence flowed through a flat and unattractive agricultural landscape, but below Quebec City, as the river widened before emptying into the Gulf, the scenery changed, and tall, rugged cliffs produced a setting of spectacular beauty. An additional attraction (particularly in a time when

air-conditioning was unknown) was the refreshing coolness of the summers. While wealthy New Yorkers were choosing the banks of the Hudson River and Newport, Rhode Island, as the site for their large summer mansions, well-to-do Montrealers fixed on the lower Saint Lawrence as their personal holiday ground. They were joined by many American visitors, who could now comfortably travel to Montreal and Quebec City by train—President Taft, for example, owned a summer house on the Saguenay River. Sir John A. Macdonald, Canada's first prime minister, also summered in the area. Resort hotels sprang up in the most picturesque spots along the north shore of the Saint Lawrence, places such as Murray Bay and Tadoussac, the site of the oldest fur-trading post in Canada. The romance of a holiday in "the wilderness," although in comfortable and well-appointed surroundings, was heightened by the nature of the transportation—the final stage of the journey was made by leisurely paddle-wheel river steamer.

The closest seacoast to Montreal was in New Brunswick, on the Bay of Fundy. Beginning in 1889, the Intercolonial Railway linked Montreal to Halifax, and it was railway tycoons, led by Sir William Van Horne, builder of the trans-Canadian line, who made Saint Andrews, a charming coastal town near the Maine border, into a favorite resort of both Boston-

ians and Montrealers. But even by rail, the distance to Montreal was much too great for short visits, and most people went to Saint Andrews by the Sea, as it came to be called, at the beginning of the summer and stayed for the season.

Halfway to the Maritime Provinces, about four hundred miles from Montreal, the Intercolonial Railway passed a small resort village on the south shore of the Saint Lawrence River. Metis Beach was the farthest outpost in the chain of summer resorts along the river. It had been settled by Scots, and beginning in the 1850s attracted summer visitors from Montreal. They came for the beautiful scenery, for boating and fishing, and for the fresh air—Metis Beach was advertised as having the highest level of ozone on the continent.

The first vacationers came by road, or by river steamer, but it was the railway that ensured the growth of the summer colony. Trains made travel both faster and more comfortable. The train to Montreal stopped in Metis Beach at ten o'clock in the evening and reached the city the next morning. Seeing friends and relatives off at the station on Sunday night was a weekly ritual. In its heyday, during the 1930s, Metis Beach included four hundred private homes—both cottages and mansions—nine large hotels, two golf courses and tennis clubs, four churches (all Protestant), and a library. Like Canne de Bois, the settle-

ment stood empty during the winter, or almost so; the summer population of three thousand shrank to two hundred permanent residents.

During the early 1900s, more and more people started coming to Metis Beach by automobile. At the time this seemed like an extra convenience, but in fact the car would spell the end of the primacy of exclusive upper-class country resorts such as Metis Beach and Saint Andrews. Automobiles enabled people to travel to many more places than were served by railways or river steamers. They could, for example, if they were New Yorkers, drive to the end of Long Island, like Jay Gatsby and his friends, or into the Catskills. If they were Montrealers, they could easily visit the Laurentian Mountains or the pretty lakes in the Eastern Townships.

If the car's only role was to allow the rich to vary the location of their recreations, it would be merely a footnote in the history of the country retreat. It was not so much the car that altered leisure habits as the popularization of car ownership. The first cars were expensive and could be afforded only by the well-to-do; after 1914, when Henry Ford began mass-producing automobiles, everyone could buy a car, and did. By 1939 there was one car for every four inhabitants of the United States—the highest rate of ownership in the world (fully three quarters of all the cars in the world were owned by Americans); Canada was

close behind, with a car for every eight inhabitants.* Both were far ahead of the leading European countries such as England and France (one car for every eighteen people) and the Third Reich, where there was one car for every forty-two people.

The automobile is "the most wonderful of conveniences," in historian John Lukacs's words, "not so much because of its comfort (which is limited in even the most luxurious of cars) and not even because of its reduction of distances, but because it allows its owner to be the master of his time rather than of space; he can leave whenever he wants, and return whenever he chooses; he does not depend on schedules of public transport." It is precisely this freedom that made the car the prime instrument of leisure.

Now that more and more working people had acquired a car, they also had more free time to use it. That was Henry Ford's reasoning for introducing the shorter workweek in his factories. The five-day week took longer to achieve popular acceptance than he had anticipated, but that did not diminish the attraction of car ownership. The automobile was first and foremost a plaything, not a means of transportation—that would come later. Eventually the combination of the

---

* The other leaders in automobile ownership at the time were also ex–British colonies: New Zealand (a car for every six inhabitants) and Australia (one for every nine).

two-day weekend and the automobile proved irresistible. The automobile is frequently blamed for the spread of suburbs, although the earliest planned suburban developments in America, such as Riverside, Illinois (1869), and Bronxville, New York (1890), predated the inexpensive cars and were both linked to Chicago and New York City, respectively, by railways. There is no question, however, that the automobile created a less visible extension of the city. The modern metropolis assumed a new and unexpected form: the city proper, and, many miles away, its rustic counterpart—weekend-cottage country.

Every Canadian and American city is now surrounded by a generous sprinkling of weekend settlements—a rustic mirror of itself. Or maybe a better metaphor would be the two vessels of an hourglass. Every fifth day the glass is rotated, and the sand pours from one side to the other; two days later, it is tilted again, and the sand pours back. Each Friday night, in cities across the continent, hundreds of thousands of families transpose themselves to their country retreats, to mountains, lakes, rivers, and seashores, or, as these fill up, to less picturesque sites like Canne de Bois. Unlike the nineteenth-century railway resort, cottage country is not concentrated but spread over the landscape, and it is no longer limited to the wealthy.

One shouldn't confuse cottage country with coun-

try; rural life is less affected by the weekend. Even as I write this, on a summer Saturday morning, my neighbor is hard at work, spraying his apple orchard. The weather—it looks like rain—does not allow him to wait. Nor do the cows of my other neighbor take weekend holidays; they must be attended to seven days a week. Farmers here still take their leisure according to the seasons—during the winter many go to Florida—and holidays tend to occur on rainy days—except, of course, for marriages and funerals, for which all work stops. That is to be expected, for the weekend, like the weekend retreat, is an urban habit. The two developed in tandem as consequences of city life—a time to escape, a place to escape to.

eight

Pastimes

A recent Japanese study comparing working men and women in Tokyo, New York, and Los Angeles found that although the typical time for relaxation at home after work varied from three hours (Tokyo) to four (Los Angeles) and five hours (New York), residents of all three cities named the same activity: watching television. In a similar vein, a 1989 national survey indicated that three quarters of Canadians adults reported that their major free-time activity was watching television—an average of 3.1 hours per day.

Whether it's a hot or cool medium, and whatever its lowbrow content, television has one attribute that is so obvious that it is often ignored: it is voracious. Three hours a day devoted to watching television means twenty-one hours weekly—half a workweek— a staggering and unprecedented amount of time devoted to one pastime. Few societies anywhere have ever spent so much time on a single type of amuse-

ment—not the Romans on their circuses (of which there were usually only eight each year), not the Middle Ages on their carnivals and feasts, not even the Georgians on their animal baiting, prizefighting, and horse racing.

There was one eighteenth-century leisure activity, however, that probably demanded almost as much time as watching television, and that was reading. Just as watching television has dramatically altered the nature of leisure in the second half of the twentieth century, so did reading books in the eighteenth. The printed book had already existed for two hundred years, but only during the 1700s did cheaper paper and faster presses—technical developments that also made possible the newspaper and the magazine—reduce printing costs enough to make books available to a larger audience.

The popularity of books was not just due to technology. Until the sixteenth century most printed books were in Latin; the international language of both clerics and scholars. Eventually translations appeared in various European languages, which meant that book reading began to spread to a broader public. Obviously, it was a public that could read. Between 1500 and 1800, literacy grew quickly in northern and northwestern Europe, which was culturally more advanced than the rest of the continent. By the mid-eighteenth century, it has been estimated that almost

187

all the adults in some countries—Scotland, Sweden, and Denmark, for example—could read (although not necessarily write). The Reformation undoubtedly played a role, for Protestantism placed great importance on individual reading of the Scriptures; so did the growth of cities, where literacy was always higher than in the countryside, and the increasing popularity of schooling for children.

The evolution of the book as an inexpensive commodity (it had previously been a luxury) influenced its subject matter. Since printers and booksellers worked for profit, the content of books, unlike that of hand-copied manuscripts, was a direct reflection of public tastes. The first books were chiefly religious— not surprising, since most book buyers and readers were clerics; works of medieval philosophy and theology, as well as legal texts, found a smaller market among scholars and lawyers.

By the sixteenth century, people had begun to read not out of religious devotion or scholastic vocation but for pleasure. History was a popular subject, especially the classical histories of Livy, Plutarch, and Julius Caesar. According to the French historian Lucien Febvre, "The same large public which had an insatiable appetite for history, and often preferred legendary histories to objective accounts, the public which, for example, took such an interest in the legend of Troy, was equally fascinated by imaginative

literature." The thirst for fiction fueled the continued popularity of medieval romances such as the *Morte d'Arthur* and the *Roman de la Rose,* and also prompted new works such as *Amadís de Gaula,* a chivalric tale of which there were more than sixty Spanish editions during the sixteenth century, and which became a best-seller throughout Europe. Eventually *Diana,* a Spanish pastoral romance by Jorge de Montemayor, and the burlesque tales of François Rabelais set the stage for the modern novel. The point has already been made that the novel signaled the arrival of a new type of leisure activity—introverted, personal, and private. What changed was not only the availability and the nature of reading material but also something else: the *way* books were read.

Between the sixteenth and eighteenth centuries more and more people acquired a new skill: the ability to read without pronouncing the words as they were read. Most people read aloud when books were rare, and many readers, lacking the ability to write, had to laboriously pick their way through the unfamiliar texts. And through unfamiliar orthography—spelling was not yet standardized and was often left to the whim of the typesetter. Moreover, reading aloud was customary; before widespread literacy, books were more often read *to* people than *by* people. Reading was a public, social activity.

Once people learned to read silently, reading be-

came an act of quiet and solitude. Silent reading made it possible for the reader to rapidly internalize what he was reading. It was also an intensely intimate activity, as reflected in the changed subject matter of books, which now dealt with the interior life of individuals. Silent reading removed one from the surrounding world, a mental separation that eventually became physical. During the fifteenth and sixteenth centuries few people (generally churchmen or lawyers) owned private libraries. By the end of the seventeenth century, it was not unusual for a bourgeois individual such as Samuel Pepys to have a considerable collection of books, and to keep them at home in a special private room set aside for solitary reading and writing.*

The eighteenth-century study, despite its name, was less a place for study than for private relaxation. The lone figure with a book had long been a favorite subject for painters, but whereas medieval artists depicted readers who were scholars or hermits, painters like Chardin portrayed bourgeois men—and, more commonly, women—in an atmosphere of idleness and repose instead of studiousness.

The privatization of reading has been called one

---

* Silent, personal reading had a counterpart in personal writing—diaries, journals, and memoirs also made their appearance in the seventeenth century.

of the major cultural developments of the early modern era. It was also a milestone in the history of leisure. Solitary reading is the ideal vehicle for individual leisure. The reader can do something—or nothing. He can pick up one book or another. He sets the pace, reading uninterruptedly or leafing through a book at random, letting his imagination free to make what connections it will. Reading requires long periods of calm—at the comfortable rate of two hundred words a minute, it takes about fifteen hours to complete a typical novel. Reflection, contemplation, privacy, and solitude are also associated with reading books. And withdrawal. Both withdrawal from the world around one, from the cares of everyday life, and withdrawal into oneself.

The privatization of reading in the eighteenth century was nowhere as advanced as in the United States, where individual literacy was widespread and the public demand for books was correspondingly great. When Thomas Paine's anti-monarchist tract *Common Sense* was published in 1776, it sold more than a hundred thousand copies in two months. (Most editions numbered no more than two thousand copies.) In all, about four hundred thousand copies of Paine's book were eventually printed. This was in a country with a population of only 3 million persons; a book

would have to sell about 24 million copies today to do as well. "Only the Super Bowl could produce such collective attention in today's America," Neil Postman ruefully observes.

There are now tens of millions of people who cannot—or do not—read books.* The large number of books published each year (more than fifty thousand titles in the United States alone) camouflages the fact that book buyers are an extremely small group, perhaps as small as ten percent of the total population. In the Canadian survey referred to at the beginning of this chapter, only eighteen percent of respondents said they read a daily newspaper, and a mere sixteen percent spent some of their leisure time reading a magazine or a book.

The criticism is often made that watching television is passive. This is true when it is compared with active recreations such as jogging or playing tennis. But watching television is no more passive than observing a landscape, listening to music, or reading a book. Like reading a book, it's a withdrawal, but a withdrawal of a different kind. Television tells a story in a way that requires no imagination; the picture on the screen and the sound provide all we need to

---

* It is estimated that as many as a third of Canadians and Americans are "functionally illiterate"; less obvious but equally disturbing is the large number of people who can read but do not—"aliterates," in Daniel Boorstin's phrase.

know—there is nothing to fill in. Television watching should more properly be called television staring; it engages eye and ear simultaneously in a relentless and persistent way and leaves no room for daydreaming. That is what makes watching television such an inferior form of leisure—not that it's passive, but that it offers so little opportunity for reflection and contemplation.

At the beach—or reading a book, or listening to Vivaldi—our attention shifts from sight to smell to sound at will. The mind wanders in and out of the scene. The physical sensations stimulate thoughts, memories, and reflections. These interruptions are an integral part of the experience of relaxing. Watching television, on the other hand, is focused, structured, and scheduled. Commercial breaks occur at preordained intervals. If the attention is distracted, the story line is lost; one cannot move in and out at will. Freedom, a key ingredient of leisure, is missing. Some latitude is restored to the viewer by the remote-control device, and even more by the videocassette recorder, which lets the viewer set the schedule and accelerate, slow, or stop the action altogether. But these are crude techniques, cruder than rereading a sentence in a book or stopping to think about what one has read. In the final analysis, compared with reading a book, television (although it is a diverting form of recreation) is a poor sort of leisure.

There's another important difference between reading a book and watching television. Serious book readers read almost daily, from habit and because of the demands of the form. A nineteenth-century novel, for example, with its dozens of characters and intertwining plots, requires close attention; it cannot be put aside for too long or the reader risks losing his place in the story. The same applies to a serious work of nonfiction, whose ordered arguments must be retained from one reading to the next. Not that books are intended to be read at one sitting; the organization of books into chapters provides convenient stopping places.

The ability to read a book presupposes the availability of short but frequently recurring periods of free time. The reduction of weekday leisure time for many people makes it difficult to find time for regular reading. Weekends don't help; they're too far apart. At least they do not help book reading, although the prevalence of intermittent, weekend reading may explain the recent explosion in the number of magazines—fast food in book-reading terms. The popularity of the blockbuster summer novels that are taken on vacation and consumed on the beach suggests that book reading has not altogether lost its attraction, only its congruity with modern leisure time.

Television's schedule is better suited to the pace of modern life. Except for daytime programs, which

air daily, dramatic television programming follows a seven-day cycle. Once a week an established cast of characters enacts an independent plot, analogous to a short story. Even when a story is carried through from one week to the next—as happens with a mini-series—each show begins with flashbacks and a synopsis, as a reminder of what came before. Nor is the viewer required to follow the entire series—unlike the chapters in a book, the segments are often self-contained and can be enjoyed on their own.

The crowded work schedules of most people demand a form of leisure that can be squeezed into irregular intervals during the week—or postponed until time becomes available on the weekend. This has not had a beneficial effect on book reading, but there are leisure activities other than television watching that can also be taken up intermittently. Listening to music, for example—the entire *Four Seasons* lasts only about forty minutes. Other pastimes—stamp-collecting, building model ships, laying bricks—can also be felicitously indulged in at odd intervals, and for varying amounts of time.

Stamp collecting and model building are usually described as hobbies. "Hobby" is a curious English word that has no equivalent in other European languages. Its root, "hobbin," was medieval—like Dobbin, an affectionate name given to cart horses—and the original meaning of hobby was a small horse or

pony. A hobbyhorse also referred to the horse mannequins that pantomimers and morris dancers carried
around their waists. Because of this association with
play, the term was used to describe the small wooden
toy horses, some on rockers, some merely a horse's
head on a stick, that were given to young children.*
As early as the seventeenth century, "riding one's
hobbyhorse" was an expression that referred not to
children but to adults, and not to playing with a make-
believe horse but to indulging oneself in what appeared to outsiders to be a trivial pastime. Eventually,
in the nineteenth century, the noun "hobby" began
to be used to describe a particular kind of leisure
activity.

The prototypical nineteenth-century hobbyist
was a collector. The pastime of collecting things (especially old things) was a Victorian passion—the
museum was an early-nineteenth-century invention—
and well-to-do men and women amassed large col-
lections of Oriental porcelain, Japanese prints, and
other exotica. The collector of modest means collected
pressed flowers, matchboxes, and, above all, postage
stamps.

---

* Hobbyhorse was also the name given to the precursor of the
bicycle. It consisted simply of two wheels joined by a crossbar on
which the rider sat, and propelled himself forward by pushing with
his feet on the ground. Hobbyhorses were a short-lived craze in both
Europe and America at the beginning of the nineteenth century.

The first adhesive postage stamp was the famous "Penny Black," which featured a portrait of Queen Victoria and was minted in 1840. By the end of the decade, most major countries had begun to issue stamps, and people began to collect them. The earliest reference to stamp collecting occurs in 1841, in an advertisement that appeared in the London *Times*. "A young lady, being desirous of covering her dressing-room with cancelled postage stamps, has been so far encouraged in her wish by private friends as to have succeeded in collecting 16,000. These, however, being insufficient, she will be greatly obliged if any good-natured person who may have these (otherwise use-less) little articles at their disposal, would assist her in her whimsical project." Soon there were enough different varieties of stamps to use for something more interesting than wallpaper. By the early 1860s stamp collecting had become an international fad. Between 1860 and 1863, the first stamp catalogs were issued (in Belgium, Britain, France, and the United States), specialty magazines for stamp collectors appeared in several countries, a Frenchman published the first stamp album, and another Frenchman coined the term "philately," which replaced "timbromania" as the name of this popular pastime.

This kind of personalization and privatization of leisure was unusual before the nineteenth century, but it became increasingly common thereafter. "Riding

one's hobbyhorse" had been a term tinged with de-
rision, like having a bee in one's bonnet; "having a
hobby" was respectable. George Santayana once characterized England as "the paradise of individuality,
eccentricity, heresy, anomalies, hobbies, and hu-
mors." That was putting the hobby in the right company, for what distinguished hobbies from other
recreations was that the hobbyist was devoted to his
private passion out of all proportion to its real importance. It was a way of doing something and nothing at the same time.

A personal confession at this point. I had several
hobbies as a boy (a model railroad, a stamp collection,
a puppet theater), and I suppose that my adolescent
career as a drummer qualified as a hobby, but I am
always at a loss when asked to name my hobbies
today. Books and music are too much a part of my
everyday life to qualify as hobbies. I enjoy carpentry,
but I would be just as happy to buy a bookshelf as to
build one. Several years ago I tried to resuscitate my
Canadian stamp collection, but I found that stamps
had lost their glamour; I was merely reminded of the
dismal state of the Canadian postal system. When I
first acquired a personal computer, I thought that
playing computer games would become a hobby; it
took only a few hours of Adventure and Space Pirates
to cure me of that delusion.

The closest I have come to a hobby—it is really

a weekend diversion—is rowing. This nineteenth-century pastime lets me fulfill my fascination with boats with the minimum fuss and bother. Rowing, unlike sculling, is a relaxing activity, although there is a small amount of mild physical exertion, just enough to satisfy my sedentary guilt. If you are not going far, a rowing skiff—mine is a replica of a type built in the 1920s for trout fishing on New York's Finger Lakes—is a leisurely way to go; it's less noisy than a motorboat, and considerably less complicated than a sailboat. And it allows one to share what Paul Theroux has called the secret of boating: the absolute difference of being on water instead of on land, the discovery of a different world—which is, I suppose, what hobbies are about.

What is "the purest of human pleasures . . . the greatest refreshment to the spirits of man"? The answer, according to Francis Bacon, who wrote these words in 1625, the year before his death, was not reading books or listening to music or even the diversions of a leisurely row. What the famous philosopher was describing was gardening.

Gardening is an indulgence, but it is an ancient one. The oldest work of literature in existence, the Gilgamesh Epic, mentions a landscape garden, and all the great civilizations of antiquity—the Mesopotamians, the Egyptians, the Persians, the Romans—built palace gardens of great beauty and sophistication.

These were usually grand, and resembled parks. The best-known gardens, such as those surrounding Hadrian's villa at Tivoli, were immense, and reflected the wealth of their owners. Even the landscaping of a smaller country estate like Pliny's required the labor of many workers; likewise the thirty-acre "princely" garden that Bacon proposed in his essay.

The history of the small domestic garden—as distinct from the great gardens of the aristocracy—remains to be written. It would be a task made difficult by the lack of physical evidence, for while the celebrated gardens of Isfahan, the Alhambra, and Vaux-le-Vicomte exist in nearly original form, the gardens of ordinary people of the past can be only known at second hand, from paintings or written descriptions.

There were undoubtedly modest gardens in ancient times, for at the heart of every Greek and Roman house was a courtyard surrounded by an arcade. Every room in the house would open onto this space which contained potted trees and flowers and often a pool of water. The court-garden house remained an Oriental prototype (it is also found throughout the Middle East, as well as in India) but in medieval Europe it was replaced by the narrow row house, with a garden at the rear. The ancestor of the small medieval garden was the close, or walled garden, which was initially attached to monastic buildings, a pattern derived from Byzantine churches. These cloister gar-

dens were known as "paradises," like their Persian predecessors, and they were symbols of both the Virgin and virginity, as well as of paradise lost. Walled orchards (the Middle Ages was as security-conscious as our own time) also had romantic overtones, for they were associated with lovers' meetings.

Eventually the close became a household fixture. The walled domestic garden behind the house was almost secretive, a magical place, not least because it provided privacy. Before the home was subdivided into specialized rooms, gardens were already "refuges of intimacy," in historian Orest Ranum's charming phrase, and afforded an opportunity for the solitary contemplation of nature—especially flowers. Roses were especially popular, and, as in Pliny's time, so was the scent of violets. The flower garden (there was usually a kitchen garden elsewhere) was intended for leisure—it was specifically called a "pleasure garden"—and was the perfect place for "doing nothing." There was usually a bench, often set in an arbor, which provided a congenial setting for private conversations and romantic encounters.

Edward Hyams, the English author of *A History of Gardens and Gardening,* maintains that the seventeenth-century Dutch were the first to develop the small suburban garden. These formal gardens were miniature versions of French parterres, with clipped box hedges and extravagant topiaries; the ground was

often covered in scrollwork shapes, outlined in colored earth, shells, and rocks. In the spring there were tulips, of course, but the Dutch garden, with its white-painted tree trunks, its glittering gewgaws and lifelike painted figures (also a French fashion, and the origin of the gnomes and flamingos that still decorate suburban lawns), was anything but natural. These gardens were meant for show—they were located in front of the house—not for idling, which is why, when Dutch painters wanted to portray intimate domestic scenes, they located them indoors, rarely in the garden.

All gardens are attempts to establish a happy and meaningful equilibrium between humankind and nature. According to Charles Moore, the author of *The Poetics of Gardens*, "in all of human history there seem to have emerged just two basic notions of how to do this." The first is the walled paradise garden, which keeps the outside world at bay and re-creates a perfect, orderly paradise within. The traditional walled garden of Persia was ideally a square, divided into four quarters and further subdivided by paths and watercourses. From this standard, which had endless permutations possible, came the great gardens of Islamic Spain and Mogul India. The paradise garden reoccurs in a modified but still geometric form in Renaissance Italy, and in seventeenth-century France and Holland.

The second idea, equally ancient, is of a garden ordered not according to geometry but to the natural world—asymmetrical, crooked, diversified, picturesque. Such gardens were seen first in China and Japan, and came into the European consciousness thanks to the English gardeners of the eighteenth century. They produced such masterpieces as William Kent's Rousham, begun in the 1730s. Kent, whom Horace Walpole credited with originating the new style of garden, was also an architect, but his gardening ideas were influenced by his knowledge of painting. His gardens were conceived of as a carefully orchestrated series of views—and viewing points—not only of trees and water but of many classical objects: gazebos, temples, bridges, and statues. Unlike the formal garden, whose symbolic geometry could be appreciated intellectually and at a glance, the natural English garden demanded to be walked through and seen, not just once but at different times of the day and year.

Kent and his famous successors Capability Brown and Humphry Repton were professional landscape architects, but Walpole suggested that gardening was best left to amateurs, for the owner of a garden "sees his situation in all seasons of the year, at all times of the day. He knows where beauty will not clash with convenience, and observes in his silent walks or accidental rides a thousand hints that must escape a person who in a few days sketches out a pretty picture,

but has not had leisure to examine the details and relations of every part."

The eighteenth century was a period of dilettantism—Walpole himself was a noted amateur architect, whose Gothic improvements to his own house at Strawberry Hill established that style as a domestic fashion all over Europe—and nowhere was this more visible than in gardening design. John Aislabie, a politician who withdrew to Yorkshire as a result of his embroilment in the South Sea Bubble scandal, spent his latter years creating an extraordinary water garden at Studley Royal. William Shenstone, a poet and the author of *Unconnected Thoughts on Gardening,* retired to his family's country seat for his health and made a beautiful garden called "*a ferme ornēd.*" The most famous amateur gardener of the time, however, was neither a poet nor a patrician, but a banker. Henry Hoare's father had built a Palladian villa, but he died before completing the grounds. Hoare spent thirty years laying out Stourhead, a grand composition around a twenty-acre artificial lake, considered by many to be the greatest of all eighteenth-century English gardens.

Few amateur gardeners had the means to achieve works on the scale of Stourhead. Still, accessibility was one of gardening's attractions. Gardens were not just for princes or rich bankers; anyone could have a garden. This sentiment is evident in the first garden-

ing handbook in English, the *Systema Horticulturae, or Art of Gardening*, which was published in 1677. Its author John Worlidge described the small personal gardens of his day: "There is scarce a cottage of the southern parts of England but hath its proportionable garden, so great a delight do most men take in it, that they may not only please themselves with the view of the flowers, herbs, and trees, as they grow, but furnish themselves and their neighbours upon extraordinary occasions, as nuptials, feasts, and funerals, with the proper products of their gardens." John Abercrombie's 1766 guide to gardening was explicitly aimed at the small householder—it was called *Every Man His Own Gardener*.

Small gardens, then as now, combined practicality with beauty—that is, vegetables with flowers. Chesterton once wrote that he liked his kitchen garden because it contained things to eat. There is something timelessly satisfying about digging up a potato or pulling a carrot out of the ground, and growing one's own food is undoubtedly one of the chief pleasures of gardening. The small garden remained common in the country, but town dwellers had to wait until the end of the nineteenth century and the allotment-garden movement. This movement originated in Germany and spread quickly across the Continent and to England, encouraging municipal authorities to acquire wasteland on the fringes of cities and towns and

along railway tracks and make it available as small plots for the working populations who lacked their own gardens. The original aim of the movement was to provide an opportunity for healthy outdoor recreation, but allotments coincided with the advent of the Saturday half-holiday, and small suburban gardens soon became a focus for weekend leisure. They became retreats, sprouting sheds and cabins resembling dollhouses—the first weekend cottages. By the 1930s, there were more than half a million such gardens in Britain, and the number increased during World War II as a result of the "Dig for Victory" campaign.

A resurgence in allotment gardening occurred recently in Poland, where it is estimated that more than a million town households cultivate allotments and another 1.5 million are on waiting lists. The popularity of these gardens, which are often several miles outside the city, is a result of the sudden availability of free time on Saturdays and of the lack of other diversions. Growing fruits and vegetables has economic advantages, especially in Poland, where food shortages are common, but the small plots also offer people a chance to build small homemade cabins, which transform the gardens into weekend retreats. According to Anna Olszewska, a Polish sociologist, "their cultivation has become a common way of passing weekends, and they have also become sites for social and family gatherings."

In North America the growth of allotment gardening was limited by the postwar spread of single-family suburban houses, each on its own plot of land. Now everyone really could become his own gardener. In 1952, Americans spent more than a billion dollars on flowers, seeds, potted plants, and garden tools, an expenditure that had increased steadily for the previous two decades—close to twice as much as they spent on books. The 1980 census revealed that more than a hundred million Americans, more than forty percent of the population, live in suburbs. The vast majority have gardens.

The pattern elsewhere is similar. In Britain, where two thirds of all dwellings are now owner-occupied, gardening (like other home-centered hobbies) has grown steadily in popularity. A recent Hungarian survey of blue-collar workers indicates that although watching television has become the main recreation, gardening remains the chief outdoor leisure pastime. A 1978 study of the recreational use of suburban gardens in Adelaide, Australia, found that gardens were used an average of twenty-two hours a week for recreational activities in addition to gardening, and concluded that private gardens were used more intensively and flexibly than any other outdoor recreational facility in the city.

Cultivating one's own patch of ground will continue to be a popular pastime for a long time to come. Gardening fits in easily with the five-and-two time-

table. Tending a garden does not require a rigid schedule, and is exactly the kind of activity that can be indulged in on weekends and at weekend country retreats. As cities become denser and more people live in apartments, it is the country place—however small—that will provide the locale for gardening. Even the small plots of land at Canne de Bois have little parcels of garden, clumps of rosebushes, or ornamental flower beds.

Gardening is undertaken voluntarily, for one's own amusement, and it fulfills Johan Huizinga's three criteria for true play: it represents freedom, it stands outside everyday life, and it contains its own course and meaning (which, like that of most play, can be serious). But it's a special kind of play. Unlike spectator sports, most games, and recreational pastimes such as dancing, gardening is not social—it is usually private. The gardener is a solitary figure, who, like the book reader, withdraws from the real world into one of his own creation.

The capacity to be alone is a valuable character trait, often associated with creative individuals. But it may have a broader application. Anthony Storr, a psychiatrist who has written about the importance of solitude in the development of creativity, maintains that any balanced person will find the meaning of his life not only in his interpersonal relationships with family and friends but also in the solitary pursuit of

personal interests. Cultivating a garden may, to use Pliny's analogy, be a way to cultivate oneself.

Gardening is solitary, but it also involves outdoor physical activities (digging, planting, pruning) that make it an attractive antidote to the mechanized—and mechanical—clerical work that characterizes most modern jobs. In that sense, the garden offers possibilities for both recreation (working in the garden) *and* leisure (sitting in the garden).

Gardening is ill suited to instant gratification—a good garden cannot be rushed. Despite the cost of lawn mowers, cultivators, and seeds, gardening is not chiefly a form of consumption, and its persistence suggests that traditional leisure may be somewhat resistant to modern influences. Gardening was conveniently ignored by those critics who foretold a society increasingly obsessed with leisure goods—Veblen, for example, chose to leave gardening off his list of "conspicuous consumptions." Christopher Lasch also neglects gardening in his *Culture of Narcissism*, which argues that modern leisure is an extension of commodity production and an appendage of industry. Gardening may yet confound them both.

The Problem of Leisure

In 1919 the Hungarian psychiatrist Sándor Ferenczi published a short paper entitled "Sunday Neuroses." He recounted that in his medical practice he had encountered several neurotics whose symptoms recurred on a regular basis. Although it's common for a repressed memory to return at the same time of year as the original experience, the symptoms he described appeared every week. Even more novel, they appeared most frequently on one day: Sunday. Having eliminated possible physical factors associated with Sunday, such as sleeping in, special holiday foods, and overeating, he decided that his patients' hysterical symptoms were caused by the holiday character of the day. This hypothesis seemed to be borne out by one particular case, that of a Jewish boy whose symptoms appeared on Friday evening, the commencement of the Sabbath. Ferenczi speculated that the headaches and vomiting of these holiday neurotics were a reaction to the

freedom that the weekly day of rest offered. Since Sunday allowed all sorts of relaxed behavior (noisy family games, playful picnics, casual dress), Ferenczi reasoned that people who were neurotically disposed might feel uncomfortable "venting their holiday wantonness," either because they had dangerous impulses to control or because they felt guilty about letting go their inhibitions.

Ferenczi described the Sunday holiday as a day when "we are our own masters and feel ourselves free from all the fetters that the duties and compulsions of circumstances impose on us; there occurs in us— parallel with this—a kind of inner liberation also." Although "Sunday neurosis" was a clinical term, the concept of a liberation of repressed instincts coupled with a greater availability of free time raised the menacing image of a whole society running amok. Throughout the 1920s there were dozens of articles and books of a more general nature, published by psychiatrists, psychologists, and social scientists in both Europe and America, on the perils of what was often called the New Leisure. There was a widespread feeling that the working class would not really know what to do with all this extra free time.

The underlying theme was an old one: less work meant more leisure, more leisure led to idleness, and idle hands, as everyone knew, were ripe for Satan's mischief. This was precisely the argument advanced

by the supporters of Prohibition, who maintained that shorter hours provided workers with more free time which they would only squander on drink. Whatever the merits of this argument—and undoubtedly drinking was popular—one senses that this and other such "concerns" really masked an unwillingness to accept the personal freedom that was implicit in leisure. The pessimism of social reformers—and many intellectuals—about the abilities of ordinary people to amuse themselves has always been profound, and never more so than when popular amusements do not accord with established notions of what constitutes a good time.

In *Work Without End,* Benjamin K. Hunnicutt describes how such thinking had an important effect on reinforcing employers' opposition to the Saturday holiday in pre-Depression America. The shorter workday had eventually, and often reluctantly, been accepted by management; one reason was that studies had shown how production increased when workers had longer daily breaks and were less tired. The same did not apply, however, to the weekend. "Having Saturdays off," Hunnicutt observes, "was seen to offer the worker leisure—the opportunity to become increasingly free from the job to do other things." And if these "other things" were not good for him, then it was only proper that he should be kept in the workplace, and out of trouble.

The Depression saw this paternalistic resistance

set aside, or at least modified. Although both employers and Roosevelt's administration opposed the thirty-hour week (which effectively meant a two- or three-day weekend) proposed by labor as a work-sharing measure, the Thirty-Hour Bill was debated by Congress in 1933. The idea was watered down by the National Industrial Recovery Act, but the pressure for some sort of work sharing was too great to ignore. Many industries adopted a shorter day and reduced the length of the workweek from six days to five.

There were different views as to what people should do with this newfound freedom. Some economists hoped the extra free time would spur consumption of leisure goods and stimulate the stagnant economy. Middle-class social reformers saw an opportunity for a program of national physical and intellectual self-improvement. That was the message of a book called *A Guide to Civilized Loafing*, written by H. A. Overstreet in 1934. Despite the title, which in later editions was changed to the more seemly *A Guide to Civilized Leisure*, the author's view was that free time was an opportunity, and the book described a daunting array of free-time activities, from amateur drama to volunteer work. Overstreet was prescient in some of his recommendations, like bicycling and hiking, although other of his enthusiasms—playing the gong, for example—have yet to catch on. If his

suggestions for "loafing" seem at times obsessive, it is because there were now so many free hours to fill. Overstreet, like earlier reformers, had a narrow idea of leisure—he neglected, for example, to list two favorite American pastimes, hunting and fishing, and, despite the repeal of Prohibition, he did not mention social drinking.

The two goals of filling leisure time—one economic and one cultural—appeared to many to be incompatible. Walter Lippmann's 1930 article in *Woman's Home Companion* entitled "Free Time and Extra Money" articulated "the problem of leisure." He warned that leisure offered the individual difficult choices, choices for which a work-oriented society such as America had not prepared him.* Lippmann was concerned that if people didn't make creative use of their free time, it would be squandered on mass entertainments and commercial amusements. His view spawned many books and articles of popular sociology with titles such as *The Challenge of Leisure, The Threat of Leisure*, and even *The Menace of Leisure*.

Much of this concern was based on the widespread assumption that the amount of available free time was

---

* More than a quarter century later, in *The Human Condition*, Hannah Arendt echoed this view: "What we are confronted with is the prospect of a society of laborers without labor, that is, without the only activity left to them. Surely, nothing could be worse."

greater than ever, and that the "problem of leisure" was without precedent. Before the Depression, an American working a forty-hour week spent less than half his 5,840 waking hours each year on the job— the rest was free time. By comparison, a hundred years earlier, work had accounted for as much as two thirds of one's waking hours. But as Hannah Arendt observed, this reduction is misleading, since the modern period was inevitably measured against the Industrial Revolution, which represented an all-time low as far as the number of working hours was concerned. A comparison with earlier periods of history leads to a different conclusion. The fourth-century Roman, for example, with 175 annual public holidays, spent fewer than a third of his waking hours at work; in medieval Europe, religious festivals reduced the work year to well below the modern level of two thousand hours. Indeed, until the eighteenth century, Europeans and Americans enjoyed *more* free time than they do today. The American worker of the 1930s was just catching up.

Most critics however, preferred to look to the future. What they saw was further mechanization, as well as technological innovations such as automation, which promised continued gains in efficiency and productivity in the workplace. "The old world of oppressive toil is passing, and we enter now upon new freedom for ourselves . . . in an age of plenty, we can

look forward to an increasing amount of time that is our own." Overstreet wrote this the year after the Thirty-Hour Bill debate, and to him, as to many others, it appeared that the shortening of the working day was a trend that would continue for some time. "It would be a rash prophet who denies the possibility that this generation may live to see a two-hour day," wrote another observer.

How wrong they turned out to be. Working hours bottomed out during the Depression, and then started to rise again. Job creation, not work sharing, became the goal of the New Deal. By 1938 the Fair Labor Standards Act provided for a workweek of not thirty but forty hours. As Hunnicutt observes, this marked the end of a century-long trend. On the strength of the evidence of the last fifty years, it would appear that the trend has not only stopped but reversed. In 1948, thirteen percent of Americans with full-time jobs worked more than forty-nine hours a week; by 1979 the figure had crept up to eighteen percent. Ten years later, the Bureau of Labor Statistics estimated that of 88 million Americans with full-time jobs, fully twenty-four percent worked more than forty-nine hours a week.

Ask anyone how long they spend at work and they can tell you exactly; it is more difficult to keep track

of leisure. For one thing, it is irregular; for another, it varies from person to person. For some, cutting the lawn is a burden; for others it is a pleasurable pastime. Going to the mall can be a casual Saturday outing, or it can be a chore. Most would count watching television as leisure, but what about Sunday brunch? Sometimes the same activity—walking the dog—can be a pleasure, sometimes not, depending on the weather. Finally, whether an activity is part of our leisure depends as much on our frame of mind as anything else.

Surveys of leisure habits often show diverging results. Two recent surveys, by the University of Maryland and by Michigan's Survey Research Center, both suggest that most Americans enjoy about thirty-nine hours of leisure time weekly. On the other hand, a 1988 survey conducted by the National Research Center of the Arts came to a very different conclusion and found that "Americans report a median 16.6 hours of leisure time each week." The truth is probably somewhere in between.

Less surprising, given the number of people working more than forty-nine hours a week, was the National Research Center's conclusion that most Americans have suffered a decline in weekly leisure time of 9.6 hours over the last fifteen years. The nineteenth-century activists who struggled so hard for a shorter workweek and more free time would have

been taken aback by this statistic—what had happened to the "Eight Hours for What We Will"?

There are undoubtedly people who work longer hours out of personal ambition, to escape problems at home, or from compulsion. The term "workaholic" (a postwar Americanism) is recent, but addiction to work is not—Thomas Jefferson, for example, was a compulsive worker, as was G. K. Chesterton—and there is no evidence that there are more such people today than in the past. Of course, for many, longer hours are not voluntary—they are obliged to work more merely to make ends meet. This has been particularly true since the 1970s, when poverty in America began to increase, but since the shrinking of leisure time began during the prosperous 1960s, economic need isn't the only explanation.

Twenty years ago Staffan Linder, a Swedish sociologist, wrote a book about the paradox of increasing affluence and decreasing leisure time in the United States. Following in Lippmann's steps, Linder observed that in a prosperous consumer society there was a conflict between the market's promotion of luxury goods and the individual's leisure time. When work hours were first shortened, there were few luxury items available to the general public, and the extra free time was generally devoted to leisure. With the growth of the so-called "leisure industry," people were offered a choice: more free time or more spend-

ing? Only the wealthy could have both. If the average person wanted to indulge in expensive recreations such as skiing or sailing, or to buy expensive entertainment devices, it would be necessary to work more—to trade his or her free time for overtime or a second job. Whether because of the effectiveness of advertising or from simple acquisitiveness, most people chose spending over more free time.

Linder's thesis was that economic growth caused an increasing scarcity of time, and that statistics showing an increase in personal incomes were not necessarily a sign of growing prosperity. People were earning more because they were working more. A large percentage of free time was being converted into what he called "consumption time," and mirrored a shift from "time-intensive" to "goods-intensive" leisure. According to *U.S. News & World Report,* Americans now spend more than $13 billion annually on sports clothing; put another way, about 1.3 billion hours of potential leisure time are exchanged for leisure wear—for increasingly elaborate running shoes, certified hiking shorts, and monogrammed warm-up suits. In 1989, to pay for these indulgences, more workers than ever before—6.2 percent—held a second, part-time job.

Probably the most dramatic change is the large-scale entry of women into the labor force. In 1950 only thirty percent of American women worked

outside the home, and this primarily out of economic necessity. Beginning in the 1960s middle-class women, dissatisfied with their suburban isolation and willing to trade at least some of their leisure time for purchasing power, started to look for paid employment. By 1986 more than half of all adult women—including married women with children—worked outside the home. Nor are these trends slowing down; between 1980 and 1988, the number of families with two or more wage earners rose from 19 to 21 million.

"Working outside the home" is the correct way to describe the situation, for housework (three or four hours a day) still needs to be done. Whether it is shared, or, more commonly, falls on the shoulders of women as part of their "second shift," leisure time for one or both partners is drastically reduced. Moreover, homes are larger than at any time in the postwar period, and bigger houses also mean more time spent in cleaning, upkeep, and repairs.*

Even if one chooses to consume less and stay at home, there are other things that cut into free time. Commuting to and from work takes longer than it used to. So does shopping—the weekly trip to the

---

* The average size of a new American home in the 1950s was less than 1,000 square feet; by 1983 it had increased to 1,710 square feet, and in 1986 had expanded another 115 square feet.

mall consumes more time than a stroll to the neighborhood corner store. Decentralized suburban life, which is to say American life, is based on the automobile. Parents become chauffeurs, ferrying their children back and forth to dance classes, hockey games, and the community pool. At home, telephone answering machines have to be played back, the household budget entered into the personal computer, the lawn mower dropped off at the repair shop, the car—or cars—serviced. All these convenient labor-saving devices relentlessly eat into our discretionary time. For many executives, administrators, and managers, the reduction of leisure time is also the result of office technology that brings work to the home. Fax machines, paging devices, and portable computers mean that taking work home at night is no longer difficult or voluntary. Even the contemplative quiet of the morning automobile commute is now disrupted by the presence of the cellular telephone.

There is no contradiction between the surveys that indicate a reversing trend, resulting in less free time, and the claim that the weekend dominates our leisure. Longer work hours and more overtime cut mainly into weekday leisure. So do longer commuting, driving the kids, and Friday-night shopping. The week-

end—or what's left of it, after Saturday household chores—is when we have time to relax.

But the weekend has imposed a rigid schedule on our free time, which can result in a sense of urgency ("soon it will be Monday") that is at odds with relaxation. The weekly rush to the cottage is hardly leisurely, nor is the compression of various recreational activities into the two-day break. The freedom to do something has become the obligation to do something, just as Chesterton foretold, and the list of dutiful recreations includes strenuous disciplines intended for self-improvement (fitness exercises, jogging, bicycling), competitive sports (tennis, golf), and skill-testing pastimes (sailing, skiing).

Recreations such as tennis or sailing are hardly new, but before the arrival of the weekend, for most people, they were chiefly seasonal activities. Once a year, when vacation time came around, tennis racquets were removed from the back of the cupboard, swimwear was taken out of mothballs, skis were dusted off. The accent was less on technique than on having a good time. It was like playing Scrabble at the summer cottage: no one remembers all the rules, but everyone can still enjoy the game. Now the availability of free time every weekend has changed this casual attitude. The very frequency of weekend recreations allows continual participation and continual improvement, which encourage the development of proficiency and skill.

Skill is necessary since difficulty characterizes modern recreations. Many nineteenth-century amusements, such as rowing, were not particularly involved and required little instruction; mastering windsurfing, on the other hand, takes considerable practice and dexterity—which is part of the attraction. Even relatively simple games are complicated by the need to excel. Hence the emphasis on professionalism, which is expressed by the need to have the proper equipment and the correct costume (especially the right shoes). The desire for mastery isn't limited to outdoor recreations; it also includes complicated hobbies such as woodworking, electronics, and automobile restoration. All this suggests that the modern weekend is characterized by not only the sense of obligation to do something but the obligation to do it *well*.

The desire to do something well, whether it is sailing a boat—or building a boat—reflects a need that was previously met in the workplace. Competence was shown on the job—holidays were for messing around. Nowadays the situation is reversed. Technology has removed craft from most occupations. This is true in assembly-line jobs, where almost no training or experience, hence no skill, is required, as well as in most service positions (store clerks, fast-food attendants) where the only talent required is to learn how to smile and say "have a good day." But it's also increasingly true in such skill-dependent work as house construction, where the majority of parts

come ready-made from the factory and the carpenter merely assembles them, or automobile repair, which consists largely in replacing one throwaway part with another. Nor is the reduction of skills limited to manual work. Memory, once the prerequisite skill of the white-collar worker, has been rendered superfluous by computers; teachers, who once needed dramatic skills, now depend on mechanical aids such as slide projectors and video machines; in politics, oratory has been killed by the thirty-second sound bite.

Hence an unexpected development in the history of leisure. For many, weekend free time has become not a chance to escape work but a chance to create work that is more meaningful—to work at recreation—in order to realize the personal satisfactions that the workplace no longer offers.

"Leisure" is the most misunderstood word in our vocabulary. We often use the words "recreation" and "leisure" interchangeably—recreation room, rest and recreation, leisure suit, leisure industry—but they really embody two different ideas. Recreation carries with it a sense of necessity and purpose. However pleasurable this antidote to work may be, it's a form of active employment, engaged in with a specific end in mind—a refreshment of the spirit, or the body, or both. Implicit in this idea of renewal—usually or-

ganized renewal—is the notion that recreation is both a consequence of work and a preparation for more of it.

Leisure is different. That was what Lippmann was getting at when he contrasted commercial recreation with individual leisure. Leisure is not tied to work the way that recreation is—leisure is self-contained. The root of the word is the Latin *licere* which means "to be permitted," suggesting that leisure is about freedom. But freedom for what? According to Chesterton's cheerful view, leisure was above all an opportunity to do nothing. When he said "doing nothing," however, he was describing not emptiness but an occasion for reflection and contemplation, a chance to look inward rather than outward. A chance to tend one's garden, as Voltaire put it. That is why Chesterton called this kind of leisure "the most precious, the most consoling, the most pure and holy."

Bertrand Russell placed leisure into a larger historical context in his essay "In Praise of Idleness." "Leisure is essential to civilization," he wrote, "and in former times leisure for the few was only rendered possible by the labours of the many. But their labours were valuable, not because work is good, but because leisure is good." Russell, a member of the aristocracy, pointed out that it had been precisely the leisure classes, not the laborers, who had written the books,

invented the philosophies, produced the sciences, and cultivated the arts. But he was not arguing for a continuation of the class system; on the contrary, he proposed extending the leisure that had previously been reserved for the few to the many. This was an explicit attack on the work ethic, which he considered a device to trick people into accepting a life without leisure. In his view, the trick hadn't succeeded; working men and women had no illusions about work—they understood it was merely a necessary means to a livelihood.

Russell's underlying argument was that we should free ourselves from the guilt about leisure that modern society has imposed on us. Hence the use of terms such as "idleness" and "doing nothing," which were intended as a provocation to a society that placed the highest value on "keeping busy." Both Russell and Chesterton agreed with Aristotle, who considered leisure the aim of life. "We work," he wrote, "to have leisure."

"In Praise of Idleness" was written in 1932, at the height of the Depression, and Russell's proposal of a four-hour workday now appears hopelessly utopian. But the weekend's later and sudden new popularity in so many societies suggests that leisure is beginning to make a comeback, although not as fully as Russell desired, nor in so relaxed a way as Chesterton would have wished. I cannot shake the suspicion that some-

thing more than mere functionality accounts for the widespread popularity of the weekend. Can its universal appeal be explained by a resonance with some ancient inclination, buried deep in the human psyche? Given the mythological roots of the planetary week, and the devotional nature of Sunday and the Sabbath, the answer is likely to be found in early religious attitudes.

Mircea Eliade, a historian of religion, characterized traditional premodern societies as experiencing the world in two distinct ways corresponding to two discontinuous modes of being: the sacred and the profane. According to Eliade, the sacred manifested itself in various ways—how physical space was perceived, for example. The profane, chaotic world, full of menace, was given structure and purpose by the existence of fixed, meaningful sacred places. Sacred places could occur in the landscape, beside holy trees or on certain mountains, but they could also be man-made. Hence the elaborate rituals practiced by all ancient people when they founded settlements and erected buildings, rituals not only to protect the future town or building but to delineate a sacred space.

The prime sacred space was the home, for houses were not merely shelters but consecrated places that incorporated cosmic symbolism into their very construction. The Navajo Indians, for example, affirmed that their homes—hogans—were based on a divine prototype. The conical shape of the hogan resembled

a mountain in New Mexico that the Navajo called "the heart of the Earth." They believed that God had created the first forked-stick hogan using posts made of white shell, turquoise, abalone, and obsidian. When a new hogan was built, pieces of these four minerals were buried beneath the four main posts, which also corresponded to the four points of the compass. In this way the builder interrupted the continuity of the everyday world by creating a separate magical space.

A person stepping out of the desert sun into the dark, cool interior of a hogan was entering a space that was a part of the ancient past, and thus he was entering not only a sacred space but a sacred time. According to Eliade, profane time was ordinary temporal duration, but sacred time, which was also the time of festivals and holy days, was primordial and mythical, and stood apart from everyday life. During sacred time, the clock not only stopped, it was turned back. The purpose of religious rites was precisely to reintegrate this past into the present. In this way, sacred time became part of a separate, repetitive continuum, "an eternal mythical present."

Eliade characterized modern Western society as "nonreligious," in the sense that it had desacralized and demythologized the world. For nonreligious man there could be only profane space and profane time. But, he pointed out, since the roots of this society lay in a religious past, it could never divest itself completely of ancient beliefs; remnants of these remained,

although in camouflaged form: for example, movies
employing mythical motifs, such as the struggle between hero and monster, descent into an underworld,
or the cleansing ordeal. Even in our homes, which
no longer incorporate cosmic symbolism in the
comprehensive way of the Navajo hogan, rituals have
not altogether disappeared. Giving a housewarming
party, carrying the bride over the threshold, receiving
important guests at the front door instead of at the
back door, decorating the exterior at festal times of
year—these are all reminders that although we treat
our houses as commodities, the home is still a special
space, standing apart from the practical world.

Is it fanciful to propose that the repetitive cycle of
week and weekend is a modern paraphrase of the
ancient opposition of profane and sacred time? Obviously the weekend is not a historical remnant in any
literal sense, since it didn't even exist until the nineteenth century, and its emergence was in response to
specific social and economic conditions. Nor am I
suggesting that the secular weekend is a substitute for
religious festivals, although it is obviously linked to
religious observance. But there are several striking
parallels.

Weekday time, like profane time, is linear. It represents an irreversible progression of days, Monday
to Friday, year after year. Past weekday time is lost
time. Schooldays are followed by workdays, the first
job by the second and the third. I can never be a

schoolboy again, or a college student, or a young architect anxiously waiting to meet my first client.*
Not only is weekday time linear, but, like profane time, it encompasses the unpredictable. During the week, unforeseen things happen. People get promoted and fired. Stock markets soar or crash. Politicians are elected or voted out of office. One has the impression that history occurs on weekdays.†

The weekend, on the other hand, is, in Plato's words, a time to take a breather. It's a time apart from the world of mundane problems and mundane concerns, from the world of making a living. On weekends time stands still, and not only because we take off our watches. Just as holidays at the beach are an opportunity to re-create our childhood, to build sand castles with the kids, to paddle in the surf, to lie on the sand and get a sunburn, many of the things we do on weekends correspond to the things we did on weekends past. Weekend time shares this sense of reenactment with sacred time, and just as sacred time was characterized by ritual, the weekend, despite

---

* Several years ago I attended a high-school class reunion, which could be described as an attempt to recover weekday time. Revealingly, the subject of conversation was sports and extracurricular activities, not what we had done in the classroom.

† The notable exception is war, which often begins on the weekend, when it is least expected. The German blitzkrieg of 1940 was launched on a Saturday morning; the Japanese attack on Pearl Harbor occurred on a Sunday; the Egyptians started the Yom Kippur War on the Sabbath.

being an opportunity for personal freedom, is governed by convention: raking leaves, grilling steaks on the barbecue, going to the movies, Saturday night out, reading the Sunday paper, brunch, the afternoon opera broadcast, weekend drives, garage sales, weekend visits. The predictability of the weekend is one of its comforts.

Although Eliade described examples of sacred time from different societies and periods of history, the specific rites and rituals varied. An event could be holy in one culture and have no meaning in another; a festival could be a taboo time because the day was considered unlucky, while elsewhere it was observed for exactly the opposite reason. The myths of their sacred histories differentiated societies.

The conventions of weekend leisure, too, vary from place to place. In Europe, for example, northerners read more books than southerners, Germans and Danes spend more than others on musical instruments, the British are the greatest gamblers, the Italians the greatest moviegoers, and everyone favors tennis except the French. Canada and the United States, which have many similarities, differ in their attitude to leisure, and surveys have consistently shown that Americans believe more strongly in the work ethic than Canadians do. Probably for that reason, Canadians give personal leisure a higher importance and have been much slower to accept commercial intrusions such as Sunday shopping.

The differences in national attitudes toward leisure are arresting because we live in a world where the character of work is increasingly international. Around the world, in different countries, what happens between nine and five during the week is becoming standardized. Because of international competition and transnational ownership of companies, the transfer of technology from one country to another is almost instantaneous. All offices contain the same telephones, photocopiers, word processors, computers, and fax machines. The Japanese build automobile plants in the United States and Canada, the Americans build factories in Eastern Europe, the Europeans in South America. Industries are increasingly dominated by a diminishing number of extremely large and similar corporations. The reorganization of the workplace in Communist and formerly Communist countries, along more capitalist lines, is one more step in the standardization of work. And as work becomes more standardized, and international, one can expect that leisure, by contrast, will be even more national, more regional, more different.

Leisure has always been partly a refuge from labor. The weekend, too, is a retreat from work, but in a different way: a retreat from the abstract and the universal to the local and the particular. In that sense,

leisure is likely to continue to be, as Pieper claimed, the basis of culture. Every culture chooses a different structure for its work and leisure, and in doing so it makes a profound statement about itself. It invents, adapts, and recombines old models, hence the long list of leisure days: public festivals, family celebrations, market days, taboo days, evil days, holy days, feasts, Saint Mondays and Saint Tuesdays, commemorative holidays, summer vacations—and weekends.

The weekend is our own contribution, another way of dealing with the ancient duality. The institution of the weekend reflects the many unresolved contradictions in modern attitudes toward leisure. We want to have our cake, and eat it too. We want the freedom to be leisurely, but we want it regularly, every week, like clockwork. The attraction of Saint Monday was that one could "go fishing" when one willed; the regularity of the weekend—every five days—is at odds with the ideas of personal freedom and spontaneity. There is something mechanical about this oscillation, which creates a sense of obligation that interferes with leisure. Like sacred time, the weekend is comfortingly repetitive, but the conventionality of weekend free time, which must exist side by side with private pastimes and idiosyncratic hobbies, often appears restrictive. "What did you do on the weekend?" "The usual," we answer, mixing dismay with relief.

Waiting for the Weekend

We have invented the weekend, but the dark cloud of old taboos still hangs over the holiday, and the combination of the secular with the holy leaves us uneasy. This tension only compounds the guilt that many of us continue to feel about not working, and leads to the nagging feeling that our free time should be used for some purpose higher than having fun. We want leisure, but we are afraid of it too.

Do we work to have leisure, or the other way around? Unsure of the answer, we have decided to keep the two separate. If C. P. Snow had not already used the term in another context, it would be tempting to speak of Two Cultures. We pass weekly from one to the other—from the mundane, communal, increasingly impersonal, increasingly demanding, increasingly bureaucratic world of work to the reflective, private, controllable, consoling world of leisure. The weekend; our own, and not our own, it is what we wait for all week long.

Acknowledgments

I have wanted to write a book on leisure for several years—my earliest outline dates from 1986. Another book intruded itself in the meantime, but I must admit that I was happy to be distracted for I was having trouble getting started. Since Veblen broached the subject, in 1899, so much has been written on leisure that the subject appeared to me exhausted, wrung out, mined dry. Still, the matter nagged. I am not sure why leisure held such a fascination—perhaps because I tended to agree with Noël Coward, who said, "Work is more fun than fun." I enjoyed my work, but one couldn't work all the time, and what exactly was the meaning of the periods in between? Were they really just rest periods, or something more? It was as a result of the encouragement, prodding, and raised eyebrows of Carl Brandt, who is also my agent, that I persevered. I exchanged several letters with John Lukacs on the subject, and his observations were stimulating, as always. Dan Frank, at Viking, was both

235

gently critical and supportive, in turn. For a splendid job of copyediting, my thanks to Harriet Brown. Lastly, my appreciation to the helpful staff of McGill University's McLennan Graduate Library.

March 1989–December 1990

Notes on Sources

This is not intended to be a work of research, more like an extended essay. Nevertheless, I have relied on the work of many scholars, and it seems only fair to gratefully acknowledge my chief sources.

1: Free Time

Information on Vivaldi is from Marc Pincherle's *Vivaldi: Genius of the Baroque* (trans. Christopher Hatch, New York, 1962). Background on the history of the Sunday paper is from Sidney Kobre's *Development of American Journalism* (Dubuque, Iowa, 1969). G. K. Chesterton's essay, "On Leisure," is contained in *Generally Speaking* (London, 1928). Churchill's bricklaying is described by William Manchester in *The Last Lion: Winston Spencer Churchill, Visions of Glory, 1874–1932* (Boston, 1983). Lewis Mumford's views of

meaningful work are contained in *The Pentagon of Power* (New York, 1964). Anyone interested in the relationship between leisure and work is obliged to read Josef Pieper, chiefly *Leisure: The Basis of Culture* (trans. Alexander Dru, New York, 1952), and *In Tune with the World: A Theory of Festivity* (trans. Richard and Clara Winston, Chicago, 1965).

2: Week After Week

Information on the origin of the seven-day week is drawn largely from F. H. Colson's delightful *The Week: An Essay on the Origin and Development of the Seven-Day Cycle* (Cambridge, 1926), and from Hutton Webster's classic *Rest Days* (New York, 1916); also from *Hidden Rhythms: Schedules and Calendars in Social Life* (Chicago 1981) and *The Seven Day Cycle* (New York, 1985), both by Eviatar Zerubavel. On ancient calendars I have consulted Benjamin D. Meritt's *The Athenian Year* (Berkeley & Los Angeles, 1961), Agnes Kirsopp Michels's *The Calendar of the Roman Republic* (Princeton, 1967), W. M. O'Neil's *Time and the Calendars* (Sydney, 1978), David S. Landes's *Revolution in Time: Clocks and the Making of the Modern World* (Cambridge, Mass., 1983), and Daniel J. Boorstin's *The Discoverers* (New York, 1983).

The French revolutionary calendar is described by Si-
mon Schama in *Citizens: A Chronicle of the French
Revolution* (New York, 1989); details on Soviet efforts
to restructure the week are from *Soviet Labour and
Industry* (London, 1942) by Leonard E. Hubbard.
Jeremy Campbell outlines recent discoveries in
chronobiology in *Winston Churchill's Afternoon Nap:
A Wide-Awake Inquiry into the Human Nature of Time*
(New York, 1986).

3: A Meaningful Day

Hannah Arendt's observations on work are contained
in *The Human Condition* (Chicago, 1958). The number
of holidays in various cultures is drawn chiefly from
Hutton Webster; the results of the study of Tokyo
residents' vacation time was reported by the *Montreal
Gazette:* "Tokyoites more tired, stressed than residents of N.Y. or L.A." (July 31, 1989). The World
War I study on longer hours is contained in S. Howard
Bartley and Eloise Chute's *Fatigue and Impairment in
Man* (New York, 1947); on the subject of fatigue:
Angelo Mosso's *Fatigue* (trans. Margaret Drummond
and W. B. Drummond, New York, 1906), and the
more recent *Psychological Aspects and Physiological Cor-
relates of Work and Fatigue* (Ernst Simonson and Philip

C. Weiser, eds., Springfield, Ill., 1976); the British author who observed the production fall-off at the end of the week is Donald Scott in *The Psychology of Work* (London, 1970). On tabooed days, I have (again) relied on Hutton Webster; Thorstein Veblen's book is, of course, *The Theory of the Leisure Class* (New York, 1979). The various traditions of the market week are chiefly from Martin P. Nilsson's *Primitive Time-Reckoning* (Lund, 1920), also F. E. Forbes's *Dahomey and the Dahomans* (London, 1851), and C. R. Markham's *First Part of the Royal Commentaries of the Yncas* (London, 1871). Colonial American Sabbatarianism is described by Winton U. Solberg in *Redeem the Time: The Puritan Sabbath in Early America* (Cambridge, Mass., 1977). The debate over Sunday-observance in Quebec is recounted by David Rome in two monographs: *On Sunday Observance, 1906* (Canadian Jewish Archives No. 14, Montreal, 1979) and *The Jewish Archival Record of 1936* (Canadian Jewish Archives, No. 8, Montreal, 1978). It is also referred to by W. D. K. Kernaghan in his unpublished Ph.D. thesis, *Freedom of Religion in the Province of Quebec, with Particular Reference to the Jews, Jehovah's Witnesses and Church-State Relations 1930–1960* (Duke University, 1966).

4: Sunday in the Park

There are many sources for material on Seurat; I have consulted John Russell's *Seurat* (London, 1965), and *Seurat* (Oxford, 1985) by Richard Thomson, whose analysis of *Grand Jatte* I have drawn on. For information on Parisian life of the time I have consulted Eugen Weber's admirable *France, Fin de Siècle* (Cambridge, Mass., 1986). Scholarly research on leisure in eighteenth-century England is prolific. I refer to Hugh Cunningham's *Leisure in the Industrial Revolution* (New York, 1980), and much of the material is drawn from two outstanding essays by J. H. Plumb: "The Public, Literature, and the Arts in the Eighteenth Century" (in *The Emergence of Leisure,* Michael R. Marrus, ed., New York, 1974) and "The Commercialization of Leisure in Eighteenth-century England" (in Neil McKendrick et al., *The Birth of a Consumer Society,* Bloomington, Indiana, 1982). The history of the circus is described by Ruth Manning-Sanders in *The English Circus* (London, 1952). On food and drink: J. C. Drummond and Anne Wilbraham's *The Englishman's Food: A History of Five Centuries of English Diet* (London, 1939), and Fernand Braudel's *The Structures of Everyday Life: The Limits of the Possible* (trans. Sian Reynolds, New York, 1981).

5: Keeping Saint Monday

Much of the historical material in this chapter is drawn from Douglas A. Reid's essay, "The Decline of Saint Monday 1766–1876" (*Past and Present*, 71, 1976). Other sources for the Saint Monday tradition and eighteenth-century leisure are: E. P. Thompson's "Time, Work-Discipline, and Industrial Capitalism" (*Past & Present*, 38, 1967), and Michael R. Marrus's "Introduction" to *The Emergence of Leisure* (Michael R. Marrus, ed., New York, 1974). Thomas Wright's contemporary account is *Some Habits and Customs of the Working Classes by a Journeyman Engineer* (London, 1867). On the Early Closing Association, Wilfred B. Whitaker's *Victorian and Edwardian Shopworkers: The Struggle to Obtain Better Conditions and a Half-Holiday* (Newton Abbot, 1973); and on Victorian leisure, Peter Bailey's *Leisure and Class in Victorian England* (London, 1978), Ralph Dutton's *The Victorian Home* (London, 1954), and Colin MacInnes's charming *Sweet Saturday Night* (London, 1967), which is the source for the music-hall song.

6: A World of Weekends

On the shortening of the American work week, I have relied on Joseph S. Zeisel's "The Workweek in Amer-

ican Industry 1850–1956" (*Monthly Labor Review*, 81, January, 1958), Daniel T. Rodgers's *The Work Ethic in Industrial America 1850–1920* (Chicago, 1974), David R. Roediger and Philip S. Foner's *Our Own Time: A History of American Labor and the Working Day* (New York, 1989), Roy Rosenzweig's *Eight Hours for What We Will: Workers and Leisure in an Industrial City, 1870–1920* (Cambridge, 1983), and Marion Cotter Cahill's *Shorter Hours: A Study of the Movement Since the Civil War* (New York, 1932). The social study of Westchester County is contained in *Leisure: A Suburban Study* (New York, 1934) by George A. Lundberg, Mirra Komarovsky, and Mary Alice McInery. On the early history of the movies: Lary May's *Screening Out the Past: The Birth of Mass Culture and the Motion Picture Industry* (New York, 1980). Benjamin Kline Hunnicutt's valuable study, *Work Without End: Abandoning Shorter Hours for the Right to Work* (Philadelphia, 1988), provides an overview of the period 1920–1940. For the emergence of the fascist Saturday, I am indebted to Victoria de Grazia's fascinating study, *The Culture of Consent: Mass Organization of Leisure in Fascist Italy* (Cambridge, 1981); the German material was based on L. Hamburger's *How Nazi Germany Has Mobilized and Controlled Labor* (Washington, D.C., 1940), Richard Grunberger's *The 12-Year Reich: A Social History of Nazi Germany 1933–1945* (New York, 1971), and Wallace R. Deuel's *People under Hitler* (New York, 1942). For European information on

Notes on Sources

leisure I relied on Anthony Edwards's *Leisure Spending in the European Community: Forecasts to 1990* (London, January 1981); on the French weekend, Joffre Dumazedier's *Sociology of Leisure* (trans. Marea A. McKenzie, Amsterdam, 1974); on Israel, Elihu Katz and Michael Gurevitch's *The Secularization of Leisure: Culture and Communication in Israel* (London, 1976). For the appearance of the Polish weekend, on Neal Ascherson's *The Polish August: The Self-Limiting Revolution* (New York, 1981) and Anna Olszewska's "Poland: The Impact of the Crisis on Leisure Patterns" in *Leisure and Lifestyle: A Comparative Analysis of Free Time* (Anna Olszewska and K. Roberts, eds., London, 1989). The last anthology also contains a useful essay on Japanese leisure: Sampei Koseki's "Japan: Homo Ludens Japonicus." In addition, not being able to visit Japan, I gleaned useful information from Herman Kahn and Thomas Pepper's *The Japanese Challenge: The Success and Failure of Economic Success* (New York, 1980), Ezra F. Vogel's sociological study, *Japan's New Middle Class: The Salary Man and His Family in a Tokyo Suburb* (Berkeley, Calif., 1963), Jared Taylor's *Shadows of the Rising Sun: A Critical View of the "Japanese Miracle"* (New York, 1983), James Allen Dator's "The 'Protestant Ethic' in Japan" in *Selected Readings on Modern Japanese Society* (George K. Yamamoto and Tsuyoshi Ishida, eds., Berkeley, Calif., 1971), "Protection Racket," *The New Republic* (202, 18, April 30,

244

1990), and James Fallows's insightful "The Hard Life," *Atlantic* (263, 3, March, 1989).

7: Retreats

John Habraken drew the parallel between shanty-towns and campgrounds in "Aap Noot Mies Huis/ Three R's for Housing," *Forum* (XX, December 1, 1966). The description of Pliny's seaside villa is contained in Book II, Letter XVII of *The Letters of Pliny the Younger* (trans. Betty Radice, Harmondsworth, 1969); Leon Battista Alberti's views on country houses are contained in *On the Art of Building in Ten Books* (trans. Joseph Rykwert et al., Cambridge, Mass., 1988). The Mumford reference appears in *The City in History: Its Origins, Its Transformations, and Its Prospects* (New York, 1961). On the summer houses of Victorian Montrealers, see France Gagnon Pratte's *Country Houses for Montrealers 1892–1924: The Architecture of E. and W. S. Maxwell* (trans. Linda Blythe, Montreal, 1987). The material on Metis Beach is drawn from Jessie Forbes's unpublished *Metis Beach Past and Present* (undated) and from Samuel Mathewson Baylis's *Enchanting Metis* (Montreal, 1928). Metis Beach survives today, but in much diminished form. The grand hotels are all gone; only a few of the original families

maintain their country homes. I have quoted John Lukacs from his absorbing and stimulating *Outgrowing Democracy: A History of the United States in the Twentieth Century* (Garden City, N.Y., 1984).

8: Pastimes

The comparative study of Japanese and American cities was reported in "Tokyoites more tired, stressed than residents of N.Y. or L.A." (*Montreal Gazette*, July 31, 1989); Canadian data is from "How long does it take a Canadian to get through the day?" (*Montreal Gazette*, March 20, 1989). I consulted Lucien Febvre and Henri-Jean Martin's *The Coming of the Book: The Impact of Printing 1450–1800* (trans. David Gerard, London, 1976), and Yves Castin's fascinating "Figures of Modernity" in *A History of Private Life: Passions of the Renaissance* (Roger Chartier, ed., trans. Arthur Goldhammer, Cambridge, Mass., 1989), on the early history of the book. Neil Postman's vigorous critique of modern American culture is *Amusing Ourselves to Death: Public Discourse in the Age of Show Business* (New York, 1985). Information on stamp-collecting came from the entry on "Philately" in the *Encyclopaedia Britannica* (Chicago, 1949). The literature on

gardening is an old one and includes Francis Bacon's *Of gardens* (London, undated), Horace Walpole's *Essay on Modern Gardening* (Canton, Pa., 1904), and W. Carew Hazlitt's *Gleanings in Old Garden Literature* (London, 1887). I also consulted Danielle Régnier-Bohler's "Imagining the Self" in *A History of Private Life: Revelations of the Medieval World* (Georges Duby, ed., trans. Arthur Goldhammer, Cambridge, Mass., 1988), and Orest Ranum's "Refuges of Intimacy" in *A History of Private Life: Passions of the Renaissance* (Roger Chartier, ed., trans. Arthur Goldhammer, Cambridge, Mass., 1989). There are many histories of landscape architecture, including Edward Hyams's *A History of Gardens and Gardening* (New York, 1971), and *The Poetics of Gardens* (Cambridge, Mass., 1988), by Charles W. Moore, William J. Mitchell, and William Turnbull, Jr. On national gardening habits: Max Kaplan, *Leisure in America* (New York, 1960); K. Roberts, "Great Britain: Socioeconomic Polarization and the Implications for Leisure" in *Leisure and Lifestyle* (Anna Olszewska and K. Roberts, eds., London, 1989); Gyorgy Fukasz, "Hungary: More Work, Less Leisure" (also in *Leisure and Lifestyle*); and on Australia, Ian P. B. Halkett, "The Recreational Use of Private Gardens" (*Journal of Leisure Research,* 10, 1, 1978). I mention Johan H. Huizinga's *Homo Ludens: A Study of the Play-Element in Culture* (Boston, 1955) here but it was a book that influenced me throughout.

Anthony Storr's engaging study is *Solitude: A Return to the Self* (New York, 1988).

9: The Problem of Leisure

Sándor Ferenczi's essay on the Sunday neurosis is contained in his *Further Contributions to the Theory and Technique of Psycho-Analysis* (trans. Jane Isabel Suttie, New York, 1952). Lippmann's article appeared in *Woman's Home Companion* (57, April 1930). Two books of many on leisure that were published in the thirties are: H. A. Overstreet's *A Guide to Civilized Loafing* (New York, 1934) and Arthur Newton Pack's *The Challenge of Leisure* (New York, 1934). Statistics on the recent increase in the length of the work week and the decrease in leisure time are from Peter T. Kilborn's "Tales from the Digital Treadmill" (*New York Times,* June 3, 1990) and Jerome Richard's "Out of Time" (*New York Times,* Nov. 28, 1988). The University of Maryland and Michigan surveys are cited by Louis S. Richman in "Why the Middle Class is Anxious," *Fortune* (May 21, 1990). The theory of a shift to goods-intensive leisure was put forward by Staffan B. Linder in *The Harried Leisure Class* (New York, 1970). Arlie Hochschild's penetrating study *The Second Shift: Working Parents and the Revolution at*

Home (New York, 1989) is indirectly referred to. Bertrand Russell's "In Praise of Idleness" is only partly tongue-in-cheek; it is contained in *In Praise of Idleness and Other Essays* (London, 1935). The idea of sacred and profane time was proposed by Mircea Eliade in his classic *The Sacred and the Profane* (trans. Willard R. Trask, New York, 1959); descriptions of Navajo hogans are from Peter Nabokov and Robert Easton's exemplary study, *Native American Architecture* (New York, 1989). The suggestion that the weekend might be linked to sacred time is made by Anthony Aveni in *Empires of Time: Calendars, Clocks, and Cultures* (New York, 1989). On European leisure habits: Anthony Edwards, *Leisure Spending in The European Community: Forecasts to 1990* (London, 1981); and on the difference between Canada and the United States, Seymour Martin Lipset's *Continental Divide: The Values and Institutions of the United States and Canada* (New York, 1990). Finally, I am indebted to my friend John Lukacs for the insightful suggestion that the worlds of work and leisure may have come to represent two cultures. Indeed, they have.

Index

Index

Index

Index

leisure, 15–22
  Chesterton's views on, 15, 19, 118, 225, 226
  choice and, 16–17, 118, 214
  class structure and, 82, 100–4, 106–8, 225–26
  commercialization of, 98, 121
  defined, 15, 118, 224–25
  democratizing influences on, 102–4
  differences in national attitudes toward, 231–32
  in England (1700–1750), 88–101
  free time vs., 15, 19, 118
  happiness and, 21–22
  as idleness, 15–16, 22
  in Mesopotamian calendars, 26
  in nineteenth century, 81–88, 101–108
  privacy and, 93, 101–2, 189–91
  problem of, 210–34
  public vs. private, 93, 101–2, 107–108
  recreation vs., 224–25
  reform movement and, 99–100, 102–3, 121–25, 127, 133, 137–138, 146, 213–14
  relationship of work and, 21–22, 225–26
  in *Sunday on the Grande Jatte*, 84–85, 87, 88, 104–8
  "universal," 20
  women and, 113, 138, 140–41
  see also weekend
leisure industry, 218–19
  Saint Monday tradition and, 117, 121
Leisure Society, 20–21
Ley, Robert, 147–48
libraries, 91, 102, 103
Ligue du Dimanche (Sunday League), 78
Linder, Staffan, 218–19
Lippmann, Walter, 214, 218, 225
literacy, 187–88, 191
London, 89, 91, 94, 176, 178–79
  bull running in, 111, 113
Lord, Thomas, 96
Lukacs, John, 183
lunar cycle, calendars and, 23, 26, 27–28
"lunar weeks," 25–26
Luther, Martin, 72

Lutheranism, 72–73
luxury goods:
  growth in popularity of, 89–90
  leisure time vs., 218–19

Macdonald, Sir John A., 180
magazines, 91–92, 95, 121, 187, 192
Maggiora, Dr., 57
Marie Antoinette, Queen of France, 94, 174–75
market days, 67–71, 80
Marrus, Michael R., 118, 130–31
Mars, 30–32, 41
Marx, Karl, 21
Maryland, University of, 217
mathematics:
  Mayan calendar and, 27
  number seven and, 30
May, Lary, 140
Mayan calendar, 27
Mercury, 30, 32, 41
Mesopotamian calendar, 25–26, 28, 32
Metis Beach, 181–82
Metropolitan Early Closing Association, 122–25, 145
Mexico:
  holidays in, 54
  markets in, 68
Middle Ages, 54, 60, 137
  gardens of, 200–1
  Sunday in, 72
middle class, 82, 220
  in England, 89, 100, 101–2, 122–24
miners, 114, 128
Mique, Richard, 174
Mithraism, 36, 37, 43, 70
Mithras, 36
Monday, 34, 37, 38, 41, 42
  see also Saint Monday tradition
"Monday-morning blahs," 59
money, saving of, 127
month, length of, 23–26
Montreal, 170, 177–81
moon, 25, 38
  as planet, 30, 32
  waxing and waning of, 23, 26, 27–28
Moore, Charles, 202
mortality rates, 99
Mosso, Angelo, 56–58
movies, 13, 78, 79, 136–41

255

Index

Muhammad, 33, 34
Mumford, Lewis, 19, 22, 176
museums, 103, 117, 122*n*, 196
music, 1–4, 8–9, 94–95, 195
music halls, 94–95, 130
music rooms, 94, 121
myth, 227–29, 231

Napoléon I, Emperor of France, 90
National Industrial Recovery Act, 213
National Research Center of the Arts, 217
Native Americans, 30*n*, 227–28, 229
nature:
  eighteenth century's idealization of, 3
  gardens and, 202–3
  retreats and, 174, 179–80
Navajo Indians, 227–28, 229
Nazi Germany, 147–48, 183
neurosis, holiday, 210–11
New Deal, 144, 213, 216
newspapers, 91, 95, 134, 187, 192
  author's job on, 6–7
  Sunday, 14–15
New York, N.Y., 134, 139, 176, 184, 186
New York *Sunday World*, 14–15
New Zealand, 183*n*
nickelodeons, 136–39
Nigeria, 70
Nones, 26–27
Notes and queries, 109
novels, 92–93, 189, 194
numbers, magical, 30
nundine, 67–68, 71
Nyren, Richard, 97

Observer (London), 14
Olszewska, Anna, 206
Orléans, Third Council of, 71
Overstreet, H. A., 213–14, 216

Paine, Thomas, 191
Pamela (Richardson), 92
paper workers, 125
Papyrus Sallier IV, 60
paradise gardens, 201, 202
Paris, suburbs of, 81–88. 104–8
parks, 103, 105
part-book publishing, 92–93

parties, upper-class house, 128
pastimes, 186–209
  gardening, 199–209
  hobbies, 195–99
  reading, 91, 92–93, 187–94
  television watching, 186–87, 192–195, 207
Paulet, Alfred, 86
Pepys, Samuel, 190
Persia, gardens of, 201, 202
Peru, markets in, 68, 69
Petit Trianon, 174–75
physical activity, as weekend enterprise, 13–14
Pieper, Josef, 21, 59, 75, 233
planetary week, *see* seven-day week
planets:
  astrology and, 30–31
  seven, 30–32
  see also specific planets
Plato, 50, 230
play, 196
  change in attitude toward, 18–19
  freedom and, 137, 208
  Japanese and, 157, 158
  letting go and, 137
  social opposition to, 136–37
  summer houses and, 172
  work vs., 112, 131
Pliny the Younger, 166–70, 172*n*, 173, 175, 200, 209
Plumb, J. H., 91, 98
Poetics of Gardens, The (Moore), 202
Poland, 206
  weekend in, 152–55
Polynesia, *tapus* (*tabus*) in, 61, 63*n*, 64
Post Boy (London), 95
Postman, Neil, 192
printers, 99*n*, 127
printing and publishing, 133–34, 142, 187, 188
privacy, leisure and, 93, 101–2, 189–191
prizefighting, 100
production, work and, 55–56, 58–59
profane vs. sacred, distinction of, 227–31
professionalism, 17–18, 223
Prohibition, 212, 214
prosperity, leisure and, 54–55, 88–90, 112–13, 155, 218
prostitutes, 107

256